RETURN TO THE HOLLOW EARTH

THE SECOND NARRATIVE OF
MASON ALGIERS REYNOLDS OF VIRGINIA

RUDY RUCKER

Transreal Books, Los Gatos, California
www.transrealbooks.com

ALSO BY RUDY RUCKER

SF NOVELS

Million Mile Road Trip
Turing & Burroughs
Jim and the Flims
Hylozoic
Postsingular
Mathematicians in Love
Frek and the Elixir
Spaceland
The Hollow Earth
Master of Space and Time

TRANSREAL SF NOVELS

The Big Aha
Saucer Wisdom
The Hacker and the Ants
The Secret of Life
The Sex Sphere
White Light
Spacetime Donuts

THE WARE TETRALOGY

Realware
Freeware
Wetware
Software

HISTORICAL NOVEL

As Above, So Below: Peter Bruegel

For Martin Gardner,
My parents Embry & Marianne,
My wife Sylvia,
My children Georgia, Rudy & Isabel, and
My grandchildren Althea, Jasper, Zimry, Desmond & Calder

Contents

1. Cape Horn

On March 4, 1850, my wife Seela and I left Baltimore for San Francisco. Seela was nearly six months with child. We were cutting it fine, trying to reach California before the birth, but Seela was game. The Hollow Earth flowerpeople are a hardy lot.

During our five months in Baltimore, people viewed Seela and me as Negroes. We two had been crisped dark by the glow of the woomo—the huge, ancient, sea-cucumber-like beings who live at the core of the Hollow Earth. I would have preferred that we be treated as white.

Now six months had passed, and our skins had faded—but in Baltimore we were still viewed as black. This opinion was by now engraved in the locals' minds. If we wanted to be white, nothing would do but to go and make a fresh start in California.

We made our way by stagecoach from Baltimore to the wharves of New York City, and on March 9, 1850, we boarded a schooner for California, a fubsy craft called the *Purple Whale*. The other emigrants were uninterested in the past or future shades of our skin. A rough spirit of equality reigned aboard the *Purple Whale*. Many of us had tangled pasts, and all of us dreamed of golden futures.

A pilot rode aboard and guided our captain through the currents and shoals to the harbor entrance. As we neared the open Atlantic, a small pilot boat scudded to our side to pick up our guide. A final, laggard passenger was aboard the pilot boat, and he made his way up a long rope ladder to the *Purple Whale*. He was dressed in a well-cut brown suit, and he carried a small bag.

Our sails filled with wind and we scudded to sea. Seela and I leaned against the taffrail, admiring the horizon ahead and the city behind, with our faithful dog Arf at our feet.

"Wonderful," I said to Seela. "We're free."

"I feel trapped," she said, glaring at the open sea. "We're stuck on this big wooden cradle. Rock, rock, rock." She glanced around at the other passengers. "Seedy. What fool wants to dig for gold?"

During our six months together in Baltimore, Seela and I had begun speaking very openly to each other. Her English had greatly improved, although she sounded, at times, illiterate. But what of it? I had a growing sense that Seela was smarter than I'd ever be. The honeymoon was over, and the marriage was underway.

"No cradle yet," I said. "A big ship. Hull, deck, sails." I held out my arms. "Feel that clean, salty wind. Be glad!"

"You wave your arms, but you don't fly," muttered Seela. "We're stuck in this tub."

Inside our Hollow Earth, where Seela comes from, the people are weightless. Our Earth is a big egg full of air—with critters, blobby lakes, and tangles of plants drifting around on the inside. Inside our Hollow Earth, the gravity from the different parts of the Rind cancels out. Seela's tribe—the flowerpeople—they fly by making fins out of flower petals and kicking themselves through the air.

"No answer about being stuck?" said Seela, increasingly peevish.

"Fine, we can't fly," said I. "But at least we can swim."

"I don't like to swim," said Seela. "Your ocean is cold and nasty. And we're on this ship for—how long, Mason?"

"Three or four months," I replied. "The days will speed by. And in California we'll have our fresh start."

"And my baby will come," said Seela, mollified by this thought.

"The three of us," I said. "It'll be lovely."

"And when do we go home to see my folks?" probed Seela. This was a sore point. A return to the Hollow Earth loomed large in her mind.

"It's not so easy," I said with a sigh.

In principle, a hollow planet has two large holes in its shell, or *Rind*—which I prefer to capitalize. One hole at each pole. But our South Hole was clogged with a miles-deep plug of ice. There was, however, a North Hole in the form of a huge maelstrom. We'd seen it from inside the Hollow Earth. And here on the surface, Seela and I had discussed the chances of sailing or ballooning through the North Hole. But for the moment it didn't seem like a realistic prospect. Things would have been different if we still had the reckless and resourceful Edgar Allan Poe with us. But he was dead.

"I know you're thinking about that North Hole," said Seela. "But listen to me. When you brought me here from the Hollow Earth, we floated up through a hole in the bottom of the ocean. Why can't we do that again? Instead of floating up, now we sink down. Get in a waterproof box, tie on an anchor, and there we go."

"We'd need *woomo* help," I said. "We'd need some of those air-plants they gave us before. I don't see any *woomo* around just now."

"They'd come if we had enough tekelili to call them," said Seela. *Tekelili* was the Hollow Earth term for a psychic power that made one sensitive to others' thoughts. "We used to get tekelili from our rumby gems," continued Seela. "And tekelili from making love." Lately there hadn't been much love-making, what with Seela's morning-sickness, and with our anxieties about the trip to California.

"I miss making love," I said, wrapping my arms around Seela's rounded waist. "You're my magic egg. Almost ready to hatch. I bet we can still make love. I won't push hard."

Seela cast an impatient look at the other passengers on the deck. "Do it with this sad crowd around? Not likely. And, Mason, tell me you're not going to be a gold miner. I don't want a digger dungbeetle."

"I mean to be a literary man," I reassured her. "Like Eddie Poe."

"Poor Eddie," she said. Five months ago, we'd sunk his dead body into the Baltimore harbor.

Next to us, a lean, travel-worn man lounged against the rail, as if eavesdropping. He looked to be about thirty. I recognized him as the one who'd arrived aboard the pilot boat. He seemed better dressed than the other passengers, more prosperous. He drained a flask of nerve tonic, studied its label, and tossed the empty into the sea.

The traveler flashed a smile my way. "I'm Connor Machree," said he. "You're wise not to be a prospector. I have reason to believe you've got wider horizons."

"I'm Mason Reynolds, and this is Seela," said I. "I'm hoping to work for a newspaper in San Francisco. I can set type, and I write."

"Fancy plans," said the man with a laugh. "Not so dumb for a country boy." He had a Virginia accent like mine.

"Gold is what's dumb," put in Seela. "We've got better rocks where I'm from. Heavy rocks like you never seen."

"Now, that's what interests me," said Connor Machree, cocking his head. "Heavy rocks and heavy gems. Would you guide me to your homeland?"

I didn't like the abrupt turn the conversation was making. Had Machree learned of the two Hollow Earth rumby stones we'd sold in Baltimore?

"We're not miners at all," I repeated.

"Yes, yes, Mason" said he. "I heard you. You seek to work at composing and printing a newspaper. A refined, but low-paying craft." Exhaling a plume of smoke, he gestured toward the other passengers. "I wonder how many of our fellow Argonauts can read?"

"Seela and I will get along fine," I said. "We'll make a new life."

"I'll hazard you two aren't legally married," said Machree, as if wanting to goad me. "Seeing as how you're black."

"Seela is indeed my wife," I assured him. "And you have no reason to call us black. We faded white in Baltimore."

"I know that," said Machree. "I know all. You lived in Baltimore, but you were born in Virginia. I'm a Virginian as well. I'm from Lynchburg. A town you frequented. Perhaps we once met."

"You're tedious," said I, liking this man less all the time. "Be gone."

"We were married by the tekelili of the *woomo* inside the Hollow Earth," put in Seela. She loved to talk about the Hollow Earth, although few understood her meaning.

But Machree was attentive, even avid.

"The Hollow Earth," he echoed. "Your homeland, eh Seela? I've read of it, but I don't fully understand. It's a true reality? Not a tale?"

"What are you nosing for?" I asked Machree point blank. "What's your trade?"

"Assayer and jeweler," said he. "I shear golden fleece from the bleating flock. I unsnarl their wool-wrapped jewels. I mine the miners." He paused and lit a short, thin cigar. "Mark this: I seek rumby gems."

My stomach sank. I had a growing sense that this man had come aboard the *Purple Whale* expressly to meet us. Silently I shook my head.

"Machree got hold of one of our rumbies from the Hollow Earth," exclaimed the forthright Seela. "That's what he's talking about. It's clear."

"I long to enter your Hollow Earth," said Machree. "The unknown Eden where you harvested your gems, eh, Mason? The land where you found your fresh, fruitful, red-toothed Seela. Happy man thou art."

My mind in a whirl, I still declined to answer. But now Machree made his crowning revelation. "I know these things because I read your manuscript in Baltimore. *The Hollow Earth*, by Mason Reynolds."

"What!" I exclaimed, baffled and shocked.

"Indeed," said Machree. "You'd left Baltimore when I arrived. But I asked around. Everyone remembered Seela—the blonde, black woman with red teeth. I found your landlady Jilly Tackler. And her pawnbroker David Marion. And the bookseller E. J. Coale."

"That manuscript you read," I stammered. "It's a fantasia. I wrote it as if I'd traveled with Edgar Allan Poe. I'm quite a student of his work."

"*Which* Mr. Poe is the question, eh?" said Machree. "*Our* Mr. Poe died in the gutter last October. In Baltimore. As you know."

The memory of Poe's death brought with it a wave of sorrow. "I was with him," I confessed, unable to hold it in.

"In your manuscript you wrote that our Poe had a younger double," pressed Machree, staring at me, as if waiting to see what else I'd say. "Your Poe."

I felt like a cornered rat. It was past time to make a stand. "If you press further, Seela will cut your throat," I told Machree. And I meant it. Seela had her big new knife strapped to her leg beneath her skirt. She was fierce and fast. Minutes ago we'd been free—and now we were under siege.

"I won't impose any further," said Machree, taking in my words. "I'm sure your Seela remains formidable—even though her skin and her teeth have nearly faded to white. But later I hope to discuss the route into the Hollow Earth. I'd pay a handsome sum indeed, were you two to guide me." And then he was off to his cabin, strutting smoothly across the rolling deck, very sure of himself. I could hardly stand to think of such a man reading my manuscript.

"I'm saying he's got one or two of the rumbies that Jewel gave us," repeated Seela. "I can feel the tekelili."

"I traded my rumby to Jilly Tackler for our rent in Baltimore." I mused. "And we sold yours to Jilly's pawnbroker last month, to get money for the tickets. I guess Machree bought that one. I wonder what put him onto our trail."

"Our Eddie had a rumby too," mused Seela. "A third gem."

"Yes, but both the Poes are dead. We left our Eddie's rumby on him when we sank his body in the harbor. A heavy amulet on his neck."

"I should have taken it," said Seela.

"I wasn't going to do that," I said. "Maybe it helped him to the next world."

"Shrigshit on next worlds," said Seela. "Shrigshit on your stupid religions. I should have snatched Poe's rumby. Did we get good money from the pawnbroker for my rumby? Machree would have paid more. What kind of tickets do we have? First class? Take me to our cabin. I need a lie-down. This dumb wood cradle is sloshing my guts." The waves were relentless.

"It's not exactly a cabin we have," I had to tell Seela. I'd held back from explaining this before. "It's second-class steerage. That's all we could afford." I leaned closer. "You do remember that we needed money for the stagecoach from Baltimore to New York. And we bought the knife for you. And clothes. And we wanted to keep some of our money for California."

Seela herself had helped me fashion the cloth band that I now wore hidden around my waist. It had twenty Mexican silver dollars sewn inside. A pitiful sum.

"What's steerage?" Seela now asked me, poor thing.

"Let's go see!" I said feigning enthusiasm.

Most of the other passengers were already below. The dismayed Seela and I had trouble finding an unoccupied corner for ourselves. The brig's skinflint Yankee owners hadn't bothered to put in bunks—we human cargo were left to make nests for ourselves amid a tangle of sails, ropes, and bundled trade goods. Foul bilge water sloshed beneath the slats of the makeshift floor. Many of the passengers were seasick, and few were ascending to the deck. A dozen sloshing buckets held our reeking slops, and to fully perfect the hellish scene, the ship now rolled to one side, spilling every single bucket on its side. Arf nosed one of the puddles.

"I can't bear this," said Seela, on the point of tears. "It's like we're dead inside a coffin."

"Let's go over there," I urged her. "A nice pile of sails. We'll settle in and you can sleep."

"You're a shrigbrain to bring us here," cried Seela. "I want to go home."

"Gold's a-waitin!" called out a man nearby. "Californee!" He was more wistful than jolly. As scared as we.

"Go to hell, sh*thead," Seela told him. I was hoping eventually to improve the *politesse* of her speech.

"*Marry a rose—hold your nose,*" said the man, baring his teeth in a fake smile. I ignored him. All of us in steerage were at our wits' ends. It was far worse than I'd imagined.

Seela and I bedded down in our canvas nest, with our one little bundle of possessions behind us, and Arf at our feet. My disheartened wife cried against my shoulder until, blessedly, we fell asleep.

Twice a day we could fetch food from the low galley on the main deck. As part of our paid passage we were entitled to sea biscuits, salt beef, and watery tea, with a noggin of lime juice every third day. Leaving the hold was a signal pleasure. Before long, Seela, Arf and I were spending most of our daylight hours on the deck. The mates discouraged the passengers from loitering topside, but Seela's bright face, lively voice, and womanly form drew the sailors and officers into our camp. They were glad to see us out and about.

The mate kept the men busy scrubbing the deck, cleaning the spars and splicing the rigging—when they weren't reefing, setting, hauling, or striking the sails. But once in a while they had time to talk. Our best friend among crew was a lithe, well-spoken, dark-skinned youth named Crispa. He was eighteen years of age to my seventeen, and a native of Baltimore.

"We're from Baltimore, too," Seela told him.

Crispa studied us closely. "I never seen neither of you before," he said.

"We're new," I said.

Crispa reached out and touched the skin of my cheek. "You black? Run away from down South?"

"I'm getting over being black," I said.

"I'm getting over being from Baltimore," said Crispa with a laugh that showed his fine, even teeth. "It's safe at sea, Mase."

"I'm gonna live in California," I said.

"I'm ready to jump ship and go off with the Crow Nation," said Crispa in a low voice. "See how it feel to be all the way free. My grandpa was an Upsaroka Indian. Some of the crew is gonna jump ship to dig gold. But diggin ain't for me."

"Me neither," I said.

"We too good," said Crispa with a laugh.

"Mason's a writer and a printer, you see," said Seela, proud of me.

"Teach me to read?" asked Crispa.

"I need to learn that too," confessed Seela. "Been meaning to ask."

So now a part of our daily chats became lessons. Somehow Crispa got me a writing slate and a squeaky slate pencil from the ship's stores. We started with A and went to Z while running south along the coast of South America. I had the two of them writing their names by the time we passed the equator.

As you may know, the seasons are reversed in the southern hemisphere. That is, down there, April, May, and June have the weather of our October, November, and December. So when we reached a latitude of 55° S in mid-April, we were surrounded by sleet and rain, with the days turning short. The tip of the Cape lay some five hundred miles to our west, and we had a long, heavy, ugly sea running against us.

For days on end we sailed into the teeth of the unrelenting west wind, tacking southwest and northwest, making slow progress against the gales and the swells. The *Purple Whale* was an ungainly old brig, formerly used for the New York to London route, and newly pressed into service for the profitable passenger run to California.

The sodden days wore on. Every so often, we'd fall off the beat of the ocean's rhythm, and our raised bow would slam against the sea with a dead, hollow sound that made me afraid. Like the boom of a clenched fist on the lid of a coffin.

As the weather grew worse, the sailors took to wearing full Cape Horn rigs: boots, long-brimmed southwester hats, and oil-cloth suits. In exchange for one of my silver dollars, Crispa equipped Seela and me with the abandoned outerwear of two youths who'd been lost at sea in earlier journeys. Nobody else wanted the outfits—sailors are loath to wear the garb of a drowned man.

Suitably clad, Seela and I continued spending most of each day on deck. And Arf was out there too, thickening his fur at a noticeable rate. The importuning Connor Machree was often on deck as well, offering sly smiles. It irked me that this man had read my manuscript of *The Hollow Earth*. He'd taken it in entirely the wrong way, as if it were a treasure map. Fool. Why did he think we'd met before? At least, for now, he was keeping his distance. I hoped to give him the slip in San Francisco.

For days blending into weeks we beat our slow way against the westerlies. One afternoon a clean-lined cutter flew past us, tacking a clever line that sliced the waves like a knife.

"It's the *Sea Witch*," Connor Machree said, edging up beside me. "Used to be an opium clipper from India to China. Now she runs rich folks and dainty geegaws to San Francisco. Gets there first with the best. Left New York a week after us." He gave me one of his lingering looks. "I would have shipped on the *Sea Witch*, if I hadn't managed to squeeze onto the *Purple Whale*." He shook his head. "That was a near thing. I rode out to you on the pilot boat, after taking an express coach from Baltimore. I'm bent on following you."

"Why is that again?" I asked, exasperated with the man.

"You and I have a history," he said, staring at me. "We fit like two gears, eh? Don't get it? Never mind for now. I've told you I want to know where you and Seela get your rumby gems." He stepped closer and rummaged in his pockets beneath his oilskin coat. "Look."

And there it was in Machree's pale hand, Seela's rumby, the one I'd sold to the pawnbroker in Baltimore. It was even lovelier than I'd remembered, the size of a small grape, quite heavy, with a subtle pattern of pentagonal facets, perpetually shifting, clearer than the finest crystal, and shattering the daylight into full-spectrum rainbows. I felt an overwhelming desire to touch and to caress it. As well as its dazzling beauty, the rumby had so strong a tekelili aura that I could nearly read my companions' thoughts.

"It's mine," said Seela, reaching for the stone. "It knows me."

"Mine," said Machree, his hard face folding into a semblance of a smile. "I bought it." He thrust the rumby back into an inner pocket.

"You know I can kill you," Seela told him. Both Machree and I were inclined to believe her. And this knowledge was, to some extent, keeping the man under control. Seela was from a far harder culture than ours.

"Don't talk that way," implored Machree. "I'd prefer that you sell me a map to the rumby mine in the Hollow Earth! Five hundred dollars. And if you guide me yourselves, I'll pay five thousand." I doubted if, even now, he grasped that the Hollow Earth is the space inside the Earth. Machree reading my manuscript was like a dog in a Latin class. I cursed the man aloud, and from the bottom of my heart. He walked away.

Dispirited by the man's ignorant machinations, I turned my attention to the passing *Sea Witch*. She was sleeker, faster and probably better-helmed than the *Purple Whale*. She had raked, back-slanting masts, a long boom, and a sharp, V-shaped hull.

"Not like our roly-poly tub," remarked Crispa, who'd joined us. But he said this too loud, and the mate set him to repairing rigging in the highest reaches of the masts for several days. Finally, on a Sunday morning, Crispa again had an hour off.

"Might could take another week more to clear the Horn," Crispa remarked to me. We were sitting with Seela and Arf on the deck behind the galley, out of the freezing wind. Overhead the spars and the rigging were coated in ice.

"What if we can't make it around the Horn at all?" asked Seela.

"There's an inland passage north of here," said Crispa. "The Strait of Magellan. But I doubt our captain could thread it. He sank a schooner off Nantucket two years back. Half the crew drowned."

"Captain didn't go down with his ship?" I asked.

"Weren't no call for that," drawled Crispa. "Captain's married to the fleet owner's daughter." He patted Arf, who'd crawled halfway onto his lap. "I admire this tattoo on your dog's belly."

"A rough fellow needled it on, last time Arf and I went to sea," said I. "Dirk Peters. An Upsaroka, come to think of it. Same as what you said about your grandpa."

"From the Crow Nation in the Great Plains," said Crispa, tracing his finger along the dotted spiral. "I can feel the tribal spirit. Good luck."

"Wasn't good luck for poor Peters," I said. "He got crushed between two icebergs."

"Let's say the luck went to Arf," said Crispa. "And let's say he's my dog too. I don't want no cold water filling my lungs."

"You're with us," I said, and Seela agreed. We saw Crispa as a fast friend. His brightness of spirit was uplifting.

"Nobody drowns inside the Hollow Earth," put in Seela, wanting to tell Crispa more about her home. "No heaviness in there. Nothing to drag you down."

"Machree always asks about the Hollow Earth," said Crispa. "And you don't tell him. Can you tell me?"

"If you can listen," said Seela. "Earth's a hollow ball. We're close to a Hollow Earth entrance right now. The iced-over South Hole. Big *woomo* sea cucumbers down inside the core. I wish one of them would snake a feeler up through some cracks. Or send a tendril through the maelstrom at the North Hole, or through a hole in the ocean floor. We'd see a *woomo* frond in front of the *Purple Whale* like a sea serpent. A branching stalk of pink light."

Crispa looked uneasy. "I don't want to hear about no sea monsters in a place like this. Let's be scanning the sky instead."

"So—how about that black cloud coming in so fast?" I said, looking upward. "It's covering us like a lid." As well as darkness, the cloud was bringing a bank of mist and a rising wind.

"Cape Horn express," said Crispa, as if calmed by the thought of a non-supernatural danger. "Our Sunday morning meeting's done, maties. I'm glad we're friends. I've got a secret to tell you by and by."

In short order, we were plowing into the heaviest seas I'd ever seen. Blasts of spume exploded off our bow. The air glittered with dancing drops. The deck was awash with seawater that ran knee-deep through the scuppers. All afternoon and all night the storm continued.

Seela and I lay below decks on our heap of sailcloth, with our arms wrapped tight around each other, and with Arf on our legs. We sang little songs by way of keeping up our courage, some songs in English, and some in Seela's native tongue. And when we ran out of songs we whimpered. And when we ran out of whimpers we prayed to the *woomo* at the heart of the Hollow Earth. And when Seela fell asleep I began working on a sequel to *The Hollow Earth* in my head. When the endless night ended and the sun peeped up, we went topside, and found the deck covered with a foot of snow.

The wind went down, the sky cleared, and all of Monday morning we tossed in frigid calm. The ocean swells were rolling, but their surfaces were glassy smooth. The *Purple Whale* bobbed like a snowy log upon a mill pond at the bottom of the world. The scene was like a fever dream—and I had an odd off-kilter sense that my written narratives were consuming me.

Adding to the scene's phantasmagoric quality, an albatross came floating by, asleep on the surface of the rolling sea, completely white, and with his head beneath his wing, now rising on a heavy billow, and then sliding into a hollow. Our voices and the creaking of our ship's timbers roused him. The bird opened his dark, deep-set eyes and clacked his hooked, ivory beak. The ever-present Connor Machree yelled a nervous curse at the albatross. The creature spread his enormous wings, easily ten feet across, and took flight, catching a stray ghost of breeze.

As if fanned into life by the bird, the wind returned, and this time it was favorable. Our sails bulged. For four happy days we sped toward Cape Horn.

On the eve of the fourth day the wind fell, and a fresh storm approached from the west. Its thunder was a continuous grumble, and its lightning sparked all along the western verge. We reefed our sails and waited through an uncanny interval of calm. The air was alive with actinic energy, and the hairs on my skin tingled.

"Look there!" cried Crispa, pointing at the rigging.

Pale coronas tipped the yardarms, and rosy flares rode the masts like candle flames. The cold fires hissed—an intricate murmur that mixed with the plash and purl of the sea.

The crew stood in a cluster, their faces lit by the eerie glow, their eyes aglint. Crispa and Seela were at my side, with Crispa cradling Arf in his arms like a baby. Arf lay on his back, as if in a gesture of surrender, with his tattoo showing dark in the uncanny light. Connor Machree was with us as well, always staring at me with that same odd look in his eyes.

The glow lifted from the ship, massing into a streamer that withdrew into the sky. Had it been a tendril from the all-knowing *woomo* within the Hollow Earth? Had it arced up from Earth's center, and through the Rind, and across the globe's surface to meet us? I felt a strong sense of tekelili from the rumby within the acquisitive Machree's inner pocket. A dense, precious, gleaming gem that was rightly ours.

"We gotta take it off him," said Seela's voice in my head, as clearly as if she'd spoken aloud.

Perhaps we would seize the rumby amid the furor of the coming storm. Perhaps Machree would fall overboard and drown. Or, if necessary, Seela could slit his throat. Machree glared at me. The tekelili was showing him the tenor of my thoughts. He moved away.

The wind rose, the rigging moaned tense chords, the sea ahead was like a colossal furrowed field. A low moon shone through the torn clouds, silvering the crests of the towering waves, and brushing glints along their hollow bellies. The sailors clewed and trimmed our sails, keeping two small rags aloft.

And then we were for it. The ranked waves came at us like attacking troops. Lest our ship roll sideways, the mate maintained a course directly into the wind, with the bow plunging madly into the tremendous seas. Each concussion buried the entire forward part of our vessel.

As if sensing the approach of doom, Crispa ignored his duties and stayed close to my side, once again clutching Arf in his arms. He, Seela and I huddled amidships near the main mast. For the ship, each individual wave required a daring and unlikely escape. Our luck would only hold for so long.

It was a freak wave that did us in, towering above the other waves like an oak above brambles, four times the height of our masts, a grim reaper of a wave, spawned in the bottomless gulfs, and risen to bring us low. At the last moment I glimpsed a leathery orange hawser, wrapping itself around our mast and straining at it, as if to tilt our deck to precisely the worst angle at which to meet the wave.

2. Shipwreck

The unfathomable mass of water broke onto the *Purple Whale*, burying us in untold tons, both fore and aft. The savage, implacable currents whirled me and my companions into the sea. And beneath the watery tumult, I heard a crunch and a crack. The ship had split in two, right across the middle where we'd stood. The pieces belched air, turned turtle, and dove for the abyss, trailing whirlpool currents that dragged us deep and deeper into the stygian gloom, perhaps a full twenty fathoms down. My ears spiked with pain, then adjusted to the depth. It was utterly dark, and the antarctic cold was astonishing. I was growing stiff and numb, but even so, I hung onto my companions by touch—to Seela, Crispa, and Arf. We'd rise together, or not at all. But I doubted we would rise.

And then, when all was lost—here came a pink streamer of divine *woomo* light. It was lifting us upward. Dimly I saw my companions. To my surprise, Connor Machree was in our midst, quite senseless, limp as a rag. Seela lunged at our foe, wriggled her hand inside his garments and emerged with—*huzzah*—her glowing rumby gem and then—*excelsior*—a second one. It was my rumby—the one I'd given our landlady Jilly Tackler for the rent. Perhaps Machree had stolen it from her. What a find! I savored the tekelili of the dense, precious gems. A rumby sense of self. *Here we are.*

Meanwhile, of course, Arf, Seela, Crispa, and I were on the very point of drowning and freezing to death —albeit in an agreeable state of tekelili from the *woomo* light and the rumbies. But we were rising, one slow fathom at a time, flailing our cold-stiffened legs against the eddies and the vortex threads of the foundered *Purple Whale*. The pink light was bearing us upward with the inert Machree.

The gleaming underside of the sea's surface was in view. A wildly squirming orange tentacle lashed through the water, stirring bubbles in its wake. It caught Seela by the ankle and tugged her up and out of sight. One, two, eight, ninety more tentacles appeared, urgent and intense, taking hold of me, Crispa, and Arf, drawing us to the roiled sea's surface with Seela.

The *woomo* light was moving away. Machree was no longer in view. Perhaps he'd sunk back into the depths. I drew in sobbing gasps of air. The tight grip of the orange tentacles was draining all force from my hands and feet. The coldness of the water and my recent exposure to the pink *woomo* light had left my skin feeling as if it were on fire.

The implacable tentacles were pulling us higher, out of the water and into the air. A menacing form bobbed above the wind-torn waves, oh no, it was a *ballula*, a giant man-eating nautilus, buoyed by a shell full of hydrogen, a carnivorous denizen of the Hollow Earth, now lifting us toward the barn-door-sized opening of its shell, a dark smooth cave whence ninety orange tentacles emerged, plus two bollard-like eyestalks, and a horribly clacking, razor-sharp beak. By the illumination of the receding *woomo* light, I could see blood upon the *ballula* beak, and a sailor's bitten-off arm and shoulder within. The remains of Machree? No, someone else. The clothing was different. Machree—he'd disappeared.

"We dead and gone to hell!" cried Crispa, bundled tight against Seela, Arf, and me by a tangle of the smooth, strong tentacles. "It gonna eat us!"

"She's not allowed to eat us!" screamed Seela. "We've got two rumbies! Rumbies have power over these beasts!" She held the heavy gems high so the *ballula's* dead-black eyes could perceive them, with each rumby a beacon of tekelili. "Obey me, you damned shell-squid!" cried Seela. "Take us to safety! I am your ruler!" A convincing performance. I don't think I could have carried it off.

So now, rather than devouring us, the *ballula* tucked the four of us into a tangle of tentacles below her huge, parrot-style beak. I felt like a pork chop on a bed of yams—with ravening jaws overhead. Arf writhed and whimpered at my side, his eyes rolling.

The *ballula* wasn't eating us. That leathery orange hawser I'd seen before our ship sank—it had been one of these tentacles. The *ballula* had scuttled our ship, yes, and she'd eaten some of the passengers and sailors. But as for us, she was taking us…somewhere.

Through the stuttering lightning we rose, with the sinister *ballula* bearing us northwest, toward the far side of the storm, propelling herself with farting bursts from her siphon tube, and finding her way to a favorable wind. Nearly an hour passed. We four huddled together, shielded by the great shell from the rushing air, sharing our bodies' sparks of warmth, and wrapping the tentacles around us like mufflers. The stream of pink *woomo* light had long since withdrawn itself, and the weather was calm. I spotted a pair of lanterns on a three-masted schooner far below, with the ship herself visible by the light of the moon.

"The *Sea Witch*!" exclaimed Crispa. "We done caught up."

Smoothly adjusting her attitude, while blatting from her muscular siphon tube, the *ballula* swept toward the cutter like a balloonist coming to earth.

"That ship's got a big lizard on front," said Seela. Indeed, the cutter's figurehead was a carved and gilded Chinese dragon with a coiling tail, markedly fierce, and dramatically brought into relief by the moon.

And then, just like that, the *ballula's* sticky tentacles uncurled and dropped Seela, Arf, Crispa, and me to the *Sea Witch's* deck. We thumped down and slid along the planks. Rather than flying into the sky, the *ballula* sank into the sea and descended, leaving a stream of bubbles that slowly settled down.

Seela, Arf, Crispa, and I had come to rest at the base of the *Sea Witch's* main mast. Stimulated by the deck beneath his feet and the smell of chickens and pigs, Arf let out an exultant bark.

"Avast!" cried a man on watch. "Boarders!"

Moments later, Seela, Crispa, and I were in the custody of a mate with a pistol, and two seamen with swords.

"Our ship went down," Seela cried. "Have mercy."

"And you swam here?" asked the mate, thrusting out his lower chin. "Tell me another. This water would stop your heart in five minutes." He was a know-it-all Yankee.

"Two albatrosses carried us," I said. "Uncommonly large." Nobody bothered answering that one.

"All right, the truth is that we're stowaways," said Seela. It helped that she was beautiful, and great with child. Even so, the mate chose to argue.

"Then where exactly have you been hid for these last seventy days at sea?"

"With the pigs," said Crispa, pointing at the pen on deck. It had a low sty with a tiny door.

"Flaming flapdoodle!" said the mate, believing the tale. "What do we do with you three and your dog? Drown you? Shove you back in with the hogs?"

"Let us ride as passengers," I suggested. "We'll pay to smooth our way," As it happened, I still had nineteen silver dollars inside the band around my waist. I kept one of dollars and offered up eighteen. Not an imposing sum by some lights, but it was enough to cheer the mate and his men. They did a three-way split. The hooting sailors danced a hornpipe jig, jingling their coins between cupped hands. The mate smiled and shook my hand.

"My name's Stearns," he said. "Welcome aboard the *Sea Witch*. I'll bunk you three in the scribbler's cabin. Hope he don't mind."

"Scribbler?" said I.

"Fancies himself a gentleman. Little fellow with a bulging brow. Very quiet in his habits. The captain enjoys him. Mr. Goarland Peale."

I broke into a convulsive grin. Seela didn't yet get the wheeze, but the shuffled letters of "Goarland Peale" told me what was afoot, farfetched though it might be.

"I'm sure Mr. Peale will take to us," I assured Stearns.

Taking pity on us now, the sailors gave us biscuits, beef, and beer, all of a much finer quality than the grub on the late, lost *Purple Whale*. Even better, they gave us wool blankets to enfold our shivering frames.

"Bunk down before the captain gets the word," the mate told us. "He takes a change easier once it's squared away. Here, this is Mr. Peale's cabin." Stearns waggled his chin and let out a thin cackle. "The high and mighty Goarland. It'll take him down a peg to share his state room with three darkies and a dog."

Darkies? Again? Staring at Seela in the lantern light, I gleaned the hard truth. The insinuating glow of the great pink *woomo* light had baked us brown once more, with even Crispa gone darker than before. Arf was of course unchanged. Always a dog.

Yes, Seela and I had enjoyed ourselves well enough as blacks in Baltimore. In some ways, life as a Negro was congenial to me, at least when white people weren't around. And Seela herself was in the habit of viewing dark skin pigment as a sign of high status. In the Hollow Earth, the dark race who lived near the center were referred to as black gods. But, even so, to set out for a white life in California, only to find myself again relegated to a low estate.

With a peremptory knock, Stearns flung open the door of a low cabin near the rear of the deck. With a bark of laughter, he bundled us in, and slammed the door behind us.

A lantern burned within. And there, pale as wax, at his ease in a soft chair, ruminating over pen and parchment, with a small pipe and a glass of claret ready to hand, was—

"Eddie!" exclaimed Seela. "You're not dead?"

"I've been expecting you," he said.

Yes, it was Eddie Poe, the Eddie who'd traveled through the Hollow Earth with me. In his soft, familiar, tenor voice he sang the altered verse of an Easter hymn.

> *The nine sad months are quickly sped;*
> *He rises glorious from the dead;*

All glory to your risen Ed!
Hallelujah!

"But—I saw MirrorPoe murder you!" I protested. "Your double."

"A nice piece of theater, that," said Eddie, trying to control his widening smile. "My parents were actors. From my earliest years I knew how to feign a florid death."

"But he ran his blade through and through you!" I protested. "He killed you."

"Misdirection," said Eddie. "You saw him repeatedly thrust his sword—but only through my cloak, and mostly to no effect. Admittedly the first jab nicked my side, and most convenient that was, as it unleashed blood enough for horrific effect. But I contrived to avoid my besotted enemy's ensuing pokes. For the culminating effect, I smeared gore on my face, drummed my heels and expired. The Death of Poe. You were diddled, my dear Mason, tender heart that you are."

"So, you were lying doggo while we carried you to the harbor?"

"Thou sayest it, my liege."

"But then surely you drowned! I tied a rock to your ankles and sank you into the depths."

"Not so very deep as all that. Thirty feet. A sandy bottom."

"You loosened the knot?"

"A bagatelle. I braced my ankles against the rope while you bound me. In the water, I relaxed, and the binding went slack. I swam free. And surfaced behind a fortuitously anchored yawl, waiting there until you decamped in a touching state of heartfelt grief."

"You're a devil, Eddie."

"An imp," said he. "A strayed lamb. A mage." He laid a finger against his nose and winked. "I have more to tell. As I left the harbor, I found I had a pet. She was swimming in the sea at my side, the size of a house. Reaching out a supplicating tentacle toward my fine amulet. A *ballula*. Tamed by my rumby's spell."

29

Eddie touched his Hollow Earth gem, nearly the size of a gooseberry, tightly wrapped in silk thread, and tied to a cord around his neck. I could sense the rumby's psychic glow across the room. Before Seela could tell Eddie about us recovering our own two rumbies, Eddie got to his feet and brought his lantern closer to us.

"Let's have a look at you. But how the devil is it that you two are black again? Hopeless bunglers."

"The pink light of the Great Old Ones," said I. "A beam of *woomo* light plumbed into the depths to save us, dragged down in the wake of our foundered ship. Twenty fathoms down. The light exalted us. And then—and then a *ballula* carried us here."

"My same *ballula* from Baltimore," said Eddie with an air of quiet pride. "I call her Cytherea. She accompanied me from Baltimore to New York. And now she's following the *Sea Witch* to California, sometimes above, and sometimes below. She jets through the sea and rides the winds. And tonight I sent her to fetch you."

"Did you tell her to sink our ship?" I demanded.

"A ghastly loss," said Eddie, as if in sorrow. He wrung his hands and furrowed his brow. "Those inhuman *ballula*s—"

"Back up," I said. "How did you know that Seela and I were on the *Purple Whale*?"

"Someone told me," said Eddie, a twinkle in his eye. "Can you guess?"

"Connor Machree," I said.

"Well reasoned, my pup. Yes, it was he. More on Machree anon."

"So far as I know he drowned," I interjected. "But pray continue."

"I learned of your departure from Machree," said Eddie. "And I booked passage aboard the speedy *Sea Witch* expecting to reach San Francisco before the *Purple Whale*. And I arranged for my Cytherea to fetch you to my ship en route."

"Why?" I asked, uneasy at the thought of Eddie Poe making all these plans for me. Wanting a distraction, I poured out a bowl of water for Arf, and settled him onto a pillow. He drank deeply and was instantly asleep.

"I want you and your Seela to help me return," said Eddie, not quite answering my question. "A second sally through the Hollow Earth—after a brief investigatory stop in San Francisco for filling out our equipage. My goal? To journey through the Anomaly at the core of the Hollow Earth—and to claim my deserved throne as dean of letters on the original Earth. May I propose a toast to my plan?"

He raised his glass of claret, and made a gesture that we were free to help ourselves. I gladly got glasses of water for Seela and me—we two were very well-salted from our ordeal. Crispa took a glass of water and a glass of wine.

"I'm for the Hollow Earth," said Seela, raising her glass. "I keep telling Mason this. He doesn't listen."

"I'll go too!" said Crispa, raising first his water, and then his wine, and draining the two glasses in a row. "If I don't find no Indians to join. I'll start out with you at least."

"Is this fellow black all the time?" Poe asked me. "Or just temporarily?"

"Black and white be bullshit in California," said Crispa. "What I heard. Fact of the matter, I'm one quarter Upsaroka Crow. But that ain't the real surprise." Crispa paused and made a bow. "I'm a woman and not a man."

As soon as Crispa said this, I understood it to be true. Her sympathy, likeability, and ready intelligence—she'd been female all along. Disguised as a man to get a berth as a sailor on a ship to California. Of course.

Thanks to the rumbies, there was enough tekelili in the room so that all these things could be readily understood. Even so, I wasn't ready to let Eddie Poe start running my life.

"You listen to me," I told him. "Right now Seela and I are going to San Francisco. With a ship this fast, we'll make landfall in two weeks. We'll feather a nest for our baby. We'll be happy. We'll settle down."

"But we don't *have* to settle," cried Seela. "With this *ballula* being Eddie's friend—he named her Cytherea? With Cytherea we can fly down through the North Hole. The great maelstrom!"

"Oh no," said I.

"Together again," said Eddie sententiously. "It is well. Tell me the tale of your past nine months, friends. I am an ear. Large and tremulous. Strike your lyres, and freely slake your thirst with wine. I've found a bit of opium in the ship's stores as well."

"Not now," said I. "Anyway, Eddie, if anyone narrates, it should be you. You could start with what you were doing with Machree."

"Not now," echoed Seela. "Eddie, lend us your bed." She used her sweetest tone. "Soft and warm. For weeks Mason and I slept on sails with slops all around. We'll take your bed, and Crispa, you get in with us. Fun. Eddie won't mind. He's a gentleman."

"When it suits me," said Eddie, with one of his thin, inwardly amused smiles. "As it happens, I'll be up all night writing. I'm mining a fresh vein of prose. Articles I can sell as when we reach San Francisco. Reports on the antics of the prospectors in the gold country."

"And you haven't even been there yet," said I, not entirely surprised.

"Genius hath its benisons," said Eddie, pouring himself a fresh glass. "Sleep well, my two lovebirds plus one, my stormy petrels, my ravens of the night. Our skewed reunion augurs well."

We three were undressing, glad to get out of our wet, cold clothes. Crispa unwrapped a cloth she'd worn tight around her chest to hide her bosom. Seela was already in the nude, her breasts full, and her belly a wondrous fertile round.

"Look at this," she said to Eddie. "Look what I got!" She could have been talking about her baby, but no, she was showing off our two recovered rumby gems, holding them up in her hands, weighing their powers. Tekelili filled the room like sunshine in a crystal vase.

"Wonderful woman!" exclaimed Eddie. "You took them from Connor Machree? —I'm sure Cytherea honored you and Mason the more for having rumbies."

"Honored?" said I. "She sank our ship,"

"Possible," said Eddie. "Probable. Unforeseen. Not what I wished. I am no fiend, Mason, no murderer."

"You've said that before. About Virginia."

"Take me as I am! An errant wanderer, a lost soul. Let us be glad the burdensome Machree has gone to the fishes. And now you sleep. I must write."

3. Brumble

The *Sea Witch* made good time on the sail north. We arrived in San Francisco at four in the afternoon on June 11, 1850, with Cytherea the *ballula* out of sight, riding air currents far overhead. Although the harbor was crowded with ships, many of them were empty. Abandoned by their crews and left at anchor, or scuttled near the shore. The mania for gold was at fever pitch.

Before we tied up to one of the long piers, the captain called the crew together and promised a bonus payment of seventy dollars apiece to those crew members who stayed with the *Sea Witch* and sailed the next leg—which was to be a run to Singapore to fetch a shipment of china, lacquered chests, and silk for the prospering citizens of San Francisco. The captain's offer went over well, and the sailors chaffed those among us, such as Crispa, who'd made remarks about setting off on their own. Crispa, by the way, was continuing her stratagem of dressing as a young man.

"I have my sketches of the gold country ready to sell," Eddie told Crispa, Seela and me as we disembarked, with Arf at our heels. "But first I need to secure a working relationship with Edward Kemble. the editor of the *Daily Alta California*. They have a steam-powered press! I wrote Kemble from New York—but, hmm, if the mail was on the *Purple Whale*, it's a dead letter, eh?"

"Don't joke," said Seela. "We had friends on that *Purple Whale*. People hoping for a change. Oh, that dark, awful water. So cold it was slow and thick." She broke off with a sound of distress, laying her hand across her belly. Although the afternoon sea air was cool and clear, Seela looked like she might faint.

Eddie turned sympathetic. "What say we lodge in the same hostelry?" He proposed. "Help me with my luggage, would you, Mason?"

Seela, Crispa and I had no possessions at all, other than our clothes and our two rumby gems, which Seela had knotted into her garments. But Eddie had a sizable trunk, containing fine clothes, camping gear, and writing supplies. Somehow Crispa and I ended up carrying it.

"Where did you get money for this kit?" I asked him.

I'd wanted to broach this subject during our two weeks together on the *Sea Witch*, but I hadn't wanted to get Eddie's dander up. Not with Seela, Crispa, and I spending nearly all our time in his cabin—lest we have to face the ship's captain. We'd lurked in Eddie's quarters, and he'd been good enough to have the cabin boys bring us food from the galley.

"I teamed with a Manhattan widow," Eddie now informed us. "A patroness of the arts, and a force among lovers of the occult. How came I to her arms? Having escaped my watery grave, I rode my *ballula* to New York, and found my way to the literary salons. My natural hunting ground." He touched the amulet at his neck. "The force of my rumby smoothed over the fact that I appeared to be a Negro. And my name, as you know, was Goarland Peale."

"And then?" Seela asked, distracted from her discomfort by the tale.

"And there I found my companion, Annabel Whistler. She admired my sensitive profile, my pensive brow. I told *la veuve* Whistler that I was the late MirrorPoe's cousin, perforce darkly incognito, due to a curious twist of fate, and that I was due to become white quite soon. She had known MirrorPoe, it seems."

"This be the longest pier ever," said Crispa, looking around. The harbor was a shallow little inlet off the bay, with remarkable thousand-foot-long wharves going out into it like sidewalks.

Ignoring the interruption, Eddie went on with his tale. "I polished several of Annabel's mystical odes and saw them into print. And I presented her with a beautifully penned copy of my appositely entitled poem, *Annabel Lee*. India ink on fine vellum. I cadged the lyrics from MirrorPoe's obituary."

"She didn't recognize the work?" I asked.

"Oh, she knew it, but I told her that MirrorPoe had in fact plagiarized it from me," said Eddie. "She doubted this, but she relished my shadowy semblance to the great man just the same. I was Annabel Whistler's inky Bohemian imp."

"Did she give you money?" put in Crispa.

"She had none," said Eddie, still walking along this endless pier. Arf has drawn ahead of us. Now and then he paused to glance back. "Annabel misled me," continued Eddie. "Her husband left a mountain of debt, and she was on the point of losing her home. She expected to put the touch on me or, failing that, to engage me as a confederate. And so it played out. Annabel and I founded an elite occult society, a mystical hoax, a confidence game. We milked our company of seekers, some two dozen strong. The Order of the Golden Frond. We recruited our first member in mid-December, 1849. Just in time to buy Christmas dinner, and coal for heating Annabel's house. All hail the Golden Frond."

"How far must we walk!" interrupted Seela, holding her enormous belly with both hands. "I need a bed. The baby's coming." I left the trunk to Crispa and Eddie now. Seela leaned against me, uncertain on her feet, and we made the last fifty yards to shore. An afternoon fog was drifting in, giving the scene a dreamlike air. Porters, wagons, and carts were all around. We were on Montgomery Street, with the city sloping up from the docks into hills.

The buildings were a hodgepodge of three-story wood frame structures, surfaced with paint, tin, or tarpaper, and seemingly all erected in the last two years. Higher up the hills, the structures gave way to canvas-sided cabins, and peaked tents. Mingled among the lodgings were shops, pot-houses, restaurants, and gambling hells, as they were called. Dogs were everywhere, and many of the men wore guns. The nearest center of activity looked to be a clamorous square some two hundred yards off.

Eddie raised his arm and summoned a shrill-voiced young porter rolling a diminutive luggage cart, a lad no older than fourteen. His name was Pip.

"Conduct my slaves and me to your city's finest hotel," Poe instructed the porter. "I understand that to be the Parker House?"

"Fine digs, if they let you in," said young Pip, looking us over. He'd loaded the trunk onto his little cart.

"On our way, then," ordered Eddie. "This *enceinte* African woman is in some distress." He glanced over at me. "Mason! Mind the dog. And you, Crispa, take up the rear."

I glared at Eddie, but, for the moment, I let it pass. After all, I'd spoken much the same way to our Otha in my Virginia days. The thing to do now was to get Seela to shelter. She was breathing in short gasps. The baby was on the way. And so we traipsed uphill, with Eddie in the lead. Seela leaned against Crispa and me, one of us on either side. Arf stuck close to our feet. And Pip handled the trunk.

The Parker House hotel was a single-story row of wooden rooms along one edge of the square I'd noticed before—Portsmouth Square. Several restaurants were on the square, and a gambling hell called the Eldorado. With the day winding down and the fog coming in, several hundred strangers were in the square—talking, making deals, and planning their evening's debauch. Pre-assembled house frames were piled in a corner of the square, as well as a mountain of lumber. Eddie made a quick foray into the lobby of the Parker House and emerged chagrined. Not only did they have no rooms for Eddie, the clerk had said something cutting.

"Puffed up mountebank," muttered Ed, and turned again to our porter Pip. "Perhaps a more Spartan style befits us. Something along the lines of a rooming house? We may, I believe, be here for as long as a week."

Pip brushed his unkempt shock of hair out of his eyes and proposed leading us to a two-story wooden rooming house that lay three blocks further up the hill. We ascended a steep narrow street, crowded with pickpockets, drunks, fancy women, speculators, and bearded miners. Not everyone was white, there were a few blacks, and more than a few coppery-skinned Mexicans, many of them speaking Spanish.

The higher we got, the more of the establishments were makeshift canvas-walled buildings with unfinished planks for their counters. The goods on sale here were in higgledy-piggledy piles inside and outside the shops. It was like a mad fairground, although some of the rowdies were brandishing little sacks of gold dust like weighty tobacco pouches. Inside one of the tents I glimpsed a toothless rustic betting two full ounces of gold on the turn of a faro card.

Seela's pains were rolling steadily. We pressed on. It was nearly evening.

Our goal was in sight: a brown-painted pine building with *Fashionable Rooms* inscribed upon its side. In the grasp of a particularly sharp contraction, Seela gasped and stood still, leaning against me.

Looking over her shoulder, I could see into a canvas-walled saloon at our side, the awning painted in curlicues with the name *The Broken Harp*. Inside, a man on a stool was playing a screeching fiddle while a guffawing prospector did a jig with a plump woman in cascading skirts. Behind them was a wooden counter resting on two saw horses, and lined with bottles on top. A man with sallow skin, red hair and an uncommonly thin head tended the bar. And, sitting at the counter, dining on a steak, a bottle of ale and some whiskey on the side, was—Connor Machree, his skin burnt dark.

His eyes locked onto mine—and there could be no doubt this was he. Not a ghost. All too real. And with a knowing look on his face. He gestured, as if inviting me to come speak with him. I assumed he wanted to resume begging for guidance to the Hollow Earth. But how could he be here at all? I combed through my memories. We'd been in the polar water, amid the pink *woomo* light, and Machree seemingly comatose. Seela had gleaned the rumbies from him, and then the *ballula* tendrils had—

Pip's sharp whistle broke my train of thought. Arf nudged my leg with his head, as if wanting to herd me along. I was glad to follow our porter Pip's lead to the brown hotel that advertised Fashionable Rooms. A Mrs. Mackie ran the place. She was a sinewy lady of middle years, hard-bitten but not unkind.

Eddie told her he was Goarland Peale, and went on to introduce Seela, Crispa and me as his slaves, I stopped him dead in his tracks.

"Don't skylark," I told him. I turned to Mrs. Mackie. "This man is my cousin. Now that we've made a fortune in the gold fields, he wants to play the grandee."

"I see," said Mrs. Mackie. "I've heard of such family complications among you Southerners. And your name is?"

"I'm Mason Reynolds, and this is my wife Seela and our friend Crispa. Appearances can be deceiving. We're anything but slaves. And—can you put me in touch with a midwife? My wife has very nearly reached her term."

"Won't be the first babe born in my rooms," said Mrs. Mackie with a smile. "An auspicious event. I'll put you in a chamber on the second floor with fine view over the harbor." She paused, watching Seela wince against a wave of pain. "I can send for a midwife, but I expect the woman's busy tonight, the way things are. You'll have to make do. And I'll tell you now that I charge you an extra dollar for laundering the bedding after a birth."

"Never mind a midwife," said Crispa. "I can birth the baby. Done it six or seven times back home before I left. We had a big family."

"A boy for a midwife?" said Mrs. Mackie, doubting this.

"Crispa is a young lady," I told her. "In disguise so the sailors and miners leave her be."

"Men are ticks," said Mrs. Mackie with a shake of her head. "Bloodsucking parasites."

"Including me?" said Eddie.

"Surely not you, Cousin Goarland," said I. "And I'll leave you to settle the accounts. You can keep Arf in your room for company." And with that, Crispa and I helped Seela up the stairs, leaving Eddie to take the only other free room—which would prove to be a low-ceilinged rat-trap with a window on the alley behind the hotel.

Seela had to pause several times on the stairs. But then we were in our room, with the windows full of sky and the evening fog, warmed by the faint orange disk of the setting sun.

Seela's face was glistening with sweat. Before anything else, she stashed our two quietly glowing rumbies beneath our bed's mattress. And then she stripped off her clothes and sank onto the sheets. I bathed her face with a wet cloth from the basin. And, at Crispa's suggestion, I put some pillows behind her so she could sit up enough to see the view above the windows' half-curtains. Quite overwhelming, this ramshackle new city at dusk, a fairy kingdom in the fog, with the ghostly ships and bay and hills beyond.

"I feel like we're inside," said Seela.

"What?" I asked

"The sky and the sea are all around us. It's like we're in the Hollow Earth. And everything is singing."

"Maybe you're right about going back inside," I told her, patting her hand.

"Someone comin out of Hollow *Seela* pretty soon," said Crispa with a laugh.

Seela's water broke, and she gave a cry, more in surprise than in pain. The bed was soaked. I was ready to panic. But Crispa calmed me. As ever, our companion's features were calm and kind. She laid her hand upon Seela, and sat on a chair beside the bed, quietly coaching her through her ongoing contractions. An hour passed. And still no baby. A gong rang downstairs. The dinner bell? I realized how hungry I was.

"Go," Crispa gently urged me, divining my thoughts. "Eat. You have time."

Gratefully, I left Seela in our friend's care.

The dozen or so other lodgers were already at table. A polyglot crew. Californios, Oregonians, Australians, Chileans, and citizens from the East Coast. None of them seemed bent on going up into the gold country. They preferred, rather, to stay in San Francisco—profiting upon the gold-panners' gains. Among the company was a grocer, a bailiff, a clerk, a fireman, a security guard, and perhaps a thief or a pimp in the mix.

Eddie arrived in the dining room about the same time as me, with the inevitable Arf in tow. We two sat down beside Calvert Combs, a purveyor of mining equipment. Arf went under the table, awaiting scraps. Combs was a Yankee from Massachusetts. My feeling is that Yankees lack the innate nobility of Virginians. They're stingy, unscrupulous, and vain—not that they have anything to be vain about.

By way of greeting, Combs took the liberty of telling me I should eat in the kitchen with my dog, seeing as how I was a mulatto. And then he smirked at me, as if he'd lit off a stink bomb and was expecting me to go wild.

"I've heard that word before," I told Calvert evenly. "*Mulatto.* It doesn't apply to me, nor to my suffering wife upstairs, nor to our friend Crispa, and you're a jackass."

"Calling me a jackass, you whelp? Shall I box your ears?" Hearing the man's tone, Arf released a low growl.

"I see no point to fights," I said, maintaining an appearance of calm, although my pulse was pounding. "Why would I stand in place so a bonebrain can hit me in the face? No thank you. The way we do it in Virginia—if a fella rides you, you sneak into his room one night and cut a new mouth in his throat. Or you slip offal into his plate of stew. Or you pour lamp oil onto your man and set him on fire, next time he's passed out drunk in the street. Are you a heavy drinker, Mr. Combs?"

"It's hardly your place to play the inquisitor," snapped the Yankee.

"But do you take the point that I mislike fisticuffs?" I said. I held up my hand and studied the back of it as if I hadn't seen it lately. "I freely admit I'm the color of fine leather saddle. But this is a passing condition, eh? We'll all be skeletons, by and by. With no skin to bear the taint of tint."

Calvert stared at me in silence for the better part of a minute, with his head cocked to one side, as if he were a dog baffled by a strange sequence of sounds. And then he gave up on trying to understand and let out a laugh.

"You're welcome with the rest of this rum lot, Mason. I can't say I honestly give a damn what you are, as long as it ain't Chinese. And stay away from my stew! Ripe offal garnish—no thank you indeed!"

"Mason's wife is Chinese," put in Eddie, very quick and mocking. "She's from the utmost southern region of China. Beneath the central glacier of the Antarctic pole."

"Whatever you two say," went Calvert Combs, refilling his glass. "And welcome to the liars' club. You're fortunate you landed here. The food is toothsome—which is something of a wonder in a rooming house, eh, Mrs. Mackie?"

"Of course it's good," said Mrs. Mackie. "Why shouldn't it be? With all the cattle in the fields, and the fish and crabs in the bay. And my kitchen garden is flourishing. Salmon, steak, and corn chowder tonight, boys, with greens and sourdough bread."

I ate my fill, passing tidbits to Arf, and losing myself in the gut joy of the meal. It was only when Mrs. Mackie set to ladling out bowls of pudding that I remembered myself, or rather, remembered Seela. That faint high noise in the background—those were my wife's cries! I snatched up spoons with three bowls of pudding and thundered up the stairs. And this time Arf came with me. He didn't want to be in Eddie's room.

Seela had no appetite, but Crispa readily ate two shares of dessert. Seela's labor went on through the night. An hour before dawn Arf and I went out into the street for a break, and I found Eddie Poe out there as well, staring up the hillside at the rest of the town. San Francisco was waking to the coming day's activity.

"See the canvas sides of the tent houses, lit from the lamps within," said Eddie. "Dwellings of solid, geometric light. Living jewels. Quite wonderful."

"Travelers we," said I, drawing a measure of calm from my friend's presence.

"I've been awake all night, penning lines and smoking opium from the *Water Witch*," said Eddie. "Bliss. How fares your Seela?"

"She says she feels like she's being torn in half," I told him. "And I'm scared she'll die. Without Seela—I'd be a lost farmboy again."

"You're more than that, Mason," said Eddie. "You've begun to write. The Hollow Earth narrative that you left at Coale's bookstore in Baltimore! Do you deem it publishable?"

"How would I know?" I said. Somehow I wasn't ready to tell Eddie that Connor Machree had read my manuscript for *The Hollow Earth*. If Machree was dead, what did that matter? But, wait, wait, I'd seen the man in the Broken Harp saloon on the way to our hotel last night. Or had I? Perhaps it had been a trick of the light, or a figment brought on by fatigue. I pushed Machree from my mind.

"I would want to edit it, were I to stay," Eddie was saying, still talking about my *Hollow Earth* manuscript. "I'd amend the infelicities. I rather suspect you made verbal sallies at my expense. It's bad taste when a student slights his master."

"I see you didn't shed any vanity during your passage through the grave," said I.

"How sharper than a serpent's tooth it is to have a thankless child!" intoned Eddie. "The Bard. *Lear*, Act 1, Scene 4. Publish what you will, impudent pup. What have I to lose? I'm twice dead. In any case, the monstrous dungbeetle Rufus Griswold has had his way with my reputation. In California, we're beyond the backbiting literary mandarins of New England and Manhattan. Should I fail at my return to my proper Earth, we'll publish your *Hollow Earth* intact, and proceed to the sequel. The *Return*. It might be well for you to enhance the first volume with a map of the inner world. Who knows how far our narratives may lead—considering that *every word is true*.

"I'm certainly in need of money," said I. Arf at my feet was at ease, delicately sampling the myriad of smells threading along the waking city's air.

"Indeed," said Eddie, his eyes still playing across the glowing tents on the hillsides. "Three mouths to feed! A manly obligation. I myself—I may never be a father."

"There's still time," I said. "If you can pick a suitable woman. Not a cousin and not a widow."

"You rebuke my wayward heart?" said Eddie, raising his eyebrows. "Your impudence knows no bounds. But in my genial mood, I refrain from umbrage." He paused a minute, rocking on his heels, as if weighing my words. "Find a suitable woman? The shapely and forthright Jewel in the Hollow Earth, do you remember her? I would gladly deem her as suitable, if I were so allowed to choose." He touched the silk-wrapped amulet at his neck, as he was wont to do. "It is, after all, Jewel's gift of this rumby that has given me dominion over that *ballula* whom I call Cytherea. It may be that Jewel hopes Cytherea will carry me back to her dark embrace."

"But who sent Cytherea?" I asked.

"The *woomo*, I'm sure," said Eddie. "But who can fathom their tenebrous plans?"

A wail from Seela drifted from our room's window. Arf sat upright, pricking his ears and staring at the window. "Go to your lady, Mason," said Poe. "Taste life's joys and pains to the lees."

Our boy was born an hour later, with the rising of the sun. I wept with joy and relief. The babe had a wide mouth and strong lungs. His umbilical cord made a particularly strong impression on me. It was thick and twisty, engorged by a red artery and a blue vein, a glistening link that led from his belly into Seela's slippery birth canal. I had a vision of a garland through time, a cord from the boy to Seela, a second cord from Seela to her mother, a third cord from Seela's mother to her grandmother, back and back, a chain of navel cords, festooned with babies like cucumbers upon a vine!

Crispa and I cleaned up Seela, got new sheets, and remade the bed. Arf stayed well out of the way, lying in a corner of the room watching. Crispa settled down on an extra feather-erbed and fell asleep. Our new baby, this tiny wight, lay at Seela's breast, not suckling as yet, just nestled there, perfectly at ease, a bit wearied by his birth, his lips a quiet triangle. For a moment he regarded me with deep eyes of primordial mystery, unfocused and untrained, taking my measure. I would do. His eyelids fluttered and he slept. He was white against Seela's dark skin. I ran my hand across his body. Skin like silk, as if without pores.

"Do you need anything?" I asked Seela.

"I'm hungry," she said. I was glad to hear this. The labor was over. We were back to—well, not back to *normal*. With the baby, our lives as we'd known them were done. New pathways lay ahead.

I went downstairs with Arf, and the roomers were at table again. I received congratulations all around. As yet Eddie was not to be seen. I heaped Seela a plate of eggs, ham, bread, butter, and jam. Arf took up his station beneath the dining table. I bore Seela's plate upstairs with a mug of coffee. She ate and drank, smiling and laughing the whole time. We couldn't stop looking at our new baby. Such a miracle—that a perfectly formed human could have grown inside Seela. How does it happen? Life is a mystery, and every instant a miracle.

Seela and I chatted for a while, though I don't remember what we said. Sweet nothings. Two birds in a nest, admiring their hatchling.

"Can we call him Tuck?" I asked her.

"Tuck? That's a name?"

"My uncle's name. He was always nice to me."

"I like Brumble," said Seela. "*My* uncle's name."

"You uncle's really called Brumble?"

"His nickname. He has a deep voice." She stroked the baby's fat cheek with the tip of her finger and raised her voice as high as it would go. "Little Brumble." The baby shifted and made a wee sound. A coo. Seela gave me a sunny, guileless smile. I could only assent.

"Brumble he is," said I.

"Now let me sleep too," said Seela. "Hard night. Worth it." She smiled at the baby again.

"Don't roll on him and crush him," I cautioned her. "Sometimes on the farm, a sow will…"

"Oh, get on with you. And take your rumby. Just in case."

I pulled my fat, heavy, glinting rumby from where it rested with Seela's, beneath the mattress. It seemed to greet me. I put it in my pants pocket, leaving the companion for Seela. Silently the rumbies sang to us, happy to be in play. When Seela had time, she'd wrap them in thread, and they'd hang on our necks again.

I kissed Seela goodbye, and walked downstairs, mentally composing my narrative of the past day's events.

4. Roulette

Eddie was alone in the common room, with Arf at his feet, studying a newspaper and drinking coffee. "The bridegroom cometh," he said, glancing up. "The father almighty. All is well?"

"Brumble," I said, grinning like a fool. I went to Eddie and shook his hand. "You can be his godfather."

"An honor," said Eddie, miming a tip of the hat. "Brumble? An hirsute cub?"

"Soft as a rabbit," said I. "Smooth as cream. I love him already."

"Hallelujah," said Eddie, with apparent sincerity. "I envy you. Are you ready to seek employ?"

"In what sense?" Today of all days, I had no lust for going hat in hand to beg for jobs.

"The *Daily Alta California!*" said Eddie, tapping the newspaper against his hand. "Their typesetting is vile, and their writers are inarticulate. Let us hie ourselves thither and amend their ways. You recall that on the ship I concocted some fanciful reports from the gold country. I warrant they'll sell. Come to my room and we'll toff you up. You have the look of a bleary sailor on a spree."

I washed, and combed my hair, and took a clean white shirt of Eddie's. I ran upstairs to check on Seela and Brumble. They were blissfully asleep, and so was Crispa. I told Mrs. Mackie I'd be going out for an hour, and she assured me she'd watch over my precious ones.

"A baby boy in the house is good luck," said she.

"What of a baby girl?" asked Eddie.

"A baby of any kind is good luck," said Mrs. Mackie. "Take care of your cousin today, Goarland. His head spins." She wagged a finger at Eddie. It was as if everyone who met Eddie could tell what he was like. "No saloons!"

"A morning drinker is doomed," said Eddie.

At this point I realized there would indeed be trouble. Of course our first day in town would call for celebration. Of course Eddie would be drunk. And then, who knew?

I turned to my imp of a mentor. "Perhaps I'd better stay here with—"

But by now Eddie had bundled me into the street with Arf right behind us. It was about nine in the morning, with a fading blanket of fog at the mouth the bay, and a brightening sun above. The air was soft, fragrant, and elastic, with each breath like a sip of tonic. Far from being exhausted after the night's cavalcade of events, I felt exhilarated. Why not walk about with my dog and my friend?

"A fellow told me the *Daily Alta* office is on Montgomery Street next to the port," said Eddie gesturing past the tents, the canvas cabins, and the brightly painted wooden buildings. "We might have passed it yesterday."

From here I could see scores of ships, some at anchor, some tied to the piers of the harbor's little cove. The abandoned vessels among them were like decaying, empty houses, but the others were clean and bright in the morning sun. The trim hull of the *Water Witch* winked a hello.

"Curious town," said I, as we descended toward Portsmouth Square. "Grown up like a mushroom fairy ring. From a few hundred souls to twenty thousand in one year."

"We'll have an easy time cozening the lads at the *Daily Alta*," said Eddie. "They're rawhide Westerners, and we're men of ink and pen. They'll sign us onto the *Alta* payroll, I'll give them my gold country pieces, we'll get fat advances, we'll take the rest of the day off. And perhaps before doing any further work at all, we'll leave town. In any case we'll have established a contact for our projects to come."

"I can be the muse for you two *writers*," said a bold girl with a husky voice. As she passed, she elbowed Eddie and brushed her hip against my leg. She was about my age. "Come see me at the Broken Harp," she said. "I brim with tales of weal and woe." A few steps uphill she glanced back over her shoulder, gauging her effect. Her lips were heavily rouged, and her eyes held an unspoken question. "Ask for Ina Durivage," she said. "That's me. I need a knight." She strode on her way, leaving Eddie in an amorous tizzy.

"Little chance of *you* courting a street girl like that," he told me, almost spiteful in his tone. "Leave her to me, my boy. After we visit the newspaper offices, you'll speed back to your mother hen and your downy chick. A faithful patriarch at age seventeen, poor lad. Caught in the trap. Meanwhile I'll spend a few hours in doubling our holdings via my mathematico-logical understanding of faro and roulette. With gold pouch full, I'll assemble the equipage for our foray to the Hollow Earth." Eddie pointed toward the sky. "Our celestial chariot awaits, richly lined with mother of pearl, eh? I've rethought our schedule. I propose we set out tomorrow at dawn. I'll arrange our supplies by dusk and then, during my last night in San Francisco, I'll pay court to the antic Ina. Quite my style, this saucy coquette. Disturbed, declamatory, decadent, doomed. Even more to my taste than the dark Jewel of the Hollow Earth. And—"

"Wait," I interrupted. "You say dawn tomorrow? We can't leave so soon as all that. Not with Seela and a newborn babe."

"Seela can manage," said Eddie. "She's wild, uncorrupted, and from a truly natural world. Unencumbered by the fripperies of civilized woman and man."

"Maybe," I said. "I can talk to her about it. But, you, Eddie, you're half out of your head. If you want to travel tomorrow, you need to rest. Not sit up all night writing and smoking opium."

"Perhaps I'll be sharpening my pen in Ina's bed," said Eddie. It was quite unlike him, such a ribald remark. But I laughed just the same.

"You dog," said I, getting into my friend's reckless mood. We were on the verge of another epic journey, and ready to slip our moorings again.

As it happened, we never made it to the offices of the *Daily Alta* newspaper. Upon entering the lively Portsmouth Square, Eddie, feeling in his pocket, observed that he still had a ten-dollar gold eagle coin left from the hoard that he and the widow Whistler had amassed in New York. He reasoned aloud that, since he would be repeatedly doubling his stake at the faro table, ten dollars was as good a start as a hundred. So really there was no need to visit the *Alta* office at all.

"My mind is keen in the early morning," added Eddie, easily throwing his arm across my shoulders. "When my night of intoxicated wonder ends, I feel a jangle in my nerves. The workaday world's details slap at me like combers against a cliff. My psyche is a raddled shower of sparks. *Ergo* let us hie ourselves to the Eldorado!"

This was the moment when I again remembered my glimpse into the Broken Harp the night before. "I saw Machree in a saloon near our hotel," I blurted out. "The man we left to drown. Not a ghost. He was real. He recognized me."

"Oho," said Eddie, halting his progress. "The plot thickens." His face went blank while his powerful mind assayed the possibilities. "The *woomo* light!" he presently exclaimed. "It carried him here. And he is burned quite black?"

"Indeed," said I, wondering at Eddie's acumen. "But why would the mighty *woomo* save a conniving jeweler? Tell me all you know, and have done with playing the Sphinx."

Eddie drew a breath and began. "First of all, the jeweler Machree is my disciple. A Crozier, as I term him, in the Order of the Golden Frond, a society invented by Annabel Whistler and me, with a congregation approaching twenty. My followers call me the Tulku. He who is reborn. I've told them my tale of being stabbed and drowned and resurrected."

"It's not grand enough to be a writer?" I said.

"I'm destined for more," said Eddie. "I am the Tulku and Machree is my Crozier. He helps me tend my flock. It's hard to be sure if he fully grasps the wheeze, not that I've been overly frank with him. He's a fellow with a wide circle of friends, and a steady need of funds. Very useful."

"So you've started a religion," I said, trying to sort this out.

"Not a religion, per se. Something more like the Scottish Rite, or like Mesmerism. But with a sting. Annabel, Machree, and I have crafted a liturgy for our occult rites—and the ceremonies culminate in psychic contact with our august friends the *woomo*."

"Wait, tell me about the occult rites," said I.

"The usual bill of fare," said Eddie, with the sly smile of a jaded roué. "Wine, hashish, and copulation—to the tune of *la Whistler's* harp arpeggios and Machree's thunderous organ music. Being the Tulku, I preside."

"You preach?"

"Often I contribute a literary recitation, such as 'The Raven.' And then, with my plump and thinky rumby gem to hand, I summon the *woomo*. The mighty sea cucumbers' tendrils find their way to us from the Hollow Earth's core, and the golden fronds illuminate my rumby. The gem twitches like a sleeper ready to awake. And my followers enter a state of ecstasy."

"Do you take advantage of your subjects when they swoon?" asked I.

Eddie looked abashed. "Not always in the coarse, animal way. Even in the absence of physical touch, I can attain a sense of intimate contact with my adepts. Samples of their life essences are physically transferred from their bodies into mine. The *woomo's* subtle tendrils extract the samples from my flock, you see, and they store these living cells within my generative organs." He lowered his voice to a whisper. "I feel a growing lump within my sack. A library of human forms."

This was not a topic I cared to pursue. I moved on. "And Connor Machree wants a rumby of his own."

"All the more reason to depart at the morrow's dawn," said Eddie.

As if conjured up, the little porter boy from last night appeared before us. Pip of the unruly hair. Arf greeted him effusively, putting his feet on Pip's chest and licking his face.

"Settled in well, gentleman?" piped the boy, framing a winsome glance through his bangs. "Any errands I can help with today?"

"We're likely to go shopping for expedition supplies this afternoon," Eddie told Pip. "You might come to Mrs. Mackie's and ask for us."

"Digging in the gold country, eh?" said Pip. "Some of the tenderfeet end up like that quiz over there. A onetime Harvard student, as he used to say."

Pip directed our attention to a forty-year-old man sitting alone on the ground in a corner of the square. He was wrapped in a rough blanket, his matted hair hung across his wasted face, and his eyes glared steadily forward. He wore an expression of hopeless suffering, and he was muttering to himself.

"Traded his digging-spot for a meal," said Pip. "And then the gold came in. The man drank bad whiskey and went mad."

"How do you know?" I asked.

"He was my father," said Pip. "Not that he recognizes me anymore. Useless fool." It was sad to see so young a boy feign such hardness.

"We're not planning to dig for gold at all," I gently told Pip. "And I'm sorry about your father."

The smudged urchin made a razzing noise and skipped away. Arf followed him for a few steps, then came back to us.

"A cold, predatory child," mused Eddie. "Aged beyond his years."

"Why don't you finish telling me about Machree and the rumbies?" I said, putting Pip from my mind. "So I know what we're in for."

"Very well." Eddie steered me to one side of the square's foot traffic, and we found a perch on the mound of unsold house frames I'd noticed before. Their owner, a little man in a dark suit, fixed us with a watchful eye.

"The sum that Machree offered for my personal rumby, although largish, was unconvincing," Eddie continued. "I told Machree I would prefer to sell him advice on how to obtain a rumby of his *own*. Machree acceded, and in return, I instructed him to seek out Mason Reynolds and his woman

Seela in Baltimore. I assumed you two were still there, and that a physical description of Seela might suffice. She hides not her light beneath a bushel. Machree boarded a stagecoach for Baltimore. This was on the first of March."

"Go on," I said.

"Machree arrived in Baltimore on March the fifth, only to learn that you two had departed for New York on March the fourth. Machree stole or purchased your two rumbies in Baltimore, and he learned that you meant to ship to San Francisco aboard the *Purple Whale*. I gleaned these details via a note from Machree which I received in Manhattan on March the ninth. By the time I got the note, you and Machree were on the high seas. I resolved to follow. I didn't want you and Seela at my covetous disciple's mercy."

"That is, you didn't want to miss out on what we did."

"If you will. I thought you and Seela might soon bolt for the Hollow Earth. And I, too, wanted to revisit that eldritch landscape or, better yet, pass fully through it and return to the Edenic Earth from which I came."

"A method in your madness," said I. "Continue."

"I boarded the *Water Witch*, a faster ship than the *Purple Whale*. And I bid Cytherea to follow along. And, soon after my ship had rounded the Horn, I petitioned my good *ballula* to ferry you and Seela from your ship to mine. In this wise we three would arrive in San Francisco before Machree. We'd have time to see the city, to garner supplies, and then to embark upon our return to the Hollow Earth without that venal, tiresome man in tow. That was my plan."

"But the *woomo* saved Machree," said he. "And he got here before us."

"Refined and devious are the sea cucumbers of the Hollow Earth," said Eddie, shaking his head in bemusement. "They sped Machree northward like a signal upon a telegraph wire."

"And again I ask *why*. Why do the *woomo* help first you, and then Machree?"

"Are we in court, Mason? Are you taking a deposition?" Eddie shrugged. "Perhaps the *woomo* value the tuneless, yawping hymns of the Order of the Golden Frond, paeans composed by Machree himself. Perhaps my cult is no hoax at all? *Nescio.* I do not know. For now, our task is to raise a grubstake for a return to the Hollow Earth. An expeditious departure is of growing urgency, with the tedious Machree on the scene."

The owner of the stack of house frames had been studiously eavesdropping. But our tale made little sense to him. Weary of Eddie's opaque farrago, the merchant nudged us on our way. Miners, swindlers, speculators, and vaqueros were streaming past, everyone talking at once. I roused Arf, then stood and turned slowly around, staring into the corners and recesses of the square.

"No sign of Machree," I said.

"It may be that he's engaged cat's-paws to watch for us," said Eddie, with a touch of unease. "The man is devious. Thanks to the *woomo*, he's had nearly a month here to lay snares." He fondled his weighty rumby gem, which he wore, as always, in an intricate wrapping of silk threads upon a cord around his neck. "I sense that you have your own rumby to hand?"

"I do."

"It is well," said Eddie. "This doubles our power of tekelili. And Seela's stone?"

"It's with her. Under our mattress. Do you think Crispa might steal it? Should I go back to our room?"

"And miss our impending financial coup?" said Eddie. "Seela, Brumble, and Crispa can wait. Grant me an hour of your time, my boy. Accompany me into the Eldorado, San Francisco's premier gambling hell. We'll perform lucrative legerdemain."

"How so?"

"We'll use our rumby tekelili for exchanging signs, for remote viewing, and mayhap to engage the hylozoic inner soul of the roulette wheel. Tekelili has untapped potency, Mason. Mind pervades matter." Meaning to offer a demonstration, Eddie fell silent and stared at me while the crowd continued swirling past.

The rumby in my pocket gave a shudder and a shake. Very faintly I heard Eddie's smooth voice in my head, asking if I could hear him. I nodded, and now Eddie sent an image. I saw a playing card, a ten of diamonds, very clear, hanging in the air. I named the card aloud.

"To victory!" said Ed, and we marched into the Eldorado. The doorman, or bouncer, refused to let Arf inside, but I persuaded the dog to lie quietly on the ground outside the door. What with my rumby, and with all that Arf and I had been through in the Hollow Earth, he did at times seem to understand what I wanted him to do.

The Eldorado's outer walls were rough wood, but the inside was sumptuous. The so-called hell was a single, large, high room. A row of fluted columns ran down the middle, with a massive, polished redwood bar along one side. The games dominated on the floor—tables for the card games faro and monte, a pair of elegantly clicking roulette wheels, and three spinning chuck-a-luck bird-cages with dice within. Eddie told me that chuck-a-luck was for greenhorns.

"We'll build a stake at faro, and make a killing at roulette," he told me.

Worn-out gamblers and languid women relaxed on the cushioned and gilded furniture. The room was illuminated by dangling crystal chandeliers, with no frank rays of sunlight allowed. Mirrors, China silk hangings, and paintings of nude women adorned the walls. I'd hardly ever seen paintings before.

Before starting at the tables, Eddie approached the bar. A comely girl in a close-fitting black silk dress awaited us. Her slender fingers were adorned with rings.

"My cousin and I would rather fancy a pick-me-up," Eddie told her. "May I charge it on account, my dear…"

"Persephone," said the smiling maiden, with a modest air. "No credit here. Open your poke and I'll take a pinch of gold dust. That's the rate for idlers."

"I, ah, have a coin," said Eddie. "But I'm loath to cut into it. I'll let Dame Fortuna make the change."

He strode over to a nearby faro table, and set down his ten-dollar gold eagle on a layout that showed each rank of card, from Ace to King. Eddie bet on the ten. The dealer brandished a card holder, known as a *shoe*, and dealt out cards in pairs. The members of each pair signaled a losing number and a winning number. Presently ten was anointed as a winning number. Barely containing his nervous glee, Eddie rejoined me at the bar, with his gold eagle and a trimmed-down gold doubloon in hand.

"Now cake and brandy for two," he told the girl with the rings, setting his mangled doubloon on the bar.

"It's on the house," said Persephone, waving off the coin. "As long as you keep playing." She gave a low laugh. "Maybe you'll hit big, maybe we'll take all."

The sweets were of a kind I'd never had before: square little iced cakes that Eddie termed *petits fours*, glancing to see if the alluring Persephone marked his command of French. But she didn't seem to care.

As Eddie and I stood there, enjoying our cake and brandy, he watched the faro game, intently eyeing the dealer's shoe of cards. At a given moment, he strode over and put his two coins on the Jack. Moments later he'd won again. Four gold coins now: two eagles, a doubloon, and a guilder. He gave me the two eagles.

The rumby in my pocket warmed. I saw a Queen card in the air. An image from Eddie. I myself was unable to see into the dealer's deck, but Eddie was in a high state of psychic clarity. I bet on the Queen, and I won on the next pair of cards from the shoe. In short order we'd amassed a hundred and ten dollars.

"Now for the roulette," Eddie said to me as we leaned against the bar, gloating over our eleven gold coins. "I'll imbibe another small brandy before I explain the plan."

"Are you sure you should keep drinking?" I asked him.

"Frightened farm boy," said he. Eddie could turn ugly very fast.

"Drinks on the house," repeated Persephone, her voice sweet.

Stepping aside to let Eddie take his pleasure, I carried a scrap of cake to Arf, lying by the wall just outside the entrance. And then back inside for me. It was nearly noon, and the Eldorado was filling up. Across the big room a young boy was lighting a full-sized cigar, an odd and unwholesome apparition. As the tousled child exhaled a great plume of smoke, I realized it was our porter once again, little Pip. Catching me looking at him, he mimed a salute and made his way over, attempting a swagger in his walk.

"Do you have a mother?" I asked him. "Does she know you're here? Does she know your Pa's gone mad?"

Speaking of family matters, about which I knew so little, I was suffused with a pang of shame. Why was I with Eddie in a gambling hell and not with Seela and Brumble?

"Pa's nuts, Ma's dead, and I don't need coddling," said Pip, closing down the topic. "You working gaffs?"

"Gaffs?"

"Gambling tricks," said Eddie, gliding over from the bar with a plume of alcohol on his breath. "The boy imagines we're sharpers." Daintily Eddie nibbled a pink *petit four*. "Currants with cream," he reported.

"If you ain't miners, you gotta be sharpers," said Pip.

"Never mind what we are," I said, misliking the intentness of the boy's glittering eyes. He was like a shrill, predatory insect. My fatigue and my glass of brandy were getting to me. "Get away from us," I snapped. "You're a jinx."

Pip sneered, blew another cloud of smoke, and headed over to cozen a drunken miner at the chuck-a-luck dice. No doubt Pip hoped to pick the man's pocket. It was a sorry class of people in here.

"I want to leave," I told Eddie. "It's too much. I need to be with Seela."

"Wait!" he hissed. "We're at the climax. One single turn on Fortuna's wheel. I'll bet our stake. We have a hundred and ten—well, no, a hundred, as I tipped Persephone. You'll stand as close to the wheel as possible. Hold your rumby in your hand, and focus the full power of your tekelili on the number we bet."

"Which number?" I asked, intrigued by Eddie's plan.

"A deeper wrinkle here," said Eddie. "*The wheel will tell us.* We'll work together—you, the wheel, and me. It pays thirty to one. We'll win three thousand dollars."

"It is well," said I. "And God help me, Eddie, once we win, we'll leave immediately, with no more drinks, and no more bets, or I'll bash your noggin in." I rapped a knuckle against his pale, bulging brow, and gave him a shake. "Do you hear me, you demonic charlatan?"

"The nest is best," crooned Eddie, as if addled from his drinks. "Back to the hen and chick for you, eh? But first we peck!"

I slipped my bare hand into my pocket. I held my fat dense rumby, and merged into its tekelili. The gem tingled against my skin, as if barbed like a burr. Colors flowed up my arm and into my eyes. Meanwhile Eddie laid his left hand across his silk-wrapped, neck-worn amulet, in conversation with his own gem.

Unexpectedly I heard a squeaky woman's voice in my head. "Twenty-three," she said. The voice of the wheel, and who knows how I heard it. Via tekelili, I shared the number with Eddie, and I heard his silent hosanna.

Eddie slapped our really rather pitifully small pile of coins onto the roulette layout. The croupier spun the horizontal wheel, and whirled a little white ball into the encircling bowl. The ball clattered against the slots and danced. Red, black, red, red, black. I fixed my eyes on the red twenty-three, and Eddie did the same. I could feel our tekelili power. Impossibly fine tendrils veined the air around us.

The red slot of the twenty three was like a polar maelstrom drawing in the tiny traveler that was the ball, or like a sun pulling down a moon, or a serpent swallowing a mouse, or a tornado pulling us into its eye. *Click, clatter, click*, and a low exclamation from those around us. We'd won three thousand dollars.

The croupier told us that the Eldorado gold was worth twenty dollars an ounce, and, with some prodding, he paid us our winnings in the form of fifteen ounces of glittering dust. Nearly a pound! I had the man bag it into two deerskin pouches, approximately equal in size, one for Ed, and one for me.

For a wonder, Eddie was willing to leave the gambling den. I think, like me, he was feeling skittish about Connor Machree. We made our way into Portsmouth Square, a little stunned by the intensity of the pure sunlight. Arf was right at our heels, sniffing us to see if we'd brought food from inside.

"I'm coming with you gents," said the barmaid Persephone, appearing beside us, and twining her arm around Eddie's waist. "I've worked enough today. I can get us a private dining room at the Delmonico. Entrance in back. We'll have a spree." Delmonico was a fancy restaurant just across the square. But I doubted we'd be getting any food if we followed Persephone there.

"Guard your pocket," I warned Eddie, and he pushed Persephone away.

"You're mistaking me for an entirely different class of person," Eddie told her, always glad for a chance to tell some thumpers. "My cousin Mason and I are tending to his wife and their newborn baby. We only came out for diapers and clabber. We entered the Eldorado by mistake—Mason here thought it was a church. He's quite pious, you know. As for the roulette, well, twenty-three was Grandmother's birthday. We're grateful for her holy blessing. But we have no lust for low jinks. Do mark that I already tipped you. Sojourn on, young woman, and may the Light be with you."

"You sober up fast, don't you?" said Persephone with disgust. She turned on her heel and flounced back into the Eldorado. Eddie pulled out his poke of gold, loosed the rawhide around the pouch, and stared in, as if wanting to confirm it was real.

"Stop that," I told him. "People are looking. Some thief is going to jostle you."

"Indeed," said Eddie, gathering his wits and pocketing his gold. "Up the hill to Mrs. Mackie's. And to Mason's wee chickabiddy. You named him—what was it?"

"Gramble, I think," said I, that single shot of bandy still buzzing in my ears. "Or, no, it was Brumble." How could I forget my son's name? Tears started into my eyes at the thought of his tiny fuzzed head. And somehow the sight of Arf's kind, liquid eyes with his mobile, sympathetic eyebrows was like a knife in my heart. I had to bring my life into order.

Taking tight hold of Eddie's arm, I swept him up the hill toward the hotel. I had a bad moment as we passed that cloth-walled saloon, the Broken Harp. The girl who'd approached us this morning—Ina—she was in there conning a miner who had precisely half of his teeth missing. The left half. Standing behind the counter with a dour expression was the thin-headed red-haired man I'd seen before. Inevitably Ina's eye caught mine, and she gave me a beckoning wave.

"That's where I saw Connor Machree," I told Eddie.

"Looking to find him?" shrilled a voice just behind us. "Want me to bring him to your room?"

Naturally it was Pip. "What does it take to get rid of you?" I cried.

"Gold," said he. "I've got a ready sack. In my spare time, I gather specks of dust off the streets. But *you're* giving me a full ounce."

I leaned back and lifted my foot, preparing to kick him, and before I knew it I'd fallen heavily onto the muddy street. Pip had shoved me off balance. The little boy was a tiger. He was on me, trying to work his hand into my pocket, meaning to steal my pouch of gold, robbing me in the full light of day. Arf snarled and nipped at Pip, but the covetous urchin thrust the dog aside.

Eddie, never one for physical fisticuffs, called for help from the patrons of the Broken Harp. The thin, cold-looking proprietor of the Broken Harp was watching us, but he made no move to interfere

"That's the boy, Pip," urged the streetwise Ina, standing in the opening that was the saloon's door. "Hold them tight. Machree's coming out from our room."

Hearing this, Eddie turned to start uphill, but Pip hooked one of his feet around Eddie's ankle, sending him to the ground as well. At this point, Arf got a really good bite into Pip's calf, and the boy yelped. And then Machree was standing over us, still dressed in his brown suit. His skin was as dark as my old companion Otha's had ever been. He looked more peaceful than before.

"The sorcerer and his apprentice," said Machree exaggerating his Virginia drawl. "Simmer down, Pip, leave them be." He turned his attention to my companion. "The boy's like a pond leech, eh, Eddie?"

"You know full well my name is Goarland Peale," said Eddie. "I'm the Tulku of the Order of the Golden Frond, and you've had the privilege to assist me as the order's Crozier."

"Come now, Edgar Allan Poe," said Machree putting on a jovial air. "Hasn't this ruffian Mason told you I read his full manuscript in the back room of E. J. Coale's bookstore in Baltimore? *The Hollow Earth*, or, *The Narrative of Mason Algiers Reynolds of Virginia*. I know the whole story. You can't bamboozle me. I'm traveling with you to the Hollow Earth, and that's that. I'm meant to be a part of your dodgy schemes."

"Perhaps," said Eddie, as if thinking this over.

I got free of Pip, rose to my feet, and addressed Machree myself. "Why don't you ask the *woomo* to carry you to the Hollow Earth on a tendril of light? Like they did for you when the Purple Whale sank. You don't need us, and we don't need you. Go it alone."

"We're having a forthright honest conversation now?" said Machree. "High time. Yes, a *woomo* ray bore me to San Francisco. Evidently the Great Old Ones see value in me. But I wouldn't know how to ask them to carry me onward to the Hollow Earth. Especially not with my rumbies stolen by you and that—"

"Mason, Seela, and I are planning to ride in my *ballula*," interrupted Eddie. "Cytherea. Didn't you see her rescuing Mason and Seela at sea?"

"I wasn't seeing anything," said Machree, all traces of a smile gone. "I'd been robbed and left to drown. At least Seela had done me the kindness of not slitting my gullet."

"Find your *own* rumby in the Hollow Earth," I told Machree.

"If Eddie lets me come," said Machree.

"I propose we meet at our hotel tomorrow morning," said Eddie. "Crack of dawn."

"You should give Seela and the baby a little more time," I told Eddie again.

"And I told you not to fret," said Eddie. He turned to Machree. "My plan is to make my way back to my original Earth and to resume my literary career. And it's now crossed my mind that you might do well as my literary agent over there. You're hard-scrabble enough to make me rich. And bully enough to fend off my fiendish literary foe Rufus Griswold." Poe glanced over at me. "Don't be envious, Mason. You're not low enough for the job."

"Flattery greases no skids, Mr. Poe," said Machree. "And hear me when I say I'm coming with you right now, and I'll be sleeping in your room."

"I'm coming too!" put in Pip.

"No," said Eddie, Machree, and I—fully united on this one point. "You're not."

"Ounce of gold?" wheedled Pip.

"Hold out your pouch," said I, and I tipped over some dust.

"What about me?" called Ina, emotion welling in her voice. "Machree's been cadging space in my room for three weeks. Promising the stars and the moon. And as romantic as Saturn and the cinders. And meanwhile the villain Cruickshank, I mean that worm-headed man behind the bar, with his red hair and dead heart—he collects a procurer's fee from men like Machree, and still he says I owe him money. I'm a prisoner here, boys, a crushed rose. I once had hopes to enter high society—now dashed. Step forward and save me, Mason and Eddie!"

"Watch your tongue or you're back in the street," said Cruickshank from behind the bar.

"Help yourself to some of Pip's gold dust," Machree coldly advised Ina. "I'm leaving your orbit now."

"Bedbug," said Ina. "Whinger. Leech."

Pitying Ina, and admiring her fine, high invective, I gave Pip a supplemental tablespoon of gold, taking care lest Arf snuffle it up with his wet, probing nose. "Share this with your friend," I told Pip.

"Can Ina and me help you shop for supplies?" petitioned the boy.

"*On verra*," said Eddie, fixing Ina with an inquisitive eye. Clearly she fascinated him. "One will see."

And with that, Eddie, Machree, Arf, and I broke free of Pip and Ina, making our way up the hill to Mrs. Mackie's hotel.

5. Cytherea

I ran up the steps to our room, and there they were, Seela and Brumble, awake now, with Seela holding Brumble to her breast, the baby sweetly content, intent as a little animal, making the tiniest of grunts and sighs, and occasionally jerking his arms. A rich entertainment. Seela had found an open nightshirt to keep her shoulders warm.

"My darlings," I said.

"Brumble doesn't know how to nurse," said Seela, staring down at the baby, and smoothing his fine hair with a finger.

"Takes a couple of tries to start," put in Crispa, who was still there.

Arf pushed into the room and ate some scraps off a plate of Seela's on the floor. Lunchtime had come and gone. I wasn't hungry myself, not after the petits fours at the Eldorado.

"I won a lot of gold," I told Seela, showing her my pouch of dust. "Over a thousand dollars. Eddie won too."

"You didn't get a job?" said Seela. A wifely question. Not that her heart was in the role.

"This is the Gold Rush," said I. "If you're sharp, there's no need for work."

"Gold," echoed Seela, shaking her head. "So how did you win your sparkly dust?"

"We guessed a number on a turning wheel," I said.

"Did you and Eddie find a way to cheat?" asked Crispa. Aboard the *Water Witch*, I'd regaled her with my tale of Eddie and I counterfeiting Bank of Kentucky bills in Virginia.

"Sure we cheated," I said. "We put tekelili pressure on the ball. And it worked."

"Will the gamblers come after you?" asked Crispa.

"No," I said. "They don't know what we did. Even so, we might be leaving soon. Eddie's about to outfit us for an expedition."

"Oh yes!" exclaimed Seela, sitting up in the bed. "We're going to the Hollow Earth?"

"I think we should wait a week or two until you and Brumble are quite strong," I said. "But yes, we'll ride Eddie's *ballula* through the North Hole. He's pushing to go tomorrow, but I told him that's—"

"Tomorrow is fine!" said Seela, stretching out her arms, and kicking her legs beneath the sheet. "I'm a tough, wild flowerperson from the Hollow Earth. I've already been out of bed. My muscles are fine, and I'm not bleeding."

"What about Brumble?"

"He'll be in my arms."

"Can I hold him for a minute?"

Brumble's limbs were tiny, and his skin slack, as if he needed inflating. His gums were starkly bare, his nose like two holes, and his eyes cloudy. The bones on the top of his skull hadn't yet grown together, although the warm skin felt tough.

I put the tip of my finger into his mouth, and he sucked on it with some force. I tested the thickness of his cheek muscles between my finger and thumb. Impressively powerful. He'd be fine. I held him against my shoulder, cupping the back of his head with my hand. His smell was intimate and warm. Our little baby, fully formed.

Meanwhile Crispa had run downstairs to talk to Eddie about the trip. She wanted to be sure that she too was going along, even if only for part of the way.

Seela was smiling at me and the baby, taking us in.

"Well?" she said.

"Wonderful," I said. "And you grew him in your stomach."

"And now I'm my own right size again. And we can show him to my people in the Hollow Earth."

"But—really leave tomorrow?" I said, looking down at Brumble. He was asleep, with his little face closed up like a bud. I sat down beside Seela on the bed, and we laid Brumble on the sheet between us, taking in his infinitesimal changes—a pout, a dimple, a wince, a wiggle of the finger. Still deeply weary from last night, we laid ourselves flat, still staring at the baby, then fell asleep with him between us.

It was nearly dusk when we woke. We'd slept the afternoon through. Brumble was mewling, waving his little arms in a disorganized way, and mixing in yawns, hiccups, and single sneezes.

"Hello, tiny," sang Seela. She drew him to her bared breast, and this time he latched on, and, how wonderful, began to nurse, with a stream of minute grunts and swallows. Pale milk was visible at the verges of his lips.

Someone downstairs was calling my name. It was Connor Machree.

"What?" said I, upon rising from the bed, opening our door, and leaning into the stairwell.

"It's your friend Eddie Poe. I took a nap after lunch. I had a wonderful dream of the *woomo*. And now Eddie and Crispa have been gone three hours with Pip and Ina. Do you think Eddie imagines he can give us the slip?" Machree's face was a dim, anxious oval.

I checked in my pocket, and my pouch of gold was intact. It wasn't likely the light-fingered Poe would have left it in place if he was skipping out. "Don't worry," I called to Machree. "Eddie will be loading his magic seashell during the night. I reckon he'll come for us at dawn. You can depend on Seela and me."

"Would that were true," said Machree in a low tone. I was getting the impression that his ride in the *woomo* light had changed more than his skin. He seemed meeker now, more inclined to accept that he was a pawn or a cog—a bit player in the ever-expanding machinations of the *woomo*. As was I.

"Just wait in Eddie's room," I advised Machree.

"You and I are paradox incarnate," said Machree, staring up at me. "A fulcrum to pry the Earths in two. The axle of fate's turning wheel."

I had no idea what he meant by this—nor did I want to. I closed our door.

"You told Machree that he can depend on us?" said Seela. "Who even said he can come along on our trip?"

"Eddie said," I said. "Turns out Machree is Eddie's—I don't know—deacon? In a religion that Eddie made up. The Order of the Golden Frond. And Eddie's like their pope. Or no, he's the Tulku? They worship the *woomo*."

"I want us to get away from Eddie when we're in the Hollow Earth," said Seela. "I've never liked him, not really." She got out of bed and stood with Brumble against her shoulder, gently patting his back. Across the bay, another sunset was coming down.

"A fresh adventure tomorrow," said I. "It never stops."

"Changes mean you're alive," said Seela. "If we're going on a trip with those rascals I want to hang our rumbies safe upon our necks again." She paused for a moment in thought, caressing Brumble all the while. "Fetch a spool of thick, strong thread from Mrs. Mackie or, better, ask for two spools of contrasting colors. So that the amulets look well."

Machree was nowhere to be seen when I went down to get the thread. Remembering Eddie's advice to draw a map of the Hollow Earth to go with my manuscript, I managed to cadge a pen and a sheet of vellum paper from Mrs. Mackie as well as the thread. Tomorrow our party would set out aboard the redoubtable Cytherea, but I'd leave my map in our room, in the hope it might someday accompany a published edition of *The Hollow Earth*.

Back in our room, I began drawing, enjoying myself with the task, and Seela set to work with the threads. I went down again an hour later to have my dinner, and to fetch a full plate and a flagon of ale for Seela. It's well known that beer is a specific for nursing mothers. Before long, my little map was done, and we two were wearing our heavy, wrapped-up rumbies on our necks again. Seela was very nimble with her fingers. I signed my map "M.R. 1850."

As night fell, we lit a candle and sat admiring the baby some more, with Seela nursing him whenever he took the whim, and with me fetching us further food and drink from the hotel kitchen's larder as needed. Eddie and Crispa were out all night. Seela and I slept, the baby woke us, we slept again, the baby woke us, we slept again—and so it went till dawn. Busy Earth, busy Sun, busy Seela, busy Mason, busy Brumble.

In the dawn's cottony glow, we sat up in our bed with the baby. Fog blanketed the city. The hidden sunrise's radiance lent the mist a warm tone. I couldn't see the next building over, so thick was the haze. But, closer than that, above the street, something was moving, a dim bulk the size of a hot-air balloon, with an inchoate filigree of faint tendrils below. Arf began barking. The shadowy curves flexed, grew, came into clarity, and reached toward us, fastening onto our window frame.

"It's Cytherea!" cried Seela. "Eddie and his *ballula*." She jumped to her feet and moved nimbly around the room, gathering her few garments, with Brumble in the crook of her arm. "Quick, Mason," she urged, opening the window sash. "We'll climb aboard."

The edge of the huge floating nautilus shell clattered against the outside wall. The shell's opening was fully twenty-five feet across, and the shell itself was a spiralled disk some seventy-five feet in diameter. Quite properly large. The hydrogen-filled shell could lift a heavy load. I peered into the queasy mass of twisting orange tentacles. Amid them were Eddie, Crispa, and, yes, Connor Machree, a mixture of greed and terror on his face.

Arf was growing hoarse. I nudged him and demanded silence. He pointed his dark nose at me, his eyes expressive. He was panting from excitement. He didn't like this at all.

"You go out the window," I told Arf, making a gesture. "It's safe. We're all coming. Same *ballula* as before." Grudgingly Arf hitched up his back legs and balanced on the window sill. He gave me another heartfelt stare. Crispa called sweetly to him from her nest amid the tentacles. Arf hopped over.

Seela went next, with some clothes under one arm, and with tiny Brumble in the other. She was wearing the nightshirt and a pair of pants, and—like me—her rumby on her neck. I meant to help Seela over the windowsill, but she exited on her own, with quick agility, springing into the *ballula's* open shell, graceful as a dancer, even now. The baby made a gurgling yodel. I followed Seela close behind.

Some early risers in the street had noticed the great hovering ammonoid. A young woman, calling out. A boy's voice as well. A cart was rolling by, and it was hard to hear them. And the fog was so dense that I couldn't make out their forms. Presumably they could see our huge shell's outline against the brightening sky. Now I heard a man's voice as well, blurred from a full night of drinking, angrily berating the woman.

I settled myself onto the heap of tentacles. Rather than being slimy, they were dry, and a bit adhesive. Cytherea was responsive enough to sculpt me a comfortable perch.

"Crew accounted for, and our vessel equipped," said Eddie, as if dictating a captain's log. He sounded well pleased with himself. "Our stores lie deeper in the shell, Mason. All is well. But—Ina's not in your room? I'd told her to—"

Below us in the fog, the man and woman were quarrelling, and now a sudden gunshot cracked. A bullet ripped through the air nearby. Cytherea wasn't one to flee a fight. She lashed down with a fifty-foot-long tendril and pulled it back with the tip wrapped around the struggling shape of—the desperate Ina Durivage. Streamers of saliva poured from the *ballula's* foul beak as she drew the woman closer, preparing, perhaps to bite off her head. Ina's cries and curses were fierce beyond all imagining.

"Halt!" cried Eddie, and Seela echoed him, very queenly in tone, and holding her hand against the dreaming rumby at her neck. Her and Eddie's grape-sized gems emitted pulses of psychic energy that caused the *ballula* to—set Ina down beside us. Though quite out of breath now, she looked well pleased.

The unseen man in the befogged street hollered something coarse and stupid. It was of course the slaving Cruickshank, the owner of the Broken Harp pothouse. A second gunshot boomed. This time the bullet ricocheted off the edge of the *ballula's* shell, knocking loose a chip. If this murderous, drunken procurer were to puncture the main body of Cytherea's shell, the hydrogen would rush out and our trip would be done.

The unseen boy in the street cried out to us. Pip.

"I conjure thee to rise," Eddie coolly said to Cytherea. He stared portentously into one of the *ballula's* great black eyes, and the eye stared back, wobbling on its short stalk.

"Do as Eddie says," I chimed in. "Rise!" I could feel the tekelili power of my own rumby at my neck, and, ever so faintly, I could feel the fabric of the *ballula's* crude mind. It was a meager consciousness, a taut web of hunger and rage.

Piqued at being ordered about, Cythera flew upwards so abruptly that I might have tumbled out backwards from the shell if Ina hadn't wrapped her arms around my midriff.

"Who *are* you?" Seela demanded of Ina. She didn't like seeing me in the embrace of this sly, loose woman of the Gold Rush streets.

"A lost lamb," said Ina. "A poetess. A man trap. And now, I hope, your friend."

"Miss Ina Durivage is from a fine New Orleans family," put in Eddie. "A free spirit, and not without literary skills. She's told me that she came to San Francisco with her journalist father, and when *père* Durivage died in an affair of honor, Ina befriended the homeless boy Pip—and they made common cause. Crispa and I spent last night with Ina and Pip, roaming the streets, assembling our equip."

"And sharing some sweet moments *à deux*," added Ina.

"I only rejoice that Pip didn't come aboard," said Machree. "Ina is much more to my humor."

"But you're not to *my* humor," huffed Ina. "I decree an end to your addled and impotent flirtations, Machree. Eddie Poe is my liberator!"

"And not I?" I sallied, so piqued was I by Ina's reckless, worldly demeanor.

"*Not* you," said Seela, and handed me our baby. Brumble was crying. Perhaps the rapid ascent had pained his wee ears.

"Indeed," said I, coming to my senses.

We'd reached the limits of the fog. The golden lamp of our Sun greeted us in our pearly chariot, the rush of light as palpable as a kiss. Peaks and mountain ranges projected from the cloud cover, with redwood forests upon the hills.

Further inland lay slopes dotted with oaks, and open fields, already sere and yellow, though it was but June.

We had six adults in our party: me, Eddie, Seela, Crispa, Machree, and Ina Durivage—with the addition of Brumble and Arf. A thousand-pound load at the very least. This meant that our full weight was well over a ton, taking into account the mass of the *ballula* herself, along with whatever casks, bales, tarpaulins, and crates Eddie had stowed at the base of her tentacles. I marveled that the lifting power of the hydrogen in Cythera's chambered shell was sufficient to keep us aloft.

How were we to reach the North Hole? This is where Cytherea's siphon came into play. It was a tube the size of a culvert, muscular yet flexible, nestled amid her tentacles. Rhythmically and repeatedly, the *ballula* drew in air, then forced it back out in a whistling stream, driving us forward. Her shell was well-adapted to this motion, and we made good speed, a forward progress enhanced by a favorable current that Cytherea located within the sky's sea of air.

Ina was full of questions. She'd had no plan of coming on the trip, but now she was excited at the prospect. Taking pleasure in the young woman's attentions, Eddie filled her in on the story of the Hollow Earth, and the Order of the Golden Frond, and our plans to descend through the North Hole. And, almost in passing, he told Ina that he was the younger double of the famous and recently deceased Edgar Allan Poe. A double from another world.

Connor Machree got in on the conversation as well. Having read my manuscript for *The Hollow Earth*, and having travelled to San Francisco aboard a tendril of *woomo* light, he had some sense of what we were in for. He did his best to clarify Eddie's extravagant claims.

But Ina kept thinking they were bragging, or speaking in jest. "Our Earth is like an egg or a womb?" she said. "What would be hatching inside? Baby suns? Come now, Mister Fake Edgar Allan Poe. Where are we *really* going? I hope it's New York."

"You'd cut a fine figure on Broadway," said Eddie. "And we'll get there when I publish my next book. But first we'll visit the brilliantly illuminated interior of our orb, eh, Mason?"

"Through the throat of the giant maelstrom," said I, projecting more confidence than I felt. "We saw it from inside the Hollow Earth."

"You were really and truly inside?" asked Ina, looking uneasy.

"Yes," said Seela. "The Hollow Earth is my home. And I've seen the North Hole maelstrom from below."

"Will it make a noise?" asked Ina.

"A low, unending moan," said Eddie, enjoying Ina's consternation. "The aggrieved groan of a fallen angel."

We progressed steadily northward and perhaps a bit to the east, with a landscape of mountains, forests, and plains unrolling below. Eddie rooted amid the stores in the depths of the shell, and produced a joint of ham, a roast chicken, some loaves of bread, several bottles of ale, and even a relatively intact chocolate cake. We feasted at leisure, wondering at the scope of the journey we'd begun.

"Never seen so much empty land," said Crispa, peering down at the lakes and prairies. "This is where grandpa come from. I can feel it." She was perched between Seela and me.

As she'd told us aboard the *Purple Whale*, Crispa had been raised in poverty by freed slaves in Baltimore. And her grandfather had been a Crow Indian. "How long ago was it you left home?" I asked her. "I forget."

"Five years," said Crispa. "I stove out a man's brains with a brick. He forced himself on me. A month later he did it again. And then I wouldn't stand it no more." She paused for effect. "Maybe I should have scalped him."

"Were you punished?" asked Seela.

"Would have been, but I run away," said Crispa. "Cut my hair, dressed like a boy and went to sea."

"None of the other sailors noticed?" I asked her.

"If they did, we generally made common cause," said Crispa. "And any skunk who put the muscle on me, well, pretty soon some rigging snapped and he'd fall in the drink and drown."

"Crispa's my kind of woman," said Seela. She smiled and dandled Brumble. "Your nanny's as bad as your ma," she crooned.

"Don't count on me to be nanny much more," said Crispa, lying on her belly the better to stare at the lands below. "I done told you I have a hankering to be an Upsaroka like grandpa. And I think I see a Crow camp down below. Teepees and smoke and, yeah, they got horses. They riding after buffalo. I rode a horse once in Baltimore."

"Will you join the Crow as a woman or a man?" I asked. "If you're a woman, you might not get to ride."

"People have a way of comin round to my way of doing things," said Crispa, undaunted. "If I want to ride, they'll let me."

"What about the Hollow Earth?" I asked.

"Don't like Eddie's talk about that giant whirlpool," said Crispa. "A sailor don't like hearin that at all. I'd just as soon this big farting shell set me down here right now."

As if responding to Crispa's words, the *ballula* began descending. Surprised, I used my rumby power to dip into Cytherea's crude mind, and learned it wasn't Crispa's plans that motivated Cytherea. She was hungry, ravenous, and bent on tearing into one of those bison that the Upsaroka were hunting.

We came in at a shallow angle, gliding above the wooly, thundering herd, with the shell side of the *ballula* first, her tentacles trailing, and the hiss of her siphon slowing down.

At the sight of Cytherea, the Upsaroka horses shied and galloped away. And the buffalo were in a frenzy of fear. Cytherea lashed out her tentacles, nearly knocking us off our perches in her shell. With quick, skillful movements, the *ballula* lassoed three of the bison, catching them round their bellies, and she forced extra tentacles down their throats to block off their air. Minutes later the three dead bison were jouncing along in the flying nautilus's wake. The survivors drummed away.

Cytherea drew one of the bison to her great clacking beak. Blood gushed over us as she consumed the creature, which may have weighed a ton. I was inclined to abandon my nest in the *ballula*'s shell while the great shellsquid fed, but Eddie and Seela held me back.

"She might make a precipitate departure," cautioned Eddie. "It would be unfortunate to sacrifice your great journey to a squeamish sense of propriety." Half his face was covered in hot bison blood, but he didn't seem to mind. Eddie, after all, had a taste for the ghastly. For her part, Ina was laughing steadily, as if at a loss for any other response. Machree, who seemed to be losing his nerve, was at the rear of our chamber, huddling against the curved mother-of-pearl that walled off the hydrogen-filled lifting chambers. Arf, of course, was scavenging scraps.

Crispa shook my hand and hopped down from the edge of the *ballula* shell to the prairie grass. "I'm sayin farewell," said she. "God speed, Mason, Seela, Eddie, and Ina. You're good people." She couldn't bring herself to say the same to Machree.

"Here's a Bowie knife for you," said Eddie, extracting the large blade from his supplies. "I've savored your company, Crispa."

"I'm gonna tell the Upsaroka I killed one of these buffalo myself," she responded, glad to have the big knife.

Casting aside the cracked-open skull of the first bison, the slobbering Cytherea tore into a second beast. Making efficient use of her dark, raspy tongue, she ate the brain, liver, heart, and kidneys, as well as the fatty muscles of the bison's hump—and then she cast the gory, rag-doll remains aside and—fully satiated—left the intact third bison to serve as Crispa's trophy. Crispa slit this dead animal's throat so that it would bleed out, and she struck a pose with one foot on the wooly creature's haunch.

The *ballula* adjusted the hidden rear parts of her body so as to increase the volume of the hydrogen chambers. And then, with her heavily taxed digestive system in loud percolation, we lifted off.

As we rose, a hail of arrows bounced off the great shell. Fortunately the aperture of our unprotected compartment was facing away from the Upsaroka tribe. And, even more fortunately, the easily-angered Cytherea chose not to launch a retaliatory attack. She was ready for a nap.

Soon we were hundreds of feet above the prairie. Looking down, I rejoiced to see Crispa making friends with the natives. No doubt they were impressed by her knife and by her self-possessed demeanor. I sensed that she wouldn't have to pretend to be a man. She'd be in a class of her own. A woman from the sky.

Meanwhile, having maneuvered her great shell into a highly favorable air stream, Cytherea cleaned the blood and gore from our quarters with quick motions of her feelers, then let her eyes grow dull, slackened all but two of her tentacles, and fell asleep, her siphon faintly whistling. Her still-active pair of tentacles extended to a length of a hundred feet in our wake. These graceful swaying limbs bore small steering-paddles on their ends—it seemed Cytherea could reflexively guide her path as she slumbered.

The northbound river of air swept us along at a fine rate, exceeding that of a clipper ship or even of a locomotive. The western prairies gave way to lakelands, to forests, to mountains, to tundra. Still Cytherea snored. The day was wearing on.

I nestled with Seela and gloated over our darling Brumble. He began fitfully wailing.

"He's cold," said Seela, pressing him between her breasts. "And I'm hungry."

Eddie and I broke out more food, and Machree passed around furs and blankets. We'd drifted high above the clouds, which extended below us on every side, a bumpy field of white, lit by the afternoon sun, bright into the preternaturally blue sky. We'd been underway for perhaps nine hours.

"I still don't grasp where we're going," said Ina. "Or how long it will take."

"Ten or fifteen more hours," said Eddie. "And then we'll begin a descent through a hole in the sea. The North Hole."

"It'll be night time," said Seela. "Dark."

"The arctic sun never sets in June," said Eddie.

"Will it be dark on the inside?" asked Ina. "Inside that Hollow Earth?"

"*Lux aeterna*," said Eddie. "Perpetual light."

"Because we'll be dead?" said Ina with a nervous giggle.

74

"Light from the *woomo*," said Eddie. "You'll see."

Another couple of hours went by. Ina told us a bit more about her childhood. Her father Joseph Durivage had been a journalist for the New Orleans *Picayune*, and, upon the death of his wife, he'd travelled overland to San Francisco with Ina, his sole child, passing through Mexico and Death Valley en route.

"And then he died in a duel," concluded Ina. "I was watching. A girl of fourteen. At dawn on the ocean beach. It was horrible."

"Last night you said it was an affair of honor?" said Eddie.

"Oh, what does that phrase even mean?" said Ina. "It's whitewash on a putrid grave. My father was murdered. One of the seconds who assisted at the duel told me father's pistol held no lead." She stared into the distance, her face working.

"What wretch did this?" asked Eddie.

"You can't guess?" said Ina. "Cruickshank the saloon owner. A procurer. A land speculator. A thief. Father revealed in the *California Alta* newspaper that Cruickshank was selling lots that lay below the tide line."

"Cruickshank a murderer," mused Eddie. "But how came he to enslave you?"

"Cruickshank forged a will assigning the custody of my father's child to him. So great is this man's baseness. It was me he sought."

"And not as a wife?" I said.

"As a low woman to buy and sell," said Ina with peculiar relish.

"Had I but told Cytherea to kill him," said Eddie.

"Indeed," said Ina.

"But you're well out of that now," said Eddie.

"Indeed," said Ina once again, batting her great eyes at Eddie.

"Enough of this dumb-show," interrupted Seela. "Play the waif for Eddie, my girl, but—mark you this—leave my Mason clear of your plans."

"Indeed," said Ina yet again, and unleashed one of her odd laughs, a ululating tone that rose into high chirps. A crafty, unstable adventuress, well-matched to Eddie Poe.

Some gaps had formed in the blanket of clouds beneath us. Far, far below, a cold gray ocean glinted in the dusky light of the low sun. We'd floated north beyond all of Canada and were embarking across the Arctic Sea with its irregular jumble of icy, barren isles.

"The air's as cold as it was off Cape Horn," grumbled Machree, who'd been studiously silent as Ina told her tale. "Ask the *woomo* to send a ray to warm us, Eddie. I miss their light. Or might this cold-blooded shellsquid find a way to kindle some heat?"

"I'd advise letting her sleep," Eddie told Machree. "When Cytherea wakes, she's in a foul temper, and…peckish. She might eat one of us who lacks a rumby—and that would be Ina or you. Or she might dive down to kill another kind of animal."

"A buffalo like before?" said Ina. "There's no more land."

"A walrus," I suggested. "A dolphin."

"I don't want to go in that water!" cried Seela.

"Let Cytherea sleep," repeated Eddie.

As the sated *ballula* dreamt, she continued guiding our path with the spade-like tips of her long tentacles. The hours went by. I did a little mental work on my projected second narrative—*The Return to the Hollow Earth*. Midnight came and went, but even so it wasn't dark. Finding a spool of twine amid Eddie's supplies, Seela took the time to weave sturdier coverings for the dense rumbies owned by Eddie, her and me—encasing our thread-wrapped stones with decorative, sailor-like knots that hung upon our necklaces. Machree and Ina watched with a certain envy, although Machree was confident he'd find his own rumbies within the Hollow Earth.

As the air grew colder, we sat closer together, snacking and chatting. Everyone was being nice to Brumble, even Ina and Machree. Seela made a little hat for Brumble by cutting off the tip of a loaf of sourdough bread and tearing out most of the bread from within the tip's crust. The cap fit nicely on the boy, cushiony and resilient, and it stayed on tight.

In our unease about this journey, the baby became a source of cheer. Seela began showing him off to Ina—whom she'd by now befriended after all—showing off Brumble by holding him up like a doll or a puppet and pretending to speak for him, using a high squeaky voice to utter odd words from the Hollow Earth flowerpeople's tongue.

"*Flaxxon moompf grooble*," said Seela, and Ina gaily mimicked her.

Brumble was—well, the boy was less than two days old, so it would have been unfair to expect any reasoned response. His unfocused eyes glinted, and the little O of his mouth opened and closed. Perhaps he was ready again to nurse? Seela hugged him against her bare breast.

At this point I noticed the sound of the North Hole. It was much as Eddie had predicted, a dirge-like drone with deep bass overtones. I felt the more profound tones as vibrations in my belly and chest. Cytherea's shell was delicately vibrating in concert with the low song as well. The *ballula* awoke with a shudder of her tentacles. It was about three in the morning, but, as I say, the sun remained above the horizon.

In silent unity, Eddie, Seela, and I used the tekelili power of our rumby gems to project a sense of purposeful calm into our outlandish bearer's mind. She hungered, yes, but not so very keenly. The bison meat was still working its way through her body. She extended her eyestalks, and changed the angle of her shell, taking the measure of the strange zone ahead.

Eddie lay slouched in the rear part of the shell with Machree and Arf. He'd brought some of his opium along, and the two men had been smoking. Eddie gazed at me with a dreamy smile on his face.

"Let me describe what you see," he intoned. "The near edge of the vast Hole is like a depression in the horizon, bounded by a white band of foam. Above the depression is a sea of mist, dotted with thunderheads and penetrated by antic tendrils of *woomo* light. Beyond the clouds is the obsidian slope of the maelstrom's far rim—like a giant cataract rolling into the sea. And yet further is the open Arctic ocean, the true horizon, and the polar sky. Surely you discern these things, Mason and Ina? Seela?"

"I see it," said Seela. "We're going home. *Volivorco gooba'am*, Brumble."

I saw the pattern too, but for the moment Ina and Machree were baffled. The hole was so large that it required a flip of mental perspective to perceive it as a single thing. The width of maelstrom matched, I believe, the breadth of my native Virginia, that is, it was two hundred miles across.

We were a few thousand feet above the Arctic Sea, and some hundred miles from the edge of the Hole. The atmosphere around the North Hole was whirling as strongly as the sea below, drawing us closer and swirling us in a convergent spiral. The ocean's surface was beginning to tilt, as if we were nearing a waterfall.

"We're going to die," said Ina. "Why couldn't you crackpots have left me alone?"

"You begged us to save you," I said. "You said Cruickshank shot your pa and made you a wagtail."

"And if I said that then, does it mean this is better? I think not. But here we are. Whirling down the drain." Ina unleashed her reckless laugh. Somehow the sound heartened me—like a war whoop. Better to laugh than to cry.

6. Maelstrom

Steering us with her siphon and her long tentacles, Cytherea rode the spiraling winds ever closer to the Pole. We were close to the ocean's surface, and below the level of the scattered thunder clouds, like dark islands in the air. The low sun's rays sliced beneath the clouds, sending glints across the water.

Round and round we swirled. The ocean slanted in an ever-steepening curve, and somewhere up ahead it disappeared from view, presumably plummeting into the open throat of the planetary maelstrom, the great North Hole, its entrance as yet hidden from us.

Unsteady pink streamers of *woomo* light were dancing up through whirlpool's core. Occasionally a pink tendril would play over our faces, taking our measure and approvingly caressing us—setting my hairs on end and further darkening my skin.

And then, at last, we could see down through the Hole. We were as motes of dust amid this vast tableau, sweeping headlong into an abyss, lit by the *woomo* streamers and by the polar summer sun. Our helical descent began.

Ina had joined Machree and Arf in the furthest recess of our vestibule in the *ballula's* shell. For his part, Eddie was now with Seela and me at the shell's edge. Having traveled through Earth's South Hole a year and a half earlier, Eddie and I weren't overly dismayed by the North Hole, even though this hole was the throat of a vast maelstrom. I might also add that Eddie was bolstering his courage with repeated puffs from his opium pipe, periodically striking sparks from a silver tinderbox.

Seela seemed at her ease. She'd grown up amid the vast and untrammeled landscape within the Hollow Earth. Eddie liked to call Seela's homeland *Htrae*, that is, *Earth* spelled backwards, and he said he was writing a heroic epic about it, composing the work in his head—much in the same fashion I was mentally composing my *Return to the Hollow Earth*.

In any case, for Seela, the North Hole was a familiar feature of the inner world's vault, and it was a handy passageway that would lead us closer to the great flower where her tribe lived. But now she said something troubling.

"I hope the empress ant will stay in her place," said she.

"What do you mean?" I asked, feeling a pulse of fear.

"The creature who lives in the water around the maelstrom," said Seela. "She swims in a circle to keep it swirling. I'm sure she won't notice us. She's too big. And don't tell Eddie about her. He's always so quick to lose his head."

"But—"

"Hush." Seela turned away from me, focusing on Brumble.

Wanting at least to reassure myself that Cytherea could navigate the throat of the maelstrom, I used the power of the rumby stone at my neck to look into the *ballula's* primitive mind. She seemed fully confident about our route—perhaps she'd even traveled it before. And as an amphibious being, she had no misgivings about possibly ending up underwater. If the chaotic winds drove us against the twisting waters of the maelstrom's wall, and if the hungry currents were to tear loose Cytherea's passengers and her cargo—well, that was no great matter for her. And if, indeed, we humans drowned, we'd no longer be bossing the *ballula* with our rumbies. And then the *ballula* would eat us. Unless the empress ant got to us first.

With a supreme effort of will, I closed down my conscious thoughts and focused my attention on the wavering song of the whirlpool, letting the subtly shaded tone take over my mind. I was part of the chant, and it was part of me. We'd been en route for a full day. Bemused and torpid, I

"You see?" I told Ina as Arf wolfed down his catch. "It'll be easy here."

"A melon for now," said Poe, rapping a perfectly round green orb against a branch. It split it two, revealing creamy orange flesh like that of a cantaloupe. I cut the two halves into slices with my knife and passed them around. The *woomo* light tendrils flickered among the trees, rising around us in a pleasant maze.

"Let's sleep here," said Seela, pointing out a stack of four or five large shelf-mushrooms on the titanic trunk of an oak. We settled in as if in bunk beds, with Eddie and Ina between an upper pair of shelves, and Seela, Brumble, and I between a lower pair.

There was no such thing as night inside the Hollow Earth—the light tendrils never stopped. But on our fungal shelves we felt safe from drifting off. With the baby between Seela and me, there was, of course no question of us two sleeping *well*. We made it through some six or seven hours—with two feedings of the baby along the way—and then my own hunger pangs compelled me to rise.

While the others slept on, Arf and I managed to catch six stubby-finned fish from a glob of water some twenty feet across. He swam about in the middle, herding the fish to the surface, and I stabbed them as they flopped onto branches, meaning to scuttle away. Extracting the sleeping Eddie's tinderbox from his coat, I got a little fire going inside a dry hollow spot in our tree trunk, and by the time the others awoke, we were able to breakfast on two roast fish apiece, complemented by melon and some banana-like fruits that Seela found.

In the near-zero gravity of this zone, the fire's smoke tended to linger, and the flames oozed around rather than flickering. I'd learned that as long as I occasionally fanned a Hollow Earth fire, it could stay alive for a day or more. But in this damp jungle there was little risk of a runaway forest fire.

A great hubbub emerged from the shrig colony, hardly visible beyond the jungle leaves. I left our fire slowly smoldering inside its hollow, and we four bounced a quarter mile through the jungle—where it ended beside the bare rocky stared at the sparkling funnel that enclosed us on every side. My mouth was slack and half open. My chin was slick with drool. I drowsed.

"Hey, you," said Seela, waking me with a nudge. Once again she handed me our baby. Brumble was like a talisman—in important ways more powerful than a rumby gem. As I took hold of his little body I returned to conscious thought. I nestled him in the crook of my arm, and let him suck the tip of my finger. So tiny, this wight, and so focused upon the task of staying alive. Such a wonder to see the awkward motions of his stubby limbs. One of the *woomo* tendrils rose through the maelstrom, licked against us, and was gone.

"I can see through the hole," cried Eddie. Indeed we could now see the glow of the Hollow Earth's pink-lit interior. The airy whirlwind within the maelstrom was sweeping us in narrowing circles. The sun-glinted water walls were very nearly vertical by now, and the open throat below us was not much wider than a mile—which was tight enough to provoke unease, but spacious enough for a viewport.

Evidently the whirlpool's spindle opened out again below the center—in the manner of a double funnel. And for this reason we couldn't see the maelstrom's lower walls from here. We saw the Hollow Earth's seas and lands, its mighty jungles, its Umpteen Seas, its flying shrigs, and the giant *woomo* at its core.

"I'm looking for flowers," said Seela. She meant the immense sunflowers growing upon the Hollow Earth's inner surface. Her original home had been the surface of a flower like this. She took Brumble back from me, and gently held his little cheek against hers. "See, baby, see?"

It could well be that Seela meant to settle permanently into the Hollow Earth with Brumble. And if she stayed—whither I? Might I live in the Hollow Earth for the rest of my days? Or return to San Francisco with Arf? Or—somehow take up with Ina?

I glanced over at that quirky woman. Intrigued by our talk of seeing into the Hollow Earth, she was making her way forward to join us. I was taken by the negligent grace of her motions, and by the mixture of irony and intelligence on her face. Might I win her away from Eddie? But how could I entertain such a faithless thought? Seela was my everything, no?

Machree followed on Ina's heels, and now the five of us were together at the lip of Cytherea's shell, with Brumble in Seela's arms, and Arf wedged between my feet. As our *ballula* descended into the maelstrom's central throat, her shell began rocking more strongly than before. I used my rumby tekelili to petition Cytherea to brace us in place by wrapping tentacles around our waists. With Eddie and Seela reinforcing my psychic admonition, the *ballula* obliged.

The winds at the maelstrom's core were turbulent, but the waters of the walls were not so much rough as they were *ropy*. That is, the surface was as glassy as in the upper regions, and lit by the summer sun, but in this central zone, the flows were so intense that the water was corrugated or gnarled, with striated bulges angling down through the hole. Even relative to the hole's mile-wide aperture, the ridges of water were quite substantial, several hundreds of yards high, like folds in a giant's handkerchief, or like ridges in a titanic twist of dough, with the crests winding around the throat of this, our upper funnel, and flowing to the surface of the as yet unseen funnel below. A mighty streamer of *woomo* light came flickering through. Inconceivably great forces were in play.

Seela, Machree, and I exchanged glances, silently sharing memories of the *Purple Whale* foundering off Cape Horn. No, the North Hole wasn't a savage riot of monstrous waves. But perhaps it was, in its own way, even more sinister.

Blatting her siphon, Cytherea caught hold of a rogue air current that carried us to the still eye of the tornado-like whirlwind within the maelstrom's constricted throat. In relative calm we drifted down along the central axis of the hole. On every side of us were the bulging, clear ridgelines of water upon the maelstrom's wall. The flexed, embossed currents wriggled from side to side, like rivulets of rain on a windowpane.

So powerfully urgent were the water flows that we saw no hint of foam. Lit by the *woomo* streamers and by the polar sun, the pellucid waters were like a mass of molten glass. As we passed through the narrowest part of the neck, we saw something within the transparent sea, a glowing leviathan in rhythmic motion—

"Behold!" cried Ina, extending a pale, elegant arm, and leaning her body against Eddie's. Actually, her arm wasn't pale anymore. The *woomo* light had taken its usual effect. To all appearances, Ina was now a mulatto. But that didn't seem to faze her. She smiled up at dusky Eddie. "Does the monster mean to devour us, my dear?"

"That's the empress ant I was talking about," said Seela, as if this were an ordinary thing. "The creature who spins the whirlpool at the North Hole. She's swims in a circle. We call her Jormungo."

"Like the fabled Ourobouros," exclaimed Eddie. "The great world snake who bites his tail."

"Jormungo is an *ant*," repeated Seela. "She has wings, six legs, and a stinger on her rear, With twitchy antennae, and crushing jaws on her head, She's nested here for centuries. Slowly, slowly, she's hatching her royal eggs."

Stepping away from Ina, Eddie leaned out from our flying shell, hungry for a better view of the prodigious beast. And then, unsatisfied with that—and in an act of extreme recklessness he bade Cytherea to grasp him with a tentacle tip and to dangle him in the empty air. Never would Eddie have done this if he hadn't been smoking opium. Normally he had a morbid fear of heights, and a deathly terror of falling.

But now, here he was jiggling at the end of a fifty-foot *ballula* tentacle, waving his arms and holding forth on the wonders of what he saw. Arf stood at the edge of our shell, furiously barking—not that we could hear either him or Eddie over the noise of the maelstrom, which at this point had reached a stunning pitch. It was as if we were inside an alpine horn sounding a deep, solemn, sustained blast.

And what of the empress ant Jormungo? She was relatively narrow, and a bit over three miles long, wrapping all the way around the maelstrom's throat. Like any ant, she was segmented into head, thorax and gaster. Her great head was like a long-stretched African mask. She had great, faceted eyes, and narrow wings half a mile long. Her surfaces were a dark iridescent purple with touches of green. And her segments were but two hundred yards across. A very slender ant indeed. Even so, her six legs were active and strong, with feet like great oars.

The ant lay sideways in the water around the maelstrom's hole, positioned like a bracelet, with her legs pointed inward. As I say, she was bent into a full circle, and with her vast toothy mandibles clamped onto the base of her onyx stinger. She was continually beating her legs and sculling the water with her veined wings. By dint of these dogged, obsessive motions the empress ant kept the whirlpool spinning.

Why? Perhaps she did it to irrigate the dozen large, golden eggs adhering to the underside of her dark belly.

Initially I supposed that our tiny presences made little impression on the empress ant. I focused on the rumby at my throat and felt for the ant's vibrations. Her mind was ancient, vast, and flickering with activity. Like a city that burns but never collapses. I seemed to see a vast round coliseum, filled with galleries and radial rooms, and within each room was a lambent yellow flame, and the flames held dark central spots that were astral eyes. Jormungo was watching us after all.

And then we were through the maelstrom's throat, with the lower funnel opening up around us, and the wondrous high arch of the Hollow Earth in view, and the central *woomo* firing off light streamers as if in greeting. Eddie was at my side, gesticulating and cheering, both of us well-lodged in Cytherea's tentacles.

At this point I want to remind you of an aspect of the Hollow Earth that is little known. The naive expectation is that inside the Hollow Earth one will walk around on the inner surface with one's head pointing toward the center of the planet. But no less a man than Isaac Newton has proved this is not the case. Within a hollow shell one feels no gravitational force whatsoever. At all points within the shell, the mass of the shell above one's head counteracts the attraction from the shell beneath. You don't walk upon the inner surface of a Hollow Earth. You drift about within a great sphere of air.

This entails, perforce, that when you fall down a vertical passageway through the Hollow Earth's Rind, your speed lessens as you near the tunnel's lower terminus. You coast to a stop.

And thus our *ballula's* rate of fall diminished as we moved downward through the lower funnel of the maelstrom, traversing the two or three hundred miles that separated us from the inner surface of the Hollow Earth. In order to aid our progress, Cytherea was steadily jetting her siphon. By now it was perhaps nine in the morning in San Francisco time. I'd gone a whole day with but one hour of sleep. Not that I could possibly think of sleeping just now.

It was helpful that the winds and waters in this lower zone of the maelstrom were spiraling in the same direction as in upper zone—and were thereby flowing out from the maelstrom toward the inner surface of the Rind.

We passed our time in conversation, raising our voices to be heard above the whistle of the siphon and the maelstrom's waning drone. Eddie was pointing out features of the Hollow Earth to Ina and Machree. And Seela was exclaiming over the clumps of her race's sunflowers that she claimed she saw. She insisted she could even see the home flower where she was born, not far from the South Hole.

"You can't see the South Hole from here," I told her. Our view to the antipodal side was occluded by the busy center of the Hollow Earth, that is, by the jiggling jewels of the weightless Umpteen Seas, by the light streamers flowing out of the mighty *woomo*, and by the warped space of the Central Anomaly at the core.

"I see past the center well enough." said Seela. "Look at the sea by the edge of the southern jungle. *That's* where my home flower is."

"Even if you do see that spot, remember that your home flower isn't actually here," I told Seela. "You grew up on the other side of the Anomaly. You came from inside Earth. We're inside MirrorEarth."

We'd talked about this before. But Seela didn't want to understand. Yet again I told her that the Hollow Earth comprises two globes called Earth and MirrorEarth, each with its own hollow world inside, and that the two hollow planets are connected via a Gate within their shared Central Anomaly. Seela brushed my tidy logic aside.

"Jibber jabber yak wak," she said. "Backwards, upside-down, inside-out. Maybe the flower on this side is different, and maybe it's the same. I wonder if Yurgen is here. I wonder if he misses me."

I tensed. Yurgen had been Seela's suitor when I first met her on her home flower. A slender musician with great cachet among the flowerpeople—he played an instrument called a reverb tube, and his music put his listeners into a trance. Superficially a charming man, he was in fact sly and unkind. That's why Seela had chosen me over him. And it helped that I was exotic. I'd carried her off to a new world.

But maybe now Seela was tired of me? Or, more charitably, just tired. She'd given birth to our baby, and the next day she'd rushed into this mad journey. I brought to mind how much in love we'd been, lying on our bed looking at Brumble, and that was only the day before yesterday. I softened my heart and gave Seela a kiss.

"How would you get all the way to the south?" broke in Ina, taking an interest in our discussion. "All the way to the other side of this—Hollow Earth? Our planet is truly a big empty ball? So very peculiar."

"Phantasmagoric," said I. "Mind boggling."

"I'm flummoxed," said Ina, as fond of words as I. "Nonplussed. Bowled over. And to think that the Hollow Earth has always been here, and that none of us ever knew. What are the people like?"

"Like me, some of them," said Seela, looking down at herself. "Except whiter. And the ones in the middle are darker. We call them the black gods. You'll like the black gods, Ina. They're jolly. They live with giant floating lakes all around. They make love."

"We're going there?" asked Ina.

"Eddie's wish," said Seela. "And it's handy for Mason and me as well. The easiest way to cross the space of the Hollow Earth is to drift inward to the Umpteen Seas—and to ride a lightstream back out."

"Fine with me," said I. "But I don't want to go near that hungry Gate inside the Anomaly. Eddie can do that on his own. I'm happy to stay out here in MirrorEarth. We'll pick up some rumby gems, have some new adventures I can write about, and then back to San Francisco. We'll be happy there, Seela. I'll write for the paper, and publish *The Hollow Earth* and the *Return to the Hollow Earth*. We'll have more children. We'll build ourselves a little house."

"They know the editor at the *California Alta* newspaper," put in Ina. "Thanks to my father. Perhaps I can help you get in there, Mason."

"I thought you were going through the Gate with Eddie," said Seela.

"We'll see," said Ina airily.

"Yes, we will see," said Seela, getting angry again. "We'll see that you leave Mason alone. And, Mason, don't be too sure that I'm going back outside the Hollow Earth again. I like it better in here."

"We'll see," I said. So many wills around me, and everyone pulling a different way. I looked at little Brumble in my arms, and to myself I was wondering if, should Seela refuse to return to San Francisco, she might let me take our son. Seemed unlikely. He was the dearest thing I'd ever seen.

And now Eddie had to stick his oar in. "I'm going the whole hog," he reaffirmed. "I'll pass through the central Gate to old Earth, and there I'll resume my proper career. Starting with the publication of my masterwork *Htrae*. My versified travel account that will take its place beside Homer's *Odyssey*."

"Everyone back on Earth will be a lot older than when you left," I said. "We lost twelve years going through that Gate the first time, Eddie. We were like bees in slow honey, with the world spinning round. That'll happen again on the way back."

"I snap my fingers!" exclaimed the defiant Eddie. "I bite my thumb. Your cavils mean nothing, Mason. They'll marvel at me on old Earth. I'm still in my early thirties, and my erstwhile rivals will be fifty years old and more." He raised a finger for emphasis. "The old Earth shall be mine. With no vile MirrorPoe to usurp me. I brim with tales, I creak with logic, I jingle with poesy."

"Fine talk," I said, somehow goaded to provoke Eddie. "You'll drink brandy, smoke opium, and copy out the MirrorPoe's works from the MirrorEarth anthology."

"Fiddle-dee-dee," said Eddie. "I abandoned that fusty tome in Mrs. Mackie's hotel. You say I shall be a besotted voluptuary and plagiarize stale tales? Nay, my friend. I'll spin fine new fantasias. And, unlike the debauched MirrorPoe, I'll moderate my vice."

"When does the moderation start?" I shot back. "You were smoking opium ten minutes ago."

"Insolent pup!" cried Poe. "I'll create an oeuvre like none has ever seen."

"How very audacious," said Ina, hanging on Eddie's arm. "Go it, my dear! And, yes, I'll come with you to the old Earth and be your muse."

"I'm with you too," Machree told Poe. "I'll be your agent, as you say."

"My epic *Htrae* will far surpass Mason's feeble tome *The Hollow Earth*," said Eddie, casting a frown at me.

"You dream in vain," said I, roused by the prospect of competing with the notorious Poe. "To cap my initial narrative, I'll scribe the sequel. *Return to the Hollow Earth*. I'm already working on it."

And by this I meant, as I've mentioned, that I'd begun formulating a clear account of our current trip in my mind—fixing the order of the events and working out felicitous phrasing for key scenes. I found this a soothing, meditative process. It felt as if I were speaking aloud to an unseen listener.

"You fancy yourself to be Poe's equal?" scoffed Machree. He gave me a piercing stare. "I'm your true rival, Mason. Our deaths ratified the split between Earth and MirrorEarth."

"What do you mean by that?" I asked, caught by surprise, and roiled by a sick feeling.

"Ask the *woomo*," said Machree shortly. "But enough of ontological cosmogony. At root, I'm a jeweler with a lust for rumbies. Can we simply discuss my hope to inaugurate trade between Earth and Hollow Earth?"

For the moment, none of us cared to reply. The wondrous Hollow Earth was slanting up on every side of us, fabulous beyond imagining. By now the waters of the maelstrom's wide opening were nearly level with surface of the inner sea's surface. The accompanying whirlwind had died to a caressing breeze that wafted us along.

Branching and swaying streamers of pink light were continually illuminating the Hollow Earth's open space. The seas and continents upon the great Rind were like images on a map, although with contours quite different from those of the familiar Earth. The oceans were a fine shade of aquamarine, with occasional dark blue patches that betokened benthic depths that ran through to the outer Earth. Wrinkled mountain ranges wandered across the continents, with deserts, grasslands, and, above all, jungles. I saw no signs of human cities or roads.

The vast atmosphere held mighty flocks of flying beasts— leathery birds with enormous beaks balanced by crests on the backs of their heads, the penguin-shaped carnivorous fowl called harpies, jeweled hummingbirds the size of fists, and, shades of Cape Horn, gliding albatrosses. In the far distance were *ballula* shellfish like Cythera. And a miles-long flock of shrigs was gathered nearby, several thousand of them—wheeling in the air, roaring, farting, perching, feeding, mating.

We were just off the coast of a Hollow Earth landmass. Its jungled shore adjoined a ring of titanic cliffs surrounding an immense volcanic butte. The cliffs were honeycombed with enormous caves. And this was where the shrigs made their nests.

These creatures would have been entirely comical, were they not a bit fearsome as well. A shrig's form is that of an immense boar's head mounted on a body curved and sectioned like that of a shrimp. The younger ones are the size of airborne cows, and the grizzled patriarchs and matriarchs have the heft of hovering frigate ships, perhaps a hundred and fifty feet long.

Normally the shrigs feed on offal, whatever they can find, and they spend much of their time near the core of the Hollow Earth, where debris tends to gather. But when they wished to mate and to produce young, they gathered around the towering mesa nearby. Beating their flat tails and twitching their foolish, tiny legs, the shrigs were engaged in a ponderous social gavotte, moving from cave to cave, inquisitively sniffing each other, flirting with slaps of their tails, confabulating via grunts and squeals, and then inevitably copulating—a singular sight, richly enhanced by the participants' triumphant bellowing. To behold twenty or a hundred shrigs in rut—it was a staggering and, I blush to confess, at times an erotically stimulating spectacle, although I freely grant that the great beasts are ungainly and unclean.

The mouths along the shrigs' mighty pig-snouts were lipless and toothless, giving the effect of a knowing smile. But, as I well knew, the normally placid shrigs could become savage when confronted by their arch-enemy and occasional prey: *ballula* shellsquid such as Cytherea, within whom we were rather conspicuously on display.

For the moment, the shrigs were a safe distance away, and fully preoccupied with their own activities. It bears mentioning that these animals are profoundly unintelligent.

Meanwhile Cytherea was doing her best to make landfall at some distance from the sky-darkening swarm, and I was glad for her caution. A trio of smallish, newly-fledged shrigs, were flying about nearby, and I could sense that Cytherea, being hungry as usual, would have liked to devour them. But even her crude intellect could grasp that, were she to follow her passions, she would suffer for it.

At this point we noticed something moving in the clear waters of the sea.

"I hope that's not the ant's husband," said Seela.

"Why do you say such a thing?" I cried.

"Everyone knows about the ants," said Seela. "The empress in the maelstrom, Jormungo, she doesn't have time to forage. Her special worker, or husband, or prince consort—we call him Fafnir—he swims around this region and gathers food. He's as big as her. And he can fly like Jormungo. He's fast and strong."

"He eats shrigs?" I asked.

"And how. His legs are hollow. He sucks the juices from their bodies.

"Does he eat *woomo* too?"

"No, no, the royal ants are friends of the *woomo*. Partners. They're not like those farmer ants. The pale, creamy ones. The farmer ants want to eat the *woomo*, but they never get a chance. They're not much bigger than dogs. They'd probably eat a person if they had a chance."

"We shouldn't be here!" I said.

"No," agreed Seela. "Only a shrig would be stupid enough to nest near the North Hole. But I didn't want to warn you. I wanted us to come through."

For now we didn't see the empress ant's husband. The nearby moving life in the sea turned out to be a pod of whales. They began leaping out of the water, and hanging for a rather long time in the low-gravity air, wriggling their bodies as if for pure joy. Perhaps they were simply shaking off parasites, but I had a rumby sense that they were happy, and I mentioned this to the others. Observing the square cut of the disporting animals' brows, Eddie said they were sperm whales.

Frustrated over not having attacked the baby shrigs, the ravening Cytherea unleashed her native savagery. With an unbelievably rapid motion, the shellsquid jetted forward and splatted against the muscular body of a disporting whale— who was nearly three times her size. Scattering most of our supplies into the air, Cytherea stretched out her tentacles to their full extent, wrapping them around the midriff of the whale. And then she began digging her great beak into the top of his head, perhaps meaning to break it open and feed upon the hundreds of gallons of waxy spermaceti oil therein.

We five passengers held fast to the bases of the mad *ballula's* tentacles, hoping only to stay aboard. It was much as we'd done when Cytherea slew the buffalo. I pressed baby Brumble against my chest, Arf was cowering by my feet, and Seela was screaming, with Machree chiming in. Ina Durivage was again laughing in that half-mad manner she had, while Eddie had his eyes squeezed shut, and was perhaps trying

to send calming rumby tekelili into Cytherea's tiny brain—
something I was too distracted to even attempt.

Blood and water spray splashed across us, and now came
the retaliation. The whale beat his tail and flippers against
the air, twisted his body, blasted steam from his spout, and
tossed off Cytherea. Before the *ballula* could try to jet away,
the enraged cetacean had seized her shell in his great toothed
jaws. A resonant crunch, a high whistle of escaping hydrogen
gas, and now our flying charioteer was a twitching tangle
of orange flesh, with scraps of her shattered shell drifting
weightlessly in the brilliant sea. Cytherea's body muscles
were clenched in pain.

The whale, despite a shallow gash on the top of his head,
was fully intact. He devoured the unfortunate Cythera with
two snaps of his long, saw-toothed jaws. And then he fixed us
with a baleful glare from a high-mounted and by no means
jolly eye, quite black, and the size of a cantaloupe.

What the whale beheld was of little interest to him—five
adult humans, a baby, and a dog, ineffectually wallowing in the
aquamarine waters. With a contemptuous spout of mist, he
turned flukes and dove deep into the sea—possibly heading
back to the Arctic Sea and the upper exit of the North Hole.
His fellows followed in his wake.

As I've said, at the surface of the Hollow Earth's inner sea,
we were in a zone of neutral gravity, with no forces pulling
us up or down. As a result of our sea battle, jiggly globs of
water hung suspended all across the surface, and the surface
itself was pocked with divots where water had been scooped
out. Slowly the liquid's natural flows were smoothing the
dents over.

But not everything that rose came falling back. Indeed,
most of the casks and bundles which Eddie had brought along
were suspended in the air, and were very gradually rising
higher. As I've mentioned before, once something moved far
enough away from the Rind, a gentle and secondary attraction
from the core's Anomaly came into play.

The sea's shore was perhaps two miles off, a muddy overgrown bank with a labyrinth of thickets and vines dangling
upward—or rather *inward*—toward the core. The jungle

extended inward for something like thirty miles, an overwhelming and formidable sight.

Balanced at this precise neutral zone, there were no forces dragging me into the depths or, for that matter into the sky. But I had an intense fear of drowning and, even more, I was exceedingly concerned about Brumble. Steadily I fluttered my legs, keeping myself upright, but not leaping wholly out of the sea and into the empty air. I kept the lower part of my body submerged, and held the baby well above the surface in my two hands. The newborn was flexing his legs and arms, and making little noises, as if warming up for a crying jag. He didn't feel safe, and he wanted his mother. I very much wanted her as well. She was a hundred yards off, although I had no real hope of swimming that distance without the use of my arms.

But soon Seela was at my side. She'd scavenged a large, curved fragment of Cytherea's shell, serviceable as a dinghy, and she was wielding a thin fragment of shell as a paddle. With great relief, I handed Brumble over to her. The exasperated baby made a spluttering noise, then settled against Seela's breast, softly grunting as he nursed. Not wanting to risk overturning Seela's coracle, I floated at its side, kicking my legs to propel us toward the overgrown shore of the promontory with the shrig's great rookery. As it happened, the current around the outer edge of the maelstrom was sweeping us in that general direction.

Beating his legs and with snout held high, Arf was very nearly managing to walk on the water. I set him into the shell with Seela. Naturally he insisted on rising to his feet and giving his body several heartfelt shakes—a process which, in this weightless zone, sent him tumbling into Seela, who scolded him severely. But she was laughing at the same time, so happy was she to have the precious Brumble in her arms. I lay on my back in the water and swam along at the floating shell-fragment's side, now and then nudging or tugging it to keep it with me. As we went along, I managed to rub my face and body with my hands, cleaning off some of the gore from the slain buffalo, the wounded whale, and the destroyed *ballula*.

What of the others? Eddie, Machree, and Ina were bunched together, making for landfall, lying on their stomachs and stroking their arms against the sea like oars, thereby gliding across the surface of the water, much as I was doing. Machree was less dexterous than the other two, and he was lagging behind, and even calling out that he might drown, not that this was especially likely.

The pink light of a *woomo* tendril fell across us, illuminating a zone several hundred yards wide. Did the *woomo* mean to carry us to safety? The light streamer focused, grew brighter and—lifted up Connor Machree alone, bearing him into the sky and toward the Hollow Earth's core.

"See you laaaaater," the illuminated figure called down to us, his voice rising as if in ecstasy.

"Go to blazes!" shrieked Ina. "*Damn* you, Machree! Why is this low worm exalted?"

What was it Machree had said to me back in San Francisco? "*You and I are paradox incarnate. The axle of fate's turning wheel.*" He'd also said that he'd encountered me in Lynchburg, Virginia—the town where my first journey to the Hollow Earth had begun.

In a flash, I finally saw who Machree was—as clearly as if a stroke of lightning had illuminated a beclouded landscape. My revelation took the form of a syllogism.

- On Earth, Mason killed the stableboy.
- On MirrorEarth, the MirrorStableboy killed MirrorMason.
- Therefore Machree is the MirrorStableboy.

I didn't bother trying to explain this to the others, nor did I share my further line of logic—which seemed to explain why the *woomo* were aiding Machree in his journey to the core.

- Having both Mason and Machree on MirrorEarth is an imbalance.
- The *woomo* are intent on keeping the worlds in balance.
- Mason intends to remain on MirrorEarth.

- Therefore the *woomo* wish to move Machree to Earth.

QED, as graybeard Euclid might say. *Quod erat demonstrandum.* I'm not as ignorant as city slickers think. As a boy, I studied a copy of Euclid's *Elements* on rainy winter days, lying on the plank floor by the fire in Pa's cabin. And I'd perused a Latin primer as well. Not to mention the *Southern Literary Messenger*, replete with Eddie Poe's essays and tales.

But, as often happens in the heady realm of pure reason, one of my assumptions was wrong, as were the ensuing deductions. The *woomo* cared nothing about my specious notions of balance between the worlds. The *woomo* were helping Machree because they wanted him to fetch rumbies from the Hollow Earth and to ferry them to the surface.

Why? Read on.

7. Ants

I sculled along, swimming on my back beside Seela in her shell boat, with my bone-deep exhaustion like a bag of sand inside my chest. I focused my attention on my senses to keep from nodding off.

Any droplet of water which rose more than about six feet would keep on falling inward toward the center. Just as it had been when we'd come through the South Hole on our first expedition. And those valuable bundled provisions that Eddie had brought along—they were fairly high in the air by now, and not coming back. A pair of large shrigs were in fact feeding on this equipage, engulfing whole barrels and bales with their blandly pleased snouts, while guiding themselves through the air with thunderous farts and with flicks of their flattened tails. A few dozen shrigbirds fluttered around the shrigs, hopping onto them and pecking up parasites as the opportunity arose, the shrigbirds a bit like terns.

I kept worrying about the purplish-green royal ant called Fafnir—but saw no sign of him as yet. In any case, I had a simpler problem to occupy my mind: I didn't want Seela and me to fall into the sky. If we did, we might tumble for four days before reaching the Umpteen Seas at the core. The distance to Earth's center from the Rind is three thousand miles. What with our bodies' drag against the air, the gentle effect of the core's pull wouldn't bring our speed to much more than thirty miles per hour. Which meant a hundred hours of falling—about four days.

On my first trip to the Hollow Earth, I'd fallen to the core while riding upon a sunflower blossom the size of a city. The great mass of the flower had allowed it to plow through the air like a dreadnought, reaching a terminal velocity of something like a hundred miles per hour. That fall had taken only thirty hours. But on our own it would be longer.

Seela and I wouldn't starve to death or die of thirst during a four-day fall—provided we brought along fruit, a supply of dried meat, and some leaf-wrapped water globs. And even if we fell without supplies, we might make it. But there was another problem. Adrift in the vasty volume of the Hollow Earth, we'd be easy prey.

A wide range of creatures ply the fecund Hollow Earth's sky. The low-flying harpy birds, the spear-billed leather-wings, the ravenous *ballula*, and floating colonies of pale, irritable farmer ants.

When Seela and I reached the water's edge, we were glad the shore was overgrown with mangroves—leafy shrubs that rested on tall, branching, stilt-like roots. We could hold onto them. I wedged my feet into the sandy mud—lest I accidently drift upward—and I helped Seela to step out of her makeshift shell boat, with Brumble in her arms. Immediately Arf set to rooting in the undergrowth.

The mangroves grew much taller here than on the islands I'd seen during my sea journeys on Earth's outer surface. In here, everything grew high. Mounting up beyond the mangroves was every manner of tree and vine, and through a gap caused by a spit of rock, I could glimpse the monumental butte, nearly a mile high, with the cliff-dwellings of the shrigs, and the populous, ever-shifting flock of them, trailed by the shrigbirds who fed upon their parasites. It's hard to judge such a thing, but Eddie suggested there might be seven thousand of the shrigs. I was very glad they weren't man-eaters.

Little purple crabs perched upon the mangrove roots. They had long feelers and asymmetrical claws, and, when disturbed, they were quick to spring down to the ground. I wished I wasn't barefoot. I'd shed my shoes in the *ballula*, and, as I say, at this point everything we'd carried was lost—although, yes, Seela, Eddie, and I still had our dense and potent rumby stones wrapped in threads and twine upon our necklaces.

"Welcome home," said Seela, as if to herself. She dimpled and took a bow—which sent her drifting up a few feet to some overarching mangrove roots above us. "Now, dear husband," she continued, addressing me from on high. "Now you'll help me travel to the opposite pole."

"Is it so important to see Yurgen again?" I asked, staring up at her.

"That boy means nothing to me," said Seela. "I only want to show Brumble to my parents."

"I thought you said you don't know who your father was. And that your mother left your home flower to join a different tribe."

"Why are you cross with me, Mason? We have a new baby!"

Right around then, one of the little crabs pinched my toe. I screamed, leapt, banged my head on a thick air-root, and yelled a curse. A funnel-shaped leaf tipped a bobbling glob of water onto my head. I had to use both hands to get the water off my face. Low comedy. Seela laughed merrily. I had a distinct feeling she'd used her rumby tekelili to guide the crab my way.

"Look at Daddy!" Seela cooed to the dozing Brumble, who was floating next to her in the air. "Daddy gets red. *Big* old crab."

"Here we come," called Ina's voice from afar. She and Eddie were some distance down the shore. Eddie had shown her how to swing weightlessly through the low branches of the mangroves. A minute later our two companions were at our side.

"Our goodies are gone!" said Ina. "Into the sky and eaten by shrigs. It's bad."

"We'll forage food and drink easily enough," said I. "The Hollow Earth is a land of plenty." Balls of water shone in the misty jungle ahead of us. Fruits like grapes dangled from a nearby vine, with fist-sized berries on a branch just beyond. Slugs writhed upon the trunks, and quick, bright-eyed creatures peeked from behind branches.

More of those fledgling shrigs were snouting at the mud. They were not unlike black, hairy pigs, save that they had no legs, and their bodies were ridged into segments which tapered to a horizontal shrimp-tail.

One of their number, about the same size as me, was busying himself less than fifty feet away. He seemed to have found a dead fish, or perhaps even a piece of the unfortunate Cytherea. Or maybe it was a tangle of decayed seaweed. In any case the shrig threw back his head, convulsively gumming down his fodder with his toothless jaws.

"Slaughter him for us, savage Seela," said Eddie. "Roast shrig meat is toothsome. And it dries to make an excellent pemmican."

"But what of the shrig's mother?" asked Ina. "They're fierce when protecting their young, one would suppose."

"The grown shrigs can't see us down here amid the trees," said Eddie. "And the little one won't have time to squeal. Pretend you want to feed it, Seela. Lure it close and slit its throat. There's the girl. Mason will mind the baby. I see that you have your knife."

Indeed, both Seela and I had thought to strap our knives against our legs. But she demurred. "Shrigs disgust me," said she. "That one you want me to butcher, he has manure crusts all over his body. What I want to eat is flower-leather. *Gooba'am*."

"Why not roast a bird?" proposed Ina, cocking her head. "I hear some in the jungle. One of them's very loud. *Awk-kwawk?*"

"That's a harpy," said Seela. "They're killers. And they taste horrible. You don't want to deal with them."

"Fruit would suit me very well," said I. "Let's eat something easy, and then sleep. No intricate preparations. I'm at my rope's end. After we sleep, I'll show you how to fish in the water globs, Ina, and we'll roast them, and we can take the measure of this congeries of shrigs. I suppose we can ride one to the center. Either get one to swallow us, or mount its back and hang onto the bristles."

"It's best to *glue* yourself on," said Seela. "If needs be. There's a cactus in the jungle with a juice you can use. Pancake cactus, it has no thorns. But I worry about riding a shrig with Brumble along. The shrigs have lice as big as turtles. That's what those shrigbirds are eating."

"I'll squash the lice," said Ina. "I'm good at that. From living in Cruikshank's foul den."

"Mason, Brumble, Arf, and I won't be riding with you and Eddie," Seela informed her. "We'll ride straight to my flower. You two should pick an especially stinky shrig for your ride to the Umpteen Seas. Stinky shrig, stinky Ina, stinky Eddie."

"I thought we were friends now!" exclaimed Ina, a little hurt.

"I don't like the way you smile at Mason," said Seela.

"You and I will do as you say," I told Seela, meaning to mollify her. "We'll fly straight to your flower with the baby. And perhaps we'll see Eddie and Ina again later on."

I was trembling with exhaustion, and I wanted peace. Certainly I had no lust to remind Seela yet again that her true home was inside *Earth* and that we were now, strictly speaking, inside *MirrorEarth*. But perhaps a village on some mirorflower on this side would be much the same as her home. At this point I didn't care.

Nor did I have the spunk to tell my companions of the great insights I'd had about Machree and me, that is (a) Machree and I had murdered copies of each other, and (b) the *woomo* wanted Machree to travel from MirrorEarth to Earth in order to promote balance. If I told these things to the others, they'd go blank (Ina), or deny (Seela), or attempt to pick holes in my crystalline logic (Eddie).

But now, thinking of Eddie's possible attacks, my convictions regarding balance began leaking away. By now any precise balance between the worlds was an impossibility. MirrorEarth's Eddie Poe was dead, but our old Earth's Eddie Poe was not only alive, but here with me in person. And forget not the vexed nexus when I killed the stableboy on Earth and, simultaneously, the MirrorStableboy on MirrorEarth killed MirrorMe.

A long-forgotten image came to mind. When I'd been running away from the stable in Lynchburg—I'd envisioned a fat worm with tendrils reaching out to me, and I'd nearly stumbled. Was it not obvious that the worm had been a *woomo*, witnessing my transition via tekelili?

Any notion of balance was a delusion, a will o' the wisp, and I was foolish to even think of it. We were deep into the authorial ink indeed. But who was writing the plot?

I followed the others, worming our way a deeper into the jungle and a bit further from the Rind, avoiding the winged lizards and the pale, haughty ants—Seela said these were a species distinct from the royal ants or the farmer ants. The jungle, as I may have mentioned, extended inward for thirty miles, not that we could see anything like that distance while in the thick of it.

We passed a long, twisty branch with exceedingly long thorns upon it. Seela pointed them out to me, and said the flowerpeople word for "rapier." Indeed, I remembered having Seela's folk use these spikes as weapons. I wondered if they'd greet us gently, if and when we reached the mirrorflower.

Preferring to think of something else, I feverishly returned to my delusional speculations about the *woomo's* plans. Might it be that the *woomo* would want to *retroactively* repair the broken balance? Was that even possible? What if they killed Eddie, Machree, and me? And what of Seela's MirrorEarth double, the MirrorSeela whom we'd surely encounter before long. Food for thought.

In the distance, the randy shrigs were rutting on the cliffs. Their thunderous wheenks were a paean in praise of physical love, which had the effect of shunting my mental focus from abstract ruminations about cosmic balance, and toward dreamy visions of making love to Seela and Mirror Seela at the same time.

Seela nudged me, and I realized that, thanks to rumby tekelili, she knew what I was thinking. She didn't mind. Everything was fine. We were free of the dangerous *ballula*, and at large in this Edenic natural world. We were Adam, Eve, and Brumble—and soon we'd have a MirrorEve as well. Surely everything would work out.

We entered a clear region amid great trees. Arf emerged from a thicket with a fish in his jaws. He hadn't forgotten the tricks he'd learned on our first trip through the Hollow Earth.

foothills that mounted to the shrigs' cliffs. We were four adults in number with Brumble in Seela's arms, and Arf making his own way. From our new vantage point I could see an enormous hole in the center of the slightly slanting butte—which was, I now realized, a volcanic vent, no longer flowing with lava but, rather, being used as a passageway by—the second giant ant whom Seela had been telling me about.

"Fafnir," she said, satisfied to have her suspicions confirmed. "Jormungo's husband. He's coming out. Look at his wings."

The narrow ant was, like his spouse, over three miles long and some two hundred yards wide. His iridescent form writhed against the sky—a narrow-bodied silhouette, with elegant wings and six devilishly lively legs in play. The royal ant's L-shaped antennae were like pennants, and the great joints of his tripartite body hinged wildly back and forth. He was vital as a flame. The twitching legs were several hundred feet long, and he was using them to skewer shrigs.

Once he'd impaled a shrig with a leg, the victim would begin sagging and dwindling—Fafnir's legs served as hollow feeding-tubes and, vampire-like, he was draining the juices of his prey. Periodically he'd bend himself double and tear at the wizened, folded-up husks of those shrigs he'd impaled upon his energetic limbs. He was dark as night and very shiny, with sheens of purple and green. The colors were continually shifting with his body's nimble play.

Directing my inner sight through the lens of my rumby stone, I picked up a somewhat confused sense of the consort ant's personality. Like Jormungo, Fafnir had a chaotic psyche, seething like a cauldron or like a storm at sea, crowded with patterns that merged and parted like the dust devils on an arid field. I was unable to decide if Fafnir was aware of me as an individual.

Meanwhile the thousands of clumsy, flying shrimp-pigs whirled in a storm, wildly roaring, striving to find safety in the center of their herd or, less successfully, to fly off on their own.

As I mentioned in my first narrative, when a shrig wants to travel a long distance, it uses an explosive means of propulsion, that is, it sets afire the thunderous gasses that emerge from its anus, in effect flying upon the propulsion of a burn-ing fart. But several of the large shrigs attempting this ruse were brought down by the male ant. He was exceedingly nimble and very cunning in his moves, far more so than the bumbling, dimwitted shrigs.

We beheld, in short, a scene of great carnage. By the time that Fafnir the royal ant had eaten his fill, he'd consumed a hundred shrigs or more. And even then he granted his prey no surcease. Continuing with his same finicky urgency as before, he skewered a hundred more shrigs upon his pointed, hollow limbs. But these he did not drain dry. These were to be carried intact to his mate.

With deft twitches of his shiny, translucent wings, Fafnir headed back into his gore-stained tunnel, bringing a fresh meal to his wife Jormungo, that is, to the undulating, three-mile-long empress ant whom we'd seen nested in the sea, endlessly swimming her circuit in the waters around the throat of the North Hole's great maelstrom, with her slowly-maturing gold eggs aligned upon her belly.

As if goaded into blood lust by Fafnir's onslaught, a platoon of four harpy birds dove at us, meaning to tear apart our flesh. I'm proud to say that I dispatched the first harpy by plunging my long knife into the beast's heart. Ina sheltered baby Brumble in her arms while Seela slew a second harpy. And then, squawking with baffled fury, the other two harpies turned tail and flew to a sinister bare-limbed tree half a mile from our perch.

We eased back into the jungle a bit, but not so far that we couldn't keep watching the show.

"Quite a death toll for so early in the day," said Ina, passing Brumble back to me. "Those poor shrigs. I wish I had some brandy."

Eddie sighed. "The cask is gone. My opium as well. And Fafnir has indeed frayed my nerves. I'll be glad when we can hop a shrig and fly to the Umpteen Seas. The center's steady play of *woomo* light is a salubrious tonic."

Not that there was much chance of Eddie and Ina mount-ing a shrig just now. Although Fafnir had retreated from sight, the blimp-like shrigs were highly agitated. They wheeled and roared, chorusing their dismay. Looking higher up, I could see a haze of shrig dung drifting into the sky.

"How often does Fafnir come here?" I asked Seela.

"He eats every day," she said.

"Our native guide is well versed," observed Eddie.

Seela turned to Eddie. "As I told Mason, all the people in the Hollow Earth know about Fafnir and Jormungo," said she. "But I didn't like to mention it before our trip. Especially not mention it to a coward like you, Eddie Poe. And, you see, we came through fine. Perhaps tomorrow we'll ride a pair of shrigs away from here. It might be best to do it just after Fafnir feeds again. When the shrigs are giddy and stunned."

"I'm not a coward," said Eddie, fastening on that word. "I'm merely rational."

"I'm not leaving until we kill that cruel giant ant!" cried Ina. "It's the least we can do. Eddie can find a way to do it. He's so clever."

"It will be so," said Eddie, wanting to play the hero in Ina's eyes. "We'll right the wrong, my lady, and slay the dragon. What say you to *that*, doubting Seela?"

"I *can* think of a way to attack Fafnir," she said. "But I'm not sure it's wise. Why kill a glorious and iridescent, royal ant for the sake of some stupid, manure-coated shrigs? We have a legend that the royal ants hollowed out this great space. And they split it in two."

"What a story!" I exclaimed. "Why didn't you tell me?"

"Well, I never fully understood the legend before," responded Seela. "But now that I've been to the surface, I understand that our world is a hollow ball. Who hollowed it out? The royal ants! Listen to the legend. At the dawn of time, Jormungo and her babies were inside an apple, eating and eating, and shitting into a crack in the air in the middle of the apple. Jormungo made the apple hollow, and the crack in the air was still here. They put so much shit into the crack that it pried the apple into two apples. And that's why the Earth is hollow, and that's why there's an Earth and a MirrorEarth." Seela smiled. "See?"

Ina wasn't listening, or wasn't understanding.

"I do so love those shrigs," she crooned. "They're jolly and gay. They make me feel like a happy girl again. We have to save them from Fafnir."

"And then what happens?" I said to Ina. I was still holding Brumble against my shoulder. He was half asleep. "If we kill Fafnir, who feeds Jormungo? Seela says Jormungo is the empress ant, and the ants made the shape of our world. Weren't you listening? The royal ants are like gods."

"The wild, ignorant legends of Seela's tribe mean nothing," said Eddie. Knowing him, I think he was annoyed he hadn't come up with Seela's speculations first. "Let the widowed Jormungo seine algae, shrimp, and kelpweed from the sea she swirls," he continued in a lofty tone. "The great insect's fate is not our concern."

"I'm quite sure Eddie is right," said Seela with a sly, demure smile. She gave me a calculating look as she reached some internal decision. "Very well then. We'll cut off Fafnir's head. Tomorrow morning. All we need to do is find a thread vine. In fact I saw one near our camp. And we'll gather some pancake cactuses as well. For gluing us to the shrigs when we leave."

My bloodthirsty Amazon tucked our baby against her breast. And then our group swung through the branches, vines, and water globs to the safety of our shelf-mushroom bunks. Arf appeared in our wake. My little fire was still glowing in its hollow branch.

"That one there," said Seela, pointing to a snaky vine with purple, mouse-ear leaves. It ran along the giant tree with the shelf-mushrooms, and inward toward the core. "We'll need three hundred yards of it, Mason, and we'll use a torch to cut it."

"No knife?" said I.

"You can't cut this vine," said Seela. "The thread—the strand running along the vine's center—it's unbreakable. But you can burn it in two."

"I want to catch fish," put in Ina, uninterested in the practical details of the Herculean task that she had set in motion. For whatever reason, Seela was intent on carrying it out. Even though, to me, it seemed a reckless whim.

"I'll show you how to fish," Eddie told Ina. "It's best if we shed our clothes. Does modesty forbid?"

"My modesty's gone," said Ina, preening. "Quashed by the slaving saloon-keeper Cruikshank, murderer of my Pa." I was beginning to have doubts about Ina's veracity. I felt she was acting a role—in this case, playing the orphan in need of rescue by a heroic male such as Eddie Poe.

Perhaps Eddie sensed this too, but was enjoying himself, casting aside his usual somberness and breaking into a smile. Moments later his and Ina's clothes were floating in the air, and the two were splashing in a nearby water glob the size of a church. Arf joined them. My eyes were drawn to the quick motions of Ina's pale brown limbs.

"Mason!" said Seela, demanding my attention. "Make a torch."

I broke a short length of dead branch off a tree, and stuck the end into the glowing nest of embers in the trunk. Using a leafy branch, I fanned the fire into renewed life, and now one end of my branch was alight. A torch. I waved it in the air, admiring the odd motions of the low-gravity flame.

"Now you burn a gap," said Seela, leading me to the smooth vine with the purple leaves.

The thread vine was turgid with sap, and not corky or pithy at all. I set to charring it through. As I reached the center of the vine a vein of some odd substance emitted a percussive crack, propelling a shower of sparks from the torch. I'd burned the thread through. I paused to rest, letting the torch hang all but weightless in the air at some distance from me. Due to the listless flow of air currents here, the heat of the torch was somewhat burdensome.

Seela had the avid Brumble at her breast. Eddie and Ina were laughing in the water. I didn't like to stare at them, but it seemed possible that they were making love, or trying to, although I recalled my Uncle Tuck's claim that a man can't do the deed while underwater. I had, in point of fact, successfully accomplished this feat with Seela in the Umpteen Seas last year. It's a matter of using rapid motion, which provides sufficient warmth to preserve love's tender glow. Of course I'd been a lively sixteen years, unlike Eddie Poe, now doddering into his twenty-ninth. Given the opportunity, I'd be glad to try the trick again. But not with Seela still on the mend from delivering herself of Brumble—had it been three days ago? Surely I'd need to wait a month until—

Seela's lips were moving. "Are you deaf?" she was saying. "I'm telling you to climb up three hundred yards, burn through the vine up there, and pull the whole length back down. I can't do it for you. You can see I'm busy with Brumble."

Indeed. A dutiful husband I, aged seventeen. Ina and that old coot Eddie continued disporting themselves, but never mind. I hopped along to a point three hundred yards further inward on the tree—really quite some distance—and then I burned another gap, and then, bracing myself against nearby branches, pulled the vine's rootlets away from the tree, freeing up a flexible, three-hundred-yard segment which I coiled into a massive ring of loops. I lugged the unwieldy load back with some effort and presented it to my wife.

"Now hold the baby," said she.

I'd been feeling a bit put upon, but my heart melted anew as I beheld our tiny folded flower-bud of a baby. I wondered at his little yawns and at the sweetly random twitches of his legs and arms. I settled him against me and he slept.

Meanwhile Seela had unsheathed the large knife that she still wore strapped to her leg. Taking the vine, she whittled away some of the vine's outer rind near one end, exposing the all-but-invisible thread that ran along its central axis. She worked on the other end of the vine as well, as if fashioning a handle at each end. The three-hundred-yard thread that ran along the center of the vine was still under cover—Seela said it was too dangerously sharp to uncover right away.

"We'll yank the thread loose tomorrow," she told me. With a small sideways motion of one handle, she showed me that, if we pulled in the right direction, the hidden thread could cut its way out of the sheathing vine.

"We'll stretch the thread across Fafnir's burrow?" I said.

"Yes. You and I will be hovering there, Mason. We'll each hold a handle, and we'll pull the cutting-thread taut between us, and when Fafnir sticks his head out of the tunnel—*zack*."

She swept her free hand across her throat and lolled her head to one side. As if she'd been guillotined.

"Ghastly," I said. "This is madness, Seela. Who am I to kill so magical a beast? It's not my place. I know nothing of the Hollow Earth."

"Maybe those royal ants have been awaiting a jolt," said Seela. "Expecting an attack for scores of years. Or for centuries. That's in the legend too. Our onslaught will mark the day of their children's birth. All in accordance with an ancient rhythm that's known to everyone except you and your surface-dwelling friends, Mason. Known throughout the Hollow Earth." Her smile was sly, enigmatic, mocking.

"I can't tell if you're teasing me," I complained. "I never know what's going on." I was a little worn-down by Seela. She'd been wildly unpredictable for the last few days— although I freely grant she had good reason. How strange it must be to have a child emerge from your body.

We heard laughter from Eddie, and a burst of merry song from Ina. "Come join us, Mason," she called, sweetening her voice.

"So, yes, we'll go attack the giant ant for Ina," said Seela, hardening her tone. "You can't keep your eyes off her. It excites you that she says she's a fallen woman, a little lost bird with a broken wing. Liar. She's grabbing for you with her nasty, dirty claws! Just when I need you the most."

Falling silent now, Seela tethered our looped coil of vine to a branch, stripped off her clothes, and leapt from the branch were we stood, arrowing thirty or forty feet through the leaves and into the great ball of water where the other two swam. From Seela's expression, you might have thought she was going to kill them.

Brumble remained behind, hanging in the air beside me. I scooped him up and set to gathering fruit, talking to the baby as we moved around.

The day went slowly, with the four of us chatting, eating fruit and fish, and poking twigs at the beetles and the alert, pale beige ants who came lolloping by. These weren't the farmer ants that Seela had talked about, these fellows were a lesser breed, less than two inches long. But it wouldn't do to try and hold one. They were quick to nip with their jaws, and they had sharp stingers on their rears.

Eddie, who was in a talkative mood, reprised a published story of his about a balloon journey to the Moon. Not that, in my opinion, Eddie's jejune hoaxing tale, which I'd read several years ago, could hold a candle to the journey we were presently on, nor did it compare, in my estimation, to my narrative, *The Hollow Earth*, which was penned, I might remind you, while I was still but seventeen years of age. So which of us two was the genius?

When I posed this question to Eddie, he told me I was a vainglorious dunderhead, and he retreated to the back of his shelf-mushroom bunk, where he busied himself with a parchment-like leaf, a thorn pen, and the ink of a crushed berry. Perhaps he was outlining his epic poem *Htrae*. Not that I'd actually heard or seen a single line of it.

The mood improved when Seela undertook the task of outfitting us with the air-kicking fins that she and her tribe called *pulpuls*. Seela had found some good-sized flowers higher up in the jungle, blooms like large chrysanthemums, and their individual petals had hollow bases that you could stick your feet through, as if into boots. Using her steel knife, Seela trimmed off the main bodies of the petals, creating shapes like paddles, and making little slits for securing the tips of our toes. And now we had rather efficient airfins. Eddie and I already knew how to beat our way through the air with these *pulpuls*, and the lithe Ina was quick to learn. Laughing as she worked, Seela even put some wee *pulpuls* on Arf, something she hadn't thought of doing on our last trip through.

We played tag for a while, in and around the glens and passages of the jungle, with Brumble reacting to the goings-on with fitful grimaces, kicks of his legs, and blinks of his eyes.

Arf got overly curious about the beige ants and trailed them to their colony a hundred yards off, a swarm of them living inside a great hollow tree. The dog snouted open a hole in the bark, revealing masses of the large, feisty, and territorial ants, all of them intent on repelling his attack. They nipped and stung him more than a few times, but, thanks to his doggie *pulpul* fins, he managed to escape them, and returned alone to our little camp. I took off his fins, and he settled into our bunk to lick his paws.

By now my little spat with Seela had faded away. I was doing my best to make it clear to her, by words and by deeds, that she, and no other, was my life's great love. Eddie, too, was back on good terms with me. He'd managed to write a poem on that leaf, and he read it to us with gusto. I showered him with praise. The poem was called "The Haunted Palace." The theme was, as would be customary for Eddie, a great mansion that falls under a curse. The last stanza sticks in my mind.

> And travellers now within that valley,
> Through the red-litten windows see
> Vast forms, that move fantastically
> To a discordant melody;
> While, like a rapid, ghastly river,
> Through the pale door
> A hideous throng rush out forever,
> And laugh — but smile no more.

"You're worried about the giant royal ants?" I said to Eddie, noticing the bit about something ghastly rushing through a door. "Just remember—it's Seela and me that will be going up against them."

"We'll tend Brumble," said Ina.

As if rehearsing tomorrow's ambush of the consort ant—Seela managed to behead a winged snake. I roasted the meat in my fire pit, which remained aglow. The serpent's flesh proved more than acceptable. It was whitish and dense, with a taste of butter and mint. We licked our fingers when we were done.

At no point did it ever get any darker here, but eventually we deemed it time to lie down and get another night's worth of sleep. Seela dropped off almost immediately. I lay awake for some time, engaged in my daily process of placing my memories in order, in preparation for eventually writing my *Return to the Hollow Earth*. More strongly than ever, I had a sense that some unseen higher being was recording my thoughts, lest my labors be lost. Would that it were so. And then I too slept, although not continuously. Every few hours

Brumble would rouse Seela so he could nurse, and oftentimes I'd awaken for a spell as well. Everything about Brumble and Seela interested me.

The animals of the Hollow Earth had their own rhythms, alternating between sleep and activity all day long. We woke with the shrigbirds chirruping and the shrigs placidly calling each to each. The slow-witted giants showed no sign of anticipating the deadly Fafnir's daily visit.

Our party breakfasted on fruit, augmented by a seedpod that had something like the stimulating effect of coffee. We four made our way to the jungle's far edge, where Seela and I parked Brumble and Arf with Eddie and Ina. Kicking ourselves into the air, Seela and I unrolled the thread vine and then, with a twitch of the handles, let the central thread cut its way out. The husk drifted into the sky. The thread itself was essentially invisible, but to test it out, Seela and I kicked our way along the edge of the jungle with the thread stretched tight between us—as if we were clearing the edge of a road.

We sliced shrubs, vines, and branches of trees, avoiding those hefty, pinching beige ants that could appear out of nowhere. I felt no tugging from the thread. It was as if the jungle plants were phantoms of the air. Urging me on, Seela kicked her way to the inner, jungle side of a five-mile-high breadfruit tree. I kept pace with her, passing the diamond-patterned trunk on its outer side. At contact, I again felt no reaction from the thread, even though the titan of the forest was soon cut in two. It seemed likely the vine's thread could cleave the ant Fafnir's chitinous head from his body.

Urged ever so slowly by the faint gravity, the miles-high crown of the breadfruit tree drifted free of the jungle and into the sky. A flock of shrigs gathered to feed on it, going after its lumpy fruits and lobed foliage.

Seela and I continued kicking our fins, traversing the two-mile gap between the towering jungle and the opening of the tunnel in the top of the butte. On the way, a party of inexperienced young shrigs mistook us for drifting food and flew toward us. I don't think they'd ever seen live humans before. With a skillful kick of her *pulpuls*, Seela adjusted our trajectories so that our wire cut the leading shrig in half, from nose to tail, like a small loaf of bread being cut along its length for a catfish sandwich at the side of the James River. A great fart rushed out and shrig dung scattered, along with gouts of the straw-yellow fluid that serves shrigs as blood.

The other shrigs in the party shied away from us—and began feeding on their companion's remains, starting with sniffs and nibbles, and progressing to gobbles and gulps. Shrigs are inelegant to the highest degree.

Seela and I passed on, directing our kicks to keep us at a steady distance from the Rind, studiously avoiding the fate of falling into the sky. As always in the near-free-fall conditions of the Hollow Earth, there were no particular directions that one felt compelled to call down or up. The words in and out were consistently more useful here—*in* meaning toward the center, and *out* meaning toward the Rind. Whether we flew with our bellies facing in or out was a matter of indifference, although, all in all, it seemed more useful to fly with our eyes facing the Rind.

Approaching the great volcanic butte, we could see into the caves wherein the shrigs nested. Inflated mothers bobbled against the ceilings of the caves, with baby shrigs nursing upon them from below. To Seela and I, the shriglets' grunts and squeals seemed harmonious, and even cozy. The chirping shrigbirds were everywhere, continually grooming their hosts. I glanced back at the tangled green wall of the jungle. I could make out the tiny figures of Eddie and Ina minding Brumble, although the baby himself was too small to see.

Unlike the fledgling shrigs who'd thought to try eating us, the adult shrigs let us pass. The mature beasts had a sense that humans were best left alone, just as we humans know not to disturb wasps.

And so Seela and I progressed, passing along the lumps and ridges of ancient lava that sloped to the lip of the butte. We flew with each of us holding one end of the cutting-string, and with the string stretched taut between us, lest a stray loop or bight sever a limb. So we were three hundred yards apart. The air was calm and relatively quiet, save for the steady background mooing and wheenking of the shrigs, and, with the help of our rumby tekelili, it was just barely possible to converse.

"You're truly set on doing this?" I called to Seela.

"A lark," she sang back. "I like change."

"But you don't like change enough to stay in San Francisco," I said.

"Live in the present," admonished Seela. "Today we cut off Fafnir's head."

"Are you quite assured the string can do it?" I said. "Perhaps the royal ants are like hammered steel—or some yet starker alloy. Not like soft shrigs."

"Let's test our thread's power," said Seela.

Just outward from us was a spire of petrified lava—shaped like the pile of mud that a crawfish makes outside its hole in the bottom of a stream. Seela said the lava was of an adamantine hardness, indeed it may have been composed of the preternaturally dense minerals that lie at the Rind's core. Keeping an eye on each other, Seela and I rose outward and swept along on either side of the spire.

Again I felt no vibration, no tremor, and no slowing in the thread. Silently it moved through the tower of lava, which was easily fifty feet wide. Slowly, the severed, stony tip drifted free of the base, and inward toward the Hollow Earth's core.

"Fafnir is doomed," declaimed Seela as we alit atop the great vent. We took our positions on either side of the great ant's tunnel.

8. Tallulah

So there we were, Seela and I, hanging head-down from a volcanic vent upon the Earth's inner surface, hanging like bats on the ceiling of a cave, but not a dark, small cave, no, this was a pastel planetary "cave" filled with flickering pink light streamers from the *woomo* sea cucumbers at the Hollow Earth's core, the great inner surface patterned with continents and wonderful blue seas. If I flipped my mental sense of perspective, we weren't hanging head-down, no, we were standing up. Or projecting out to the side. In any case, we had our feet wedged into cracks of the lava so we didn't drift into the sky.

The consort ant's crawl-hole was some three hundred yards across, just the length of our thread. Although the royal ants were three miles long, they were only two hundred yards wide, so he'd slide smoothly from the hole. Seela and I had positioned ourselves on diametrically opposite points of the rim of the hole, and we had our deadly-sharp vine thread pulled taut.

The simplest idea was that, as Fafnir scrambled out of his hole, he might ram into the thread and immediately split his head in two. Like a meat cleaver hitting him in the forehead. The other idea was if he came out wholly on one side of the thread, Seela would jump free and kick her fins, sweeping the thread across the opening, thus guillotining the ant.

Why were we doing this? It had started as a peevish request by Ina, and then Eddie had advocated for it, if only to make himself seem big, and then, for whatever veiled personal reasons, Seela had said we'd get it done. As for me, I'd simply been drawn along.

My faint rumby contacts with the ants Jormungo and Fafnir had shown me that these beings weren't anything like the bovine shrigs. The royal ants had complex and, for me, barely comprehensible inner lives. Seela said they'd hollowed out the Earth. Were, then, the royal ants not worthy of worship?

I'd decided I was not going to slaughter Fafnir. Far from holding the thread taut, I was going to yank it out of Fafnir's way when he appeared. I held this thought deep in my mind, lest Seela see it via our tenuous rumby link.

I felt a vibration in the adamantine stone of the volcanic vent, and I heard a faint, echoing roar. A joyful sound, a riotous squawk from, as Seela had it, one of our world's creators.

Fafnir's psyche was like a bonfire, an inner roar, the consuming pyre of a thousand saints—albeit saints who enjoy killing and eating shrigs. Amid the turmoil, I sensed Fafnir's love of his wife Jormungo, and his exultation that, at long last, her brooding upon her eggs was coming to term. I found it passing odd that Seela and I had arrived on this particular day. Odd or—as Seela had seemed suggest—fated.

Yes, I repeated to myself, Fafnir must live. As a new father, I felt full sympathy for the giant ant. Nothing must spoil his joy at the hatching of his wife's eggs.

At my first sight of the tips of Fafnir's gleaming purple-black mandibles, I pulled my feet free and kicked away from the tunnel's entrance. But—oh no!—the cunning Seela had anticipated my move. She was kicking *her* limbs as well, moving in precisely the opposite direction from me, so that our stretched thread was rotating above the tunnel's hole like a great compass needle—rather than being yanked to the side.

In order to save Fafnir, I might simply have released my hold upon the thread, but I was leery so to do, dreading a disastrous encounter between my body and the deadly-sharp line. But now these considerations became moot. Fafnir rammed into our stretched thread with his long, massive head and the effect upon him was—nil.

I wasn't entirely surprised that the ant's armor had a hardness and a solidity unknown among Earth's normal creatures. Why not? This was, after all, a being from the dawn of time.

Perhaps by way of teaching us a lesson, Fafnir gave our vine string an abrupt yank. The handles were torn from my grasp and from Seela's. The thread coiled invisibly into the surrounding air. My luck held, and no bight of the freed line happened to decapitate me. With all his surfaces and protuberances intact, Fafnir shook out his long wings and flew free of the butte.

Although Seela and I were tiny relative to the leviathan, we were aglow with our rumby tekelili. *And* we were the ones who'd been holding the vine thread. Fafnir marked us with a flash of his eyes—but for now he let us be. He had larger plans.

Moving in elegant swoops, the flying purplish-green ant impaled a succession of a hundred or more shrigs upon his fearsome legs, draining their bodies rapidly as his own body swelled. The spectacle was similar to his attack the day before—but with ten times the noise. Fafnir's grainy cries were like the harsh caws of a bird of prey. And now, unfathomably, the exultant royal ant began beaming a brilliant red ray from the great stinger at his rear—directing the blinding, needle-like beam inward toward the basking *woomo* at the core of the Hollow Earth.

Inevitably the ray and the distant clamor attracted the attention, and perhaps the opprobrium, of the *woomo*. A dense, burning streamer of light focused upon Fafnir's flickering form, following his gyrations with barely a lag. The impaled and drained bodies of the shrigs were crisped into ashes. Fafnir's body glowed first red, then yellow, and then white. But he didn't seem to mind. Indeed, he seemed to be enjoying himself. He flapped his illuminated wings; he danced like a bonfire. His cries grew louder, more harmonious, more jubilant. And he continued goading the distant *woomo* with his tail-stinger's red beam.

Drawn by her husband's clamorous cries, Jormungo now made her appearance, wriggling out of the volcanic tunnel upon the butte and buzzing free. All the while, Seela and I were frantically kicking our airfins, wanting to make our way back to the shelter of the jungle.

A particularly bright *woomo* beam played across Seela and me, lingering rather longer than was comfortable, perhaps even for a full two minutes, and in that time, Seela and I were once again cured to a total ebony blackness, which was seemingly to be my recurrent fate for the rest of my days. The good news was that the light stream moved away from us before we were roasted like pigs or kindled into flame.

The *woomo* had homed in their primary target by now, and their intolerably intense light streamers were playing across the white-hot Fafnir from one end to the other, over and over. But, as I say, the light seemed to do the ant no harm. Remember that—if Seela was to be believed—Fafnir and Jormungo were primeval, nearly god-like creatures, capable of hollowing out a planet and splitting space in two. For beings like these, the heat of a *woomo* light beam might even be agreeable. Perhaps the *woomo* knew this. Perhaps they were not in fact trying to kill the royal ant. Perhaps they were caressing him.

Jormungo flew to Fafnir and seized him in a full-body embrace, never flinching from his heat, and indeed, writhing against him as if in ecstatic transport, their flame-like bodies as one. And as they embraced, Fafnir shared with her the steaming vapors of his ingested shrig juice. The two of them caromed off the surface of the Rind. With joyful twitches and snaps of their shimmering bodies and wings, Jormungo and Fafnir propelled themselves across the lava fields, past the jungle, and into the aquamarine sea, sending up a dense explosion of steam, which was quickly followed by a dozen loud reports, as if from the detonation of twelve bombs. The eggs? Events were unfolding very rapidly indeed.

The cloud of steam had developed into a great bank of fog, which put an end to the efficacy of the *woomo* light beams. All around us the shrigs were bellowing in the expanding mist. No longer could I see our way to the jungle. But Seela took hold of my hand, and led me with unerring instinct, guided in part, I suppose, by the tekelili of Eddie's rumby. As soon as we reached our friends amid the branches and vines, Seela seized baby Brumble. And I took hold of Arf.

"What have you done?" Ina demanded in a petulant tone. "You shouldn't have stirred up the giant ants like that. And now you're blacker than ever. I spoke in jest when I said to kill Fafnir. What madness have you unleashed?"

I could sense Seela's strong emotions. She'd gone beyond disliking Ina. She despised her. And so she favored the woman with no response.

"We're leaving," Seela said to Eddie. "Mason, Brumble, Arf and I are riding a shrig to my flower."

"We'll await you at the Umpteen Seas," said Eddie. "But only for a time. Before I return to my ancestral home."

"Mason and I will stay on my flower forever," said Seela. I didn't agree with this plan, but my wife was in no mood to be contradicted.

Off in the nearby sea, the pair of royal ants were excitedly chirping. It was perhaps like an operatic duet. Not that I'd ever heard an opera.

"I don't want to go to any Umpteen Seas," wailed Ina. "Nor go to some other Earth. I want to go home to San Francisco."

"This remains your choice," said Eddie. "But first I pray you accompany me to the Hollow Earth's core. It's like a waking dream, Ina, a sublunary paradise with heavy teke-lili. The black gods—they're beyond compare for flash and fancy. You'll bid farewell to me—and I'll journey on through the Central Anomaly, perhaps with Machree for company, if he's not too busy harvesting rumbies. And, Ina, if you will it, the *woomo* can send you back to your California, perhaps aboard a fried-egg flying disk. Seela may well stay on her dull flower with her pup. But I ween the young Mason will accompany you to San Francisco. He'll be overdue for a new woman—and a seaport spree."

I chose to ignore Eddie's divisive and impolite badinage. A beam of *woomo* light was playing across the befogged jungle. I wondered if they were looking for us. Two great, lost shrigs were mooing nearby, with their shrigbirds fluttering around them.

"Quickly now," Seela said to me, smearing her dark hands and feet with sap from one of those thornless pancake cactuses. They were common around here. "Do as I do. This plant-taffy can glue you to the back of a shrig. We'll use our rumbies to direct our shrig to my flower. The shrigs stink, and they have lice, but they'll do. We need to get out of here now. Come, Mason."

Without a word for Eddie or Ina, Seela was kicking away from the jungle. She had Brumble in her arms, the baby's face a spot of white against his black mother. I had no choice but to follow. I bid godspeed to Ina and Eddie, crushed a fat lobe of cactus, smeared the juice onto my arms and legs, and followed in Seela's wake, towing Arf by a small vine tendril I'd tied to one of his feet.

The shrig that Seela and I found was a big one, a female, subdued by Fafnir's rampage, not to mention the thunderous explosions of the eggs and the sudden blanket of mist. Seela and I infiltrated the shrig's psyche with our rumby tekelili, and she allowed us to land upon her bristly hide. Kneeling on her back and deploying our sticky sap, we fixed our positions, with Seela cradling Brumble in the crook of one arm, and me holding Arf as if he were my son. Using her rumby tekelili, Seela ordered the flying shrimp-pig to rocket us away.

The shrig—her name was Tallulah—responded with a grumbling groan and, for the moment, took no action. But I had a sense that, on the whole, the shrig didn't mind having us guide her getaway. By now she'd already spawned and released her season's quota of fry, and surely she was ready to leave—particularly with Fafnir and Jormungo on a rampage.

What Tallulah didn't as yet grasp was that Seela would be directing her toward the South Hole, rather than toward the Hollow Earth's core. In the mist and the low gravity, navigation was tricky. Especially for a shrig.

Seela repeated her order, and now Tallulah fired up her rocket. That is, she began leaking out a steady stream of fart which she set alight—by striking a spark with a pair of flint stones that she carried at all times in the prehensile tissues near her anus. And then we were on our way, leaving the shrigbirds behind.

Looking back, I saw that Eddie and Ina had imitated our actions. They'd boarded the other shrig, glued themselves down, and their shrig was rocketing toward the Hollow Earth's core. I waved farewell. Presumably they'd find 'Machree already at the Umpteen Seas.

Our initial velocity was not so great as to prevent Seela and me from getting a good view of what the giant ants were up to. The cloud of fog had drifted away from the sea. Below us, Fafnir and Jormungo were cavorting in the water—with the dozen newly hatched royal ants at their side. Fafnir was no longer directing his red beam of light at the *woomo*, and the *woomo* had suspended their rays as well.

The newborn ants were like their parents—but in a juvenile stage—ten yards long, with bright eyes, and with paddle wings. Their dark skins scattered highlights of purple and green, reminding me of the emperor staghorn beetles I'd seen on our manure pile in Hardware, Virginia. They had little bumps where their legs would so grow, and as yet they had no mandibles. But they were alert and they could fly, moving about like gnats, albeit gnats three times the size of cows.

The sea here had been circling the great maelstrom that ran in from the North Pole. But the maelstrom's swirl was dying—for the empress ant Jormungo was no longer at the great whirlpool's throat, and was no longer driving its rotation by her swimming. As a result, the passageway through the central hole was narrowing fast.

Somehow I hadn't anticipated this. But Seela had. She flashed me a fierce grin, a mixture of passion and possessiveness.

"You won't get away so easy now, Mason Reynolds! You'll stay with me in my cozy flower home."

I was speechless. Surely, if I tried, I might find a way to float up through hundreds of miles of cold, black sea. But ballooning through back the North Hole would have been so much simpler.

At this point the North Hole's throat was still just barely open. Did the family of royal ants mean to fly through it? Outwards from the core they flapped, rising in a helix, entering deeper and deeper into the narrowing strait, the two adults and the twelve juveniles. They moved with startling speed, and then—*thip, thip*—the parent and eleven of the children dove into the maelstrom's sidewall, just below the throat.

"Why did they do that?" I asked Seela.

"They'll paddle sideways to get into the middle layers of the Rind. People say that's where the royal ants have their big nest."

And just about then the maelstrom's throat pinched shut. The North Hole was gone. It remained only for the vast dimple in the sea to rebound.

I studied the last of the twelve royal ant juveniles—a restive dot just short of the maelstrom's closed-off throat. Changing his vector of motion, he was arcing away from the Rind, as if heading inward toward the Hollow Earth's core. I wondered what kind of reception the *woomo* would give him.

Meanwhile Seela was exhorting our shrig Tallulah to blast herself away from the Rind. And with good reason. As I say, once the maelstrom's throat closed over, the seawaters were due to rebound. For a single still moment a great aqueous dimple covered the hole where the whirlpool's mouth had been. But then, due to water's natural tendency to smooth itself, the surface began tautening toward us. With a certain physical exuberance, the onrushing mass of water overshot its mark, and rose high above the aquamarine surface of the inner sea—becoming, for a few moments, a continent of water thirty miles high, and thereby submerging the nearby jungle, as well as the cliffs with the nests of the shrigs, and indeed rising so far that this domed sea came nearly within touching distance of the rocketing Tallulah. Whether the rogue ant juvenile escaped the flood, I did not see.

As the sea settled back, damping herself with a series of dwindling oscillations, we continued on our way. Seela and I had seated ourselves just behind the shrig's large head, which shielded us from the wind of our rapid passage. I tied Arf's leash to an especially large shrig bristle, lest he drift away. Seela and I took the glue off our hands and sat in place with spots of glue holding our rear ends in place.

"Tell me more about the ants," I said.

"The story is that every thousand years, Jormungo hatches a clutch of royal ants to help start a new colony on another world. The *woomo* like it when the empress ant is brooding over her eggs and keeping a North Hole maelstrom open. Makes it easier to send out their tendrils. But now that won't happen for a while." She leaned over and gave me a kiss. "You were right, wanting to save Fafnir."

"Why didn't you admit that before?" I asked.

"Well, I did think it would be fun to get Jormungo excited," said Seela. "Give her a jolt. I was hoping she'd go ahead and hatch her eggs. And I wanted to see the maelstrom close." She smiled. "For the reason I told you."

"You're a sly one," I said

"I mean to keep you," said Seela. "You suit me well." She kissed me. I liked her with the dark skin.

"And what about that one juvenile royal ant who got away?" I said after a bit.

"Supposedly whenever they hatch a royal litter, they send one of the juveniles to visit with the *woomo* at the core. To tell them it's time for what they call a Bloom. That's when they send some *woomo* and some royal ants out together. Inside a couple of those fried egg ships. To colonize a new world. I'm not exactly sure about the details."

"The *woomo* and the royal ants are partners?"

Seela laughed. "Like you and me. I'm the *woomo* and you're the ant."

"I'll bite you," I said. "I'll pinch you hard!"

"I'll zap you! I'll sting you with my fronds!"

We got into an inconclusive amorous tussle, then burst into laughter and let the hours pass. As so often happened in these new days, Brumble was the focus of our attention.

"Four days old," said Seela. "I think he's opening his eyes a little more."

"He doesn't really see me," I said. "But maybe he sees you."

"He knows your voice," said Seela. "He waves his arms."

Arf pressed forward and licked Brumble on the face.

"Baby's bath," said Seela. "Keep an eye out for shrig lice, Mason." She pointed along Tallulah's hide. "There! Like a crab. See? It matches the shrig's skin. If it bites Brumble, I'll kill you."

"Can you calm down?" I said. "You've got everything you wanted. We're back inside the Hollow Earth, the North Hole is closed, and we're flying to your mirrorflower. Just you and me and Arf and Brumble. With Eddie and Ina and Machree out of the picture."

"That's all fine, but we don't have food, which *does* bother me," said Seela, taking herself seriously. "Now be a man, Mason, and kill that shrig louse before it gets the baby!"

I caught hold of the shrig louse and pulled. It came loose from the shrig's hide, leaving a dribble of pale yellow shrig blood. The louse didn't look at all like food. I snapped it in half and tossed it into the wind. I felt something like the ghost of a thank-you. From Tallulah? Perhaps the shrigs had an inner mental life after all. Probing back, I seemed to hear a steady note of song. As if the shrig were singing to herself as she flew, content with her task, meditatively moving on.

We were getting ever further from the curved Rind as Tallulah continued her route across the Hollow Earth's great round cavity—and toward the environs of the South Hole. Our path was very nearly a diameter or, more precisely, a chord of the sphere.

"Let's cuddle now," said Seela, her mood changing once again.

"You mean have sex?"

"Maybe," she said. "But no poking. I'm as sore as if I fell down a flight of stairs in Mrs. Mackie's rooming-house. Another reason it's better in the Hollow Earth. No stairs." She smiled at me as if expecting something.

"You were talking about cuddling," I said, feeling my way. "And then I said sex, and you said no poking, and now?"

"I'm saying we're tired, but we can, you know, kiss and touch, To help us bounce back."

"Like the sea from the maelstrom hole."

"The mount of love," said Seela, cheerfully bucking her pelvis. She still had Brumble curled in her right arm. "You don't see any shrig lice, do you?"

"Nary a one," said I, smearing some of the cactus glue onto the backs of my black shoulders and gluing myself flat on my back. "Have at me, Seela. Play me like a fiddle."

"A country tussle," she said, her face suddenly very close to mine. "Like with Yurgen. On the flower. When I was a virgin girl and he was the pied piper."

Clumsily we spent our passion, dozed off, and then I woke to Brumble crying. My shirt was wet with Seela's milk. This was the same white shirt of Eddie's that I'd taken from his room at Mrs. Mackie's hotel in San Francisco a week or so before. And my pants were still the same gray twill. Both garments were much stained by travel, and by our encounters with the Hollow Earth's outlandish inhabitants.

The better part of another day had passed. We were in an empty zone, midway between the Rind and the core, headed south rather than inward, with Tallulah making for a green spot of jungle beside the sea at the South Hole, this being where Seela's mirrorflower lay. Tallulah's flame still burned, but her gas supply was dwindling. Her inner song was wavering. She needed a meal.

I myself was hungry as well, and thirsty too. Thanks to the wild chaos brought on by Fafnir and Jormungo, Seela and I hadn't been thinking clearly when we'd left. We hadn't even thought to bring a water glob, let alone a supply of fruit.

But now fate smiled upon us again.

"Look," said Seela pointing ahead to a shoal of curious shapes—fuzzy blimps, whirling pods with whip-like tails, and long green chains of green sausages, tangled around like vines. The blimps, pods, and sausages glowed. The blimps were the size of Tallulah, the sausages were the size of my arm, and the pods were somewhere in between. There were a lot of these critters—or were they plants? They were heaped up like a tangled mound of garbage, and managing not to fall inward toward the Hollow Earth's core, thanks to the beating fuzz on the blimps, the thrashing tails on the pods, and the sparkling bubbles within the sausages.

"Brobdingnagian cryptozoa?" I said, drawing fine words from my *Southern Literary Messenger* store of learning. I meant that these creatures seemed like overgrown versions of the tiny plants and animals that scuttle about beneath the debris of a forest floor.

"Brob *what?*" said Seela, laughing. "This is an antfarm, tended by farmer ants. They're mean and creamy-white. They're a reasonable size. They grow these things you see: ant-sheep, ant-pigs, and ant-plants. Poach as much as you want, but don't let the farmer ants catch you."

"What exactly do you mean when you say the ants are a reasonable size?".

"Like big dogs."

"I don't see any of them."

"They're hiding on the other side of all this junk," said Seela. "They're scared of Tallulah. But soon they'll rush in for an attack. We have to eat fast The ant-plant sausages are especially good. Look at our shrig go."

Tallulah had focused on a tangle of those green sausages, and she was harvesting bushels of them with her open mouth. Periodically she'd pause to crunch her catch, bursting the sausages, releasing the verdant, effervescent slime within. Tallulah grunted with pleasure as she gulped down her questionable cud.

Seela leaned out from our perch on Tallulah's back to snag a foot-long ant-plant sausage herself. Nimbly Seela sliced it across the middle, popping something at its center. The sausage stopped glowing and went limp. Seela handed me half—like a floppy goblet. I lapped and sipped at the foamy ichor within, spilling out dancing droplets for Arf to snap from the air. The slime was grassy, but sweet, with a slight pungency, and bearing an odd tingle. The goo slid readily down my throat, slaking my thirst and restoring my energy. I snagged a second ant-plant sausage and then a third. A capital form of alimentation.

"Now for meat," said Seela, brandishing her blade. "A hunk of that sky-whipping guy's tail. We call that an ant-pig. The tail's a special treat."

Although none of the ant-sheep or ant-pigs had eyes, they were aware of our bulky shrig's progress—I suppose they were alerted by our smells, our jostling, our sound vibrations, and perhaps our psychic emanations. The blimp-like ant-sheep in particular were tracking us rather closely. They were glorious creatures, illuminated from within, with rainbow highlights shimmering along their cilia, and they had colorful globules of food and fat and water within their gelatinous flesh.

"Are those brains in the middle of these things?" I asked Seela. Each of the whirling ant-pigs and fat ant-sheep had a round, flickering mass at the core of its translucent body.

"Those are stomachs," said Seela. " It's not just the ant farmers you have to worry about—their livestock is dangerous too. If one of those critters happens to wrap itself around you, it'll start in on digesting you right away."

And with that, Seela set off on the hunt. Her intended prey was a whip-tailed ant-pig, and she was steering our shrig its way. Sensing our approach, the creature beat its flagellum, spinning its body like a top, and caroming off whatever came in contact. Seela rose to her feet, checked her airfins, and handed Brumble over to me. Choosing her moment with care, Seela plunged into a void amid the bustling population of the antfarm, kicking her legs to speed her way. With no solid matter nearby, I feared Seela's sally might go badly awry, with her missing her mark, losing her fins, and endlessly tumbling inward toward the Hollow Earth's core.

But Seela had precisely timed her leap so that her body would interrupt the sweep of the targeted ant-pig's tail. Seizing this thick, ropy strand in one hand, Seela slashed off a three-foot segment of the tip. And then she held the still-twitching bit of tail at such an angle that it propelled her back to our shrig. Cradling Brumble in one arm, I used my free hand to catch hold of Seela's leg.

She glued herself to our shrig again, and held up her prize, that is, a severed length of the tail. After some diminishing shudders, the tail-tip fell still. Seela cut off a bit and began eating it, all the while grinning at me and exaggerating her chomps.

"Try it, Mason. We're masters of the Hollow Earth. Conquerors of the antfarm. And remember to eat fast. Those farmer ants are gonna come after us any minute."

I accepted a piece of her odd, fibrous catch, whatever it really was. The substance was very chewy, like aged pemmican, with what I would call an off or a "high" taste, like spoiled meat. Its tingling juices had the property of numbing my lips and tongue. I spit out what was in my mouth, and gave the rest of my portion to Arf. Of course the dog loved this offal, and he begged Seela for more.

Stunned by Seela's abrupt attack, the ant-pig was moving crookedly. Again I had a sense of contact with Tallulah the shrig's mind. Her energy was mounting like a wave. She sensed an opportunity. As Tallulah's mental activation peaked, she executed a great wallowing lunge, and seized the narrow end of the ant-pig with her toothless but powerful jaws. The glowing ant-pig failed to spin free. Tallulah burst a hole in its hide—and slurped down perhaps a hundred gallons of the wounded creature's gelatinous body mass. But then the ant-pig's central digestive organ came slopping out along with the slime. The stomach—if that's what it was—glowed an angry yellow-white.

Emitting a sharp squeal, Tallulah backed off. The odd, hot sphere from within the dying ant-pig flew past us and collided with one of the fuzzy, fat, ant-sheep. In a transition that I found hard to understand, the glittering ant-sheep widened itself at one end and engulfed the stomach-ball—which united itself with the other glowing core that was already present in the ant-sheep's core. Like two whirlpools merging into one.

Meanwhile Tallulah was bellowing in triumph, celebrating her kill and her escape. Swept into a close sympathy with my new friend, I raised my voice with hers, twisting my cries into mad squeals.

"What is *wrong* with you?" said Seela.

At this point about a dozen pale white, dog-sized ants came after us—some of them winged like Jormungo, and all of them clacking their jaws and wielding their stingers. One of them bit Tallulah in the ass, and another one stung her. The beleaguered shrig's roars turned to wild, screeching wheenks.

"Flame on!" steady Seela ordered the shrig, and we were off again, riding a burning plume of fart.

I, for one, was weary of death-matches with fantastical beasts. To my relief the rest of the trip to Seela's mirrorflower went smoothly. Tallulah got into her meditative inner hum. Seela nursed Brumble, then napped again. The sated Arf was sleeping as well. And I sat awake, watching for shrig lice, and killing seven of them. I felt a bump of approval from Tallulah with each one. The attack of the farmer ants had set the lice to crawling up Tallulah's body toward her head.

As we approached the sea and jungle near the South Hole. I squinted my eyes, hoping to make out some pinpricks of color along the jungle's edge—these would be the flowers where Seela's folk and their rivals lived. And one particular yellow flower would be the mirrorflower we sought, that is, the twin to the home flower where Seela had been raised and where I'd won her love.

Despite my reluctance to settle on this mirrorflower for good, I was looking forward to the visit. I liked the flower-people. And after the wild twists of the last few days, I was ripe for a rest.

Perhaps in a week, with energy renewed and terror sub-dued, I'd find my way to the Hollow Earth's core, there to bid farewell to Eddie before he and Machree passed onward through the great Gate or Central Anomaly, bound for the old Earth where Eddie and I had been born

My feverish thoughts returned to my fantasies about balancing the two worlds. Machree would go, and I would stay. Admittedly, he and I had already broken the two worlds' balance with our crisscrossed acts of murder. But perhaps it was important for the two of us to live on opposite sides? Probably not. The more basic truth was that I misliked Machree, and I wanted him to go.

And what of Seela and MirrorSeela? What if I coaxed both of them into the core with me? And then I'd talk Seela into travelling through the Rind and back to the surface of MirrorEarth with me. Was there any chance I could bring MirrorSeela to San Francisco with us as well? San Francisco would be better for us than, god forbid, the South. Thanks to the intense *woomo* light at the Hollow Earth's core, Seela and I would be even blacker than now, and MirrorSeela would be black as well. And we'd remain black for half a year or more.

But how exactly would we pass out through the Rind? The South Hole of this MirrorEarth was plugged by ice, and its North Hole maelstrom was gone—thanks in part to our own actions. *Oh la*—fate would provide. I felt strangely happy. My plans were all nonsense anyway. I could only watch the adventure unfold. I spooned against dear Seela's side, and fell asleep yet again.

I woke to the sound of Seela's voice comforting Brumble, followed by a heavy thump echoing through the gassy body of our shrig. Tallulah had landed against an enormous sunflower blossom, a curved, patterned surface, easily two miles across, yellow in the middle, with gently waving white petals around the rim, with a large glittering glob of water resting delicately upon the center, and with smaller globs twinkling all around.

"How did you find it?" I asked Seela.

"It was easy," said she. "It's almost as if Tallulah knew the way."

The flower was affixed to an enormous stalk that wound out from a fantastical jungle that was, once again, thirty miles high, with vine upon bush upon fungus upon waterglob upon tree upon moss upon stone.

Seela was holding Brumble and fluttering her finned feet, gliding off Tallulah's back and onto the flower. Arf had already landed. The flower faced the Rind, which meant that the Hollow Earth's gentle inward pull tended to hold us to the flower's face, albeit very weakly.

Before joining the other two, I drew upon my growing sense of empathy with Tallulah. "You go hide!" I told her, using images rather than words. I added a scene of the shrig eating wildly for days. "Food in the jungle," I said aloud. "And then we fly to the *woomo*."

Seela was good enough to support me. "Do as Mason says," she thought to the shrig. "Wait until we call." Even though Seela yearned—or thought she yearned—to settle down upon this flower, she was wise to the ways of the world, and she appreciated the value of having an exit.

I fluttered clear of the beast's grubby hide and came to rest upon the springy, sweet-smelling, two-mile-wide surface of the flower.

With a fart and a joyful roar, Tallulah flew off into the staggeringly huge tangle of the southern jungle. Like Seela,

I had a sense the shrig had been here before. Yes, I had a growing rapport with the shrig—potentiated by my rumby tekelili—and she knew that I wanted her to stay. But her primary motivation may have been that she knew this jungle, and she wanted to forage. From where we rested, I could spot at least ten species of fruit upon the tangled vines and trees.

Shrigs had an ability to take on weight very rapidly, and if Tallulah really went at it, she might increase her size by as much as a third in the course of a single gluttonous week. And this would please her well. A shrig's status was strictly dependent upon its heft.

"Look!" cried Seela, pointing past the great ball of water that rested in the blossom's center. "Here they come."

A pair of flowerpeople were flying toward us across the broad, yellow surface of the flower, a man and a woman, with the woman in front and the man behind, the two of them kicking their legs against their airfins, and carrying long, sharp thorns.

9. MirrorSeela

The two who came to meet us were MirrorSeela and MirrorYurgen. A coincidence? More likely it was an inevitability—and yet another of the slightly-off-kilter harmonies between Earth and MirrorEarth. After my first visit to the Hollow Earth. Seela and I had emerged on the surface of MirrorEarth with Eddie Poe in our company—and almost immediately we'd met the MirrorPoe. Opposites attract, and ever the twain shall meet.

MirrorSeela had never seen me before. And initially she didn't seem to recognize her young double Seela. Seela and I were, after all, completely black again, thanks to our exposure to intense *woomo* light during the scene with the royal ants and the shrigs.

For their part, MirrorSeela and MirrorYurgen were creamy white. MirrorSeela's stomach was a bit soft, and the muscles on her legs were hard. Her green/brown eyes were the same. Her skin was slightly oily, and somehow very comfortable looking, like the leather of a cherished deerskin glove—although that simile is neither chivalrous nor fully apt, for the demeanor of the MirrorSeela was by no means that of an old glove. Indeed, with her rapier at the ready, she looked capable of killing the two of us on the spot. I longed to touch her before I died.

MirrorYurgen was keeping most of his body behind MirrorSeela's. I recalled that Yurgen was, if not a coward, exceedingly meticulous about his safety. I was surprised he'd come out to meet us with MirrorSeela. Probably she'd made him.

"Don't you recognize me?" Seela called to MirrorSeela. She spoke of course in the language of flowerpeople, rather than in English. But after my earlier time on Seela's flower, I knew a bit of the native tongue.

"Why should I know you?" replied MirrorSeela. "You're black gods who flew here on a shrig, and now the shrig is hiding in the jungle. We've seen her here before. Tallulah, no? What do you want? Are you here to loot?"

"Would I bring my baby on a raid?" exclaimed Seela. "And you should know me because I'm you, *blaga'am*. But twelve years younger." She propelled herself closer to her double. "My man is Mason. Our baby's name is Brumble, and he's five days old. Our dog is Arf."

"*Dog?*" echoed MirrorYurgen, missing the gist of the message and focusing on the unfamiliar word. They had no dogs in the Hollow Earth. "Does he bite?"

Seela's old suitor wasn't aging well—a front tooth was missing, his hands trembled, and his once luxuriant hair was thin. He was like the glove that you throw away, the one with its finger-tips worn off. Seela didn't bother answering his question. Her attention was focused on her double.

"*Gooba'am*," said MirrorSeela very slowly. She lowered her rapier. "How is it so, my twin sister? How are you young?"

"Your world is a mirror of ours," I told MirrorSeela. "Twelve years twinkled past as we came through."

"You're pretty," MirrorYurgen told Seela. "I like you black."

"Ah, dear Yurgen," said Seela, flirting. "Do you still charm the tribe with the reverb tube? I remember our golden days. Before I left with Mason."

"Tell us why you've come," interrupted MirrorSeela.

"I missed my home," said Seela quite simply. "Is old Ogger still alive?"

"Gone," said MirrorYurgen. "He fell asleep in the open, and a *ballula* ate him. How he screamed."

"We'll bring you to the village square as guests," MirrorSeela told us. "We'll celebrate. MirrorYurgen will play the reverberator tube, and we'll all eat *juube* and get to know each other." She gave me a look.

"I wonder—I wonder if we'll make love?" I found myself saying. MirrorSeela laughed gently, as if approving an answer by a slow student, and my Seela herself tittered in amusement.

"The four of us!" cried MirrorYurgen

I hadn't been including this broken-down bard in my daydreams. I had a sudden, demented impulse to dart forward and plunge the blade of my knife into his gut. As if sensing and forestalling this possibility, Seela spoke up, her voice mild and controlled.

"It's pleasant to imagine such idylls, but remember I just gave birth. I'm sore."

"Of course," said MirrorSeela. "Men imagine there's a rush to have sex, but there isn't." She tucked her rapier into a sheath upon her back, and fluttered forward to have a closer look at Brumble, who was nursing at Seela's breast. Mirror-Yurgen moved a bit further back.

"Such a baby it is," said MirrorSeela. "So sweet. So white against your skin."

"The *woomo* light cooked Mason and me yesterday," said Seela. "And just then Brumble was in the arms of two friends."

With domesticity entering the picture, my simple-minded, lust-maddened wish to kill MirrorYurgen was fading away. He and I even exchanged a look of mutual sympathy. There wasn't going to be an full-on orgy anytime soon, and we were sad about that.

"You don't have children?" Seela was asking MirrorSeela.

"She's barren," called MirrorYurgen, quick to place the blame on his partner.

"The problem is you," snapped MirrorSeela. "You waste your force on *juube*. And you put what's left into your resonator tube. With me you're often limp."

"No man truly knows what gets a woman with child," protested MirrorYurgen. "Perhaps it's the *woomo* light, or what the woman eats, or the sting of an airshrimp. There's no call to take me to task."

"I'd forgotten," Seela said to MirrorSeela in a low tone. "Forgotten how stupid the men on this flower are. That's why I left with Mason. How quickly the mind makes the past sweet. I shouldn't have returned."

"I'll leave with you if I can," murmured MirrorSeela. "On your friend, Tallulah the shrig. She's eating in the jungle as usual. I see the trees shaking from here."

"Depend on us, sister," said Seela. "But first a night of rest." She detached Brumble from her breast, fastened up her blouse, and shot a smoldering look at MirrorYurgen, as if testing her powers.

"Seela and I have an extra chamber you can use," said the musician, fluttering his fins.

"There may be some fun for you yet," Seela told him, parting her lips and waggling her tongue. She hadn't acted like this in Baltimore! But now she was back home. I didn't have it in me to be jealous. The situation was too fantastical and absurd. Foremost in my mind was the fact that we two would be sharing a dwelling with the potentially pliant MirrorSeela—and never mind what MirrorYurgen did.

"Let's eat, drink, and fly to the village," I proposed.

The great flower's surface was tiled into hexagonal cells, like on a common sunflower, except these cells were about thirty feet across. Each cell had a hole in the middle, with a more-or-less empty chamber beneath. A ring of stubby, yellow growths surrounded each hole. I suppose you could call these petals, although they were nothing like the large white true petals around the flower's outer rim.

I used my knife to harvest a handful of these secondary petals and offered them around. Tender flowerleather. Seela ate with gusto, very pleased to be tasting this staple again. For their part, MirrorSeela and MirrorYurgen weren't hungry— but they were fascinated by the sharpness of my steel knife. They'd never seen one before. The flowerpeople lived like cavemen.

There happened to be a waist-high glob of water trapped in the middle of the next cell, and Seela and I drank deeply from it. And then we sat down to rest with MirrorSeela and MirrorYurgen. I dandled tiny Brumble on my lap, letting him suck the tip of my finger. Arf nosed about, snapping at the shiny beetles that came buzzing by.

Around this time, MirrorSeela sensed the import of the tight-wrapped amulets that Seela and I wore at our necks.

"I had a rumby myself," she exclaimed.

"How would *you* get one?" asked Seela, doubting her.

"Rumbies come from beyond the Umpteen Seas. There aren't any down here on this…this old flower." She was losing her enthusiasm for being here.

"The *woomo* sent me the rumby," said MirrorSeela, drawing herself up. I could tell this had been one of the great events of her circumscribed life. "I was dizzy with *juube*, staring into the sky. A beam of light swooped down like a bird, this way, that way, coming straight to me. The light was carrying a rumby for me. I held it in my hand like a little plum. It was heavy. It gave me tekelili. It was alive." Absorbed in her memory, MirrorSeela clasped her hands against her chest.

"Where's the rumby now?" asked Seela.

"You'll see," said MirrorSeela, her tone exalted.

And then MirrorYurgen turned to me and asked if he might borrow my knife. Weighing my options, I handed him the blade. He accepted it with a graceful bow, then squeezed down through the hole at our cell's center. After about five minutes he popped back out, bearing a *juube* bean the size of a roast turkey. Such beans were the unripe seeds of this great flower. Moving with purpose and agility, MirrorYurgen carved up half the bean like a watermelon.

I well knew the intoxicating effects of these dripping chunks, and I partook very sparingly. This was not the time to lose my edge. Seela and MirrorSeela each had but one slice as well. We'd be facing the whole tribe soon.

But MirrorYurgen exercised no restraint. He wolfed down three, four and then five hearty slices of *juube* and began to laugh, to sing, and to howl into the sky, as if trying to bounce an echo off the planetary Rind. To complete his performance, he removed his breechcloth and showed us his member. An unprepossessing sight.

"My Yurgen is difficult," said MirrorSeela, shaking her head. "But he's an angel on the reverberator tube. His great skill. You'll hear him later. It's concert night."

"But—" began Seela, and broke off. MirrorYurgen was crawling on all fours and pressing his nose up against Arf's.

"The tribe honors him still," said MirrorSeela. "And this makes him useful to me. His status shields me from low, importunate men. I pick who I want. Come now, let's kick fins to the village."

"But—" said Seela again.

"We'll leave Yurgen here," said MirrorSeela. "He'll find his way back for the concert. Or drift into the sky. Or be eaten by a *ballula*. Like Ogger. I pick bad men for sex."

"You did it with *Ogger*?" said Seela with a laugh. "I never—"

"You were lucky," said MirrorSeela. "You left the flower young. I stayed and I got bored. And I hoped Ogger might get me with child."

"Even if he was your father?" said Seela.

"He said he wasn't," said MirrorSeela

"Perhaps Mason can help," said Seela lightly. "He bursts with seed."

MirrorSeela gave me an appraising glance, then drew close and kissed Seela on her mouth, long and deep and leisurely. Seela seemed to enjoy it.

I was standing there holding the baby, Arf was nudging me with his nose, and MirrorYurgen was lying inert on his back. My brain—and other parts of me—were about to explode. Have I mentioned that I was seventeen?

The women broke apart, breathing hard. MirrorSeela spoke. "In a few days we we'll all be leaving together on Tallulah, yes Seela dear?"

"Perhaps," said Seela. "Look at Mason. So excited."

The women laughed at me, and then the three of us kicked our way across the pleasant-smelling expanse of flower. But before we left, I retrieved my knife from MirrorYurgen. In the air, I held Brumble, and MirrorSeela carried Arf, making much of him, and holding him out in the air as if he were flying on his own.

"Stop here!" called MirrorSeela as we came to the truly enormous glob of water that rested upon the great flower's center. "We'll swim."

Held together by the tension of its surface, the glassy button slanted up on all sides from where it lightly touched the flower. Seela and I were once again ripe for a bath—what with the cactus glue, the ichor from the smashed shrig lice, the slime of the primeval ant-plant sausages—and our bodies' own secretions. We would have liked to swim together, but Seela didn't feel comfortable leaving Brumble alone with MirrorSeela who, after all, had no children of her own, and might possibly wish to steal our baby. So first the two women swam together, and then I swam with Arf.

I can't say that I'd often seen truly clear water in Virginia. Muddiness was the norm. The floating ponds and lakes of the Hollow Earth were nothing like. Think of distilled corn whiskey in a clear glass. Or air that is a liquid that wets your skin. The view from inside the mirrorflower's great central lake: stupendous.

Arf and I swam within a living lens, with the pulsing pink-lit Hollow Earth on every side—its vast skies rich with life, its Rind embossed with seas and jungles, the warped mystery of the Central Anomaly like a navel at the core. The water blob itself was populated by legged fish, schools of them like glittering scarves, darting and veering, and occasionally leaping through the water's membrane, crawling across the flower, and finding their way back in. Arf tried in vain to catch one.

Seela had once said you can't drown while swimming in the Hollow Earth, but if you're a blockhead you can. Your weight isn't dragging you into the depths, but, contrariwise, your buoyancy isn't lifting you to the surface. When short on air, you need to swim to the edge. But, having been here before, Arf and I knew this. Beating our legs, we dove and surfaced again and again, rejoicing.

As a practical matter, the clean water was most welcome upon my soiled and crusted skin. Of course I stayed black just the same. Not that being black was in any way a burden here. As I've mentioned, the flowerpeople referred to the *woomo*-blackened natives of the Umpteen Seas as gods. When I left the pool, MirrorSeela again eyed me with approval.

Carrying Brumble and Arf in our arms, the two Seelas and I kicked onward to the cleared-out hexagon that was the commons of the local tribe. This clearing was at the flower's far edge. A pair of guards flew out to meet us, with rapiers and shell knives at the ready. Their names were Kurt and Kong. Tough characters with ragged beards, well-known to MirrorSeela, but not her friends. They accompanied us to the village green, which was a spot where the flowers' yellow cells had been torn away, leaving bare the blossom's verdant lower layer. Open-doored cells surrounded the clearing— these were the dwellings of the tribe.

Twenty or thirty locals appeared: men, women, and children, with handsome faces and well-formed limbs, lightly dressed in breechcloths and tunics of leaves, petals, and soft bark. The flowerpeople were keen on meeting us, initially taking us for black gods. When I told them we were from somewhere yet further away, beyond the sky, and on the other side of the Rind—that made us only the more intriguing. They marveled that I spoke their tongue, and even more did they wonder to see that my Seela was a young, dark double of theirs.

Just as when I'd visited Seela's original home flower, Arf was the great sensation. Everyone wanted to pet his fur and, in the manner of the flowerpeople, to lick his nose. The noble hound suffered their ministrations with dignity. In return, they fed him scraps of dried fish and meat.

I'd expected, or rather dreaded, that we'd have to face a ruler of some kind, perhaps a peevish queen who might, on a whim, ordain our execution. But the leader, or icon, or mascot, or god of this tribe was something odder than that.

"Look," said Seela, pointing past the flowerpeople. Something bulged over there, metallic and shiny.

"A fried egg craft!" I exclaimed. Seela and I had seen one before, and I'd based my name for it on its shape, that is, the fried egg was a disk-shaped object some forty feet across, with a central dome fifteen feet in diameter. And I knew by now that the locals called it a *veem*. Its dome was a cabin with a big window, two small portholes, and a door that was presently closed.

"It's the very same one," said Seela as we kicked toward it. She was right. I recognized the hieroglyphs and the pattern of holes upon its rim. The very same fried egg that Seela, Eddie and I had fished out of the Umpteen Seas about a year ago—a year, that is, of my own body's time.

The fried egg, or *veem*, was inscribed with symbols upon its flat rim and upon the inner walls of its cabin. Having studied these pictographs, we'd determined that the fried egg was an alien space craft which had brought the *woomo*—and us humans—to this, our Hollow Earth.

When we'd first found the fried egg, we'd been intent on making our way back to the outer surface of the Hollow Earth. And so Eddie, Seela, and I had settled into the domed cabin with Arf, and we'd prevailed upon a helpful *woomo* named Uxa to hurl us across the Hollow Earth's inner sky, thus landing us in an ocean upon the inner side of the Rind. Eddie had then contrived to close the fried egg's door and, buoyed by the air in the cabin, the craft had wobbled up through the sea, emerging in the Chesapeake Bay. When we debarked, we'd left the door open, and the *veem* sank, presumably all the way back to the surface of very sea that arched up across the inner Rind. And now here it was on this flower, and we were next to it. Once again, causes and effects were intertwining.

"I see something inside it," said Seela peering through the *veem's* window. "Like a big soft yam lying on the floor. A larva or grub worm or a slug."

I would have liked to go inside, but the fried egg's door was closed, and I felt uneasy about trying to open it.

"That's a baby *woomo* asleep in there," said MirrorSeela, joining us. "Her name is Nyoo. We worship her."

So the flowerpeople had a queen of sorts after all. But—a *woomo*?

"Tallulah dragged the *veem* here last year," added MirrorSeela. "Your shrig friend. The *veem* was Tallulah's gift to us so that Karl and Kong don't hunt her while she feeds in the jungle. She brought the *veem*, yes, and after a few days I took the notion to put my rumby inside the *veem*. The rumby was talking to me about it, not with words. With tekelili. I put my rumby in the *veem*, and at first—nothing. But then, a day later, a ray of light came from the *woomo* in the sky. It went inside the *veem* and tickled my rumby."

Seela nodded, enthralled. "The rumby hatched?"

"A baby *woomo*," said MirrorSeela. "Little Nyoo. Thanks to me. Look. She makes pink light." She rapped the hilt of her shell knife against the fried egg's window. The little shape inside writhed, then lifted one end. The end was puckered. Nyoo the *woomo* flexed her body and pushed out a—branching tree of flesh. Like soft coral, or like fungus, and the branches were flexing, and they had fronds at the ends. A faint glow formed along the branches, a pale pink aura, and then came a steady stream of pink light, smooth as milk pouring from a pitcher, flowing from the *woomo* and playing across the inner walls' hieroglyphs, and the cabin's silvery surfaces, and the broken-off control upon the panel within the fried egg. The beam focused, then lanced out through the glass of the fried egg's window, etching a bright line across the Hollow Earth's sky. The flowerpeople cheered, but with an undertone of awe or even fear.

"*Nyoo!*" they cried. "*Gooba'am Nyoo!*"

"We're the only flowerpeople whose queen is a *woomo*," said MirrorSeela with pride.

"Was your old queen called Quaihlaihle?" I asked.

"Yes," answered MirrorSeela. "She wanted to forbid me from putting my rumby inside the *veem*. She wanted Kurt and Kong to stop me. My rumby called Tallulah, and Tallulah ate the queen."

"I thought shrigs don't eat people," I said.

"Tallulah did anyway. Kurt and Kong say it's another reason they should eat Tallulah."

"Lots of eating," I said to Seela in English. "Not safe here."

"Don't you let Brumble out of sight," said Seela, also in English. The baby was crying in her arms. He was hungry and he didn't like the rough, jumbled noise of the crowd. "You watch over Brumble even when you start rutting on MirrorSeela."

"Who says I'll do that?"

"You don't fool me one bit, Mason Reynolds. You're slobbering over MirrorSeela, jaded old prick-pocket that she is." This was similar to the line of attack Seela had taken regarding Ina. "Not that I mind," continued Seela, throwing in a heartbroken shrug. "It's fine, I'm sure. I'm in no shape for sex. So it's natural for you to run after any woman who crooks her finger. It's a knife in my heart, yes, but I'll grin and pretend I'm wanton too. You're a man, and—"

"Should we just leave right now?" I interrupted. "I don't care about MirrorSeela. You're the one for me, Seela. Always. Should I call Tallulah for a ride?"

"Too tired." said Seela mustering a weak smile of triumph. She held tiny Brumble against her shoulder, patting him. "Let's go into that grabby hag MirrorSeela's cell and rest."

MirrorSeela was watching us, not quite sure what we were saying, but surely catching the drift. But she was in fact a much kinder person than Seela was making her out to be. She led us to her apartment—which was two adjacent flower cells off the main square—and she made us comfortable. And then she went back out with Arf, wanting to show him off to her friends.

Seela and I refreshed ourselves with water, flowerleather and dried eel, and I told her I loved her, and made much of her, and agreed that men are worthless. And then we talked a little about the fried egg and the *woomo*, not coming to any real conclusions. We were too tired to work out any plans. As we talked, Seela nursed Brumble to satiation, and then we lay down and napped on the soft floor, with our arms around each other and dear baby Brumble in between.

By the way, I realize it sounds as if we were sleeping very often, but events were coming at us in an unrelenting torrent, and we needed to rest when we could. Also keep in mind that there's no night inside the Hollow Earth, and that most of the denizens alternate between sleeping and waking in short cycles.

We woke to the sound of MirrorSeela and MirrorYurgen arguing. He'd snapped out of his *juube* trance and had made his way back to the apartment, shaky and disheveled. MirrorSeela was helping him to clean himself and to don freshly-picked petals. His mood was very much worse than before. Noticing I was awake, he scowled at me with hatred. And then he went outside. A murmur mixed with cheers rose among the flowerpeople. Several hundred of them had gathered.

"I'll introduce you to the tribe," MirrorSeela told us. "And then Yurgen will play. Depending what he does, you might not want to stay here very long." MirrorSeela paused. "And I just might leave with you." She smiled ingratiatingly, as if hoping for approval. Seeing this worn woman in her moment of uncertainty, my heart went out to her.

I could sense that Seela wasn't quite happy with this, but she wasn't fully against the prospect either. MirrorSeela was, after all, her twin.

Are you quite sure you can summon Tallulah?" was all Seela said..

Laying my hand upon my dense, plump, living rumby I communed with its tekelili. Somehow the mind of a dreaming, unborn *woomo* was embodied within this curious gem. How strange. The rumby's tekelili was indeed so intense that I could reach all the way to Tallulah, off in the jungle nearby.

As I made contact, it struck me that the shrig wasn't anything like so stupid as I'd imagined. Gluttonous, clumsy, comical—but not dumb. She was devouring greasy pods that resembled varicolored bananas, although maybe they were something else. Her gut swelled with fart, but she was holding in the gas. Building up her supply. She sensed my tekelili, and wordlessly she told me she was ready to come at any time. She knew about the unborn *woomo* within my fat rumby gem. She'd known all along. Sensing a coming crisis, I urged her to begin her approach, and to hide herself beneath the underside of the flower.

Meanwhile Seela and I followed MirrorSeela out of her living-quarters, with Seela nursing Brumble at her breast. The windows of the fried egg were dark again. Nyoo the *woomo* slumbered. But the village green was lit with the unceasing warm-summer-afternoon glow of the Hollow Earth. The crowd stared at us, eyes bright, very curious, and hopping into the air, the better to see us. The mood was cheerful, with many of them holding slices of *juube*.

Someone had fastened a long, hollow plant stem so that it sloped from the flower's upper surface down to the village green. Its smaller end was tied to a branch protruding from the ground. MirrorYurgen stood beside it, at the ready, with Kurt and Kong poised behind him, as if guarding his back.

MirrorSeela took Seela's free hand, and my hand, holding them high. She spoke briefly to the crowd, saying she was glad to have us here, that Seela was her double, and that this was another a sign of divine *woomo* favor toward their tribe.

"*Ahnaa bogbog Ma'aassong lamalama Seela gloloo Brumble. Nicabange nansi A'arf! Doolango emthonjeni womculo. Jjanjee woomo? Thul'ulale sini lindile. Gooba'am!*"

The crowd roared. A dirty-faced little boy named Peepy handed me some chunks of *juube*. A voluptuous woman pressed herself against my right side, ignoring Seela on my left. A man smiled at Seela and offered her bright bits of shell. Old people cooed at Brumble. Arf perched at our feet, looking around with interest.

And then MirrorYurgen's music began. The reverb tube had a taut shrigskin membrane across its small end, and MirrorYurgen sang into a small hole in the center of this hide. Evidently there was another such drumhead across the wide end of the tube, some hundred feet off. MirrorYurgen's voice resonated inside the great tube, building up layers, with the sounds overlapping and forming beats, reminding me of crisscross waves in a current. He chanted and crooned a tune that meandered up and down a half-note at a time. It reminded me of an Oriental dirge I'd heard a Malay sailor play on a flute during his companion's burial at sea. As amplified by the reverberating tube, the effect of MirrorYurgen's song was entrancing, and even hypnotic.

The crowd was in a festive mood. Everyone was smiling at us, and at each other. The flowerpeople swayed in a slow dance, and those who were intoxicated by *juube* were caressing each other. The guardsmen Kurt and Kong were fixated upon MirrorYurgen, utterly absorbed by his performance, staring at him from only a few inches away.

But things were turning sour. Each time MirrorYurgen paused to grab a breath, he glared over at me, shooting daggers with his eyes. He was jealous about the budding relationship I had with his MirrorSeela. And, more than that, he wanted my Seela for his own.

With the consummate craft of a mature artist, MirrorYurgen began weaving his emotions into his performance. Harsh tones entered his stream of song, and his changes in pitch were abrupt, driving away any sense of comfort. Were the flowerpeople regarding me in a less friendly way than before? Yes. The woman who'd been rubbing me with her breasts now favored me with a sharp elbow to the kidney. The *juube*-bearing urchin Peepsy pulled Arf's tail. The man who'd been admiring Seela took rough hold of her shoulder, as if meaning to violate her. With a quick kick, Seela knocked the oaf off balance, and then stunned him with a knee to his head. He withdrew, bleeding from his nose. But more enemies waited. And Brumble was crying very loud.

MirrorYurgen had a gloating, saturnine air—like a cruel jester at a feast where his rival is to be slain. His music surged and throbbed. Kurt and Kong detached themselves from MirrorYurgen and began pushing through the crowd, coming my way. They carried barbed spears much longer than the rapiers they'd borne before. Somehow the baby *woomo* in the fried egg was still asleep. The windows of the *veem* remained dark.

"Call Tallulah!" MirrorSeela urged me in her tongue. "And remember that I'm leaving with you."

"It is well," said Seela. "Hurry, Mason."

No need to tell me. I was already putting my full energy into my tekelili summoning of the shrig. Here she was, bumbling through the ruff of white petals at the flower's edge, rising like a bloated moon.

Seela, MirrorSeela, and I were already wearing our pulpul airfins. It was a simple thing to hop into the air, and kick toward the edge of the flower where the baby *woomo* slumbered within the dark fried egg. MirrorYurgen's ugly, angry music was raging. The flowerpeople were out for our blood—reaching toward us and hollering imprecations. A few were airborne like us, and we managed to dodge them, but here came the formidable Kurt and Kong, hefting their weapons. Did they mean to kill us outright?

With no pause in their motion, the two guards used throwing sticks to hurl their barbed lances our way. Time seemed to stop. I noticed that the spears had long cords unwinding from their ends. Harpoons. Rather than striking Seela and me, they flew past us—and sank deep into the fatty abdomen of dear Tallulah.

Wheenk!

My tekelili told me that the wounded shrig was about to flee upon a flaming jet of fart. But in that instant Kong had already hauled himself over to her, and had slashed open Tallulah's belly with a broadsword made of *ballula* shell. The shrig's store of gas blatted ineffectually into the air, spreading a sad, miasmal stench across the village green. MirrorYurgen's music had come to a stop.

In this silent moment of dismay, the two women and I landed upon the rim of the fried egg, me carrying Arf, and Seela bearing Brumble. I executed a carefully reasoned-out gesture that Eddie Poe had taught me—a looping sweep of my hand across the outer surface of the domed cabin. My move worked—the door opened. And once we were inside, I used the reverse of Eddie's move to close the hatch behind us, blocking out Kurt and Kong.

As the two bandits pounded against the *veem*, Nyoo the baby *woomo* awoke and filled the chamber with intense pink light. Taking a quick look around, I recognized the same features as before. This *veem* was of an incalculable antiquity, tens of thousands of years in age. It had a stubby, broken stand that might once have supported a seat, and the brackets on the wall might have held bunks. Undoubtedly it had been an airship. The inside of the cabin wasn't a full hemisphere, for a section of it was walled off by a bulkhead. Eddie had said there must be a stove of some kind in there to produce the aethereal lifting gas that allowed the fried egg to fly. Friezes and cartouches of pictograms and hieroglyphs were embossed upon into the cabin's dully shining walls like tattoos upon skin.

The walls were smooth and luminous. Not metal. Too soft for that. The embossed images on the walls showed the cucumber-like bodies of the *woomo*, and their branching fans, and fried-egg craft, and some figures that were surely ants, women, and men. The ants, *woomo* and the humans had traveled together to Earth in the primordial past, long before the dawn of known history.

Kurt was bashing at the fried egg's front window with a stone axe. Seela and MirrorSeela were emphatically pointing this out to me. What to do? We needed to nudge the *veem* off the edge of the village green so that it could drift into the sky, thence falling inward to the core.

Again I put myself into tekelili contact with Tallulah. Kong had cut her throat, and her ichor was leaking out in wobbly globules. The poor beast had entered her death flurry; she was flopping spasmodically upon the village green. Some of the flowerpeople were already in the act of butchering her, carving off hunks of her tasty meat whenever she was momentarily still. Her mind was a contracting vision of the world, dark around the edges and bright at its core.

"Please push us," I beseeched the shrig, using images rather than words. "Set us free. Push the *veem*."

The good Tallulah gave one last snap of her great tail. Our ancient fried egg craft skidded across the surface of the village green and we were in free fall. On our way to the core.

10. Fwopsy

A rabble of flowerpeople came after us, wanting to drag our craft back to the village green. But their combined forces were insufficient to divert the stately path of our craft. And with the fried egg craft's door closed, we were secure from personal attack. Arf was barking and Brumble was crying, with the noise reverberating within the stuffy confines of our hull.

Slowly the *veem* was gaining velocity. The miles-thick wall of jungle was drifting past. Even so, the mirrorflower-people persisted in their attempts to save their prize. Urged on by MirrorYurgen's blasts on the great reverb tube, our pursuers tied vines to the holes in our craft's rim. With Kurt barking commands, they began kicking their air fins in regular rhythm—with disconcerting effect. Our progress slowed and halted. Kurt redoubled his cries. Slowly, slowly we began moving back toward the Rind and the mirrorflower. Eventually we'd have to open the fried egg's door for air. And then Kurt, Kong, and MirrorYurgen would kill me.

"Help," I silently implored our *woomo*. She'd filled our *veem* with a tekelili far stronger than what a rudimentary rumby could produce. Her mind was alight with energy, and she was excited about traveling to the core. But perhaps she didn't realize what was happening. I bent my will to projecting my emotions into her. "You need to save us."

The *woomo* responded with an outward rush of thought.

Sparks leapt from the outer rim of the fried egg, severing the attached vines, and scorching the hands of the importunate flowerpeople. Had the sparks come from the *woomo*, or from the *veem* itself? Hard to say. Cursing and yelling, the pirates fell away. Once more our craft began gaining speed. Mirror-Yurgen's plangent honks faded away.

Inside the freely falling fried egg, Seela, MirrorSeela, Arf, Brumble, Nyoo, and I were as if weightless. We had no tendency to settle upon any particular area of the cabin's dimly shining walls. To my eyes, by the way, the walls seemed increasingly like patterned skin. Could it be possible that the *veem* was alive?

Seela produced a strand of woven bark and fastened Brumble's foot to her wrist, lest he somehow drift away. And then I opened the door so we could have fresh air. Our motion was producing a stiff breeze. Arf knew to stay back lest he be whirled out. I noticed also that Arf kept a healthy distance from Nyoo. I don't think he liked *woomo*.

Nyoo damped down her pink glow, but by now MirrorSeela was as black as Seela and me. We all agreed the pigmentation looked well on her. We drifted at our ease, watching the Rind move away. Seela nursed Brumble and then, after a fit of hiccups, he fell asleep, floating in the air beside her. Meanwhile MirrorSeela and I were eying each other with admiration.

"But no, you're not going to poke your member into me," said told me via tekelili. Unwelcome news.

"Thank you," Seela said to MirrorSeela.

"You're my sister," MirrorSeela told her. "You're me. And that's why it means nothing if you and I kiss."

"But—but what about me helping you have a baby?" I asked MirrorSeela, playing the only card I had.

"There's plenty of men at the Umpteen Seas," said Seela tartly.

"I don't want a man," said MirrorSeela. "Just a drop of seed. I need a rest from men." She and Seela burst into laughter at this sally.

I didn't mind their teasing. I was with two women and we were on a wonderful journey. Seela and I had a healthy baby, and in a few weeks Seela and I would be making love again. Moreover, my intense tekelili contact with the two Seelas felt satisfyingly erotic. I had a constant sense that I was merging with them. Not quite like sex, but for now I was content.

I noticed that, by means of occasional twitches of its rim, our *veem* was keeping itself on an even keel. Was the airship awaking from an eons-long slumber?

In any case, rather than spinning, tumbling or, worse, swooping back and forth like a feather, we were slicing through the air edge-on. This meant that our drag was low. I hazarded a guess that we were going sixty miles per hour. Which meant we'd reach the center after fifty hours of falling. Two days.

And so we sat and chatted, savoring the intimacy of our close tekelili contact. Intermittently we dozed, or saw to Brumble's needs. Arf had his snout pointed up, continually sniffing this strange sky's airs.

As always, I delighted in the joyous curving sweep of the Hollow Earth's inner Rind—not to mention the pink streamers. the jungles and seas, the scattered clouds, the dotted flocks of flying beasts, and the odd, lensing quality of the space at the core. And with Nyoo the *woomo* aboard as our ally, I wasn't much worried about carnivorous shell-squids and the like.

But there was a problem. Stupidly enough, Seela and I had once again set out upon a long sky journey with no food or water. Food wasn't crucial—I expected us to reach the core in another day. But we did need water, particularly with Seela nursing.

Again I let my psyche mingle with our *woomo's* mind. Nyoo had a sense of pride about ushering two outer-world sojourners to the Hollow Earth's core, a nd she was pondering the friezes of glyphs that covered our rounded cabin's walls. I studied the images with her. Certainly there were images of *veem* craft—most of them round, rather than like hemispherical fried eggs. Within the craft I saw, as I mentioned before, images of *woomo* and humans and ants."

"The humans are natural pilots," said Nyoo. "I think you could do it."

"When?" I asked.

I could tell that Nyoo had some specific mission in mind, but she wouldn't share the details. The Central Anomaly was involved. I earnestly hoped I wouldn't have to go back in there.

Getting back to basics, I did my best to make Nyoo aware that we were thirsty. The little creature gave me no direct answer. Instead she crawled across the floor like a foraging sea-slug, and thrust her stubby snout into the wind rushing past our open door. She aimed a narrow pink streamer toward the core and wobbled it.

Apparently she was calling to her relatives. A thick tendril of light came our way. The forking stream of radiance reached into our vessel and played across our faces, as if getting to know us. I felt the vast calm of the Great Old Ones at Earth's core, and I had a sense of being surrounded by choral song. A spare, crooked epigram entered my mind.

> The past not now
> The future not yet
> Between two nots
> Is

Well and good, but now the fat light stream flicked out to the Rind and back, thereby fetching several hundred gallons of water into our fried egg's chamber, the water in a single mass that engulfed my legs and sloshed over the heads and shoulders of the two Seelas.

We flailed our limbs, sputtering and shrieking, more glad than frightened. The water split into juddering globs that repeatedly divided and rejoined as they danced around us—like miniature versions of the Umpteen Seas at the Hollow Earth's core.

Brumble, who'd been momentarily submerged, was in a paroxysm of fury. Arf was lapping at the globs, slaking his thirst. Seela held Brumble against her shoulder with one arm, while using her free hand to scoop water into her mouth. I gulped down a pint that I gathered with both hands, and then I took the outraged Brumble from Seela so she drink faster.

In a few minutes the bulk of the water had jounced out the door, with a only few blobs still inside the fried egg. During the inundation, Nyoo the *woomo* had used her bumpy skin to cling to the floor near the door. And now she was on the move again, creeping back to the cabin's center. She waved a cheerful tendril at me.

"Thank you," said I, bowing to the far-fetched creature.

"I hope you didn't ask for food," said Seela. "Who knows what they'd bring. How much longer will we fall?"

"Maybe twenty hours," said I.

"I *do* want food," said MirrorSeela.

No sooner said than done. Nyoo the *woomo* angled a jagged beam out the door, and the fat light stream from the core returned. Again it twitched out to the Rind—and our cabin was cluttered with those multicolored banana-like objects I'd seen Tallulah devouring in the jungle beside the mirrorflower.

The objects within the colored rinds had a redolent, meaty quality. They weren't bananas, they were pupae from some unknown insect. The pupae were oily, with a bitter quality beneath their cloying sweetness. But we ate our fill just the same. And I was quite sure I saw several of the meaty things being swallowed by slits in the *veem's* floor.

Dazed and stupefied by our unwise repast, we slept. I had a dream of sex with the two Seelas, and I awoke in a state of excitement. As it happened, MirrorSeela was in fact fondling me in an intimate manner. Amused and titillated by the game, my Seela was kissing her elder double. Floating in the air beside us, Brumble dozed.

Seeing my eyes open, the two women withdrew, and feigned an air of primness—smirking at me withal. Was their teasing an idle pastime, or did it mean more? Light-headed with lust, I brazenly finished what their lubricious play had begun. The Seelas caressed each other as they watched. I asked no more. I was seventeen, and this was heaven enow. As my sweet spasm subsided, MirrorSeela used a fingertip to ensure that a bit of my seed made its way to her womb. I was glad.

In a calm mood of exaltation, we ate some more of those bright-skinned insect pupae, and scavenged up the last few floating globs of water. Meanwhile we were passing through a zone of feeding shrigs. They tended to gather fifteen miles

152

out from the Umpteen Seas, scavenging the slowly drifting debris of the entire Hollow Earth. They feared to go very much further in, as the black gods were so fond of hunting them for leather and meat.

A couple of the shrigs nosed at us, but Seela and I, as well as the more powerful Nyoo, used our tekelili to project images of shrig-friendliness and of inedibility. MirrorSeela was in a tizzy, but our efforts were sufficient to ward off the languid flying pigs. There were, after all, many other things to eat here—corpses, offal, and the rich debris of the jungles—all of them freely adrift. The Hollow Earth's inward attraction died out in this zone,

Carried onward by inertia, we slowly coasted through the last dozen miles, closing in on the Umpteen Seas. At any given time there were between a dozen and a score of these miles-long bodies of water—they were continually merging and breaking apart. Once again I had a fond memory of how in the summers on the farm, Otha and I would throw buckets of water into the air and delight at the water's jiggles. I wondered how Otha was doing.

Beyond the Umpteen Seas was the inner zone where the ancient *woomos* lived—arranged upon the surface of that invisible and impalpable sphere known as the Central Anomaly or the Gate—the very throat of the tunnel between MirrorEarth and Earth.

Unceasing streams of pink light flowed from the *woomo* tendrils. The tekelili in the air was intense—my two Seelas' minds were warm and clear, and even Brumble's and Arf's thoughts were manifest—not that they were thinking much. I savored the comfortable joy of this heavenly zone.

I peered inward, hoping to spot some of the black gods, or even Eddie Poe and Ina. But now came an interruption.

It was that juvenile royal ant whom we'd seen hatched at the North Hole—the one who'd flown inward toward the core, rather than following the others into the sea. I recognized his psychic vibrations. He was some twelve feet long now, with a flattened round head, a tapering torso, and a plump gaster bulge at the rear. Although he had antennae, he still lacked mandibles, and his up-curved mouth was like a melon-slice cut from his head, which gave him a cheerful air. His faceted eyes were the size of dinner plates, and his skin was a rich and reflective purplish-green with an iridescent sheen. As before, his legs were still just two rows of bumps. And he had the stubby wings, and a nascent spike at his rear. He hovered by our *veem*, peering in through our craft's door at Nyoo.

Seela had said the royal ants and the *woomo* were partners. Yet I'd seen Fafnir and the *woomo* blasting intense rays at each other. So I was half-expecting a fight. But Nyoo seemed pleased to see the juvenile royal ant. The two of them had a rapid, wordless, tekelili conversation which, in its rough outlines, I might represent as follows.

Ant: I'm Skolder. You ride with humans—why?
Woomo: I'm Nyoo. We aim to gather rumbies for a Bloom.
Ant: It's past time for a Bloom.
Woomo: We need to awaken the *veem*. The one called Eddie Poe will help.
Ant: I will aid with my zap. Charge me.
Woomo: Will you eat me if I come close to you?
Ant: I have as yet no pinchers, Nyoo.

Nyoo bid us a temporary farewell, and flew out of our door. As if stimulated by the presence of the ant, the *woomo* swelled abruptly in size, growing into a warty sea cucumber some twenty feet long. The ant narrowed his shape by pressing his wings against himself and tightening the bulges of his body. Nyoo widened one of her ends, and formed a cylindrical cavity. The ant slipped into Nyoo's body like a spit into a chicken, like a sausage into a bun, like a dagger into a sheath.

Given my erotic byplay with the Seelas, I naturally took the *woomo*-ant union to be in some way sexual—but the coupling was, rather, a way for Nyoo to infuse Skolder with an extremely high electrical charge. The *woomo* were prodigious sources of electrical fluid. And, with their separated thorax and gaster, the royal ants could behave like Leyden jars, or like Volta's galvanic piles, that is, they could store a titanic reservoir of electrical fluid for an abrupt release.

As Nyoo was charging up the ant, her numinous tekelili aura reached a critical state. And for a moment, I accessed a higher level of knowledge.

- The flying fried eggs, or *veem*, are alive.
- Ants, humans, *woomo*, and *veem* work together in a symbiosis.
- Our Hollow Earth bears our four races on a journey through the stars
- Occasionally the four races send a colony to another world. This is a Bloom.
- The *veem* craft bear the colonists across space during a Bloom.
- The humans pilot and speed the *veem*.
- The royal ants hollow out the colony world for the *woomo*.
- The *woomo* orchestrate the evolution of the colony world, and guide its travels.

It was as I'd been groping in a night landscape—now illuminated by a bolt of lightning. I'd already gotten some hints regarding the nature of the Bloom, and the role of the royal ants. But the full truth had been eluding me.

I stood slack-jawed, staring out the fried egg's door, in a state of exaltation, dazed by the psychic intensity of Nyoo's tekelili, and doing my best to note the details of my revelation for inclusion in this narrative you read, *Return to the Hollow Earth*.

The two curious creatures pinwheeled away, their tekelili voices raised in silent song. They passed behind the nearest of the Umpteen Seas and vanished for a time. Meanwhile our fried egg ship had drifted to a full stop. This was the terminal zone—a gutter in space, if you will, a resting place before the inmost core. I hoped we'd find Eddie Poe here.

The nearest of the Umpteen Seas was wobbling as if it might soon engulf us. For me this was not a disturbing prospect. The miles-long, floating lakes had clean, sparkling water and edible fish. And this one contained a substantial island at its other end. We could kick our way to this bit of land with our airfins or *pulpuls*. But MirrorSeela was alarmed.

"We're fine," Seela reassured her. Like me, she'd been to the core before. "The black gods will greet us." Her voice rose. "Look! Here they come."

Two well-formed black gods were approaching, a man and woman, both of them riding the polished scraps of *ballula* shell that they called lightboards. If you positioned your lightboard along the edge of a *woomo's* great pink streamer, you could ride the wake of heated air that surrounded the tube of light. One of the black gods looked familiar. I'd known her as Shrighunter on the other side of the Central Anomaly. Presumably this was her MirrorEarth double.

And the man—he was more than familiar, he was the first friend of my youth, my companion on my initial trip to the Hollow Earth, the beloved equal whom I'd left at the core when I traveled on to MirrorEarth, and a kinsman of sorts—in that we shared a common half-brother.

"Otha!" cried I, my voice cracking.

"Mase!" called Otha, gliding up to us and stopping his motion with a kick of his shrig-leather *pulpul*. "You done rode back on this old fried egg? With *two* Seelas? And, looky here, it's Arf and a baby!"

"We call him Brumble," said Seela. "It's fine to see you, Otha. You didn't get old. Not like my twin MirrorSeela."

"Are both you women doing the juicy with Mason?" asked Otha, never one to stand on ceremony.

"Not exactly," I said. "Not in the ways I'd like."

"The ways *we* like," said MirrorSeela, touching her belly. "Mason is useful."

"Tell us how you got to this side of the Gate," Seela said to Otha.

"I come through it same as you. Lookin to find my woman. Shrighunter. We two was bundled tight. She disappeared on a hunt, Mason, and I missed her so hard, I pushed through that *woomo* Gate to see if she might be here. Watcher said naw, the two sides are mostly the same, but that ain't true, not since you and me and Eddie Poe come to stir it up. And

I *did* get Shrighunter back, see? She didn't know me none, but I worked my mojo, same as before."

"So this is *MirrorShrighunter* you're with," I primly said.

"Ain't no mirror about her," said Otha. "Go on and introduce yourself to the new Shrighunter, brother Mason."

Otha was right, it would be petifogging pedantry to Mirror-modify the name of each familiar black god we found. Suffice it to say that the Mirror versions were substantially like the ones we'd met on the Central Anomaly's other side. Shrighunter, Watcher, Jewel, Smoker, Offerer—I soon encountered versions of them all.

Thanks to tekelili, I was quickly fast friends with the new Shrighunter. She enjoyed the sampler of Otha-memories that I offered her, and she laughed at my story of the time Otha had inadvertently exploded a shrig—by slitting open its gassy gut while its butt-flame was lit.

"That story ain't funny no more, Mase," interjected Otha. "Might could be that's how the old Shrighunter died. She'd borrowed my steel knife."

I felt the pang of Otha's grief. But even so, we were soon in a festive mood—especially after he told me that, yes, Eddie Poe, Ina, and Connor Machree were already here. We found them on the large island at the end of the nearby Umpteen Sea—it was a popular gathering spot for the black gods. We met amid cheers, with greetings all around.

"You rode up on a *woomo* ray of light?" Seela asked Machree, still miffed about the jeweler's special treatment. Smugly he nodded.

The island was mostly above water just now, and coated with wiry grass and little white flowers. We'd contrived to tow our fried egg after us, and we fastened it to tufts of grass with a woven rope. I hadn't forgotten Nyoo's suggestion that we might somehow restore the fried egg or *veem* to a fully living status. That new ant Skolder might help, now that Nyoo had fed him such a powerful charge. And perhaps Eddie could do something. On our first trip, Eddie had spent days and weeks studying the *veem's* hieroglyphs.

The black gods Smoker and Watcher were here, and Jewel would soon arrive. Because Seela, Eddie, and I had lost a dozen years during our passage through the Gate on our first journey, these versions of our black god friends were older than the originals—but I hardly noticed.

Remember that, due to the salutatory effect of so much tekelili, the black gods have lifespans of three hundred years. In the face of that, a decade does little to change their appearance. Time's passage had, however, left stronger traces on the less than happy MirrorSeela. But here in the cheerful company of the black gods, she already seemed more bright and youthful.

Smoker, as always, had a wicker basket filled with choice bits of dried meats—shrig meat, fish filets, and chunks of the small sea creatures who nestled in the island's tangled grasses. He was sedulously offering his treats to MirrorSeela, and she was favoring him with warm smiles. I should mention, by the way, that the black gods were using tekelili to talk with us, and their lips didn't move when they spoke.

"Hallelujah!" exclaimed Eddie. "We stand united at the heart of eternity!"

"With the changes never done," said old Watcher.

Let me mention again that, even though the speech of the black gods was silent tekelili, I tended to hear their words as if spoken in a black accent similar to Otha's. In Otha's opinion, this indicated that black people were in fact the original, and higher, race of humans on Earth, and that their modes of speech were more correct, and to be preferred.

"Changes because of *us*?" pert Ina replied to Watcher's remark. She was nestled against Eddie's side. Ever the coquette, she threw back her head and poured out a merry laugh. "And we're just black people from California," she added—by now all of us were indeed dark-skinned. Ina focused a bright eye on me. "Looks like our Mason fished up an extra Seela!"

"Seela's older twin," I said.

"Bedazzling," said Smoker. "A ripe flowerperson. You liking it here, Seela the elder?"

"Leave out the *elder*," said MirrorSeela, extending her arms as if taking in her surroundings. "This is stunning. Vast.

Everything is everywhere. And the tekelili—so rich and strong. I know exactly what you're thinking, Smoker."

"Do it suit you?

"Well, I *am* in need of a man," said MirrorSeela, contradicting what she'd said to me in the in the fried egg. Perhaps Smoker looked to be a better long-term prospect. "I left my partner," MirrorSeela continued, and then paused, as if looking down into herself. "And, and I may be with child."

"Fast work by our Mason," trilled Ina. "Too bad young Seela has claimed him. The boy is *such* a catch!"

"Am *I* not a catch?" said Eddie, inclining his head toward his saucy flirt. "Or am I, rather, an aging, inky, half-mad scribbler?"

"Our raw nation's literary master," said Ina. "The true Edgar Allan Poe. And you've brought me to this paradise. Huzzah, my dear. I taste and savor your mind, Edgar. I'd do well at declaiming your poems onstage. You and I could go on tour. You'd manage me, under your cognomen of Goarland Peale—and I'd perform. I'm a very quick study."

"A cunning hoax," said Eddie slowly, thinking this over. "A way to make a living—short of undertaking a second passage through the uncanny Gate between worlds. The closer it is, the more I dread it."

"I fear that Central Anomaly too," said Ina.

"What say you and I return to the MirrorEarth," Poe said to Ina.

"I'll return with you two," put in Machree. "Bringing my load of rumbies."

"Don't interrupt," said Eddie. "I'm telling Ina that I see a way for us to capitalize on the vulgar notion that Edgar Allan Poe is dead." He pressed the back of his hand to his forehead, like an actor recounting a vision. "I see Ina Durivage on stage, performing Poe's posthumous work—a clairvoyant Ina, sensitive to spirit voices from the other world! First-rate flimflam. And in this wise I can decant my versified epic *Htrae* into the public ear. By Deadgar Ailing Pro." He smiled, but his expression was resolved. "I jest not."

"Very fine," said Ina, assimilating the plan. "We'll go back home together, yes. And avoid that spooky Gate. We'll—we'll get up subscriptions for our performances. Your epic, you call it *Htrae*?"

"*Earth* spelled backwards," I told Ina. "Eddie talks about it all the time. Not that I've read or heard any of it."

"I compose in my head," said Eddie, turning haughty. "Like the bards Dante and Homer. The oral tradition, where rhymes and iambs house the words. Each night I form verses in my head, and the recording angels bear them away."

Grandiose though Eddie's words were, and much as I doubted he was in fact working on his project, his underlying notion resonated with me. Lacking time or the facilities to write out a draft of *Return to the Hollow Earth*, I really had been drafting my narrative in my head.

In the near distance the bulky *woomo* creatures lolled, stretching their tendrils. They were positioned upon the oddly glowing sphere that was the Gate, or Central Anomaly, the improbable nexus which links the hearts of the two Hollow Earths. The *woomo* had a way of steadily rolling their bodies like roasts on spits, and thereby sweeping their tendrils between the worlds. Faint images of the Umpteen Seas on the other side could be glimpsed between the warty bodies of the *woomo*. Like Eddie, I had little desire to venture in there again.

"It's tolerable in there," put in Watcher, alert to my thoughts. "A fountain of youth. I can slip by fifty years in a flash."

"Skipping twelve years is enough, huh, Mase?" said Otha.

"And I went through as fast as I could," said I.

Machree cleared his throat. He wasn't quite following our discussion. By way of changing the subject, he addressed a question to the statuesque Shrighunter. "With regard to your Great Old Ones—the *woomo*? Are they friendly?"

"I expect so," said Shrighunter, a bit wary of Machree. "If they weren't friendly, we'd be dead."

"Good," said Machree. "My belief is that the *woomo* want me to gather jewels and to bring them to the Earth's surface. I'm speaking of rumby gems? The *woomo* saved me from a shipwreck, and carried me to this core—to be close to the gems. But I'm not clear if I need to pay the *woomo* for them—or what I *could* in fact pay."

"Listen at him," said Shrighunter. "The man thinks he's makin deals with the *woomo*."

"The *woomo* aren't shopkeepers," put in Watcher. "If they want something, they take it. If they want to give something, they do."

"They'll give me rumbies for free?" pressed Machree.

"It's time that all of you know that rumbies are *woomo* eggs," burst in MirrorSeela.

I think Watcher already knew this, but the other black gods were surprised.

"*Woomo eggs!*" sang out Jewel, who'd recently arrived to perch herself next to Otha. "Why didn't nobody tell me? How you find that out, Seela elder?"

"A *woomo* tendril handed me a fat rumby, down on my flower by the Rind, and then it hatched," said MirrorSeela. "Hatched inside this beat-up old thing that we rode here in." She nodded toward the ancient craft we'd tied to the grasses.

"*La no,*" exclaimed Jewel in wonder. "Can't hardly believe it."

Jewel's role among the black gods was to collect rumbies, to weave them into little nets upon string necklaces, and to supply them to her companions. It was Jewel who'd given Eddie, Seela, and me our rumbies last year—or, rather, the gift had come from Jewel's counterpart, who lived on the other side of the Central Anomaly.

That other Jewel was, as Eddie had already confided to me, a woman greatly to his liking. And presumably his feelings for this Jewel were much the same. But he was containing any signs of passion. Firstly, this Jewel had never seen him before and might not even find him attractive. Secondly, Eddie was now in the web of the eccentric Ina. Thirdly, nothing seemed important beside MirrorSeela's stunning news.

"A jewel that's an egg," mused Eddie. "A flame within the gem. A chorus of reflections. A crystalline library, with *woomo* wisdom woven in place."

"All along I thought them rumbies were *refined turds,*" said Jewel with a cackle. "Squoze down outta the *woomos'* guts, and with a touch of tekelili in them. Eggs? An egg's supposed to be soft and juicy"

Oblivious to the import of this revelation, Machree turned the conversation to his practical concerns. "Do you think we can ride that broken-down fried-egg airship back to the surface? Collect the rumbies and float up through that column of water that fills the North Hole."

"No more maelstrom in the Hole?" asked Otha.

"You didn't notice?" said Watcher. "Mason and Seela ruined it. They chased off the royal ants."

"My fault," said Ina. "I talk too much." She turned to Seela. "And I'm sorry for being unkind to you, Seela. We need to stick together, we women. I've been a little fool."

"Agreed," said Seela with a slight smile. "And do you promise to leave my Mason alone?"

"I don't want him!" said Ina, doing her all to sound sincere. And maybe she was. "It's Eddie I've set my cap for."

"Wise choice," said Poe.

"It may have been *woomo* tekelili that led you to provoke the royal ants," Watcher told Ina. "By way of bringing on the Bloom. Wheels within wheels."

"It don't matter if the maelstrom's flooded," persisted Machree, dumb as a post. "I tell you, that old fried egg will float."

"You're a bonehead," Seela told him. "Don't you understand that *the rumbies are woomo eggs*? Nobody wants to buy fake gems that hatch into giant sea cucumber gods. And what happens to Earth's surface when we have all those *woomo* flopping around? They might eat everything, or set fires, or dig holes."

"Not my lookout," came Machree's quick response. "Not if I been paid in cash."

Maybe he was teasing. We were all a little giddy here, bathed in the heavy tekelili.

"A shrewd man is our jeweler Machree," said Eddie. "I wish I had his acumen."

"That little *woomo* that we hatched," I put in. "She thinks you can fix our *veem*, Eddie. Bring it back to life. I don't think the *woomo* can do it alone."

Eddie cleared his throat, drew back his shoulders, and puffed himself up. "Yes, I may well be more adept at ratiocination than the Great Old Ones. They dream through the millennia in a mystic glow, fanning fronds of divine light. But to fix a watch, or to analyze a chess-playing machine, or to resurrect an ancient alien—yes, such tasks are best left to a man like me."

"And to a woman like me," put in Ina. "I see the *veem* patterns in your mind, Eddie. And, if you please, I have a more efficacious touch than you. You're a man of words. I stop not at words—I'm a woman of craft."

Arf was rooting in the grass, and he pulled out a small, ordinary sea cucumber, also known as a trepang or *bêche de mer*. It was about the size of a squash, green and warty, with dark purple striations. It had retracted its tendrils in fear. It was leaking water from both ends. Arf held it for a moment his jaws, considering it, and then he dropped it.

"Is that a baby *woomo*?" asked Machree.

"No, no," said Watcher. "Those things in the grass are no-account, low-down, shirt-tail cousins of the Great Old Ones. They're not full *woomo* anymore than a mouse is a man."

"Watcher's right," said MirrorSeela. "When my rumby egg hatched, it was a Great-Old-One kind of *woomo* right away. Not a sad little bag."

Smoker took the trepang from between Arf's feet and used his shell knife to slit it open along its length. Via tekelili, I'd felt the creature's tiny, pitiful spark of life wink out.

"More meat to dry!" said Smoker, scraping out the slimy innards, and stashing the body in his basket.

"I want to see that new baby *woomo* you done hatched out," Jewel told MirrorSeela. "Where's it at?"

As if beckoned by our thoughts, Nyoo came sailing around from the other side of the floating sea and landed on the island at MirrorSeela's side. She readjusted her size—perhaps by flexing or slackening her internal tissues—and now she was the size of a small dog. Her juvenile royal ant friend Skolder was with her, looking a bit more adult than before, dark and glistening, with the beginnings of mandibles at the corners of his mouth.

Nyoo bent one end upwards. The tip had a hole in it like a letter O. She was talking to Eddie—by means of silent tekelili. I could of course hear her too.

"You'll help us fix the *veem*," Nyoo was saying to Eddie. "The Old Ones say you know how. You're smart. You learned from the pictures on the *veem*. You tell me what the *veem* needs, and I can grow it with my light."

"Light into matter," said Eddie. "A sorcerer's dream."

"I'm the wand," said Nyoo. "You're the wizard, Eddie Poe."

"But what are you after?" Eddie asked.

"We *woomo* have been waiting for thousands of years for our next Bloom. And we haven't been able to do it because only two *veem* remain. One *veem* is in hiding, and this one is inert. We need to resurrect it. But none of us *woomo* has the right turn of mind to do it."

"And if I help?" said Eddie. "What then?"

"A new Bloom," said Nyoo. "Three *veem*, some royal ants, a hundred rumbies, and an Adam and Eve. Upon this reed, a new world can blossom."

"Resurrect this fried egg to start with," echoed Eddie. "Yes."

He reached out and touched Nyoo's sparkling hide. The *woomo* gave him a friendly shock. Due to tekelili, the rest of us could precisely calibrate the strength of the stimulus—a pleasant tickle.

By the way, how many of us were present? I make it sixteen. Thirteen humans: me, Seela, Brumble, Arf, MirrorSeela, Smoker, Otha, Shrighunter, Eddie, Ina, Machree, Jewel, and Watcher. And three others: Nyoo, Skolder, and the fried egg. Assuming it was fair to count the *veem* as a conscious being. And, as we soon saw, it was.

Holding Nyoo under one arm like a lapdog, Eddie hopped onto the shiny rim of the fried egg and went into the cabin. Aiming the *woomo's* tip like a hose, Eddie let its light play across the interior—guiding the *woomo* energy with his nimble and responsive mind, and taking into account Ina's clean concepts of design.

The broken column before the control panel grew like the stalk of a plant. A tulip-like seat formed on the tube's crown. It was mounted on a swivel, so that, whichever way the craft turned, a pilot could sit at any angle desired. Next, Eddie, Ina and the *woomo* healed the broken stub upon the control panel. The restored control was simplicity itself: a protruding rod with a spherical bulb on the end. A pilot had only sit in the chair and waggle the knob.

With Eddie and Nyoo's attention, the ship's weathered friezes of hieroglyphs grew bright with colors, and the symbols themselves seemed to twitch. The rim and dome flexed into more pleasing curves. But I had a sense that the cabin's rear walled-off section required a special infusion of energy.

Skolder the juvenile royal ant slipped his rear stinger beneath the base of the *veem* and released a staggeringly powerful jolt. The fried egg pulsed like a beating heart. A jagged gout of light zig-zagged out from a particular *woomo* in the Central Anomaly. Via tekelili, I recognized this *woomo* as my friend Uxa. Her energies haloed the fried egg in a radiance so great that the craft grew dark with light.

The grasses beneath the fried egg caught fire. The agile Shrighunter jumped into our Umpteen Sea and guided her lightboard into a tight circle, sluicing up a roostertail that doused the conflagration amid smoke and steam. And when Uxa turned off her torrent of light, the fried egg was fully healed and actively alive. I could sense her psyche via tekelili. Her aura had a distinctly feminine tinge.

"Gweetings," said the fried egg, actually speaking aloud. She spoke by vibrating her skin. Her lisping voice was like the soft quacking of a baby duck. "I'm weady to fly far," said she. "But first I need more to eat."

"She needs lifting salts for her hidden stove," Eddie opined. Even now he remained under the illusion that the fried egg's method of flight would be the same as that of a hot air balloon.

"Completely wong," quacked the fried egg.

"What's your name?" Ina asked her.

"Fwopsy," said the fried egg.

"How is it that you speak English?" I asked.

"I wearn fast," said Fwopsy. "I'm smart. I wearned Eng-wish by weading your minds with tekelili."

"Most excellent," said Ina. "Can you take us for a ride, dear Fwopsy? Now that clever Eddie and clever Ina fixed you?"

"Hold off on that," called Otha. "The black gods come first. Fwopsy is spang new, and we gonna be the ones to show her around."

The fire had burned away the ropes that had tethered Fwopsy to the grass. She pirouetted, displaying herself. And then she held her door open for Otha, Smoker, Shrighunter, Jewel, and Watcher to come aboard. They fit comfortably, with Jewel in the chair, and the others standing. Before Seela, MirrorSeela, Eddie, Ina, Machree or I could protest, Fwopsy closed her door and dove into the depths of the miles-wide floating sea, with Nyoo and Skolder in her wake.

Eddie, Seela, and I looked at each other and smiled. This was shaping up to be a hell of a run.

11. Uxa

Fwopsy and the black gods flew looping paths through and around our Umpteen Sea, with an excursion toward the Central Anomaly and back. From my viewpoint, the lively ship seemed to slow down as she edged into the beginning of the *woomo* zone. The *woomo* welcomed her with still more light. I myself hoped I wouldn't be going into the Anomaly at all. I wanted to get Seela and our baby back to the San Francisco of 1850.

While we waited for Fwopsy to return, hummingbirds were picking at the dried-meat basket that Smoker had left. They were little birds, filling the air with pert cheeps, their bodies blue with red throats, but their bills—I now noticed for the first time—their bills had rows of tiny, sharp teeth. I wondered if they drank blood. An abandoned ant-farmer tangle from the inner sky was drifting our way, with its twirling, slightly menacing livestock. Pterodactyls were feeding on them. Further out, a dozen *ballula* hovered. I felt unsafe.

One of the other Umpteen seas was approaching ours. The two great lakes were wildly bobbling, almost as if they were eager to meet. *Oops*, the second Umpteen Sea merged with ours, and a forty-foot-high wave came barreling across our sea's ropy, dimpled surface. The moving mountain submerged our island, of course. We had to use our *pulpuls* to kick ourselves into the air with, once again, great worries about our tiny, week-old Brumble, whom Seela held struggling against her breast. As when doused before, the little fellow began roaring with pique. And the flesh-eating humming-birds were near.

"I want a street I can stand on!" Ina yelled at Eddie. "I want a house with a roof! I don't want everything around me to be alive!"

"First we get the rumbies," insisted Machree.

Seela and MirrorSeela were calm. The hummingbirds and pterodactyls dispersed. The untended antfarm had been devoured. We hovered now amid random spawned-off ponds of water, with a lovely aurora of *woomo* light behind us, a peaceful herd of shrigs separating us from the *ballula*, and the great Rind arching in the background.

"*You* shouldn't have come to the Hollow Earth at all," MirrorSeela told Ina. "It's beautiful here in the core. I'm going to seduce Smoker, and he'll partner up with me. I can tell he's game."

"I'm glad for you," said Seela, looking down at Brumble, who'd calmly started nursing again. "Do you really think you're pregnant, big-sister Seela?"

"With all this tekelili, I can see into myself," said MirrorSeela. "It's like I'm made of clear water. Yes, I'm going to bear Mason's second son."

At some level I already knew this—but hearing it aloud was disorienting. What a responsibility! How could I live up to it? Or, more frankly, how could I escape? But I'd been raised a Virginian, and I did my best to play the gent.

"I'm deeply honored," I told MirrorSeela. "And I'll ask you again: are—are you sure you don't want to come to the surface with us? I'd be proud to help you with the boy."

"Smoker will be a good father," said MirrorSeela. "The Umpteen Seas are a good place to raise the boy."

Seela laughed a bit ruefully. "Having a baby is harder than you think."

"Why is Fwopsy moving so slow?" interrupted the fretful Ina, staring in at the core.

"It's like in Washington Irving's tale about a man named Rip Van Winkle," said Eddie. "Rip goes for a stroll in the mountains, and he meets some dwarves. He drinks genever gin with them and plays nine-pins, and he takes a nap. When he awakes, twenty years have passed. For all those twenty years, Rip was slow." Eddie gave one of his inward smiles.

"Nine-pins?" said Ina, utterly at a loss. "What are you talking about?"

"Never mind, my lady, our gilded coach arrives." And, yes, Fwopsy was swooping our way, with Nyoo and Skolder still in her wake. The carefree black gods tumbled out, talking and laughing. It was our turn.

Eddie took the single swiveled seat at the control panel of the fried egg. Machree and Ina stood behind him with Seela. In this low gravity, it was no great effort to stand. I hesitated outside with Arf for a moment, saying goodbye to Otha.

"I guess you'll stay on here," I said.

"How they treatin black people in the United States these days?" countered Otha.

"It's hard," I said. "And I'll have to go through it all over again. The *woomo* light's made me dark again."

"But you'll fade to white after a year," said Otha. "Not like me."

"I take your point, Otha. But it's not so bad in California."

"How bout if you went back to Lynchburg to look up our younger brother Purly?" Otha asked. Purly was the offspring of my father and of Otha's mother. A blood link. Otha and I had known Purly, growing up, but not well. He'd lived in town, and we'd lived on the farm.

"Would *you* go to Lynchburg?" I asked.

"Naw." Otha cracked a slight smile. "Not even for *Purly*." He'd always been a little put out over how fond of Purly his mother was. And, of course, angry at Pa for having forced himself on his mother.

"The MirrorEarth Otha lives in Baltimore," I told Otha, by way of changing the topic. "Twelve years older than us. Gray hair. Married to a woman called Juicita. And he's got a copy of Arf."

"Arf and Juicita? MirrorOtha livin well. What he do?"

"He's a waiter in a fancy hotel. Eddie Poe and I smoked opium with him."

"Like old times," said Otha, shaking his head. "I don't need none of that white mess no more. Doin good here with the tekelili and Shrighunter and the *woomo*. Hell, Mase, I'm a black god."

"Their king," I said, meaning it. We hugged.

Arf and I got into the fried egg to join the others. I truly hoped we'd go speeding outward toward the Rind—but Fwopsy was in the process of telling us that she wasn't done with her affairs here. This was fine with the low, grasping Machree. His only thoughts were of collecting rumbies.

"I'll ride with you," said Nyoo, darting into the fried egg ship with us. "I'll help with those rumbies."

"How about you?" Fwopsy asked Skolder

"I come indeed," said Skolder via tekelili. His voice in my head was scratchy. "The rumby hunt is needful for the Bloom. To this end I sought out Nyoo, dear Fwopsy, and it is for the Bloom we roused you. We'll gather rumbies, find your mate, and fly to Earth's surface where the rumbies shall be cellared until the time is ripe. I will wait by the rumbies for decades or even centuries, in full vigilance, intent that my fellow royal ants will be on hand when the Bloom is finally achieved." Skolder did a mid-air pirouette, and buzzed in through Fwopsy's door.

Fwopsy closed her door. With her body fully restored, she was generating a steady supply of air. Nearly weightless, Ina and I bounced along on the floor and leaned our backs against the wall. Seela came to join us. I put my arm around Seela, and held Brumble in my lap. Arf lay at our feet, keeping his distance from Nyoo. Eddie, still perched in the single chair, had grasped the protruding knob upon Fwopsy's panel, and was moving it with no apparent effect. Machree was leaning over Eddie's shoulder talking to him about where they might best find rumbies. Nyoo the *woomo* lay quietly in a corner, with Skolder at her side.

With a sinking heart I watched as we headed in toward the Central Anomaly. Behind us were the Umpteen Seas, spread out like a flock of blobby, wayward sheep. Due to the Anomaly's spacewarp, as we progressed, the zone of the Seas looked increasingly flat, as did the innermost zone of the Anomaly, which was the Gate itself. About sixty of the Great Old Ones were on the surface of the Gate.

My paramount concern was how many years we were going to lose by approaching the Gate. By way of distracting myself, I studied Fwopsy's refurbished interior. The friezes were much clearer than before. Now that I was beginning to know what to look for, I could distinctly make out images of spherical *veem* craft, one of them holding *woomo*, one with humans inside, and one containing ants. The royal ants, I now understood, would be the ones to hollow out the colony world targeted by the Bloom.

Another glyph caught my eye. This one showed a *woomo* with a series of chambers inside her body. Curled inside the cavities were figures like human babies. Tiny babies ripening in *woomo* wombs. How deep did the *woomo*-human partnership go? Nyoo wasn't saying.

Meanwhile Eddie was still playing pilot—waggling the stubby lever on the control panel. It didn't matter. Fwopsy was taking us exactly where she wanted to. Deeper into the damned Anomaly. We were hovering about half a mile from the Great Old Ones. Fwopsy was flexing her body and Nyoo was humming a high, thin tune. Fwopsy was slowly rotating. Her window framed a view of the Umpteen Seas above. They were speeding around like the balls on a billiard table and, being water, they were merging and splitting at a furious rate.

"What's going on?" asked Ina uneasily.

"Time is molasses in here," Eddie told her. "The closer we get to the center, the slower our time goes. It's like being drugged, or almost dead, eh?"

"Maybe it would be more apposite to say time is *faster* in here," said I. I was all nerves, and in a mood for quarrel. "Last time through, we spent five minutes here, and we found we'd hopped from 1838 to 1850. We'd travelled twelve years in five minutes. We weren't slow, we were *fast*."

Eddie shook his head. "Don't try to cogitate, Mason. Not your forte. We were *slow*. Consider this: we only managed to nibble through five minutes, while the others gobbled down twelve years. Look out there at the Umpteen Seas leaping. They're fast, and we're slow, stretched, molasses."

Knowing I was defeated, I didn't give Eddie the satisfaction of a response.

"Where are the rumbies?" demanded the obsessed Machree. "Open your door, Fwopsy, so we'll be ready to scoop them up. Fly in closer to Uxa."

"You'd piss away twenty years for twenty dollars," I told Machree. "You pig-blind fool." I gave Machree a rough shove. Fwopsy had by now opened her door for the rumbies, and Machree very nearly lost his footing and fell out.

Taking my side, Seela jeered at the jeweler. "We should squeeze you out like the big fat turd you are," said she.

We were sinking ever deeper into the Anomaly. Beneath us, the *woomo* Uxa looked as big as San Francisco, and very nearly as hilly, with great warty mesas on her primeval integument. Via tekelili she told us she was ripe with rumbies. Expatiating on this, Uxa showed me a vision that was in accordance with my eight-point revelation from Nyoo, and with the evidence of the *veem* glyph frieze.

Uxa's rumbies were to spawn into *woomo*—and the *woomo* would fly into space aboard a flotilla of three *veem* ships, one of the ships piloted by a woman and a man. Human lovers had the power to *push*, or to *yearn*—and therewith to hop across the void of space in the blink of an eye. Uxa expressed this last point with a physical sensation of Seela and I becoming a tunnel in space. As if, impossibly, I were to crawl down Seela's throat while she crawled down mine.

The plan felt like a fever dream in a fairy tale. I feared it much.

Meanwhile, rumbies were exuding from puckers in Uxa's flesh. A slow, heavy shower of them, dropping like ripe cherries. The living gems were calling each to each, excited to be on the loose—*I'm here, I'm here, I'm here.* Fwopsy drifted closer.

"Hurry and finish," I urged the *veem*. "Scoop them up!"

"Get weady," said Fwopsy. She cupped her edge like a shovel and funneled a drift of rumbies in through her open door. Three or four dozen of the dense, thumb-sized, gemlike eggs were bouncing inside our cabin, caroming off the walls. Their bright tekelili was like the cries of schoolchildren. Machree was snatching them from the air and stuffing them inside his shirt. Nyoo was doing her best to catch some with her tendrils. Skolder the juvenile royal ant was holding down a few of them with his body. Eddie and Ina were grabbing them too.

"Oh no!" screamed Seela. She was pointing away from the core and out through Fwopsy's front viewport. The Umpteen Seas were jiggling at pell-mell pace that was nightmarish to behold. We were losing months like the ticks of a clock.

"That's enough rumbies!" I cried. "We have to leave!" I flung myself at Fwopsy's door and executed the gesture for closing it. The portal closed. Dozens more of unharvested rumbies pattered against our hull.

"Damn you!" yelled Machree, punching me in the stomach. I doubled over from the blow. "Open the door again," Machree ordered Fwopsy. The *veem* acceded to his request.

A fresh clutch of rumbies bounded through the door, drawn by little Nyoo's mental force. I was still working to catch my breath. Eddie was sedulously stuffing the excited rumby eggs into his trousers. He'd tucked the cuffs of his pants into his socks to stop the gems from tumbling out. By now he and Machree must have collected more than a hundred of them.

Ina was berating Machree, but Seela's anger at the man was truly incendiary. My Hollow Earth wife! Handing Brumble to Ina for safe-keeping, Seela curved her fingers like talons, and clawed Machree's face—digging into his flesh and drawing blood.

Machree bellowed, seized Brumble from Ina, and threw our frightened, mewling infant out the open door. I had no choice but to go after the baby, and loyal Arf came after me, and then Machree threw Seela out after the three of us. And—I was grateful to see—Nyoo the *woomo* came out with us too. But Skolder the princeling royal ant stayed aboard. The fate of the rumbies was his prime interest.

Whether in response to a command from Machree, or a word from Eddie, or by her own decision—Fwopsy closed her door and left the *woomo* zone. Her apparent speed grew faster and faster, and by the time she passed the zone of the Umpteen Seas, she was a blur.

Unbelievable. Seela, Brumble, Arf and I had been abandoned here with Nyoo. And the little *woomo* had no clear plan of how to save us. I was beginning to doubt entirely that the *woomo* were all-knowing gods. Perhaps they were but strange alien creatures, albeit with high intelligence, an ability to read minds, and a curious power of extending their bodies via thousands-of-miles-long pink fronds. But divinities? No.

Floundering and at a loss, Seela and I kicked our legs, beating our *pulpul* fins against the air, hoping to work our way back to the Umpteen Seas. But we weren't strong enough to escape the unpleasantly potent attraction toward the core. We tumbled and sank—coming to rest upon one of the cupped mesas atop Uxa's hide, with Nyoo at our side. Nyoo was delighted to be in physical contact with a full-grown *woomo* such as Uxa—indeed, she was more than delighted, she was entranced, and her mind damped down to a steady glow of bliss.

I huddled wretchedly there with Seela, the two of us taking in our surroundings with frightened eyes. Although we were too shocked to talk, we were joined in tekelili, We cradled Arf and Brumble between us. Despite having been tossed around like a ball, Brumble was calmly snuggled against Seela's breast. Arf was unhappy. He didn't like *woomo*, and they were all around.

Beyond the jostling haze of the Umpteen Seas lay the distant Rind and, how frightful, I could see the seasonal light of passing summers, pulsing through the water-filled window of the North Hole. Years rushing by.

The mountainous bodies of the fifty or sixty *woomo* were on every side, great warty barrels, bedizened with suckers, puckers, and subbranching fans, steadily rolling, spreading their tendrils toward one Earth and then the other. Their steady, stately motion carried Seela and me through the Gate into the old Earth's zone, then back through the Gate to the MirrorEarth's side. From my point of view the outer world dissolved into a haze each time we moved through the plane of the Gate. We were fortunate to have Uxa's momentum carrying us through.

Uxa's vast, slow tekelili was all around, and she allowed me to visualize her race's cosmic journey. The *woomo* were bound for an impossibly huge space spindle at the heart of the starry disk we call the Milky Way. I could see the spindle in my mind's eye, a perpetual fountain of souls, rising like a Jacob's ladder to a transcendental heaven of flowers that folded in upon themselves, and opened again, eternally new, forever old, unceasingly singing the higher-dimensional music of the spheres.

By now we'd lost at least a century of ordinary time. What kind of city would we find—if we ever made it back to San Francisco? My past was utterly lost, but yet I was happy, sitting here with my Seela, the two of us secure on Uxa's rough skin, and with our baby and our dog between us.

The oceanic flows of *woomo* tekelili lulled me into a trance, and, forgetful of all around me, I once again set to work putting my narrative of my trip into order. All along it had been as if I were writing my *Return to the Hollow Earth* in my head, starting with the journey upon the *Purple Whale* and ending, for now, with an interlude at the center of the Hollow Earth. All along I'd imagined that some celestial being was remembering my thoughts—and now I realized my recording angel was Uxa.

Yes, Uxa was sedulously absorbing my narrative—although her purpose was as yet unclear. Did she mean to create the book for me? Was she on the point of transmitting my words to some distant human scribe? No matter. A calming phrase echoed in my head. *All will be well, and all will be well, and all manner of things will be well.*

With a start, I noticed someone standing ten feet away from us. It was Watcher. Somehow he'd made his way inward to us, and he'd touched down unnoticed. He raised a hand in greeting, and his voice spoke in my head.

"It's gettin on toward time to go," said he.

"How long?" I asked him. "How long have we been here?"

"One and a half centuries of Earth years," said Watcher. "And you'll lose a few more years on the way out."

"We're missing everything!" cried Seela, very upset.

"Don't matter none," said the weathered black god. "Everything's always the same. I like it in here."

"How's Otha?" I asked.

"He's passed on. He only lived a hundred and sixty years. Not long for a black god, but of course he wasn't actually born at the core. His wife's still alive, Shrighunter. Our man Otha died a great-great-grandfather. He had a good life."

"What about my sister?" Seela asked, her voice breaking. "The other Seela. Is she alive? Did she have her son?"

"The other Seela's still shakin'," said Watcher. "She named her baby Bramble—to match your Brumble. Bramble looks like you, Mason, according to the people who remember you. Bramble's in the middle of his second century, with children and grandchildren of his own."

"Lives gone in a wink," said Seela with a sigh. "As if they're nothing."

The thought of meeting my aged son and his grandchildren gave me gooseflesh—and not in a good way. I didn't want to go back to the Umpteen Seas at all.

"Get us out of here," I implored Watcher.

"Fwopsy will arrive directly," he said. "She expects to meet Duggie here. That's who you been waiting for. It took all this time for the *woomo* to find him."

"Who's Duggie?" I asked.

"A *veem* like Fwopsy," Watcher told me. "What you call a fried egg? You saw Duggie when you fell through the South Hole on the old Earth. Uxa went sifting through your memories, and finally she spotted your Duggie hit. You the key to it all, Mason. You and Seela gonna be Adam and Eve. Uxa's bringin Duggie here. Show Mason his memory, Uxa."

In a flash I saw the scene.

Eddie, Otha, and I have fallen through the ice cap that covered the South Hole. We dropped hundreds of miles, with shattered bergs of ice tumbling after us, melting as they fell. Looking up, I see what I take to be a metal ball emerging from a cracked mountain of ice. Or no, not a ball—half a ball, with a rim. Maybe it isn't metal. It reminds me of a great, shiny, fried egg—frozen and still. It disappears into the dim, drizzling mist.

"Hail Uxa," said I.

"Here they come," cried Seela. "Fwopsy and Duggie!"

Two *veem* craft were approaching, one from Earth and one from MirrorEarth, speeding toward us at a furious pace, one on each side of the Gate.

The fried egg on our side was Fwopsy. As Fwopsy drew closer, her motion seemed to slow. Her voice was silent for now, but I could hear her thoughts via tekelili. She hadn't fully abandoned us. She'd had a two part plan.

The first part involved carrying Poe and the hundred or so rumbies to the year 1860. The second part involved working with the *woomo* to find a mate for herself—however long the search might take. Meanwhile she'd stored Seela and me here in slow time. We'd be part of the Bloom. The puzzle-pieces were coming together.

Duggie was on the other side of the Gate. Fwopsy's intended mate, revived from his frozen trance by the *woomo*. He too was shaped like a dome joined to a disk but, unlike Fwopsy, he generally flew with his dome on the downward side. That is, if Fwopsy resembled an igloo on an ice floe, Duggie had the form of a lid resting upon a bowl. He slowed down to a crawl as he inched through the Gate. But as he rose toward us, his time-stream came into synchronization with ours, as Fwopsy's had already done.

Seela was like as a coiled spring, itching for escape. Baby Brumble watched us with us with sweet, wise eyes.

"Now," said Seela. "Now we can go."

"Take these," Uxa thought to us. Raising a delicately branched tendril, she handed me three—scarves? Finely-textured, greenish-beige rectangles of a textile akin to woolen felt. But slippery. They were made of matted *woomo* fronds.

"Thank you," I said, too preoccupied with escape to ask what the scarves were for.

Finally returning to activity, the little *woomo* Nyoo lifted herself off the surface of Uxa and flexed her warty body. "It's been lovely here," she intoned.

"Are you coming with us?" I asked her.

"Indeed," she said. "I'm tasked to orchestrate the Bloom. The great migration."

"You can do what you want," I said. "Me, I'm planning to settling back down on Earth."

"*All will be well*," said Nyoo, echoing Uxa's slogan, but not really accepting my answer.

Seela and I kicked our *pulpul* fins. She carried Brumble, and I bore Arf. What with the deep tekelili, I could understand my dog's inner mentations—simple but sincere. Unease about the *woomo*, curiosity about their vinegary smell, a fondness for Bumble, a wish to lick my face—which he now did. Seela and I fluttered toward Fwopsy with Nyoo floating after us. We were like marooned sailors swimming for a dory just off their desert island.

Somehow Fwopsy was a bit too far. Or perhaps the pull of the Central Anomaly was a shade too great. We weren't going to make it. Watcher floated along at our sides, somehow without having to kick his legs. He was savoring the adventure, but not offering aid. Nor was Nyoo of any help. She was back in her tekelili trance.

I prayed with all my heart—and finally picked up an answer. A psychic message from Duggie, the other *veem*. A competent creature, poised to act.

"No problem!" quoth he.

Moving in unison, Duggie and Fwopsy positioned themselves above and below us, with Fwopsy like a dome above us, and Duggie like a cup beneath us. Both dome and cup were sealed off by flat disks. To complete their coup, the two *veem* opened large round holes in the flat disks that had hidden their interiors. The *veem* were now like a matched pair of cupped hands, poised to trap six moths.

"Do it!!" called Watcher. The *veem* clapped together, dome joining cup, with the rims of their two disks merging to one. Their hemispherical cabins were conjoined into a sphere with an inner ledge like a circular balcony. Watcher, Seela, Brumble, Arf, Nyoo, and I were within. As usual, Arf was avoiding Nyoo—and I could sense he was glad to be away from Uxa.

The doubled cabin had six windows, two doors, and two control panels, each with a single swivel seat. The seats grew from the narrow ledge that ran along the spherical cabin's equator—with Fwopsy's seat oriented upward, and Duggie's seat downward. As I've mentioned, the seats were on swivels, so that the pilots could position their bodies as they pleased. And each pilot would be holding one of those ball-tipped controls. And, finally there was a flattish, closed-off volume along one side of the inner sphere. Eddie had once imagined that "lifting salts" were in there, but more likely the space held internal organs.

In any case, a lovely winding frieze of symbols covered the conjoined walls. The parade of hieroglyphs spiraled outward from the apex of one dome, wound along the central ledge, then spiraled inward to the apex of the second dome. It seemed as if one of the two depicted histories was the continuation of the other, not that—to speak truthfully—I was sure which direction represented the forward flow of time.

I should mention that the word *veem* is used in three ways. Firstly, it can refer to a single fried-egg-style aircraft, like Fwopsy. Secondly, it can be viewed as a plural form, akin to the words *deer* or *woomo*. Thus one can speak of a pair of *veem*. Thirdly, we can use *veem* to refer to a conjoined pair of the individual craft. Thus: Fwopsy was a *veem*, Fwopsy and Duggie began as separate *veem*, and after they joined themselves together they were a higher sort of *veem*.

Duggie was chatting away, his tenor voice filling the cabin. He'd managed to pick up English too. He was a livelier character than Fwopsy. A rowdy, you might say. And with a Southern accent instead of a lisp.

"We're ripe to mate!" exulted the *veem*. "I'm back from cold storage. Fwopsy and me gonna hatch out some *larvae*! We the last two *veem* on your two Earths! All our children flew away during the last Bloom."

"I'm not weady," demurred Fwopsy. "Not till we're on the outside—where we can welease our wittle ones wight away. We don't want our warvae settling on the walls inside our cabin."

"You right," said Duggie. "And we don't want no sessile ufological saucerian larvae taking root on our human guests neither."

"Where do you get those odd words?" inquired Watcher. "They're unfamiliar to me."

"When Uxa's ray woke me up under the South Pole, I tanked up on radio talk from today's Earth," said Duggie. "It's a new world up there! Get up to speed, old coot."

By now we'd escaped the Central Anomaly and were heading into the zone of the Umpteen Seas. Once again the floating lakes were wobbling at a reasonable rate. We'd rejoined Earth's quotidian flow of time.

"You left us in there too long?" I told Fwopsy. "We've lost—"

"Over a hundwed and sixty years," said Fwopsy. "Watcher told you why. Didn't you wisten? It took that wong to find Duggie."

"It's still hard to believe you'd do that to us," I muttered.

"Go ahead and drop me off here," the dignified Watcher now told the pair of *veem*. "Any place around the Seas is good. My folks will find me."

I turned to Seela. "You don't want to visit with the black gods again, do you? After all this time?"

Seela shook her head. "Too much," said she. "Let's go back to California and see what happens there. We've still got our own lives to live."

"Yes, we do," said I, liking the prospect. I had a mental image of a cozy little house with children in the yard, a garden, me writing at my desk, and Seela with a jewelry studio.

12. Twenty Eighteen

The trip went quickly. This time it wasn't a matter of passively floating up though the ocean in the all-but-lifeless hulk of a long-abandoned fried egg. Instead we were aboard a coupled pair of fully functional *veem*. Their powers of flight were extreme.

In less than an hour, we'd sped from the core to the Rind, and then upward through the seawater and the icepack of the MirrorEarth's now frozen-over North Hole. A half hour after that, we were hovering high above San Francisco. The setting sun gilded the ocean and bay.

It was odd to be dealing with weight again. Relative to the Earth's pull, Fwopsy was right side up, and Duggie was upside down. We were looking out through the *veem* viewports while standing on the inner surface of Duggie's inverted dome.

"What are those shapes?" said Seela, peering through one of Duggie's windows at the city. "All angles and lines. Buildings like teeth. Streets so smooth. A park like a green tongue. San Francisco is huge."

"And see the bridges," I said, uneasily studying the busy bay. "And the cranes and ships."

"Flying machines too," said Seela, her voice rising as she pointed at one of Fwopsy's windows. "Look out Duggie!"

Our *veem* ship twitched to one side, and a nasty metal aircraft screamed past. A hateful, violent thing, intent on doing us harm. Seen from below, it was shaped like a cross.

Our paired fried eggs picked up speed so fast that we fell on our butts. Seconds later, we were low over a beach town down the coast. It had a harbor and a river, and looked to be a more manageable size. The town had paved roads running along its cliffs, with shiny closed-up wagons speeding along them. Alive like our *veem?* Machines powered by steam? I noticed some people playing in the waves—riding boards like the black gods had done inside the Hollow Earth. But the people here were riding water, rather than flows of light.

"This is Santa Cwuz," said Fwopsy's voice, vibrating from the cabin walls. Santa Cruz had been a tiny fishing village when we'd sailed to San Francisco in 1850.

"Why's everything so strange?" I complained, knowing the answer, but wanting the words to be said.

"It's the year twenty eighteen," intoned Duggie. "Long wait since the last Bloom. That was in the year ten twenty, as I do recall. Fwopsy and I been zonked out ever since. We the only two *veem* left. It's time to feed and breed."

Twenty eighteen. Numbly I revolved the numbers in my head, trying to make sense of them—and wondering if Seela and I could fit in here.

Once again, a savage, flying metal cross flew at us.

"Quick," said Nyoo to our *veem.* "Let me out. I'll get them off your trail."

In the blink of an eye, the door irised open, Nyoo sped out, and the door closed. Nyoo flew straight at the angry metal cross, then cut to the side, leading the clumsy thing on a frantic upward arc.

Meanwhile Fwopsy and Duggie dove into the sea beside a long wharf. Moving rapidly beneath the surface, the *veem* sped some miles further south, and found shelter in a deeply shaded crack within a precipitous ocean trench. We lurked there, where no spy rays could pry. Full night fell.

It was utterly dark inside the paired fried eggs, and cold. Brumble didn't like it at all. He was crying inconsolably. And Arf was endlessly barking, as if he'd lost his mind.

"Put us ashore," Seela begged the *veem* craft. "It's enough now."

"Seela's right," came Duggie's voice inside the gloomy cabin. "Those crazy killers who were chasing us are gone."

"We'll take you to Big Sur," said Fwopsy. "The wumbies are in a tweasure chest in a secwet cave. Machwee and I put them there after we took Eddie and Ina to San Fwancisco. Skolder is watching them."

"We gonna spawn in that cave?" asked Duggie.

"Yes, dear *veem*," said Fwopsy. "That's the whole idea. We make our babies. And the wumbies there are weady to hatch into *woomo*. And we have Mason and Seela for Adam and Eve. Time for the Bwoom!"

So we rose out of the ocean and flew yet further to the south, reaching the coastal district known as Big Sur. Even after a century and a half, this was in large part a wild, uninhabited land, with few lights. The moon was up, the sky was clear, and no bullying, metal flying machines were in view. Nor, for now, was Nyoo anywhere to be seen.

"Do you know the exact date?" I asked Fwopsy.

"March 24, 2018," she said.

"So I missed my birthday," I remarked. "That was on February 2." Not much of a reaction from Seela. The flowerpeople were barely aware of the passing years, and they had no reckoning of months and days. Seela was staring at the rolling sea and the hills of Big Sur, lit by the fat moon.

"I'm going to start saying I'm eighteen," I told little Brumble, whom I had against my shoulder. I loved the smooth, warm skin of his silky head. "Right, baby? Papa's all done being seventeen. It was a short year, but a busy one."

Brumble made a single hiccup, which I took to be agreement.

We skimmed across the moon-silvered waves and rose fifty yards up a sheer coastal cliff. And here was an isolated grassy meadow, perched amid the rock faces like a shelf. Our double fried egg nestled into the inky shadows of a grove of gnarled cypress trees, hard against a steep ragged wall of stone, complete with the steaming pool of a hot spring. *This is how it's supposed to be in California*, thought I. I was glad not to be in one of those cold and overbuilt new towns we'd seen.

"The cave's over here," Fwopsy told Duggie. "Away from the hot spwing. We'll dig now."

Although the shadowed meadow seemed to meet the dry part of the cliff quite seamlessly, Fwopsy and Duggie rooted at the soil with their shared, flexible rim, scattering dirt, and shoving boulders aside, with some of the rocks rolling across the meadow and off the cliff into the foaming sea.

Soon they'd opened a low tunnel that did indeed lead into a cave, a largish one, as big as the nave of a church. Once we were inside, the two *veem* lit up. Fwopsy, who was still on top, glowed pale yellow, and Duggie shone vegetable green. Seela and I were still sealed inside them. We watched through the viewports as the conjoined *veem* settled in. I noticed a time-worn treasure chest against the cave's wall. This must be the box that Fwopsy said was full of rumbies. And I glimpsed stealthy, moving forms at the far, low end of the cave. But then the shapes retreated into deeper gloom.

"We'll hatch new *veem* to make a wittle fweet," Fwopsy lisped to Seela and me.

"What's a *fweet*?" I had to ask.

"She means *fleet*," said Duggie. "A fleet of three *veem* balls. Each of them will be a pair of our fried-egg hatchlings."

"Why does Fwopsy have to lisp like that?" asked Seela, annoyed. "If you two are so smart, why can't she talk right?'

"She thinks what she does is funny," said Duggie. "I think so too."

"Can you let us out now?" I said, really very tired of these *veem*. "I don't want to be inside you anymore."

"Just a minute," said Duggie. "We can't open our doors until we spawn. Are you ready, Fwopsy?"

"Weady, my love. I've waited ten thousand years."

The *veem* trembled at a rising rate. Duggie grunted and Fwopsy squeaked. A scent of musk and cinnamon filled the air. Then all was still.

"We done it!" said Duggie after a bit, his voice gone husky. "I'm woke and I'm lit and I squirted."

The air of our cabin was befogged by drifts of eggs and milt, with lucky larvae forming apace. This round space was alive with tiny, writhing *veem* fry.

"Look at them sparkle," added Duggie, his voice low in awe. "Feel the fizz."

"You should be bweathing through Uxa's scarves wight now," Fwopsy cautioned us, her voice languid. "The ones she gave you?"

"Don't want no flying saucer barnacles in your windpipes!" whispered Duggie.

"Flying saucers, yes," faintly echoed Fwopsy. "That's what the men in those fwying metal things were calling us. Even though Duggie and I together are like a ball and not like a fwied egg."

I wrapped one of Uxa's scarves across Brumble's nose and mouth, and covered the lower part of my own face. Seela donned a scarf too. Wise Arf curled up on the floor and stuck his snout into the fur of his belly.

My skin itched at the thought of baby *veem* settling onto me like limpets fastening themselves to a tide-washed rock. But now, thank heavens, Fwopsy and Duggie had finally opened their doors, and their spawn was drifting out.

As the verminous exodus abated, Seela, Brumble, Arf, and I disembarked as well. The cave's inner walls were cool, dry, smooth. Hundreds of the *veem* larvae were alighting on the stone. Each hatchling carried a slight spark of consciousness—I could track their locations via a trickle of tekelili from Fwopsy and Duggie. But the vast majority of the tiny new *veem* were dying. Only a very few of them would flourish and take root.

And there was something more daunting than this. The two parent saucers, Fwopsy and Duggie—their tekelili was fading. They'd fallen away from each other, breaking their embrace, no longer joined as one. Their flexing bodies were beginning to stiffen and dry. They were, if not dying, doing something very like. A final pulse of thought came from Fwopsy.

"A ten thousand year nap," she said. "Good wuck to you two." The *veem* dropped senseless to the dusty, stone floor. Their bodies had gone dark. The only light in the cave was a faint ray of moonlight angling in the door.

Seela and I stood there for a moment, taking it in.

"I liked them," she said.

"Even though Fwopsy left us at the core?" I said.

"I liked their voices," said Seela. "And their beautiful designs."

"Fwopsy says they'll be back some day," I said.

"We won't be here," said Seela.

We could hear things moving in the rear of the cave. Creepy. We made our way outside. It was wonderful in the salty, fresh, cool night air. There wasn't much of a wind.

The mouth of the cave was dark, but the moon highlighted the cliff and the seaward branches of the low trees. Mist drifted from the hot spring. Its shallow pool would be a good source of warmth against the March night.

Seela stripped off her travel-stained pants and shirt and seated herself in the pool, submerged to her waist. I quickly disrobed and joined her, then took hold of Brumble and rinsed his little body. He gaped, gurgled, sneezed, and kicked his legs like a crawfish snapping his tail. He liked the warm water. Arf came into the pool as well, picking his way slowly and carefully, with much suspicious sniffing.

When had I last bathed? Less than a day ago, by one reckoning. Or over a hundred and sixty-seven years ago, by another.

"We can stay by the spring all night," said Seela.

"Or we could go in the cave," I said.

"I don't like the scuttling," said she.

"Maybe it's something friendly," I said.

"Maybe it's something that bites."

"I wish we'd brought food," I said. "Why don't we ever remember that?"

"Trust fate," said Seela. "It's brought us this far." Raising her voice she yelled aloud, just in case there might actually be something friendly in the cave. "Bring us food!"

I could see my darling by the moonlight. Thanks to our massive doses of *woomo* light, our skins were deeply black. And Brumble was black too.

"Starting at our society's low end again," I said. "I'm tired of it."

"Why do you care?" said Seela, discerning my import. "I like dark skin. It's better."

"Not in Virginia or in Baltimore," I said.

"I've never been to Virginia," said Seela. "But you and I did fine in Baltimore. We had more fun than those pinched, anxious whites. We were free, and newlyweds, and we had no baby to worry about, and we made love all the time. And now we're in California."

"California twenty eighteen," I said.

"That's a year number?" said Seela. "You used to say eighteen fifty. I don't like numbers. The flowerpeople don't use them."

"I know," I said, putting my arm around her. Smooth, wet, warm. Brumble between us, very darling, even though he hadn't yet learned to smile. "Real things are better than numbers," I agreed. "Warmer and rounder. With colors and smells."

"Maybe you can find a job on a newspaper," said Seela. "Like you planned."

"If people will read me," I said. "I'm from the days of yore. I'll be judged quaint and skew, a pompous relic."

"Write simple," said Seela. "Learn new words. Like Duggie was doing. *I'm lit.* I liked when he said that. We'll fit in. We're sly rats. Stop worrying!"

"I'll soak my head," I said, passing Brumble to Seela so I could lie back in the water. It was good being submerged, in a primeval puddle unchanged for centuries. Me, my wife, and our baby. After a while the wife poked me and I sat up.

"You're rude," she said. "You didn't ask what I plan to do."

"Tell me now," I said. "I'm sorry. What will you do in this new world?"

"Necklaces," said Seela. "Jewelry. What I've always done. You called them money nets? I'll weave doodads onto wires and threads."

"*Doodads*," I echoed. I'd never heard that before.

"A modern word," said Seela. "Duggie's tekelili was full of them. I can't believe he came back to life for about one day and now he's already gone."

"Harsh," I said. "That's a Duggie word, too."

"Remember how in Baltimore I traded one of my money nets for a ham, and one for a dress, and one for twelve pieces of fried chicken? Jewelry."

"Sly rat," I fondly said. "Did you notice the treasure chest in there? Fwopsy said the chest is full of rumbies, right? And the rumbies are *woomo* eggs, awaiting the great Bloom."

"I know all that," said Seela. "And I hope the Bloom's a flop. The rumbies were brought here by Eddie and Machree and Ina, and those three are vile parasitic shrig-fleas, and I hate them. They left you and me at the Hollow Earth's core to die."

"But we didn't die," I said, meaning to calm her emotions. "Sure, I hate Machree too, but Ina's our friend, and Eddie—well, he's Eddie. I'm surprised the rumbies all ended up in the trunk. I thought Machree wanted to sell them."

Seela shrugged. "Maybe they're *not* in the trunk. Or maybe Machree didn't get his way. Do you think he and Eddie and Ina are still around?"

"I think they got back here a hundred and fifty years before we did," I said.

"Numbers are shit," Seela reminded me. "Numbers are numb."

"We were in the slow time longer than they were," I said, rephrasing my thought. "And while we were in the slow time, they rushed through the years in fast time. I'm pretty sure they're dead."

"Well—you can never be sure about Eddie," said Seela. "He's a weasel."

I had to agree. "We saw him stabbed and drowned in Baltimore," I recalled. "And then he was back. Drinking claret in a stateroom on the *Water Witch*."

Seela shook her head and dropped the topic. She scooped more warm water onto Brumble, then raised her voice and called out again to whatever helpful-elf-type beings might conceivably be rustling at the back of the cave.

"Bring us food!" she yelled.

Moonlight glinted off a shape at the mouth of the cave. A low creature, moving daintily as if on tiptoe, walking backwards with his head lowered, dragging something—was it a magic cougar bringing us the haunch of a slain deer? No, larger than a cougar. The being glistened in shades of purple and green.

"A royal ant!" exclaimed Seela. "With ant-plant sausages!"

Arf was barking furiously. Ignoring him, the large ant deposited a pair of plump, foot-long, ant-plant sausages beside our pool. Raising his head, he clacked his great jaws at Arf, enjoining the dog to be silent. I picked up a touch of the ant's tekelili.

He was none other than Skolder—the royal ant princeling who'd hatched near the North Hole, and whom we'd encountered near the core of the Hollow Earth. He was a century and a half older now, and perhaps not yet his full adult size, but decently large, the size of a horse, albeit a horse with six very short legs. Formidable.

"Remember me?" came Skolder's scratchy tekelili voice in my head.

"We do," said Seela. "You ditched us at the core."

"Is that all you two ever talk about?" said Skolder. "Here you are. Be happy. I've been waiting by the rumbies with my family, to make sure we get in on the Bloom. Riding off on those flying saucers to a new world. And you two are supposed to be Adam and Eve."

"No we're not," said Seela. "I'm not going."

"Perhaps your man harbors thoughts you choose to ignore," said Skolder in our heads.

"Go away," said Seela. "Stupid, overgrown ant. I'd like to crush you under my heel."

Skolder chirped something unintelligible and returned to the cave.

"I hate when others say they know things about you that I don't know," Seela said to me. "All of them sneaking and reading our minds. Are you going to leave on those saucers or not?"

"Can't we just eat? Quarrelling is so hard."

"Yes," said Seela.

We cut the sausages in half and set to. They were like the ones we'd eaten on the hovering ant farm within the Hollow Earth—brimming with a bubbly, tasty jelly that went down as fast as I could swallow. Delicious and marvelously restorative. I'd been aching all over, but soon I felt fine

Seela and I lounged beside the warm pool with Uxa's *woomo* scarves wrapped around us, and with Brumble between us. We felt comfortable and at ease. And, at least for now, I felt I'd stay with Seela forever. We'd sleep out here tonight, and tomorrow we'd find our way to one of the settlements north of here, perhaps to a town smaller than the ungainly sprawl of twenty eighteen San Francisco.

But the unresolved question remained. "We don't really have to fly off in one of those *veem* ships, do we?" Seela asked.

At one level I did want to travel on and on, finding ever newer wonders. I was born for adventure. But—now I had Seela and Brumble. So maybe I'd stay. In any case, for now it was easiest to say what Seela wanted to hear.

"I've had enough of the *woomo* and the *veem* and the royal ants," I told her. "It's as you said. We're ready for a life of our own." Using my rumby tekelili, I went so far as to show her my vision of us three in a rustic cottage—without revealing my thought that our home might be on the new colony world, rather than on Earth. I was hoping to have it both ways at once.

"Yes," murmured Seela, taking in the superficial lineaments of my vision. "A cabin like that. And with a cow." She cuddled against me and we fell asleep.

I was awakened by a thud or a splat. It was early morning, with the rising sun gilding the foggy sea. Our cliffside meadow was damp with dew, and still in the shadow of the Big Sur coastal range. Lying next to us was—Nyoo. She'd plopped down out of the sky, quite unharmed. She was full of energy and raring to go. Meanwhile Seela and Brumble were still asleep.

As I've mentioned, Nyoo was a tubular creature of variable size. Just now she was about three feet long, with branching fleshy fronds on either end, and with warts and suckers along her striped green-and-black body—very like a sea cucumber. She had no eyes—she saw solely by the power of tekelili.

"Mason!" came her lively voice in my head. "Are you ready? You'll need to round up Eddie and Ina and the rumbies for the Bloom. We'll have at least six good new fried eggs turning ripe on the cave walls in a few days. And Fwopsy said the rumbies are in a treasure chest in the cave." All this came in the form of impulses and emotions rather then as images and words.

"Do you know that Fwopsy and Duggie are dead?" I asked.

"In hibernation," corrected Nyoo, evoking a drifty sense of how Fwopsy had been when she was an inert hulk amid the Umpteen Seas. "Never mind them. Those newborn saucers will carry you away!" A sense of the cave's six baby fried-egg saucers clapping together in pairs to make three big sphere saucers.

"Seela doesn't want to go in a saucer," I told Nyoo. "I'm not sure I'm going to help any more with the Bloom. I might be finished."

"Nonsense. Look at everything we've done for you." Nyoo expressed this with a kinetic sense of my arms being laden with gifts, followed by a sense of me kneeling in gratitude.

"*Everything you've done?*" I cried. "Like throwing us a hundred and sixty seven years into the future? I'm supposed to be glad about that?"

"Thanks to me you had the opportunity to mate with Seela and MirrorSeela at the same time," said Nyoo, casting this sentiment into a transfixing erotic scene. "I know this was important to you."

"It didn't happen that way at all. You saw what it was like. You were there."

Nyoo sent a thought indicating her disinterest in the fine points of human words, or in the niceties of human courtship. She expressed this via a montage of humans speaking in barks, squeals, and grunts while twisting their bodies into shameless, unnatural displays. Done with this topic, she viscerally prodded me to accompany her into the cave. It was hard to gainsay a *woomo*'s direct order. I acquiesced.

"What—what's happening?" said Seela, awakened by the aethereal vibrations of my teeping with Nyoo. She sat up with her beautiful hair mussed. Brumble wormed his bald little head against her, opening and closing his mouth.

"I'm taking Nyoo to see the rumbies and the baby *veem*," I said, already on my feet and donning my clothes—the stained gray pants and the dirty white shirt. It occurred to me that Nyoo might not know that Skolder the royal ant was still here. I did my best to suppress this thought. If I knew something that Nyoo didn't, it might somehow help me to get free of her demands.

"Wait till I'm done feeding the baby," said Seela, who sensed that I was uneasy. "I want to come with you. Just in case you need help." With or without rumby tekelili, we two had grown so intimate that Seela was aware of my faintest ruminations. But Nyoo wasn't so perceptive. Perhaps the vaunted *woomo* weren't as knowledgeable as I'd once supposed.

So Nyoo and I waited till Seela and Brumble were ready. Rather than leaving Brumble on his own on the cliff, Seela brought him along on her shoulder, quietly hiccuping. And naturally Arf came too. He was curious about whether we'd find food in the cave.

Pink energies flickered from Nyoo's feelers and she levitated into the air. She drifted through the mouth of the cave, with us following after.

Fwopsy and Duggie lay dark and still on the floor. Nyoo played her pink rays across their gleaming hides. "We'll haul them to the core," she told me, or rather showed me. By the light of Nyoo's rays, I saw that precisely six of the newly spawned fried eggs had successfully taken root on the cave's walls. They were the size of dinner plates, or even serving platters.

The little treasure chest sat by the wall, dark with age, a box of stained wood with wrought iron fittings along its edges, and with a heavy brass padlock in its tarnished hasp.

I heard a shrill chirp. Skolder was watching us from a position high up on a cave wall to our left. Incredible that a creature the size of a horse could lodge himself there. He had strong legs and highly adhesive feet.

"Caution!" said Skolder, communicating via a mixture of tekelili, antennae twitches, and mandible clicks. "The chest of rumbies—it's not as it seems."

"Stand back," advised Nyoo, confidently aglow. Fwopsy had assured us the rumbies were here, and that's what Nyoo believed—to the point of ignoring her old friend Skolder's warning.

Nyoo tilted her stubby body and directed a zap of energy at the lock. It sprang open and fell to the ground. Skolder chirped another warning. Finally sensing something might be amiss, Nyoo urged or, rather, commanded me to open the trunk myself.

"Don't do it," called Seela. She was standing with Brumble in the cave's mouth, a shapely silhouette against the brightening Big Sur day.

Despite the warnings, I gingerly pulled upwards on the chest's convex lid. As I say, Nyoo's tekelili gave the *woomo* a certain power over me. And, boy that I still was, I was unable to resist the lure of a treasure chest. I'd expected some resistance from the lid, but the hinged top flew open in a rush, clacking against the cave's wall. Pale, shining, smudged surfaces seethed within. Nyoo emitted a silent cry of alarm and turned to flee.

But she was too slow.

Dozens, nay scores, of dog-sized white ants rushed from the open trunk, which had a slyly tunneled hole in place of its base. Farmer ants. They roiled out like pale smoke from a fire. They were the size of dogs, cunning, vicious, quick on their feet, and capable of leaping halfway across the cave in one go.

Nyoo extended a tendril and sent some rapid zaps of light at the pale ants—to no avail. The creatures' dirty-looking white bodies were highly reflective, and *woomo* beams bounced away. Faster than it takes to tell, six or seven of the farmer ants had hold of Nyoo, tearing at the *woomo* with their jaws, and repeatedly thrusting their stingers into the alien sea cucumber's flesh.

Nyoo dropped to the dusty floor. Two dozen of the pale ants were upon her. A few seconds later our friend the *woomo* was gone—entirely consumed by the savage, ravenous, farmer ants—leaving behind nothing more than a damp spot of ichor upon the ground. The *woomo* were, in the end, as vulnerable as me. It was only the intoxicating force of their tekelili that had made me deem them immortal gods. I felt lost and sad.

Still on the wall, Skolder the princeling royal ant creaked an audible sound like a dirge. Faintly luminous, the pale farmer ants stood in a phalanx, watching Seela and me. Somehow I had a feeling they weren't quite sure what manner of beings Seela and Brumble were. Maybe Seela's rumby vibrations were throwing them off, or maybe they'd never seen a human baby before. Skolder grew an intense beam of light from his stinger and played it across the eyes of the farmer ants. They stood their ground.

"I once told my friend Nyoo that I savored her," said Skolder's voice in my head. "These brutal, low-caste, farmer ants take such a thought in too crude a way. They've lurked here for years, patiently wanting to devour some *woomo* at the time of the Bloom. My royal ant siblings and cousins are in a nest nearby. We have a young empress in waiting, and I am to be her consort. We'll ride together to the new world. It is for you two to finish the preparations for the Bloom. My kin and I will block the farmer ants from claiming all the room. Go to fetch Eddie and Ina. And find the rumbies. The rumbies are no longer here." And with that, big Skolder wriggled into a hole in the upper left corner of the cave.

Still at the mouth of the cave, Seela spoke. "I've always heard there's nothing a farmer ant would rather do than eat a *woomo*. And I said it's like the way we women control you men. Remember, Mason? We joked about this in happier times. I'm like a *woomo*, you're like an ant."

The pale, whitish farmer ants studied us with their unreadable eyes. Were they going to set upon us? Unlike Skolder and his royal tribe, the farmer ants had no tekelili at all. Their antennae waggled up and down, and they were chirping. *Skritch skzz skritch.* I made my way to Seela's side.

"I know I'm terrible, but I kind of loved how the farmer ants ate Nyoo," said Seela. "So juicy. I was half-expecting it. All along I had a feeling they might be hiding in the chest."

"How did you know?" I asked.

"Well, first of all, when we saw Skolder bring the ant-plant sausages last night, I figured there had to be farmer ants around. The royal ants and the farmer ants—they fight with each other, but often they're neighbors as well. And, second of all, if the rumbies were put here a hundred and forty years ago, it figures that by now someone would have stolen them. So why not have farmer ants waiting in the treasure chest. Surprise, Nyoo!" She laughed again.

"Do you think the farmer ants carried the rumbies down to their nest?"

"Hoarding rumbies would fit with them being obsessed with eating *woomo*," said Seela. "After all, the rumbies are *woomo* eggs. Those greedy, mindless, low-caste, white ants might sit and wait for years for a rumby egg to hatch—just so they can gobble down a newborn *woomo*. But the shiny purple-green royal ants like Skolder—they understand about cooperation. You heard what he said. He's angling to get himself and his empress ant wife onto a *veem* ship of the Bloom. Even though the Bloom is probably screwed."

"This is getting so complicated," I complained.

"Let's get out of here," urged Seela. "Before any rumbies hatch, and before the ants start a war, and before those saucers on the wall wake up."

"Nyoo and Skolder said that it was up to me to find Eddie and Ina and the rumbies," I told Seela. "I feel like I owe the *woomo* that much."

"*You owe the woomo?* Why, exactly?"

I groped for an answer. "I—I mean, the *woomo* are like gods. They're always sending out tendrils to do things for us. And both the times we were at the core they helped us get through."

"They're using us," said Seela. "They shuttle us back and forth—between Earth and MirrorEarth, between the inside and the outside, and along they way they kept us in storage at the core for over a hundred years—and it's all just to help their precious Bloom. We're supposed to pilot the ships? And hatch a new race? Fuck the *woomo*, Mason. Fuck the Bloom. It's not going to work. Face facts."

"I still feel like I should try to find Eddie," I stubbornly said. But part of me was wondering if Seela were right. Had I become a *woomo* slave? No, no, I was a free agent. A young hero. Born for adventure.

"How the hell would you find Eddie?" pressed Seela. "By now he's been dead for years and years, no? He came up here much earlier than us. You're going to dig up his corpse? It's not up to you to make the Bloom happen, Mason. And we're *not* going on those saucers, right?"

"I guess not," I said, just to shut her up. Would you think me a traitor if I admitted I was already wondering if there might be a way to settle Seela in Santa Cruz—seen from the air, the town looked more congenial than San Francisco. Maybe I should leave Seela there, and ride a saucer to an entirely different world on my own? I was in complete inner turmoil.

Dressed in our dirty clothes, and with Seela carrying Brumble in the *woomo*-woven scarf she'd tied across one shoulder, Seela and I made our way up the jagged cliff, hoping to find a road. Somewhere along the way we'd lost our shoes, but that only made the climb easier.

Blessedly it was a pleasant, sunny day, as can happen any day of the year in California. As we'd flown the last part of our trip in darkness, I'd unthinkingly supposed that the road, if there was one, would be a dirt track, as it might have been in 1850.

We started hearing traffic when we were a hundred feet below the top. A growing hiss, a percussive roar, and then a hiss that faded away. Over and over again. Looking along the coast we could see bits of the dark gray road. Shiny wagons sped along it, rolling on smooth, black wheels. These were the things we heard. I felt no spark of life from them. They were machines. Were people inside them?

The slope leveled out, and we made our way onto a patch of red and yellow gravel. And there was the dark gray road, very solid, as if baked from a slurry of tar, mortar and stones. For the moment none of the glossy, enclosed wagons were in sight.

"Which way do we go?" asked Seela, who even now was a bit unfamiliar with how we oriented ourselves on Earth's outer surface.

"There," said I, pointing to the left. "Up the coast. North to Santa Cruz." I'd fixed on that town as our goal. Although I'd heard little mention of it on the *Water Witch* or during our brief time in San Francisco, I liked the look of it from the air.

One of those smooth, shiny wagons was approaching, heading north to south. Seela and I stood well back from the road and watched it pass. It was large, with tinted windows all around, and I could clearly see a man and a woman within. The entire rear area of the wagon was unoccupied. The man and the woman wore spectacles with dark lenses. Seela waved to the couple, but they offered no response. If anything, they seemed to avert their gaze.

"Let's stand on the other side of the road," I suggested. "If we can hail one of the wagons it might carry us to Santa Cruz. That's better than walking all the way."

We stood by the road for perhaps two hours, every now and then walking a bit further toward the north. The walking wasn't easy with our bare feet. Certainly some of the drivers saw us, but none of them wanted to stop, nor did they smile. To the contrary, many of them scowled, and one white man, riding as a passenger, stuck his arm out his window as if shaking his fist, but with his middle finger extended. I'd seen sailors use this sign to express disrespect.

"You were right," Seela said to me, shaking her head. "It's hard to be black in America. The whites fear us and hate us."

"Some of them are kind," I said. "In time someone will stop."

It was another two hours till we got our ride, shortly after noon. The sun was high and hot, despite the steady ocean breeze. The wagon that stopped was boxy and dirty, with worn green paint. The driver was an energetic, copper-skinned woman in yellow-lensed glasses, with a bearded brown man sitting next to her wearing darker glasses. I could see another man and woman in back, and a pair of small children.

"*Andale*," called the woman at the wheel in a friendly tone. "We got room. Don't stand with your *niño* in the sun. Look at him, *que lindo*. A little flower bud."

A side door on the wagon slid open. The door was made of metal and it clanged. After the noon sun, it seemed dark in the car. It smelled good on the whole, like food, mostly, although there was an undertone of diapers.

Our saviors were mostly talking Spanish, although they did know some English. I was pleased to realize that the tekelili of our rumbies gave Seela and me some slight ability to speak Spanish ourselves. Our new friends said they were from Mexico, living and working in Santa Cruz, and that they were returning from a trip they'd made down the coast to visit some relatives who worked on a ranch. I communicated to them that we wanted to go to Santa Cruz, and they said they'd take us all the way.

The woman driving was named Aida. She had dark, wavy hair, a noble, straight nose, and a bulky body. She was the boss, a big talker and a flirt. She beamed a few smoldering looks my way, as if testing my reactions.

"*Muy caliente*," said her husband Hector, after the second of stocky Aida's fierce, tooth-baring smiles. He laughed and nudged her, not taking this byplay seriously. "You be a proper old lady, Aida, for the sake of little Tomás."

Tomás was Hector and Aida's son, a two-year-old, wriggling in a little chair next to Maya, who was the wife of Hector's brother Rafaelo, and the mother of Frida, who was one, and was seated in another tiny chair. Our speeding wagon had three padded benches, with Seela, Brumble, Arf, and me in the middle one, along with Tomás in his chair. To make room for us, Rafaelo and Maya had moved onto the rear-most bench next to Frida. Maya wore a lacy black blouse, with buttons in it so she could easily nurse Frida. Rafaelo wore a fancy shirt with a scalloped section on the shoulders, and snaps on the pockets. He had a thick, black ponytail as long as Maya's.

It was confusing to be with so many people, but even more, it was unsettling to be flying along this narrow gray road at an unheard of speed, with other shiny wagons racing toward us, very nearly colliding with us and then roaring past. The road ran along the rising and falling edges of the cliffs, with the aquamarine Big Sur ocean throwing wild spume from the rocks below. Seela clutched Brumble tight.

Aida was an extremely inattentive driver, constantly talking, and using one hand to hold a type of small cigar with white paper wrapping. She had a round steering wheel, and a control with a handle on top, a bit like the single control on the panel of a fried egg saucer. Every minute she would turn almost completely around to assess the impact of her jokes, admonitions, and sallies upon us in the rear. All the while, furious blasts of music issued from the van's control panel—massed horns, accordions, and lamenting voices, raised in expressive arcs of Mexican song.

Seela looked at me goggle-eyed, sharing my anxiety. Rafaelo offered us something to drink, that is, he handed us two oddly lightweight little cans, very smooth-skinned, and with sharp edges around a hole in the top. I was thirsty, but I couldn't quite see the trick of how to drink from the can, nor was I sure the contents would be salubrious. I spilled a bit of the stuff onto the palm of my hand, then sniffed and licked it, sending the ponytailed Maya into gales of laughter.

Having determined that my can held thin, bitter beer—which they called Tecate *cerveza*—I tried to drink it, but I spilled most of my first mouthful onto my chin and my filthy shirt. Seeing my embarrassment, Rafaelo slowly raised his own can to his mouth, with his eyes fixed on mine, as if demonstrating a physical principle to a child, and then took a long drink, with his prominent Adam's apple wagging. Hector laughed. I think they assumed we were primitive villagers, which wasn't so far off the mark. No matter. Seela and I successfully emulated Rafaelo, and the beer was indeed welcome.

I'd been so anxious about getting a ride that I'd hardly noticed how thirsty and hungry I was, but now I could gainsay my hunger no more.

"Food *por favor*?" I inquired.

"*Tamales*," said Maya.

With an auspicious rustle, she extracted larval shapes from a box on the floor—corn husks wrapped around cornmeal patties with shredded pork in the middle, a food not wholly unlike things I'd eaten in Virginia. Gratefully, Seela and I ate several tamales, and Arf got one too, nearly choking on it, as he insisted on swallowing the thing in one gulp. Brumble began to nurse. Little Tomás watched in fascination.

"You coming north from Belize?" Hector asked, pointing at Seela and me. "Long trip."

"*Si*," I said, glad to have a ready explanation for our origin. We were to be impoverished immigrants from, I surmised, a country called Belize. But Seela felt the need to correct Hector.

"We're from the Hollow Earth," she said. "*La Tierra Hueca.*" Why did she have to make things so hard? But it was fine.

"*Fantastico*," Rafaelo said, as if he'd heard of the Hollow Earth. And with that, we let the topic go. Seela and I were destitute non-white immigrants, we spoke a little Spanish, we were their guests, and that was enough.

And so we traveled on, past the intense ink-blue sea, the round green hills, and the dry red rocks. Seela made much of little Frida and Tomás, and the Mexicans showered kindnesses upon Brumble. They kept asking Seela to say his name again, as her pronunciation made them laugh.

Houses and business establishments began appearing beside the road, low flimsy structures with large windows. Metal wagons like ours were stationed in front of them, like hitched horses. The wagons were called cars and trucks. They were everywhere. We saw very few people on foot. The pedestrians carried small rectangular objects that they stared at all the time. They seemed dazed. They wore bright clothes, with colored shoes. On their heads they had skullcaps with projecting bills.

The road widened to hold more cars and trucks, racing in both directions at insane speeds. Large green signs with instructions appeared on poles beside the roads, and on mighty horizontal bars overhead. The road's surface had changed to featureless gray stone with lines painted on it. Other roads crossed over our road by way of improbably huge viaducts that roared with echoes. Poles lined the roads, bearing sets of black wires.

A town slid by on our left, and another on our right, each of them a congeries of dun, shoddy houses, with low, sloping roofs. Unaccountable gargantuan stores were amid the houses, with short, meaningless words written large upon their sides. People teemed in and out of the stores like swarming gnats. We passed a crooked hotel by the sea, as ugly and unornamented as the homes.

The flow of cars grew heavier as we approached Santa Cruz, and the drivers more agitated. Continually our car blasted strident music that sounded sad even when it was supposed to be merry. I felt desperate and lost. Seela and I held hands and silently comforted each other via tekelili. Still more beige buildings flew by, with their crude blank walls and moronic signs. The future was horrible. We were marooned in a shoddy, overcrowded hell.

The ocean appeared again on our left. The high cliffs were gone. I glimpsed boats. Aida veered off the busy highway into a quieter street. Blessedly she slowed down. It was late afternoon. I saw a woman walking a tiny dog on a red leather leash. The woman's dark hair was dyed in stripes of yellow. She was staring at one of those shiny rectangular items in her hand.

"You get out here now?" Aida asked us.

"I don't know," said Seela, nearly in tears. "We don't know what we're doing at all. I'm scared."

"We'll be fine," I said, manfully taking Brumble on my shoulder. "Thanks for the ride."

"You don't got papers, do you?" said kind Rafaelo. "We're the same. You can stay with us."

"*Bene*," I said, shaky with relief.

"Only for a short time," said Aida, casting a stern look over her shoulder.

"Month, two month, three month," said the mellow Hector.

"And you find work," Aida told me. "Put money in the pot."

"Yes, yes," said Seela. "We will. Thank you, oh, thank you."

"And Mason can tell me about the *Tierra Hueca*," said Rafaelo. To some extent he was joking, but I could also sense true curiosity.

13. Impostor

So our Mexican friends brought us to the small, rented house that they shared, low and tan, in the sandy flats near the mouth of a small river, and near a fantastical outdoor amusement park that Maya called the Boardwalk. A great wheel in the park was turning, and small carts with people were rolling along a high track. A tower with lever arms was swinging people in the air. I'd never seen such large machines.

"It's open?" I asked Maya, wanting to go over there and explore—as if I hadn't had thrills enough this week, and as if I wasn't totally disgusted with the clangor of twenty eighteen. But, remember, I was seventeen, and the idea of a pleasure park had some appeal. But wait, I'd decided to start saying I was eighteen, as my February 2, 2018, birthday had been last month. On the other hand, I'd skipped over nine months, along with those 167 years, so—

"Yes, the Boardwalk's open today," said Maya, interrupting my number thoughts. "Sunday. Not on work days. And it closes in an hour. So never mind. Look at our house."

"You sleep here," said Hector, pointing to a large open shed adjoining their house. A stable for cars, I supposed. But they called it a garage. A well-used mattress lay on the floor at the back of the car stable. The walls were of an odd kind of wood, exceedingly thin, as if pressed flat by rollers. A lifeless machine stood near the front of the stable. It had two great rubber wheels, like those on a car, and an oily engine of some kind between the wheels. Shiny, opulent white fenders shielded the wheels. A seat cushion rested above a teardrop-shaped tank, with a pillion cushion behind. Presumably two people could sit astride the cushions and ride. It seemed very dangerous and impractical. To make the machine still odder, it had a one-wheeled pod attached to the right side, an open passenger compartment with its own small windshield and a cushion on the floor. Its wheel, too, had a curved white fender.

"My sidecar motorcycle," said Hector. "I got this rig from my cousin cause the engine *no mas* run. I dream I fix it."

"I can help," I said, wanting to make myself agreeable. My friends had resurrected a comatose flying saucer. Maybe I could do the same for a broken motorcycle.

"Let's go in and chill," said Maya, leading the way.

The first miracle was that Aida pushed a switch on the wall, and the room was filled with light. From a fixture on the ceiling. Gas? No, the light came from a small, frosted glass bulb that seemed to have a tiny sun inside it.

"E-lec-tri-ci-ty," said Maya, laughing at my expression. "*Tu sabe?*"

The house had virtually no furniture, just a lumpy divan, a mattress in each of the two bedrooms, a spindly table, and six diverse folding chairs made of lightweight metal tubes and with woven straps of a material I'd never seen.

The second miracle was that the house had water running from metal fixtures—and hot water as well, not to mention an indoor water-filled bowl in place of an outhouse. Seela and I flushed it five or ten times in a row, fascinated to see the vortex go spiraling down, carrying the little mock boats of tissue that we set upon it for drama.

One would have expected a house like this to very lavishly furnished, but the inside walls lacked cornices or framed paintings. In lieu of this, the blank walls were decorated with crude, hand-made representations of rattlesnakes, cactuses, stone gods, and what must have been a Mexican flag. "I make these," said Maya with pride. "The landlady don't know."

"Will she throw you out?" I asked.

"Hard to evict someone in Santa Cruz," said Rafaelo. "Even us illegals."

"What are the chairs made of?" I asked. "Those flat straps."

"This *vato* is from nowhere," said mother Aida, eyeing me. "You lived in a hut and pounded a log and ate bananas in Belize, Mason?"

"I myself lived on a flower," said Seela, always one for circling back to her origins. "In the Hollow Earth."

"*Loco*," said Hector.

"Plastic," Rafaelo said to me, running his hand along the yellow straps on one of the chairs. "Everywhere. Not plant, not leather, not metal. From factories in China. Our coats and shoes—plastic too. Everywhere. Like Spiderman."

"I don't like plastic," said Seela decisively.

"Don't matter," said Maya. "You in California, baby. Look here, everybody. I got still more tamales!"

We sat in the plastic chairs and ate the rest of the food. Arf got a tamale too. The beer was gone, so we drank water. In plastic cups. Tomás toddled around, and Frida crawled, the two of them accepting scraps of tamale from their parents. Tomás liked to wrap his arms around Frida and pick her up, and then she'd yell in rage. Excited by the sound of other kids, Brumble waved his arms and gurgled. And then Seela nursed him while Maya nursed Frida, who was by now nearly weaned.

The Mexicans told us about their jobs. Aida was a maid at a nearby place named the Clearlight Court Motel. Hector worked at a small restaurant called Los Trancos Taco Bar. Rafaelo was a cleaner in a building in downtown Santa Cruz. And Maya sold jewelry in a craft shop called Sparkle Wow.

"Some of them like to hire illegals and pay us under the table," said Aida. I didn't know what she meant by this. Were Seela and I illegals?

"You can work at Sparkle Wow with me," Maya was telling Seela.

"That's good," said Seela, brightening. "I can make jewelry for them."

"If Josh lets you," said Maya with a shrug. "He's the owner. Thinks he knows a lot. I painted a mural on his garage, but he didn't pay me none. He's one who takes advantage of illegals. He makes a lot of the stuff he sells. And he likes the girls. So we've got that good old pussy power on our side."

"Charming turn of phrase," I said, feeling uneasy.

"What about a job for you, Mason?" said Aida.

"I'd like to write," I said. "For a newspaper."

Aida guffawed. "A barefoot illegal from Belize, and you want a job like that?"

"My English is excellent," I said. "My penmanship is very fine."

"So let Mason try," said Rafaelo. "A new voice, *verdad*? The building where I clean, the newspaper office is there. The *Good Times*. I bring you there tomorrow, Mason, and you push in and talk *excelente* and you ask to write for them. People are crazy in Santa Cruz. The editor might say yes."

"*Si, si*, but Mason still needs shoes," said Aida. "You got so much shoes, Rafaelo. Give shoes to him."

"Air Jordan," said Rafaelo. "Twenty fifteen model. Very sharp for you, Mason."

"And take clothes from our heaps!" said Hector, waving his hand toward the mounds on the floor and at the stuffed double closet by the front door. "For *donnas y hombres*. Mason and Seela. Pick coats for sleep in garage."

Rafaelo's shoes fit me. They were huge and red. Seela selected tight, lime green pants, a blouse with large purple flowers, a puffy pale blue plastic jacket, and some furry pink slippers that were almost like shoes. I got a black sweatshirt, that is, a long-sleeved shirt with no buttons and no collar, and a matching pair of black sweatpants, plus a puffy plastic silver jacket similar to Seela's. Also a black cap with a bill, and the number forty-nine on the cap.

As the early sunset wound down, Hector, Rafaelo, Seela and I kicked around a yellow plastic ball in the front of the house. It was a game of sorts, with the idea being to kick the ball into the stable where we were to sleep. Arf sleepily watched us from our mattress, where he'd already settled in.

Afterwards Hector played the trumpet—wielding his long, thin horn with some skill. Maya and Rafaelo sang along, and then Aida joined, and then Seela and I, feeling our way through the Spanish lyrics. The music sounded better live than from the control panel of a car. We sang for a long time.

Hector and Aida went to bed with little Tomás, and Maya lay down with little Frida at her breast, and after that, Rafaelo showed me and Seela his great treasure, a piece of black glass that showed moving images of monsters fighting women and men. At first I thought the creatures were alive inside the device—perhaps via a woomo trick of space and time—but they were only pictures. The toy also emitted the sounds of roars, shouts and explosions.

"I dream someday I'll build games like this," Rafaelo told us with a faraway look. "If I can learn the tricks."

"You could make a game about the *Tierra Hueca*," I speculated. "Maybe the woomo can help."

Rafaelo continued playing with his toy, which quickly grew tedious for Seela and me. We bundled up and went to lie on our mattress with Brumble. He sneezed once and yawned. We had one of the *woomo* shawls wrapped around him. I'd worried the mattress might be damp, but it was dry, and we went to sleep right away.

At some point during the night Uxa woke me. It started as a dream. I saw a crooked ray of pink light creep in through our stable's open door—and lay hair-thin fronds across my body, with special attention to my spine and the back of my neck.

I sat bolt upright on the mattress, looking around, and, yes, I was seeing the pink main branch of the ray. It was subtler in color than in my dream, but it was real, and Uxa was wordlessly speaking to me. She showed me an image of myself on a pedestal, haloed in glory, a mighty avatar, an idol of the human race. A lure for my vanity. Lest I dream of escape, Uxa added a motion sequence image that showed how her tendrils had been tracking Seela and me ever since our sojourn upon the slick, rubbery mesas of her body at the Gate.

Thanks to the loss of the Big Sur rumbies, the Bloom wasn't going to work. The *woomo* could of course transport more rumbies to the surface. But, for whatever reason, they wanted me to be involved. And I couldn't tell how.

Did Uxa want me to drive the pugnacious farmer ants from the Big Sur cave? Was I to recruit a corps of human volunteers for the Bloom? Was I on a quest for Eddie Poe and the missing rumbies?

Uxa wasn't one to reveal her long-range plans—if she had any. Perhaps she lived only in the now. She urged me to my feet, and showed me an image of myself fixing the engine of Hector's motorcycle.

My hands were glowing. I was a channel for Uxa's *woomo* energy. I rose to my feet. Seela and Brumble continued sleeping, but Arf got up to watch. Just to test my powers, I touched my forefinger to his nose—and his fur puffed out like dandelion fluff. He gave me an accusing look, then backed away and shook himself, settling his hair into place.

I walked quietly to the sidecar motorcycle, which rested at the car stable's entrance like a stilled insect. The three-quarters-full moon was in the west, sending glints off the fuel tank of the three-wheeled machine. My mind filled with diagrams of the motorcycle's odd engine, and of the toothy gears it wore upon the axle of its rear wheel. Yes, I knew how to put this particular type of engine into working order. Whence came the knowing? Uxa showed an image of a dexterous motorcycle groom, sleeping with his tattooed wife in a low home not so far away. Within easy reach of *woomo* tekelili.

Playing on my longing for renown, Uxa fed me a blasphemous image of myself in the role of a robed Messiah, raising a dead man by the laying on of hands. The corpse was Hector's motorcycle. I stepped forward. Jagged fronds grew from my fingertips and fed into the oily crannies of the engine's innards. White hot sparks sputtered within. I had a sense of things merging and dividing. And then—Uxa's will was accomplished. I cried out in a loud voice.

"Rise, Lazarus, and sin no more!"

Understand that I said this in jest. I've never had much truck with religion. But I'd read the Bible back on the farm, and I liked the language and the strange tales. Giddy with exultation, I sat atop the motorcycle, twisted the grips on its steering bar, and used my foot to pump a sturdy lever on the thing's side. The engine popped and roared. Arf watched these things in wonder and kept them in his heart.

"The fuck you doin? Turn it off!"

It was Rafaelo, sleepily peering from the side door that led into the garage. Uxa had released her hold over me, but even so, I knew how to kill the engine. The sudden silence was deafening.

"I fixed it," I told Rafaelo, getting off my seat.

"How?" said he, greatly doubting me.

"Secrets of the Hollow Earth. Giant sea cucumbers. Crooked rays of light."

"What you smokin, dog? Go to sleep. I'll take you to my job tomorrow. Crack of early."

I woke to the sound of the motorcycle, farting and growling, its voice rising to a snarl. Hector sat astride it, turning the grip on the handle, greatly pleased.

"Aida!" he called. "We ride to work!"

She appeared in the garage, with very little paint on her face, wearing plain blue clothes, her hair in a bun, and her body the shape of a potato—ready for her day as a maid at the Clearlight Court Motel. She'd parked their son Tomás with an old lady next door.

"*Que pasa?*" she asked.

"Mason fixed the motorcycle," said Rafaelo.

"Mason da man!" yelled Hector, beaming at me. "*Bueno, amigo.*"

Aida blew me a juicy kiss, put a hand on Hector's shoulder and, rather than sitting in the low sidecar, swung her leg over the pillion cushion and wrapped her arms around proud Hector's waist. "*Andale.*"

With a concussive roar, the creamy white sidecar motorcycle pulled onto the street and sped away.

Arf barked, by way of punctuation. Brumble wailed. Seela sat up. "You did something?" she asked me.

"I'm the man," I told her.

"We gotta go to my building now," Rafaelo told me. "And, Seela, you can go with Maya when she wakes up."

"Fine," said Seela drinking some water and lying back down with Brumble. She was still tired. "Good luck, Mason."

We were close to downtown Santa Cruz, so Rafaelo and I walked. Today he was wearing a long-sleeved dark-red shirt with white shoulders. Black piping separated the shoulder yoke from the lower part. After his own fashion, Rafaelo was a well-dressed man.

I looked around the streets with interest, avidly taking them in. It was nicer to be on foot than in a car. As we crossed a busy street, Rafaelo stopped at a brightly colored food shop with large windows and thin walls. The shop's name was written in yellow letters in dozens of places on the walls, and on the plastic clothes of the employees, but somehow the name didn't stick in my mind. They had music inside the shop. Rafaelo bought us coffee and paper-wrapped buns with ham and scrambled eggs in the middle. Very welcome. The coffee was in paper cups.

Then we entered an older part of the town, with normal-looking buildings of brick and stone, although the street-level shop fronts were almost entirely glass. Signs were everywhere, with big, screaming letters. I couldn't understand what some of the shops sold. The short words on the signs didn't always make sense.

Fog shrouded the sky, and the sounds were muted. I noticed three people riding on velocipedes—metal frames with spoked wheels that they turned by pressing levers with their feet. Rafaelo called them bicycles. I'd once seen an engraving of a Parisian velocipede in the *Southern Literary Messenger*, but I'd never seen one in person.

The women wore their hair loose or in ponytails, and hardly anyone had a proper hat—just those foolish billed caps like the one on my head. Over and over I muttered the year number to myself. *Twenty eighteen.* Surely I was in a different world, but the people seemed, in their essence, much the same as in eighteen fifty. Beggars, ladies, men of the world, dunderheads, poets, merchants, termagants, coquettes—all the usual types were here. A surprise and a relief.

I hoped Seela was getting along well with Maya. And that they'd tethered Arf at the house. And that Maya's boss didn't mind that Seela would be bringing Brumble to work. Maya had said she often brought Frida, at least for part of the day, although sometimes she'd leave her with the old lady who was watching Tomás.

Rafael's building was a pile of granite, several stories high. We went in by a back door, where Rafael changed into a drab work uniform of beige pants and shirt. And then he equipped himself with a rolling bucket, a rolling trashcan, and a cart with rags and mops. His first task of the day would be to swab and polish the building's six bathrooms. I felt disheartened that that my clever, personable friend was relegated to so humble a role—in part because he lacked proper papers. Surely he sensed my feelings, and was himself in some measure abashed, but he covered it over with his fine good humor.

"You help me, Mason, and we work our way to the top, and you meet the big man at the *Good Times* newspaper."

Six bathrooms later, Rafaelo ushered me into the offices of the *Good Times*. A woman named Janelle greeted us. She wore black pants and a flowing blue blouse with white dots. Her face was sensual and a bit rough-skinned, with a layer of oily beige paint, and with her lips colored very red. This was, as I'd already noticed on Aida yesterday, an ordinary practice in the year twenty eighteen.

Janelle knew Rafaelo, and she seemed to find him attractive.

"*Hola,*" said he. "My homie Mason wants to talk to the boss."

"About?" Janelle was looking me over—black-skinned in my black sweatpants and sweatshirt, with my puffy silver coat, my enormous red shoes, and a billed hat with the number forty-nine. It struck me, in this fraught moment, that the forty-nine might be a symbol for that epochal California Gold Rush year.

"Mason's a writer," Rafaelo was saying. "He has a story about someplace weird."

"Weird is good," said Janelle agreeably. "And Noah's not especially busy right now. All he does before lunch is read email."

The editor Noah Blanker was relaxed and genial. He wore a silky shirt the like of which I'd never seen—it was pale blue with pink and green spirals and an enormous floppy collar. He spoke very slowly, almost as if he were talking in his sleep, but this was a conversational stratagem. His eyes were alert. He invited me to tell him my idea for a story, then leaned back in his chair and listened, beginning to smile as I went on.

I outlined the narrative of my first trip to the Hollow Earth. This was easy for me, given that only about four months of my personal time had elapsed since I'd finished writing *The Hollow Earth*, my book-length manuscript about my trip—which manuscript I'd foolishly left with E. J. Coale in Baltimore, 1850. But I digress. Quickly I told Noah Blanker of my trip to the antarctic with Poe, our fall through the South Hole, our encounter with the *woomo* at the Hollow Earth's core, and our return through an ocean hole in the Rind near Baltimore.

"Awesome rap," said Noah when I finally paused. "Like a happy dream. But it has nothing to do with Santa Cruz."

"I could mention that living flying saucers from the Hollow Earth have recently spawned babies in a Big Sur cave," I blithely said. As I spoke, I felt an unpleasant twinge in my spine, as if to say: *Don't talk about that.* Uxa was still watching me.

Noah Blanker was shaking his head. "No saucers," said he. "The Hollow Earth is enough. Think harder, Mason. Find a local hook, and I'll run your piece day after tomorrow. I need two thousand words."

"I—I've never counted words," I said, a little confused.

"You can learn," drawled Blanker. "You're a bright kid." He paused, studying me. "I do have one question. You talk like a white guy in a historical movie. But you look black, you're dressed like you're homeless, and it's our Latino custodian Rafaelo who brought you in. How do the pieces fit?"

"May I speak without artifice?" I said.

"Lay it on me, dude." How curiously this man spoke!

"My Hollow Earth narratives are veridical," I said. "And I am in fact white. I was burned black by the light of the *woomo* at the Hollow Earth's core. I'm from the Virginia of 1850. I lost over a century and a half in an eddy of slow time."

"The *woomo*," said Noah Blanker with a bark of laughter. "I love how you stay in character. Maybe you can turn your routine into a book." He paused, thinking. "Find the damn hook and write your piece by tomorrow morning. Tuesday. Our weekly issue comes out on Wednesday. And we've got a two-thousand-word hole. Tracy Ting was writing a piece on this year's surf scene, but then she took off for Tonga with a pro surfer she met."

"Will you pay me?"

"Peanuts," said Blanker. "A hundred bucks. But if your story works out, you can do a sequel next month and I'll pay you two hundred for that one. But, remember: you've gotta find a local hook."

"You mention surfing," I slowly said. "I believe I saw surfing on Saturday. People stand on lozenge-shaped boards and slide down the faces of ocean waves."

"You got *that* right, spaceman."

"In the Hollow Earth, we use lozenges of ballula shell to coast upon the heated air around giant moving streams of light. We call these lozenges lightboards. And the rays are from the *woomo*."

"Lightsurfing!" exclaimed Noah Blanker. "Perfect. Love, love, love those *woomo*. Your title is *Lightsurfing the Hollow Earth*. Now go write the rest."

"Might I petition for a partial advance payment of my fee?"

Blanker chuckled. I think he relished his recklessness in trusting me. "Here's two twenties," he said, handing them across the desk. My heart sang.

I went downstairs and found Rafaelo buffing a hallway floor.

"Noah Blanker is buying a story about the Hollow Earth!" I exulted. "It'll be in the *Good Times* on Wednesday."

"No way!" said Rafaelo. "You're magic, Mason. You fix Hector's motorcycle and you sell a story to a white newspaper. You gonna program my Hollow Earth videogame too?"

"Not today," I said. "I need to draft my narrative."

"Buy a pad of paper and a pen. There's a store right down the street. Palace Art. Then you go sit somewhere. A coffee shop, or the library."

"A library? That would be wonderful. I've never seen one."

"It's somewhere near here. I don't know exactly. You got money for the pen and paper?"

"Noah Blanker gave me forty dollars," I said, showing him my bills. "I get sixty more when the article comes out."

"*Fantastico*. You the goose who lay the golden egg! We'll buy us *carnitas* meat and a case of *cerveza* for tonight, *si*? Case is twenty-four cans."

"*Bueno*. But should I go and see if Seela and Brumble are safe before I start writing?"

"They'll be at Sparkle Wow with Maya till five. You go to the library, *vato*. Settle in. Then come meet me here at five."

"*Adios*," I said.

It was difficult for me to purchase the paper and the pen. Even opening the store's swinging glass door was a problem, and then I had no idea what a pen might look like here, nor how it would work, nor how a notebook of blank paper might be packaged. A kind young clerk came to my aid, a woman not much older than me. She wore a name tag that that read Shelly.

I completed the purchase, watching attentively as Shelly blinked numbers onto a glass rectangle and extracted change from a rolling drawer that was set into a chunk of machinery. Wanting to impress Shelly, I said I was going to the library to write an article about the Hollow Earth for the *Good Times* weekly newspaper.

"That's nice," said Shelly, her neutral smile flattening into a tense line. She thought I was a liar or a madman. She pitied and feared me. As she gave me directions to the library, her voice was a cold monotone.

One of the librarian ladies was leery of me as well. This was a Mary Bisby, who sat at a counter near the door. I felt she disliked my presence because my clothes were shabby and my skin was dark—and I told myself that white attitudes toward blacks hadn't changed much since eighteen fifty. This said, after I'd worked quietly for an hour, Mary Bisby switched to giving me approving nods. In her eyes I was bettering myself.

And so I wrote away in my notebook, using a fine hand so Noah Blanker would find my submission pleasant to read. "Lightsurfers of the Hollow Earth," yes. I remembered my original *Hollow Earth* narrative very vividly, and I was able to quote key phrases from it, which helped me compose at a rapid pace.

Even more—and this is a bit hard to explain—I had by now a sense that I'd already written the bulk of my new narrative *Return to the Hollow Earth*. Admittedly I hadn't yet scribed any of it in pen and ink. But, as I've mentioned, I'd been composing it in my head during the past three or four months of lived time. And all along I'd had a tekelili sense that I was somehow dictating my narrative to an unseen being. And while we were becalmed at the core of the Hollow Earth, I'd realized that my listener was in fact Uxa. The great *woomo* had a record of my whole composition thus far. It struck me that Uxa might here and now be prevailing upon some third party to commit my narrative to paper. Someone in California twenty eighteen. I did enjoy doing the writing myself, but having an astral secretary would certainly be handy.

But just now I was on my own, writing the old-fashioned way, leaning over blank paper pages and inscribing letters with my peculiar futuristic pen. Every now and then my fingers would cramp, and I'd wander among the shelves and look at the books. What a treasure trove! The art, science, history, and literature of my lost hundred and sixty seven years were ranged here for my education and delectation. If Seela and I were to settle in Santa Cruz, I would read hundreds of these books.

As I continued writing in my notebook, I felt the same creative ecstasy as when I'd written out my *Hollow Earth* manuscript, and I vaingloriously thought to myself that really I had no need to read other people's books, nor did I need further schooling. What with my unparalled adventures, and with the metaphysical illuminations I'd experienced amid the *woomo* at the Hollow Earth's core, and with my mental vision of *Return to the Hollow Earth* nearly done—with all this in hand, I was a genius complete—an author on a par with Eddie Poe. I grinned as I wrote.

By the time it occurred to me to estimate my count of words, I found I'd amassed six thousand. I flipped through my pages, X-ing out blocks of text and condensing the more florid descriptions. And then I had it down to three thousand words. That would do. I still needed to make a fair copy of what I had, but by now the sun was sinking, and the large, humming clock on the wall said it was nearly five, so I went to meet Rafaelo.

He changed back into his handsome clothes, and we had a fine fiesta at their home. Seela was in a good mood. Josh at Sparkle Wow had not only been pleasant to Seela, he'd allowed her to create two of her networked necklaces of wires and geegaws, and one of them had already sold. Seela liked Josh, and she matter-of-factly told me she could make him fall in love with her.

"Why do you say that?" I cried. "To make me jealous?"

"I'm going to find a way to stay here," said Seela. "Even if you're crazy enough to fly off in a *veem*. I can tell you're thinking about it. You don't fool me one bit."

"Let's wait and see what happens," I said, a little put out. "Don't you go jumping into bed with that man right away. Relationships work a little differently here than they did among your Hollow Earth flower tribe."

"No they don't," said Seela, turning sly and worldly. "They're just the same." Impudently she extended her forefinger and pushed it in and out of a loop she made with the thumb and forefinger of her other hand. "See?"

"If we split up, who keeps Brumble?" I asked.

"Let's wait and see what happens," said Seela, smugly echoing me. She dandled the baby on her lap. Our shared treasure.

I sat up late and made my fair copy of my condensed article, working by the light of our Mexican hosts' wondrous lightbulb.

Tuesday morning I gave Noah Blanker my article, and he took a photo of me to run with it. I spent the rest of Tuesday walking around town with Arf and Brumble while Seela worked at Sparkle Wow. I even managed to buy a sandwich and bring it in to Seela when it was time for her to nurse the baby. The new necklace-nets she was making were glorious. I didn't get a chance to size up her boss Josh. He hadn't come in for work yet.

My article was to appear in the *Good Times* with a photo of me on Wednesday morning. By the time I rose on Wednesday, Rafaelo had gone to work. I left Brumble with Seela and walked over to Noah Blanker's office with Arf. I planned to get my copy of the paper, and to claim the sixty dollars they still owed me. Arf ran to Rafaelo on the bottom floor and I went upstairs. Noah's assistant Janelle wasn't at the front desk. Peering out from his office, Noah waved me in.

He was frowning. He'd just spoken to the assiduous Mary Bisby, the librarian who on Monday had observed me writing my article in her common room. La Bisby had noticed my picture next my article this morning. Doubting my honesty, she'd canvassed her shelves for an alternate source of my material. And, oh woe, she'd found a narrative entitled *The Hollow Earth*, and attributed to a local author named Rudy Rucker.

In a trice, the spiteful Bisby had convinced herself that my "Lightsurfing the Hollow Earth" was copied from Rucker's volume—and she'd hastened to pour her poison into Noah Blanker's ear. I was a plagiarist.

"It's not plagiarism," I told Noah after he'd explained this to me. "I myself wrote *The Hollow Earth*. In 1850. It's my account of what actually happened. My name is in the book, Mason Reynolds. It's abundantly clear. Somehow my manuscript found its way to Rucker's hands. You may say he's the author, but he's only the editor."

"Doubling down on your lies, eh?" said Noah, his expression stern. "You're a plagiarist *and* an imposter. Not only did you copy from the book, you claim you're a character from it. *Mason Reynolds*. What a total crock of shit."

"You'll withdraw my article?"

"Too late for that," said Noah with a shrug. "The paper's in stacks in shops and on street corners all over town. I'll run an apology next week." His eyes were sad. "Too bad it worked out this way, Mason. Or whatever your name is. I'd thought this would be fun."

"Can I have my sixty dollars now?"

He glared, then fished out his wallet. "Obviously you need it." He handed me three twenties. "Now beat it. We're done."

As I rose to my feet, Noah's assistant Janelle came into the office, sipping a cup of coffee she'd bought herself. "Oh, good, Mason's still here. I wasn't sure. I got a written message for you this morning, Mason. This skungy street person brought it to the office."

"Can I see the note?" I asked. "Who's it from?"

"You don't have to help him," Noah told Janelle. "He's a con-man. The librarian says he copied his article. And he's not even Mason Reynolds."

"He's still kind of cute," said Janelle. "I like how he always wears the same clothes." She was making fun of me, a little bit.

"Like that guy in AC/DC," said Noah, his gloom slightly lifting. "The one who always wore the schoolboy uniform? Angus? I saw AC/DC play at the Cow Palace when I was in the eleventh grade. It was the absolute high point of my life. The women in the audience, Janelle. Beyond all dreams."

"Old much?" said Janelle.

Would I ever learn to banter like the overlords of twenty eighteen? "Did you save the piece of paper?" I pressed Janelle. "With the message?"

"I think so," she said carelessly. "Somewhere on my desk. It's cuckoo jive-talk and it's signed Edgar Allan Poe. Supposedly Poe wants you to meet him at the Evergreen Cemetery. Oh, and he needs clothes."

For a moment Noah looked intrigued. But then he shook his head. "I'm guessing our young author wrote the message himself," he said. "And he had one of his skeevy pals bring it to you. Step lively, *Mason*. Don't let the door hit you in the ass on the way out." Janelle and I exited.

In the front office, Janelle handed me my message—it was handwritten in dark pencil on a thick, dirty scrap of paper, yellow with age. The writing was unmistakably Eddie's—as was the style and, above all, the content.

Greetings Mason. It is I, the penitent Poe. Ina and I have lain in wait for one hundred and forty one years while Fwopsy sought her mate. The rumbies are ours. Their forces have preserved us like royal pharaohs. And the villain Machree is no more. Roused by *woomo* tekelili, Ina and I hail your and your lady's advent, o new Adam and Eve, o scions of the Bloom. Ina and I sit amid foul, unclean shrouds, windings, and cerements in the Evergreen Cemetery dell. Bring us raiment and, in the name of God, bring cake and brandy. Make haste, I beseech you. With heartfelt rue, Edgar Allan Poe / Goarland Peale

Pure Eddie. Keeping a straight face, I repressed a shout of joy, and shoved the scrap into my pocket. "Stuff and nonsense," I muttered to Janelle. "But, yes, I'll go. I have, as you may surmise, little else on my agenda. Can you direct me to the Evergreen Cemetery?"

"Sure," said Janelle, glancing over at Noah's closed door. "But you really do need to leave. I've hardly ever seen Noah so mad. And there is zero chance of him buying another article from you. You need to internalize that."

Janelle conjured an image onto the glass screen she had on her desk. The glowing map made little sense to me. Janelle pecked at a row of keys. A white plastic box beside her desk whirred, then spit out a warm, typeset sheet of paper with walking instructions. Janelle said it wouldn't take me more than a half an hour.

"But maybe you should wait for night?" she added with a puckish smile. "I mean, for meeting ghosts in a graveyard?"

"I don't believe in ghosts," I said, trying to salvage some dignity. "I'm a rational man."

"Of course you are," said Janelle, holding her lips tight, lest she laugh in my face.

14. Reunion

I'd risen so late that by the time I left the *Good Times* office it was nearly noon. To my relief, Rafaelo was willing to accompany me and Arf to the cemetery. I was very uneasy about what I might find. Rafaelo replaced his dull dun work uniform with his bright, joyful clothes, and he walked across town with me, eating an extra egg sandwich he had along. Today he wore black leather pants with shiny medallions along the outer seams, and a red and gray shirt with piping, pearl buttons, and embroidered dots and whorls. Atop his head he sported a stiff, white straw hat with a brim.

Using my new money, we purchased two used sweatsuits, a bottle of brandy, and a small chocolate cake. Rafaelo got a packet of those thin white paper cigars as well. Cigarettes. He offered me one. It made me cough, and dizzied me in a pleasant way.

"Pop the cap," said Rafaelo, pointing at the brandy bottle, with cigarette smoke drifting from his lips like liquid. "I'm not goin back to work today at all."

"Very well," I said. We each drank a slug. More coughing, more dizziness. I felt calm.

We crossed a wide road roaring with cars. A subtle system of colored lights indicated when we could cross. I had to bend over and lead the uneasy Arf by the scruff of his neck lest he run off.

On the other side of the road was a gravel pit, and some flimsy, beige stores with big windows. We kept walking, and came to a field with white lines on it, and then to a steep, sodden hill covered with enormous trees. Redwoods. A low iron fence ran along the bottom of the hill, with tilted, mossy gravestones and funerary monuments within. I saw two pale, bedraggled figures seated on a low cement wall beneath an immense laurel tree. I could smell them from across the street, rank and wild. Arf sniffed deeply at the air, tasting the intricacies of the high, thin reek.

"That's your friends?" Rafaelo asked me. "They look *malo.*"

Eddie tried to call to us, but his voice was so wispy I couldn't make it out. And he could barely wave his hand. He was dirty and naked, with a flattish silver box beside him, a box the size of a thick book.

"Mason," husked Ina, her voice very rough. Her hair hung down, long and lank. "You're still young. What year is it?"

"Twenty eighteen," said I,

"Don't know what that means," said Ina, very wretched. "The sun—still here. Pale and lost." She dropped her head and her shoulders shook. She was sobbing. Poor, poor thing. Her skin had turned as white as the flesh of a mushroom. She was clad in greasy scraps of shroud from the tomb.

I made my way up the low stone stairs to where she and Eddie sat, and I offered Ina a pink Goodwill sweatsuit. She waved it off.

"I need to bathe," said she. "I'm foul."

"There's a hose," said Rafaelo. "I'll get it." Quickly he had water running through a rubber tube from a metal fixture like I'd seen in their house. A faucet.

Ina drank, then played the stream across herself and Eddie. The two of them rubbed their bodies, groaning with relief, showering water across their eyes, mouths, noses, and ears; gargling and spitting, washing their crotches and armpits and feet and hair. The wet grass sparkled; the drops twinkled against the sharp, sour green.

"Thank you, old friend," croaked Eddie, accepting the yellow sweatsuit I had for him. He rubbed himself with it, then pulled it on. His hair, like Ina's, was nasty, dank, and disturbingly long. His fingernails had grown out and curled over. He had a scraggly beard. He was the very image of a creature from his tales—a ghoul, a revenant, an undead corpse. He sensed me thinking this, and he smiled a bit, as if pleased to be so theatrically ghastly.

For whatever reason, we had a fair amount of tekelili here. Oh, of course—I now sensed that Eddies' rounded silver box was full of rumbies, close to a hundred of them, clacking against each other like massive marbles.

He reached out for the bottle of brandy. I uncapped it and he deeply drank. Taking out a pocket knife, Rafaelo cut slices of our cake. Ina snatched a piece, wolfed it down, then ate a second and a third, willfully smearing chocolate icing across her deathly pale face. She drank of the brandy as well—we all did. We shared a communion of spirits and cake.

"You two were buried here?" I said. "How did you emerge?

"Wormed through the tree," said Eddie, making an intricate, expressive gesture that encompassed the towering bay laurel in whose shade we sat. It had a hole in its bole, as if from rot. Fluttering his fingers, Eddie indicated that they'd crawled up through the tree's roots and into its hollow base, having started in—and this I saw via tekelili—a bronze double casket that lay six feet below the sun-splashed grass. I stepped over to read the inscription on the ornate free-standing gravestone. Their names were in bas-relief ovals amid stone ivy leaves.

INA DURIVAGE OF LOUISIANA
DIED JAN 19, 1877.
AGED 33 YEARS
<--->
GOARLAND PEALE, A BOSTONIAN
DIED JAN 19, 1877.
AGED 44 YEARS
<--->
"WHAT LAUGHING HEART HAS DIED IN VAIN"

"You copied the epitaph from my stone?" I exclaimed. "The grave of MirrorMason in Lynchburg, Virginia. He was shot by the MirrorEarth stableboy?"

"I'm aware of this," said Eddie. "I draw upon what comes to hand. When I designed this stone, you were present in my mind. I knew we'd see you when we rose."

"By what route did you enter the grave?"

"The burghers termed it *misadventure*," said Eddie. "Meaning suicide, presumably by laudanum. In truth we benumbed ourselves with the tekelili of our mass of rumbies, and we entered a state of life-in-death. I paid an undertaker in advance to see that we were interred intact in a shared bronze casket—which contained a secret sliding door of my own design."

"Your purposes are opaque, my liege."

"We hoped to be part of the Bloom," said Eddie, pausing to hawk up phlegm, and then to drink more brandy. "And we knew it would be a long wait. When we left you and returned to the Earth's surface, the year was 1862. Fwopsy dropped Ina and me in San Francisco, and proceeded onward with Machree and the rumbies, we knew not where."

"Did you see Machree again?"

"We saw him fifteen years later, said Ina. "More on that anon. Eddie and I spent the intervening years as performers. I treaded the boards as a spiritualist trance-speaker, declaiming poems and tales that I purported to channel from that lost literary titan, Edgar Allan Poe."

"And I posed as Ina's stout, fusty, clean-shaven, bespectacled manager, Goarland Peale," said Eddie. "I sat near the stage and fed her my words via tekelili. An efficacious diddle. But I tired of the work. It's dull, pleasing dullards."

"It's thanks to me that we worked our hoax for as long as we did," said Ina. "We carried it to London and Berlin, to Tokyo, Sydney, and Honolulu. During the seasons when Eddie was having his vapors and doldrums, I'd spout fresh bluster on my own. It's easy to beat a drum, once you find the stick." She rested a cool gaze upon Eddie. "I'm your equal, Goarland Peale."

"The vixen is a virago," said Eddie fondly. "An elfin Xanthippe."

Incongruously, Ina giggled. "We should have published a book of my verse. *Happy Poe.*"

"And we could have included *Htrae,*" said Eddie. "My blank-verse epic of the Hollow Earth. I formulated great swatches of it, Mason, and Ina declaimed them to the crowds."

"But he never wrote down a single word of it," said Ina. "Too bad. And then came the climax."

"We took possession of the long-lost rumbies—and murdered Connor Machree," said Eddie, drinking yet again from the brandy bottle. "He reappeared and sent us to a Big Sur cave to fetch the rumbies where he'd hidden them. Ina and I very nearly died in the process. We were set upon by vile white farmer ants who'd recently infested the cave. Machree himself was scared to go, you understand. I managed to throw the attacking ants into a trance, Ina and I carried the rumbies back to Santa Cruz. And then Machree made as if to claim them from us by force. Ina cozened him into bed, as if for old time's sake—and she slit his throat from ear to ear."

"Well done," said I, gladdened by the death of my stableboy rival.

"With the rumbies in our possession, our role in the coming Bloom was assured," said Ina. "Una told us this via tekelili. She said we had only to await the advent of Mason and Seela."

"But now loomed the noose," said Eddie. "Our murder was in no wise a perfect crime."

"And thus arrived in the year eighteen seventy-seven our season of hibernation," said Ina, pausing to drink more water from the steadily running hose. "And there in the double-sized bronze casket we lay. Awaiting Adam and Eve."

"Here am I," said I, smiling at my friends' tangled tale.

"But where is Seela?" asked Ina. "And the baby Brumble—is he well?"

"In the pink," I responded. "He's aged less than a week since you last saw him. He and Seela are nearby with Rafaelo's wife."

Eddie had managed to light one of Rafaelo's cigarettes. "Fine tobacco, my friend," said he. "Are you quite in Mason's confidence? Do you know of the Hollow Earth?"

"He tells me something about it," said Rafaelo. "The *Tierra Hueca*. Mason say maybe I can write a video game."

"A game, eh?" said Eddie, not at all grasping Rafaelo's point. His attention turned to the cheap, worn, yellow sweatsuit we'd given him. "Is this customary garb in the year twenty eighteen?"

"For poor people," said Rafaelo, laughing. He flicked a finger against the colorfully stitched collar of his shirt. "You have money, Eddie Poe? You want to buy sharp clothes like me?"

"I have magical, living gems," said Eddie, rattling his silver box. A thudding came from within. "The eggs of gods. Would you like to see?"

"Don't spill them," snapped Ina. "You're already drunk." She glanced at me. "That's the worst thing about Eddie. Over and over. I'm so tired of men. Do summon Seela, Mason. And tell her to bring scissors. We'll cut our nails and hair. And if she brings a razor I'll shave Eddie's beard."

"Or mayhap you'll slit my throat," said Eddie, narrowing his eyes in a manner meant to be jocose. But the grimace only made him look befuddled.

With a sudden gesture, Ina snatched the still half-full brandy bottle from Eddie and shattered it against their gravestone. Arf yelped in surprise.

For a moment nobody said anything, and then Ina spoke again, making her voice very calm, as if she were in full command of the situation, even though she was barefoot, emaciated, and quite pathetic. To all appearances, Ina and Eddie were homeless, unhealthy vagrants—like the others I'd already seen around Santa Cruz.

"Eat more cake," Ina was saying to Eddie. "The chocolate will bring you back. And smoke more of Rafaelo's tobacco." She turned to us. "For god's sake, get Seela."

"I can phone my wife Maya to bring her," said Rafaelo. "Maya can bring Seela here on the sidecar motorcycle. Hector left it at home."

We three relics from the past watched as Rafaelo produced one of those glassy black rectangles from his pocket. So-called phones, for speaking across distances. And supposedly these phones were in some sense smart as well. Rafaelo poked his and it lit up. He talked into it in Spanish, then returned it to his pocket. He smiled at us.

"In ten, fifteen minutes they come," he said. "Maya brings Seela and Brumble and our little Frida too. Also some cola and *hamburguesas. No mas* alcohol. We chilling."

Accepting that the brandy was gone, Eddie let the hose water run steadily into one side of his mouth, slopping out of the other side, as if rinsing himself out. He paused now and then to swallow water, and to retch. And then he ate some cake. Slowly the light of intelligence was returning to his eyes.

We sat on in silence for a time, watching a bluejay hop around on the grass, springy on his legs, pecking at the bright bits of broken glass. Crows cawed overhead, and a faint breeze rustled in the leaves. High afternoon fog was drifting in from the sea, dimming the sky.

Once in a while someone would drive by—a small truck with garbage in the back, a dirty sedan, a bigger truck carrying a machine. I wondered if the police might come. I'd seen a police car yesterday, and Rafaelo had warned me about it, as if telling a new fish about a shark. The police cars were black on the bottom and white on top. They might not like our looks. A Mexican in a fancy shirt, a black man in a sweatsuit (me), a dog, and two decrepit beggars. The five us sitting on the wall in the sun in an abandoned graveyard. Harmless and low. But bullies homed in on people like us. I'd seen that in the South.

A roar and a beep broke my foreboding mood. It was Maya aboard the white motorcycle, with Seela in the sidecar. Brumble and Frida were squeezed into the sidecar with Seela, perched side-by-side in a special little baby-carrier in front of Seela. A cute pair of human larvae. Maya hopped off and helped her passengers out of the sidecar. Frida was quacking in excitement. She wore a one-piece yellow terry suit with a zipper, and Brumble had a similar outfit in white with stripes of red. He looked very trim. They came to us, with Seela carrying Brumble. Maya was toting some rustling paper bags that she'd had behind Seela in the sidecar. How hale and normal these four looked.

"Eddie and Ina?" called Seela. "It's you? You've lain in the ground for all these years?"

"I'm sorry we abandoned you at the core," said Ina right away.

"We'll discuss that later," said Seela, overcome with pity for Ina just now. She rested her hand on Ina's shoulder. "You poor woman. Look at you. You buried yourself? Eddie Poe's idea, I'm sure."

"What an unalloyed joy it is to encounter Seela," put in Eddie, defensive and sarcastic. "My great admirer."

Seela shrugged this off. "Never a thought of reform, eh, you wretch? But this is no time to scold you, brought so low. Meet our friend Maya and her daughter Frida."

Maya was cautiously polite to Eddie and Ina—clearly she took them for derelicts who, for whatever reason, Rafaelo and I had taken under our wing. But she had a great reservoir of empathy. She drew out a comb and a pair of scissors, briskly snipping the scissors in the air. Frida danced around in excitement.

"Let's clean you up," Maya told Eddie and Ina. "Who goes first?"

"Me," said Ina, bowing her head. "These lank corpse strands—ghastly. Trim it down to a few inches, Maya. You're very kind."

The haircut only took a few minutes. And then Maya washed Ina's head with soap she'd filched from her workplace's bathroom. Eddie came under Seela's ministrations next. She had not in fact brought a razor, but she used her scissors to minimize Eddie's nasty beard, and to trim his mustache to seemly size. And then she dried their heads with paper towels. Our friends didn't look *good*, but they no longer looked dead. Keep in mind that, in terms of actual, lived, non-casket years, Ina and Eddie were aged but thirty-three and forty-four.

"*Fabuloso*," said Rafaelo. "We gotta fatten you up, Eddie and Ina. You look like beef jerky." He smiled down at Frida. "You want to eat too?"

And so we set upon the food that Maya had bought. Fried fingers of potato, and hamburgers, that is, ground beef on buns with a red paste called ketchup. Eddie and Ina slavered and ate. And, as always, Arf got some too.

As we sipped our fizzy, sweet drinks, I explained the situation to Seela.

"Were you awake all that time in the casket?" she then asked Eddie.

"In a stupor," said he. "Pleasant enough. Cellared like tubers, we were. And the worms never came."

"Eddie was clever about our casket's design," said Ina. "He's a good man. Except when he's not."

His spirits rising again, Eddie struck a pose and declaimed a variation on the hymnal verse he'd used when we'd found him restored to life aboard the *Water Witch*.

Seven score years are quickly sped;
He rises glorious from the dead;
All glory to our risen Ed!
Hallelujah!

"Alleluia to me too," said Ina, consuming a bit more chocolate cake. A heartening touch of pink had appeared on her cheeks. "Do tell, Mason old chum. Has Fwopsy mated? Is the Bloom time come? I hope Uxa didn't rouse us in vain."

"Fwopsy found a mate, yes," I said. "Duggie. They spawned baby saucers in that Big Sur cave. The new *veem* craft will carry an expedition of people, *woomo*, and Earth ants—to colonize a new world. The only remaining problem was the missing rumby eggs."

"I just knew Eddie had stolen them," said Seela.

"Ina and I guarded them in fiduciary trust!" said Eddie. "As our reward, we'll emigrate to a new world with the ships of the Bloom!"

"I suppose so," said I, not quite sure how I felt about the immanence of the Bloom. "Supposedly the royal ants can convert a solid colony planet into a construct like our doubled Hollow Earth."

"I have a rather interesting theory about this," said Eddie.

"No theories from you," Ina told Eddie. "You're half in the bag." She glanced over at Seela and me. "The man has no tolerance for spirits. Especially today, when we're so starved down. Drink more soda, Eddie."

"As Mason says, the royal ants hollow out a planet for the *woomo*," continued Eddie, wagging a bony finger. "And then—they pry the hollow planet's space into two sheets. Like Earth and MirrorEarth. With a Gate of warped space between. A Central Anomaly that forms a proper nest for the *woomo*. I have deduced this with crystalline logic. I am in no way addled, nor subject to fits."

Eddie's speculations were, so far as I know, largely correct. And they dovetailed well with the myths of Seela's tribe. But Ina didn't want to hear about this. She silenced Eddie and turned her attention to Seela.

"Are you two ready?" she asked. "To be the new Adam and Eve? That's how it's supposed to be."

"We don't want to go," said Seela. "We want to settle down here with Brumble. On a little farm."

"With a cow," I added, smiling at Seela to make her happy. But deep down I was thinking that when the saucers left I'd be aboard.

"You and Eddie should go in the saucers instead of us," Seela was telling Ina.

"Perhaps we can be the ship pilots, but we're not fit to be Adam and Eve," said Ina, running her thin hands across her raddled face. "Cain and Lilith is what we are."

"We'll get better," croaked Eddie. "Inside a *woomo* womb."

"I'd fancy that," said Ina. "Looking as we do now, one might expect we'd spawn a skewed, unwholesome world. Like Earth before the Flood. Or worse. I don't know that I can even bear one child. Eddie never quickened me during our fifteen years together."

"I brim with life essences," said Eddie. "I house multitudes. I will be the Abraham of a new race. Mason knows what I mean, eh? The fruits of the Order of the Golden Frond. I have a third testicle."

229

Wearing a fixed, embarrassed smile, Ina made no attempt to explain. "Perhaps it might work if the four of us went on the *veem* together," she said. "And perhaps you can bring your nice new friends, Mason. Mayhap this is the Great Architect's will."

As I've mentioned, I mistrust religious talk—even after the wonders I've seen. "Did you see God while you were in the grave?" I challenged Ina. "Or an angel host?"

"I saw Uxa," said Ina. "And the shared *woomo* mind—and the Earth's mind, and the mind of the Sun, and the one great Mind beyond. Is the Mind the same as God? Might we view the planets and the stars as angels? But never fear, you fractious young freethinker, I saw no Jehovah, no Moses, no Jesus, no Buddha, no Allah, nor any others of that tedious, manly ilk."

"I quite liked being dead," put in Eddie. "The years flew by—like they must have done for you at the Earth's core, Mason."

"Let's talk about that now," said Seela, a flush of anger rising to her cheeks. "Why didn't you stop Fwopsy from marooning us? I heard her story about needing all this time to find her mate Duggie, but even so—"

"Blame Machree," came Eddie's quick response. "He was the one who threw Brumble out the door. And he was the one who didn't want to let you back in."

"Ina says she cut Machree's throat," I told Seela.

"Such a rush of blood," said Ina, with her pert and hardened air.

"I'm sure you had reason to hate Machree," Seela said to Ina. "In San Francisco he presumed to buy you from a procurer."

"It was nothing so legalistic as all that," said Ina, coolly. "I don't mind sex. No, I didn't kill Machree for that."

"So you killed him for abandoning us at the core!" exclaimed Seela. "That's what I need to hear! Vengeance done."

The contrary Ina didn't want to agree. "Truth is, I killed Machree over the rumbies. We already told this to your husband."

Eddie hefted his heavy silver box and raised the lid, careful not to spill the contents. And then he peeped inside, wearing an expression of senile gloating that made Rafaelo laugh. Again I assumed Eddie meant his display as comedic mime, but in his current state, it was hard to be sure.

"And now comes the Bloom," said Seela in a weary tone. She gave me a frank, searching look. "Are you with them, Mason? Or with me?"

And that's when the police car showed up—black and white, with a single driver, a youngish white man, not particularly zealous, but in any case intent on evicting us from the cemetery.

"Hi guys," he said, walking over from his car. "We got a complaint. You'll have to take your picnic somewhere else. There's a homeless shelter just two blocks away. Can you walk that far? Anyone need a ride? How about you, sir? Where did you get that silver box?" He directed these last questions to Eddie Poe. The scent of brandy was strong in the air.

"The question to hand being what or why?" said Eddie, temporizing. None of us wanted to get into the grilled-off rear seat of the policeman's car.

"I don't suppose you have ID?" said the policeman. "Never mind. I'm not going to ask if you're illegal. Sanctuary city and all that. All I want is for you to pick up your trash and move along." He studied Arf, baby Brumble, little Frida, and the shiny sidecar motorcycle. Complicating factors. "Whose trike is that?"

"Belongs to my brother-in-law," said Maya, flashing her best smile. "We using it today. And, yes, I have a driver's license, no *problema*. I brought my friend Seela and her baby and my little girl here for a picnic. We all old friends. We can leave." Rafaelo, working quickly, had already packed up our debris.

Brumble chose this moment to pitch a fit, unleashing howls, heartbroken sobs, and desperate gasps—with his face red and wet, his toothless mouth wide open, and his tongue folded double. Seela dandled and rocked him to no avail. It wasn't time to nurse him—she'd done that only a few minutes ago.

"You the father?" said the policeman, focusing on me. I sensed he didn't like that Seela, Brumble, and I were black.

"Yes."

"Do you and the mother have a home? Is the infant receiving proper care?"

"We've only just arrived here," I said.

"I'd like to take you and your family to the shelter down the road," said the policeman. "One of their counselors can talk to you and your wife, and we'll see about getting the infant into the system."

"We're none of your business," challenged Eddie. "Mason and I are from a mirror world, and Seela's from the Hollow Earth."

"You're going to the shelter too, Grandpa," the policeman said to Eddie. "I want the four of you in my car. And the silver box. And the dog. He's going to the pound." The policeman glanced over at Ina, Rafaelo, Maya, and Frida. "The rest of you can go. You've got a place to stay?"

"We have an apartment," said Rafaelo quickly. "We have jobs. And this thin lady, we take care of her too."

"So pile onto your trike and vamoose."

But now yet another vehicle was at the curb—a small, dark green car, dense-looking, shaped like a quick bug. The door flew open, and a lively, white-haired man extracted himself, fairly bursting with glee. He spotted me and waved.

"Mason!" he cried. "Mason Reynolds! I'm Rudy Rucker."

15. Rudy

Old Rudy strode up to me and shook my hand. He seemed to know exactly what was going on. And he wanted to tell me all of it at once.

"I knew you'd come to Santa Cruz," said Rudy. "So I drove over today, and right away I saw your story in the *Good Times*, and of course I went by their office. The woman said to look for you in this cemetery, and here you are. And you're still black. What a trip. And, oh my god, there's Poe and Ina. They look so *gnarly*. Hi Eddie! So *insane* that you buried yourself in a bronze casket for a hundred and forty years. You're *nuts*! I love it! Glad to see you've got your box. And here's Seela and Brumble? So wonderful to meet you, Seela. You're gorgeous. I know it's hard when your baby cries like that." He drew out a handkerchief, dried Brumble's face, and cooed to him in a high voice. "Did the policeman scare you? Do you need a new di-di? Can I hold him, Seela? Maybe he'll be so surprised that he stops."

Seela glanced at me, and I nodded, and she handed the baby to Rudy. Brumble emitted a single, shocked squall, and then settled down into hiccups, resting his head on Rudy's shoulder.

"And there's Rafaelo and Maya with little Frida," old Rudy continued. "Hi, guys. Thanks for helping my friends. Every detail is in place, it's perfect."

Finally I found my voice. "How do you know all this?" I asked. "I understand that you edited *The Hollow Earth*—so of course you'd know my history. But the new things—how do you know them?"

"I've been writing your next book for you, Mason, I've been working on it for nearly a year. The writing's never been easier. At first I said the Muse was helping me. But I now I can see the words are coming from you. Long-distance tekelili, radiating from Uxa at the Hollow Earth's core! I've been transcribing the second narrative of Mason Algiers Reynolds—direct from the source. I'm your astral amanuensis. Ever heard that word? It's like secretary, but more high-tone." Rudy smiled, cupped his hands beside his mouth and boomed, "*Return to the Hollow Earth!* Right? That's what I've been writing, okay? It's really happening, and we're in the story, and it's all around. I can't believe it." He leaned over to pet the dog. "And here's good old Arf. Hi, Arfie."

The policeman watched Rudy's performance with some uncertainty. To all appearances Rudy was a respectable, well-off man, nicely dressed in an argyle sweater, well-spoken, and with a good car. The fact that Rudy was greeting me so effusively was surely a point in my favor. Even though he was, to some extent, raving like a maniac. But extravagant outbursts were perhaps common in Santa Cruz.

Rudy turned and addressed the policeman on our behalf. "Mason's an old friend," he said. "I'd be glad to give him and his family and their dog a place to stay."

"Where would you take them?" asked the policeman. "To the homeless shelter?"

"They're welcome to stay at my house," said Rudy. "I'm happy to take care of them until they get things set up—if I can talk my wife into it. We live over the hill, in Los Gatos."

"Fine with me," said the policeman. "And what about this addled elder gent who likes to run his mouth? Possibly in possession of stolen property?" He meant Poe. "You going to take him too? Otherwise I'll put him in the tank at the shelter."

"Leave Mr. Poe with me." said Rudy. "We'll work things out. That box is definitely his. Believe it or not, Eddie's a famous writer."

"Believe it or not, I've got other shit to do," said the policeman. He gave us a last look. "If I see any of you in this graveyard again, you're going to jail. For reals." Therewith he got into his car and ponderously rolled away.

"What now?" Seela said to me. "You're getting yourself in deeper all the time, Mason. And I want to back away."

"I have to talk to Rudy," I said. "He's nearly finished writing my next book. I want to see what he's done."

"You two do what you like," put in Rudy. "You're the characters. I'm just the scribe."

"Let's go to our house to talk things over," proposed Maya.

So some of us piled into Rudy's car and the rest of us got onto the trike, and we drove a mile to the Mexicans' beige, flimsy house, with its walls half an inch thick. Hector and Aida were still at work. I showed Ina and Eddie the light switches and the faucets, and they liked them exceedingly. Eddie started formulating explanations, more and more like his old self, while keeping a tight grip on his box of rumbies. Maya dug up more shoes—she herself had as big a stash as Rafaelo did. Seela nursed Brumble, and Maya nursed Frida, then gave her a teething biscuit. We were ready to talk about what to do next.

But we didn't get a chance to talk right away—because Seela's rumby hatched. The way it happened was that a zigzag ray of *woomo* light meandered through the open window, and alit upon the string-wrapped bulge on Seela's necklace. The rumby. The heavy gem gave a silent tekelili cry, burst its wrappings, dropped to the floor, and—*behold*—it was a wriggling *woomo* that started out the size of a thumb, then grew to the size of a summer squash, and then, in a sudden rush, expanded into a great tubular form that ran from one side of the living-room to the other, plump and warty, bulking as high as my chest. Everyone was yelling and upset. Arf was barking furiously. He was backing toward the door with the hair on his hackles erect.

Meanwhile I'd quietly tuned in on the new arrival's tekelili.

"She says she's Uxa's daughter," I told the others. "Don't be scared. Her name is Lux."

Lux's bumps were flat on the top, a bit like suckers, and her hide was mottled in shades of green. Lux's powerful teke-lili was throbbing like a barroom band with a rowdy crowd. Very nearly overwhelming. Lux was communicating with us via feelings of motion rather than via images and words. And her message? She was going to carry us to the saucer cave in Big Sur, with some of us inside her, and some on her back like riders on a flying dragon.

Arf wasn't going to be riding on any *woomo*. Seela didn't like the idea either, and Rafaelo and Maya were very dubious as well. Eddie and Ina were all for it—this was the reason they'd taken their tortuous route to the year twenty eighteen. And I—I too was intrigued. What an adventure it would be, after all, to travel to a new planet as a part of the *woomo* Bloom.

"I'll ride to Big Sur," said old Rudy. "But no further. I need to stay here and publish your book, Mason."

A thought crossed my mind. "Will you share the money with Seela and me?"

"Sure," said Rudy. "You guys can have half of the money for the new Hollow Earth book, and I'll give you some of whatever I got for the first one. It's hard to remember exactly how much I made. I can look it up. Not a huge amount."

"Your books don't sell well?"

"They do okay, but they don't hit big," said Rudy. "Science fiction fans think I'm too literary, and the mandarins pretend I don't exist. I joke, I'm dirty, I use math, I hate the pig, and I'm old."

"What of me?" interrupted Eddie Poe. "How goes my literary career?"

"You're a titan," said Rudy. "Millions of books. Tens of millions."

"More than Nathaniel Hawthorne?" Eddie wanted to know.

"Way, way more," said Rudy. "Hawthorne's in the pantheon, sure. But really he's just for English profs. He never learned how to make it nasty and crazy like Poe. You're the king, Eddie. A demigod."

"Why are you three talking about *books*?" interrupted Seela. "And meanwhile this enormous rubbery *woomo* is about to kidnap us!"

Rudy cackled at this. "We're writers," he said. "What do you expect? Just give us another second, and then we'll let our tale's hair-raising climax kick in. Mason, I don't want to build up too much hope, but it's just possible our new book could score. I mean—it's a fucking masterpiece! Of course I always think that. But this could be the one. I'll publish it along with a reprint of our first Hollow Earth book.

"By Mason Reynolds," said I. "Put that on the cover."

Rudy shook his head. "I've developed a following over the years. If my name is on the cover, we're guaranteed to sell at least a thousand copies. And it could take off from there. And of course I'll write an Editor's Note where I say the book's really written by Mason Reynolds, and that he fed it to me via *woomo* tekelili." Rudy smiled. "Everyone will believe *that*!"

"I should get credit too," put in Eddie.

"Like you need it, you glory-hog," said Rudy, flaring up. "Give us a chance."

"My glory will be magnified beyond your ken when I engender a new human race," said Eddie. "My scrotum holds a thousand life essences, you see. Donated by the adherents of the Order of the Golden Frond, and by unwitting passers-by. My third testicle. Not unlike a third eye."

"This gets better all the time," said Rudy, taking Eddie's remark in stride. It was as if he'd set aside all belief in ordinary reality—and was glad so to do.

"Donated?" said I.

"I believe I mentioned this to you once before," resumed Eddie. "*Woomo* rays extracted cell clusters from the donors and tingled them into my sack for safe-keeping."

"Tingled?

"Slipped them through the meatus, then guided them along the urethra, across the seminal vesicle, and through the vas deferens," Eddie said, assuming a professorial air.

"Sounds like a tour of ancient Rome," jested Rudy, then made a calming gesture. "Don't be mad at me, Eddie. What you did is a good idea. You'll avoid the genetic bottleneck.

The dreaded founder effect." Rudy glanced over at me. "With only a few adults in a new Eden, one needs a source of exogamy to avoid incest—lest the population be poxed by recessive genes." I didn't recognize all the phrases, but I grasped the import.

"Inbreeding is ill," summarized Eddie. "Outbreeding is well. I have the seeds for a thousand new babies." Departing from his usual refined manner, he patted his crotch. "Some are from members of the Order of the Golden Frond. And some were *woomo*-plucked from worthy candidates we happened to see. A pensive brow, a noble countenance and—*whisk*—into Eddie's sack! No races barred."

"Who'll grow all those babies?" asked Rudy. "You can't ask proud women like Seela and Maya to serve as brood mares."

"We'll use *woomo* wombs," said Eddie. "A *woomo* can form an entirely efficacious uterus within her flesh, complete with umbilical cord and placenta, you see. A womb indeed, warmed by the *woomo's* glow." Triumphantly he raised his silver box of rumbies and rattled it. "I'll supply not only the seeds, but the *woomo* as well!"

"Zounds!" exclaimed Rudy, getting into the spirit.

Looking back, it seems hard to believe that Rudy, Eddie, and I took the time to have this conversation—what with Lux the *woomo* newly arrived in the room. As Seela had already pointed out, and was just now pointing out again, I should be discussing Lux's declared intention to rush us to the saucer cave in Big Sur. But perhaps my conversation with Rudy and Eddie didn't take as long as it seems in written form. After all, thanks to Lux, we were in intense tekelili contact, and our remarks may have been in silent psychic form. A quick flutter of sense and emotion.

In any case, Seela now had her hands on my shoulders. She was shaking me, and in fact screaming into my face.

"I don't want to fly off in those saucers!"

With a sudden motion she pressed Brumble into my arms. "You can take the baby, fine, but you can't take me. I'll stay here alone. I'll settle in with Josh, the Sparkle Wow jeweler. He says that he loves me. He'll marry me if I want.

But he'd prefer not to have another man's child on his hands."
She was crying as she said this, and her hands kept flying out
to caress the sleeping Brumble's hairless pate.

My chest felt hollow. My mouth was dry and it was hard
to talk. "Seela— "

"You can't stop me!" she interrupted, glaring at me even
as she wept. "I'm leaving you and leaving that, that noisy,
greedy baby who nobody wants. I'm not following you into
a *veem*. You made me leave my flower, you made me leave the
Hollow Earth, and now you want me to fly into the horrible
empty sky, and, no, no, no, I won't do it!"

With that, Seela turned and ran out the little house's
door, sobbing as if her heart would break, and with her thin
shoulders shaking. And still Brumble slept.

"Branch point," said Rudy at my side. "Which fork do
you take?"

I was stung by Seela's assertion that she would settle in
with that Josh character. And shocked that she was willing
to abandon Brumble. Our baby unwanted? Never! Most of
all, I grieved to see Seela in such a state. Poor, dear woman.
Arf looked up at me, uncertain.

"Go with Seela," I told him. "Be her friend." Perhaps
it was due to his dislike of *woomo*, but this was one of those
rare times when Arf obeyed a command. He took off after
Seela without looking back.

I recalled the time in Richmond that Arf had left me for
Otha. I'd been fifteen. With the ongoing rush of events, that
felt like half a lifetime ago, but it was only three years. I saw
no sign of the turmoil abating. And I liked that. But—what
of Seela's dream of a farm by a river with a cow? How could
I so coldly set myself against her heart's desire?

"You'll be fine," said the opportunistic Ina, replacing
Rudy by my side. She ran her wizened hand across my cheek.
She was about as alluring as moldy scarecrow. "Lux is going to
restore Eddie and me on the way to Big Sur," she continued.
"We'll crawl inside her and marinate in her smeel. Like babies
in the womb. I heard Eddie telling you about *woomo* wombs.
The *woomo* will make Eddie and me beautiful again. Fresh.

Turgid. Pert. We'll travel with you on the saucer. I'll be your lover. I'll teach you tricks. What fun we'll have."

"Smeel?"

"That's what we call Lux's divine *woomo* body nectar," said Ina. "I'll be lissome, I tell you, *virgo intacta*. Just wait and see. Eddie and I will be capital company. And you'll have Maya to chivvy with as well. I warrant you'll bed her."

"Be cool," Maya said to Ina. "I'm bringing my husband Rafaelo."

"You two are coming in the saucer to another world?" I asked Maya. "On your own free will? You understand what it's about?"

"We want to very much," said Rafaelo. "No more working for white people. You know what I mean, Mason. You're *negro*. They don't treat us good. This new world, it can be beautiful. Better than a videogame."

"Yes," I assented. "The *woomo* will pick a good planet. They want us to be at ease. We'll all fit. The humans, the *woomo*, the flying saucers, and the big ants."

"Ants?" said Maya. "I didn't hear nothing about ants."

"You won't notice them much," I said. "When we land, the ants will go underground, digging out space for the *woomo*. And prying the new planet in two. Into a world and a mirrorworld. To make room for the dirt they dig out from inside. Never mind. We'll live on the outside with meadows and seas and flowers and trees. We'll have children of our own, and Eddie will hatch extra babies from the *woomo*. Nobody has to marry a cousin."

Rafaelo was holding Frida against his shoulder, and I was holding Brumble. "Maybe some day our two kids—who knows?" he said, "But, you, *vato*, you need to bring your own wife for this trip. I don't want you hanging round my back door. You find Seela and beg her on your knees to come with you. You're *loco* to lose that girl."

"I—I don't know," I said. It would be cruel—and probably impossible—to force Seela to come. Yes, I'd be desperately lonely, making the trip without her. But if I didn't leave on the saucer, I might regret it for the rest of my life. I was born for adventure, wasn't I? At least I'd have Brumble with me.

And Seela would have Arf. Rafaelo was still glaring at me. "I won't bother Maya," I humbly promised him.

"As if that's up to you two," said Maya. "We'll go to Sur now and see what we see."

Meanwhile the sea cucumber Lux had opened a hole in her side.

"Heal me!" cried Ina. She shed her pink sweatsuit and scooted in, feet first. It looked dark and wet in there—one could indeed say it was like a womb. Certainly it was more welcoming than a bronze casket six feet underground. A tube dangled from the side of Lux's inner wall.

"You too, Eddie," sang Ina before fitting the tube to her navel. And then Lux opened a womb for Poe as well. Leaning on my shoulder, he too removed his sweat clothes, and I helped him in. He took his place in there, with his heavy box of rumbies clasped against his bony, naked chest.

"I hope this works," I said, showing Eddie his umbilical cord.

"A new man," said Eddie. "A nam wen." Playing with words even now, in such low estate, my worn old friend. I prayed for his restoration—but prayed to whom? To the great Mind, I suppose.

Lux sealed in Ina and Eddie. Rudy, Maya, Rafaelo, and I remained—plus the two children—Brumble in my arms, and Frida in Rafaelo's. Maya ran and filled a big laundry bag with assorted clothes. And I managed to replace my sweat pants with a pair of the blue denim trousers called jeans.

And then the *woomo* narrowed herself and wormed between our legs, cupping herself against our bottoms so that we four adults were, in effect, sitting on saddles atop a warty, eyeless, fronded slug. Lux wriggled out the door of Maya's house and sprang into the air before any of us could manage to jump free, not that any of us did want to jump free. We were drawn by the magnitude of the impending adventure, and we were a bit under the sway of Lux's tekelili.

Minutes later we were five hundred feet high in the air, cruising southward along the California coast. It was late afternoon, and clouds were piled on the horizon, with the low sun turning orange. Despite the chill, we were comfortable, as Lux was exuding a gold glow that covered our bodies and sent sparks off our fingertips. Perhaps the halos made us hard to see—in any case, no military planes were taking notice of us today, nor, for that matter, had the neighbors raised an outcry.

Rudy sat in front, then me with Brumble, then Maya with her laundry bag, and Rafaelo in the rear with Frida. I felt sadly alone. In truth, I barely knew these people. Seela was the one I knew. And we'd parted. I imagined her dear face before me, sad and uncertain, and imagined the sound of her voice: *"Is the little one well?"*

Brumble was still asleep. He had an enviable ability to ignore his surroundings. And he'd nursed his fill before Seela left. Kind Maya would surely nurse him when he woke. I studied the little slits of Brumble's closed eyes, and his tiny pursed mouth. Was it in any way reasonable to load this little fellow onto a flying saucer to another world? Could I really leave his birth mother behind?

As we angled down from the sky toward Big Sur, I noticed low buildings and a chapel atop a nearby hill. They faded from view as Lux bore us lower. We landed unobserved upon the same tiny, mid-cliff ledge-meadow as before—with the hot spring, the cave, and the stand of twisted pines.

Dusk was coming on; the air was calm. Brumble awoke, crying plaintively and without relent. As I'd hoped, Maya took him over.

"The saucers in there?" said Rafaelo, pointing at the dark mouth of the cave. "You sure this is on the up and up, Mason?"

"It should be fine," I said, hoping this was true. "I should tell you that the saucers aren't metal machines. They're alive."

"You've talked to them?"

"Not these new ones. They just got hatched. Maybe they'll fly out and say hello. Maybe we don't have to go inside the cave."

Meanwhile Lux was flexing her body. She kinked the region where Eddie and Ina were ensconced, and then— *behold*—the two of them slid onto the ground like new-foaled colts. Wet, gasping, and wholly restored—supple, clean-featured, bright-eyed, and all their wits about them.

"*Ecce homo*," said the nude Eddie, striking a pose with his heavy box of rumbies held firm in his hand. "Behold the man."

Gracefully Ina took Eddie's hand. "Husband mine," said she, setting aside her designs on me, at least for now.

Rudy, Maya, Rafaelo, and I cheered, and for a few minutes we five chattered excitedly about the transformation. For the first time since Eddie's and Ina's emergence from the grave, it seemed possible to me that they were indeed capable of being a new Adam and Eve.

After so much tekelili with the *woomo*, I'd developed a sense of duty to their cause, and a conviction that it was up to me to make their Bloom work. And perhaps I was drawn by the romantic pathos of being doomed to leave for a new world. But that was nonsense. With Eddie and Ina in fine fettle—I didn't really have to go.

My thoughts were interrupted by a section of the cliff exploding outward—some fifty feet to the left of the cave's door. Lit by the rays of the sinking sun, rocks avalanched toward the inky sea, clattering and overtaking each other. Furious, jointed forms struggled amid the dust cloud within the cliff's ragged new hole.

The combatants were, of course, oversized ants—Skolder and his cow-sized royal companions versus the nasty, creamy, dog-sized farmer ants. A large and very graceful purplish-green form was fighting at Skolder's side. Presumably this was his betrothed, the empress ant for the intended colony world. Peering deeper into the seething fracas, I perceived that the creamy ants had a queen of their own. She was demonically ripping the heads off any royal ants she could reach. Not that she had much hope of victory, for Skolder and his empress were slicing through the farmer ant troops like scythes reaping grain.

Maya was jabbering in fear, but Rafaelo was incongruously seized by mirth. Perhaps the myrmicine struggle reminded him of a jolly scene in his beloved videogames. Rudy and I, who had a fuller understanding of what was taking pace, called out encouragement to Skolder. Meanwhile Eddie and Ina sat to one side amid the gnarled pines, quietly talking about their upcoming plans. The weighted silver box of rumbies rested on the ground between them.

The focus of ants' battle progressed into hidden subterranean passageways. For a time, showers of pebbles continued emerging from the newly opened hole in the cliff. And all this while, our helpful *woomo* companion Lux was darting out rays and tendrils to deflect any wayward stones that came our way. Slowly the signs of the ant war abated. We felt a few more irregular shudders, and a final shiver of ripples patterned our hot spring's pool. I was relieved that the densely grown stand of pines had held our perch intact. I sensed that the royal ants had all but annihilated their farmer ant foes.

"For sure I'm not going in that cave," said Rafaelo.

"I can't stand ants," repeated Maya.

"Our three *veem* craft will float out," I said. "Royal ants will be in the first one. And then we'll hatch Eddie's box of rumbies to make *woomo*, and they'll go aboard the second craft. And the third one—well that's for people."

"I don't like this," said Rafaelo. The sun was down. The sky was a fading gray.

"Good news," announced Ina, rejoining us. "Lux just told Eddie and me that I'm pregnant."

"Capital," said I, relieved that fertilizing Ina was no longer a task I might be called upon to perform.

"Eddie did it!" exulted Ina. "It's finally clicked. The *woomo*—while Eddie and I were inside her, she mated us. My egg and Eddie's sperm. We're going to have a girl, says Lux. The princess of New Eden."

"Who she gonna marry?" asked Maya, homing in on the central difficulty with our understaffed colonization plan.

"She can share Mason's Brumble with your Frida!" said Ina, as if this fully solved the problem.

"And what about the next generation after that?" I ventured. "And what if Maya and Rafaelo and Brumble and Frida and I don't come along at all?"

"Maya don't like those ants," ventured Rafaelo.

"We don't need you shirkers and your children," snapped Eddie Poe. "Watch. I have powers beyond compare. I'll sire all the babies we need—and they'll have fresh heritage. Help me, Lux!"

Lux directed a branching ray of light upon the wrapped rumby amulet at Eddie's throat, haloing it in a shower of sparks. The enclosing twine burned away, and on the way to the ground the jewel morphed into a *woomo* slug. She sat at Eddie's feet, with one alert tip lifted into the air.

"I dub thee Lenore," said Eddie, still naked.

He knelt over the newly hatched *woomo* Lenore, running his fingertips along the tiny sea cucumber's hide. Lenore pressed back against Eddie, as if enjoying the petting. Continually she grew in size. Her upper surface began to smooth itself—and to flow. She was spreading like batter on a griddle.

"Oh no," said I, sensing what was coming.

"Gnarly," said Rudy. He had an inkling too. After all, he'd already transcribed the bulk of the *Return to the Hollow Earth*.

Lenore formed her body into a low platform like a bed. Embossed upon her was a simulacrum of a pale, female figure—as still and lifeless as a marble effigy recumbent upon a tomb. Eddie stared, fascinated, his eyes burning, his lips pressed tight together.

"It's Virginia?" murmured old Rudy.

And, yes, the form was the very imago of Eddie's lost child bride, Virginia Clemm. With a shriek, the unclothed poet threw himself upon the phantasmal form—and furiously copulated with the *woomo*. A repellent sight indeed.

Rudy giggled. "Exogamous children," said he. "Straight from the sack. Poe's third ball."

"*So* nasty," said Maya.

"We're bailing," declared Rafaelo. "You too, Mason?"

"Yes," I said. "Me too." Saying this, I felt a flush of happiness. All was not lost. I could still be with Seela—if she'd have me back.

"We'll find a ride to Santa Cruz," said old Rudy. "But first let's watch the Bloom."

16. Farewell

"Too much for you?" Eddie said to me when he was done. His tone was exultant and even haughty, so sure of himself was our Poe.

"Find yourself some clothes in Maya's laundry bag," I suggested. "You and Ina both."

"What a stolid burgher you've become," said Eddie. "So far, and no further, my would-be rake? It'll be paradise in the world I'm to engender. I'll be the Tulku, and you can be my Crozier. Like Machree was."

"Leave Mason alone," said Ina. "He wants to be with Seela. I don't blame him. He wants his own life."

"And you, Ina?" said I. "You're content with the *woomo* plan?"

"Perhaps I seek doom," she lightly said. "That may explain the paths I choose. But let's be sunny. I am indeed fond of Eddie. I'll welcome the clarity of a new world. Farewell to the muck and the ruck. And, yes, restored by our *woomo* Lux, I am indeed fit to be Eve."

While Ina spoke, she was rooting in Maya's laundry bag, and now she produced a pair of outfits. Red jeans and a blue frock for her, a white shirt and a black business suit for Eddie. And of course, bright athletic shoes for both of them.

"Time to hatch our rumbies!" said Eddie, once he and Ina were clad. "Help me, Lux and Lenore."

With a conjuror's flair, Eddie lifted the lid from the silver box and skimmed the lid across our meadow. It arced over the edge and downward to the rumbling sea. By now the daylight was nearly gone. Careful not to spill the contents, Eddie laid his open box on the ground beside the hot spring's steaming pool, then stepped well back. The box held eighty or so rumbies. They were excited—they glowed a bit, and a silent hubbub of their tekelili filled the air.

Lux and Lenore set to work, sending branching tendrils into the bustling rumby box. I laid a protective hand across the rumby amulet I still wore at my neck. I was concerned that it, too, might be impelled to hatch. I had an inchoate plan to hatch it later on, privily, and that my personal *woomo* would then help me and Seela on our way. Surely we two did have a future path together, Seela and I, despite that vile interloper, Josh the jeweler of Sparkle Wow. To keep my amulet safer, I took it off my neck and shoved it deep into my jeans pocket.

The eggs were hatching one by one, each of them with a pop or a hiss or a squeal. Each new-hatched *woomo* wormed out of the box and into the pool of the spring, stretching itself, sucking in water, spurting it out, nudging the others, and steadily increasing in size. The air thrilled with the auras of four score new minds, keen for adventure. Lux began advising them about the trip.

At this point the first of the three spherical *veem* craft pushed out the cave, forcing its way, enlarging the cave's mouth to ten and then twenty yards wide, excavating masses of dirt and stone on either side. This first *veem* glowed with lavender light, and was laden with young royal ants. A wondrous sight. But the craft's exit from the cave had set off yet another avalanche. Just on the other side of the cave, great blocks of stone were coming loose and tobogganing downhill.

"Come sit with us," called Eddie, perched with Ina atop the hovering *woomo* Lenore.

Uneasy though I was about my footing, I was loath to join them. For all I knew, Eddie would whisk me into one of the *veem* craft, and I'd be headed into deep space against my will. Scanning across the face of increasingly the unstable cliff, I spotted a damp, upward path to the right. It held a flowing rivulet, and was choked with grasses, bushes and moss.

"Let's go!" I shouted to Rafaelo, Maya, and Rudy.

Slipping and panting, we four wended our way up the muddy path. Rafaelo carried Frida, and I held Brumble. Off to the left the roar of the landslide grew. The ground shuddered hideously. At one point I fell. I had trouble regaining my footing, what with the bawling Brumble in my arms. Maya and Rudy lifted me up, their hands firm and kind.

Venturing a quick glance over my shoulder, I saw the spherical *veem* ship of ants hovering in mid-air, at an altitude lower than my position on the cliff, but not all that far. The craft was a good forty-five feet across, very nearly spherical, with a Saturn-like rim, and with the *veem* skin stretched so tight that I cold see the green and purple armor of the royal ants within. None of the pale farmer ants had been allowed to join the mission.

A second ship now appeared—a lambent, copper-colored orb, thirty feet across. It took up a position directly above where the ants' *veem* ship hovered. It was approximately level with where I stood. Our eighty newly hatched *woomo* flew up from the hot spring's pool and began wriggling in through the saucer's two open doors. Lux—the *woomo* from Seela's amulet—flew up with them, reducing herself to their scale.

At this point the alien sea cucumbers were about the size of human legs, intricately whorled with rubbery warts, and each of them glowing in its own unique shade. The lustrous light-emitting tendrils of the individual *woomo* were continually in motion, limning a choreography that etched an intricate tracery against the night. Added to this exquisite visual beauty was the intense tekelili I felt from these joyous, youthful beings, destined to live for millennia, and reveling at the inception of their great quest.

I'd experienced the tekelili force of a *woomo* swarm twice before—both times at the core of the Hollow Earth. But to be with this new generation of Great Old Ones at their earliest flowering, and to be witnessing the scene amid the magical, unparalleled beauty of Big Sur...the experience struck me even more profoundly than before. My soul brimmed and overflowed, like a wineglass in a waterfall.

Nevertheless, a part of my attention stayed fixed upon the quaking mire beneath my feet, and upon our struggle up the cliff. Some extra ants were on the cliff with us—both royal ants and surviving farmer ants. These were resentful, disappointed individuals who'd failed to secure passage aboard the ant *veem*. The ants were snapping at each other, and their mandibles made percussive clicks. Blessedly they had no interest in us. Their goal was only to find passageways to the remains of their nests within the ruined cliff.

"Here's the top!" called Rudy. I saw him as a silhouette against a clear sky brightened by a sea of stars. The waning moon had yet to rise. And then I was at Rudy's side. We'd reached the patch of gravel by the road. No cars were coming by. I was glad for that.

Rudy, Rafaelo, Maya, and I stood at the brow of the cliff, catching our breath and nursing our bruises. The avalanche had abated. Our footing was stable. Out past the face of the cliff hovered the large pale purple craft of the ants, and above that the medium-sized coppery sphere of the *woomo*. Meanwhile Eddie and Ina sat upon the airborne *woomo* Lenore—awaiting the appearance of the third *veem* craft, the one that would carry the humans.

Ever the showman, Eddie called out one of his Latin mottos: "*Aude sapere*," meaning, "Dare to know." A fitting phrase for this protean man of changes, undaunted by risk, seemingly indestructible. I was glad to hear the power and energy in his voice. I prayed that he and Ina would prosper and thrive upon their new world, peculiar though Eddie's methods were.

If I haven't made it fully clear: I loved Eddie from the start, and I will admire him till I die.

The third and final *veem* craft pushed free of the rubble around the collapsed cave. This *veem* ship was of a golden hue, and its flesh had the crystalline pellucidity of a jellyfish. The sphere was comfortably small, little more than fifteen feet across. It rose to a level precisely even with the top of the cliff, and not all that far away from us. I could see into it quite well.

The golden *veem* was canted back with its two viewports facing the sky. Eddie and Ina made their way inside it, and their *woomo* Lenore darted down to join her fellows in the copper-colored craft.

Eddie took one of the pilot's seats, and Ina the other. They leaned back, recumbent, with their heads pointing away from each other—staring up through their view ports at the starry heavens. With the moon still down, the ghostly stream of the Milky Way was clear to see. Somewhere out there was the next planet the *woomo* would colonize.

Eddie and Ina took hold of their rudimentary *veem* controls—those simple knobs on sticks—and instigated a process that would complete the Bloom.

I heard a low hum, and the brightness of the gold sphere increased. A circuit of energy was building. Eddie glanced over at me. I could clearly see the expression of his face. He raised his dark eyebrows, as if asking if I was sure I didn't want to come. There was still time. I shook my head no.

He shrugged and smiled. An actinic glow flowed from his sphere to the ball of the *woomo*, and thence to the ship of the ants, spilling down like a cataract. Aroused by the influx, the royal ants thrust their stingers from their ship's doors and darted rays at the craft of the *woomo*. In turn the *woomo* swathed Eddie's *veem* with crackling sparks of tekelili energy. Continuing the cycle, Eddie sent fresh energies cascading down and, once again, the lower spheres sent aethereal forces up.

As the iterated interplay intensified, the *veem* craft were drawn into contact with each other. With showers of sparks they welded themselves together at their points of tangency, producing a stack of three spheres, intensely humming with a rising pitch.

"Too loud!" cried Maya, covering her ears.

She was right—the sound was hurting my head or, worse, boring into my brain. The singing of the conjoined spheres slid up beyond the range of human ears. Arf wouldn't have liked it.

In concert with the sound, a halo was expanding outward from the three *veem*, a luminous hollow shell that rushed towards us and passed through my body as if I were air or glass. The touch set my hairs on end.

All around us the hollow shell was inflating itself, hungrily racing in every direction, above and below, soon enclosing the land, the sea, and even the stars above. A pregnant pause. A colossal clap of thunder made the welkin ring.

The shell of pale light rushed back in upon us, like a ring of breakers in a phosphorescent sea—or, rather, like the walls of a collapsing room. Again the shell passed through my body as if I were naught. It condensed into a bright, egg-like globule located above the three welded-together *veem*. It gleamed like a star above a snowman.

Flexing with arcane, eldritch energy, the egg roughened its surface and grew a single porcupine quill. Taking careful aim, the egg hurled the luminous lance above the damp, rounded hills, and high into the star-besprent firmament, leaving a hair-thin trail of light in its wake. Tekelili told me that the lance was aimed at the most promising world that the scouting shell had found.

Again a pause. No sound from the sky, the stars, the *veem*, or the pale egg. A sudden flash glared at the heavens' zenith. I held my breath, expecting a boom, but, no, I'd heard the thunder a minute ago—*before* the flash. The deep structures of length and duration were baffled by the Bloom's wild play.

A jointed arm of light reached down from the heavens and placed a spindly fingertip upon the egg. And, behold, a space tunnel opened directly above Eddie's and Ina's *veem*.

This higher-dimensional Gate was much like the one at the heart of the Central Anomaly. And, as it happened, the new tunnel led, not to a mirrored copy of Earth, but to the *woomo*'s next colony planet, very far away.

I could see through the tunnel. A sunny prospect of verdant meadows, with stubby reddish-brown creatures in the fields. Cows? Not exactly. I yearned to visit this new Eden, and sorrowed that I would not.

The linked gold, copper, and lavender *veem* craft rose smoothly toward the Gate, seeming to shrink into the distance, yet without moving very far. And then—they were on the other side, with the green field and the not-quite-cows. Eddie, Ina, the *woomo*, and the ants—all of them were on the other side. The Gate shrank back to an egg, and to a white dot. It shivered and winked out.

The *woomo*'s intoxicating aura of tekelili was gone, as was the musky energy of Eddie and Ina. The only tekelili I still had was a faint pulse from the rumby in my pocket. The Bloom was done. The ocean waves splashed on as before. I felt homely and dull. My life was but a common thing.

§

Rudy, Rafaelo, Maya, and I talked things over for a bit. We felt disoriented by the rapid changes. The time was perhaps nine pm. Our location was so remote that Rudy's pocket phone didn't work.

"There's a monastery on the hill," said Rudy. "A hermit-age. I've been there before. Nice people. Maybe we can pay one of them to give us a ride."

"Is it a long walk?" asked Maya.

"An hour," said Rudy. "Up a side road."

And so we set off, arcing back and forth with the road's bends. The tardy, gibbous moon rose. The timeless sea glinted like hammered bronze. Images of my long journey flitted through my mind.

The bateau trip down the James River from Lynchburg to Richmond. My meeting with Poe in his newspaper office. The packet boat to Norfolk, and then the clipper ship *Wasp* to Antarctica. The balloon trip with Eddie and Otha to the South Pole. The collapse of the ice cap, and the fall through the Earth's Rind. The journey across the Hollow Earth jungle to Seela's flower. My union with Seela. Our fall to the central zone of the black gods. Finding Fwopsy the fried egg. Uxa the *woomo* skimming us through the Central Anomaly and to the inner surface of MirrorEarth. The bobbling drift up through the Chesapeake Bay. The boat ride to Baltimore. The seeming deaths of Poe and MirrorPoe. Settling in with Seela like newlyweds. Our shipboard passage to the Horn, and the foundering of the *Purple Whale*. Our rescue by the flying ballula. Finding the revived Poe aboard the *Water Witch*. The birth of Brumble in San Francisco. The flight to the North Pole aboard Cytherea. Our passage through the neck of the vast maelstrom. The herd of shrigs, and the encounter with the royal ants. Riding Tallulah to MirrorSeela's flower. Recovering Fwopsy the fried egg, with the newly hatched *woomo* Nyoo inside her. MirrorYurgen and his horn. Drifting once more to the Hollow Earth's core. Dallying with MirrorSeela along the way. Bringing Fwopsy to life. Our strangely ecstatic century-and-a-half sojourn upon Uxa at the Anomaly. Flying with Fwopsy to the cave in Big Sur. Our ride with the Mexicans to Santa Cruz. Poe and Ina risen from the grave. Meeting old Rudy. Breaking with Seela. Riding Lux the *woomo* to the cave at Big Sur. Eddie's departure for the new Eden. Here I was.

"What you thinking about?" said Rafaelo at my side. I could see his face quite clearly in the light of the moon.

"I'm lost," said I. "Out of place."

"I hear that," said Rafaelo. "I don't know how long we can stay in Cruz. So many Mexicans getting deported these days."

"I'd like to leave Santa Cruz," I said. "Too crowded. Seela and I were going to look for some land." A thought struck me. "Would you and Maya want to come along? Move out into the country. Or to an island?"

"We're ready for anything," put in Maya. "But it's hard to travel with no green card and no passport."

"First we'll get back to Cruz," said Rafaelo. "And then Mason finds Seela. And then—*quién sabe.*"

Onward we walked. The cracked old road leveled out and we passed some pines. I kept glancing at the sky, as if expecting to see Eddie's new world up there.

Finally we came to the hermitage, and managed to find a monk on watch, a calm, gentle young man who seemed amused by the story we told him, not that our tale contained any actual facts. In any case, the monk readily accepted that something remarkable had happened to us—he'd seen the odd lights in the sky, and it may have been that he'd felt the tekelili touch of the massed *woomo*. His name was Brother Nguyen.

He agreed to use the monastery's van to ferry us up to Santa Cruz immediately, and for a reasonable sum. And that was that.

Weary, drained and sorrowful, I dozed for most of drive. It was perhaps one am when we reached Aida and Hector's house. Having found only the briefest of notes from Maya, they'd been wondering where we were, or if we were coming back at all,

I'd hoped that Seela might be there, but she wasn't. Evidently she was spending the night with Josh. I had an urge to run over to Josh's house and rouse them, but Maya held me back.

"Josh is flaky," she said. "Loses his temper. You need to be strong when you go in there for the showdown, Mason. And it's better for you if Seela has a whole night to think it over. So she gets sick of Josh and starts missing Brumble."

"You're on my side?" I asked Maya.

"I'm on Seela's side," she said. "And you're a better catch than Josh. He's a jerk. Bossy. He says he's PC, but he rips off his workers when he can. Lie down and sleep, Mason. What a crazy *loco* day. Those big wriggly slugs? And that nut Eddie humping one of them? And the giant ants who made a frikkin avalanche? *Hayzooz Christo*. I'm glad we didn't go in no flying saucers."

Not wanting to leave yet, old Rudy took Seela's place on the mattress at my side, with Brumble between us, which wasn't much to Brumble's liking. He yawned, sneezed, and had a fit of hiccups. The night passed like a waking dream, with me repeatedly having to carry Brumble to Maya and petition that she nurse. I was going to have to learn about bottle feeding, but blundering around a strange house in the moonlight at three am was not the time. Finally Maya just let me leave Brumble in her bed.

And then at last the sun came up, not that I could directly see it, what with the whole town shrouded in white fog, but at least it was bright out, and I could stop pretending to sleep. And go get Seela.

Josh's house was within walking distance. It was another of those flat, beige boxes in the poor part of town. The shades were down and the lights were out—no surprise, as it was only six am. I stood outside the house for fifteen minutes, looking things over and waiting to hear a sound. Josh had a nice-looking mural on the closed garage door—a flowing image of sparkling stones, waves, goddesses, and the like—and I remembered Maya saying that she'd painted it. It was a little like the murals she'd put on walls of their rented house.

One of the window curtains of the house twitched, and I saw the quick flash of Seela's eyes. A moment later she was standing on the concrete stoop outside the front door. She was barefoot, with tangled hair, and wearing a long T-shirt as a nightgown. She seemed conditionally glad to see me.

"What are *you* doing here?" she asked, holding back a smile.

The ice in my heart melted. Any doubts about staying were gone. I held out my arms and Seela came to me, her body wonderfully warm and familiar against mine. "I need you," I said.

"Where's Brumble?"

"With Maya. They didn't leave on the saucers either. It was just Eddie and Ina. He was being too—"

"Too Eddie," said Seela, with a soft giggle. "And, Mason, we can always go back into the Hollow Earth, if life here is too tame. But, you know, I'm starting to think the outside is interesting."

"I hate how crowded it is in twenty eighteen," I said.

"Maybe we'll go somewhere out of the way. Virginia?"

"Oh god, no. I'm not going back there after all this. And with black skin? We—we could go to a South Seas island."

"I bet Rudy can tell us about one. And, don't forget, he's going to give us money. For your books! I can set up a little shop on the island and make necklaces to sell."

"And I'll buy a boat," said I, getting into the vision. "I'll take up diving. I saw a dive shop here. People wear tanks on their backs and breathe underwater. I could be a guide. You'll like diving too. It'll feel like flying around inside the Hollow Earth."

The beige house's door opened again, and here was Josh. He was a bit taller than me, in his twenties, with long, braided hair and a tidy beard. I sized up his strength. Could I beat him in a fight? I didn't like that he was holding a hammer.

"I'm Mason Reynolds," said I. "Seela's husband. We two are getting back together."

"Not so fast," said Josh. "Seela told me you deserted her. And suddenly you're back? This woman needs personal time to process her feelings, Mason. I'm giving her a safe space. You show up at six am—that's an invasion. It's stalking. I'm asking you to leave. Otherwise I have to call the police."

"The police!" I exclaimed, anger flooding my veins. "You should be glad I don't thrash you. You ridiculous popinjay. Come on, Seela. Get your clothes and we'll go back to Maya's."

"You need to watch yourself," Josh told me, his tenor voice rising. "I happen to know that you and Seela and Maya and Rafaelo are illegals. I think it's totally cool that Santa Cruz is a sanctuary city, but sometimes we have to draw a line. You people are guests here, Mason, and you have to mind your manners." He was tapping his hammer against the palm of his other hand.

"What's the dumbshow with the hammer?" I said, stepping closer to him. "Go ahead and fetch your clothes, Seela. We're clearing out."

Seela slipped past Josh into the house.

"I'm seeing some mental health issues with you as well," said Josh, increasingly strident. "Seela was telling me about this fantasy life you two share. The Earth is hollow, and you've been inside? You need treatment, Mason, and so does she. We're talking fugue state and psychotic break. You're ripe for a 5150—and that means involuntary commitment. If you're man enough to walk away, Mason, I'll nurture Seela like a stray dog. Otherwise—"

Right on cue, Arf pushed the door open with his nose and slipped outside to join us. He smiled at me in that way he had, letting his pink tongue loll from his open mouth. Seela was right behind him.

"I'm ready, Mason!" said Seela, her voice bright.

Josh put his hand on Seela's shoulder. "If you think this is going to be over as easily as all that—"

"It *is* over," I said, shoving Josh's hand aside.

Josh began talking very fast, his voice even higher than before, his eyes a bit blank. He raised his hammer into the air.

Was I supposed to knock him down? And wrest the hammer from his hand? Not my usual style—but once again Uxa the *woomo* came to my aid.

A zig zag line etched its way down from the low, pearly mist—and plunged into my brooding rumby amulet, which was once again on my neck. This was the last of the rumbies. It sang a silent tekelili note—and hatched. The new *woomo's* name was Ned. Most of the *woomo* were female, but Ned was a *woomo* boy.

Initially Ned resembled a yellow banana slug, three or four inches long, clinging to my black sweatshirt. His sudden arrival gave Josh pause. And then, of course, Ned began to grow. Within thirty seconds, he was three feet long, hovering in the air between Josh and me. Arf yelped in displeasure.

As for Josh—he was scared shitless. His stopped playing the madman and scooted away from me. Just for the joy of it, Ned zapped Josh's hammer with a galvanic shock. The hammer clattered to the concrete stoop. Josh went in his house and bolted the door.

"Hooray!" said Seela. "The mighty Mason and his gallant *woomo* steed!"

Not wanting to attract undue attention, I stuffed he great sausage of a *woomo* inside my sweatshirt and tucked the shirt in around my waist. Basking in the pleasant glow of Ned's tekelili, Seela and I walked back to Maya's place with Arf at our heels.

"Quick work!" said Rudy, meeting us at the door. He tapped his head. "I'm all up to date. I'm ready to write your last chapter."

"How does the chapter end?" I asked.

I freed Ned from my shirt and he hovered in the air. Arf balefully watched the *woomo* from behind the couch. Seela was exclaiming over Brumble and rocking him her arms. She paused to glance over at Rudy.

"I know how it ends," she told Rudy. "You tell us the name of a nice island and we go there."

"I like Micronesia," said the white-haired Rudy. "I went there on a dive trip with my brother a few years back. This one particular island—Pohnpei. It's perfect. Even better than Fiji."

"We'll go there," said Seela.

"We want to come too," said Rafaelo.

"I'm not sure they invited us," said Maya.

"Mason did," said Rafaelo. "On the hike up to the monastery."

"Sure, let's all go," said Seela. "We'll stick together. None of us is white. At least not now."

"I think Hector and I stay here," said Aida. "We like to be near Mexico."

"I wonder if Ned can get American passports for all of you guys," said Rudy. "That would make things easier."

No sooner said than done. Thanks to his vast tekelili, the newly-hatched Ned was already cognizant of our government's intricate workings. He sent out a tendril, almost too thin to see, and a moment later, eight blank US passports dropped to the floor. Moving with stunning speed, Ned successively personalized a passport for each of us, even for the children. His delicate fronds tattooed our personal information onto the passports, along with color photos of us. And he sprayed on some slime to cover his additions with a shiny, official-looking gloss of faint stars.

"Be sure to copy their personal info to the chips," Rudy told Ned.

"What are chips?" I asked.

"You'll learn," said Rudy. "They're everywhere in twenty eighteen. Like lice. There's one inside the back cover of each passport."

"I have a chip in here," put in Rafaelo, holding up the black glass rectangle he used for his games. "You still gonna help me code my *Tierra Hueca* game, Mason?"

"Not directly," I said. "The trick will be to have a *woomo* help you. Uxa helped me fix Hector's motorcycle—by finding the skill in a mechanic's brain. You'll want to ask Uxa or Ned to ferret out the know-how you need. Or maybe you could study books."

"There's a two-year college in Pohnpei," put in Rudy. "It's always good to get more education."

"Me, I might do that," said Maya. "Learn business math."

"No school for me," said Rafaelo. "I'll just ask the *woomo*. We'll go back and forth, try this and try that. I'll be the game designer, see, and the *woomo* will be my coders."

"Listen at him," said Maya.

While we'd been talking, Ned had finished the passports. Beautiful work, utterly convincing, at least to me, not that I'd ever seen a passport before. Rudy said they'd work. Aida, Hector, Maya, Rafaelo, Frida, Seela, Brumble, and me—all of us were free to travel anywhere we liked.

"And you won't need special permission to settle in Pohnpei," said Rudy. "Last I heard, with a U.S. passport, you can stay there as long as you like."

Rather than planning for Pohnpei, Aida and Hector were talking about taking a road trip to visit their relations in Mexico. But Maya and Rafaelo were packing for the move. At nine am, Rudy went over to the Wells Fargo bank and extracted what he deemed to be a fair sum for my share of our two Hollow Earth books.

"Kind of hurts to give you this much," he said, handing me a sheaf of a hundred hundred-dollar bills. "But *The Hollow Earth* did pretty well, and I'm thinking *Return to the Hollow Earth* might do better."

Counting the bills, I privately wondered why Rudy hadn't given me more.

"Very kind," said Seela, giving the old man a kiss on the cheek. "Thank you. And how do we get to Pohnpei?"

"I guess you could take a plane," said Rudy. "Kind of expensive, though, with two couples and two kids."

Ned had been lolling on the floor, drawing in unseen energies and steadily getting larger. He was twenty feet long, and still growing. To fit in the room, he'd curled up one end. He broke in on our conversation with a burst of tekelili. His message came as a kinetic sense of us lying on his back and arrowing across the sky, with his *woomo* aura shielding us from the frigid air. More or less like the way Lux had flown us from Santa Cruz to Big Sur.

"Can we trust Ned?" Seela asked. "What if he ships us off to Eddie's new Eden? Or carries us back inside the Hollow Earth?"

Ned reassured us that he and his race were exceedingly grateful to Seela and me for helping to bring about the Bloom. He would most certainly take us to Pohnpei. He expansively added that he would remain in Pohnpei as our backup, and for as long as we liked. A few years—or even a century—didn't mean much to a *woomo*.

So now everything was resolved. Ned stretched himself out in the house's front yard. Rafaelo, Maya, Seela, and I began loading on the luggage and the kids. A couple of neighbors were watching. They had no idea what was going on. And even if they talked, it didn't seem likely anyone would listen to them. All of us were poor. We didn't matter.

I'd thought Seela and I would be able to coax Arf onto Ned's back, but the dog was highly recalcitrant. Rather than growling or actively fighting us, he lowered himself onto his belly, made himself flat, and whimpered, with his expression bereft and piteous. He just didn't like *woomo*.

"I'll take care of him," said Rudy, hunkering down beside Arf and stroking his fur. "I used to have a dog like this, a long time ago. Will you come live with me and my wife, Arfie? We have a sunny front deck and a grassy back yard. You'll get table scraps. And I'll give you a flea collar." Rudy paused, thinking. "Oh, I just remembered something. They eat dogs on Pohnpei! All the more reason to stay with me."

Arf stuck his snout in Rudy's face and took a deep sniff, then rose to his feet and stood at the old writer's side. The man and the dog were in agreement.

"You'll finish my book?" I asked Rudy.

"I've got everything I need," he said. "I'll mail you a printed draft. We can stay in touch by email."

"What's email?"

"Maya and Rafaelo know. Good luck out there, Mason. I'm glad we met. It's a dream come true."

§

We took our places atop Ned. The *woomo* had fashioned shallow depressions for us. And Rafaelo had thought to pack drinks and food. We rose into the air, bound for Micronesia. Ned amped up his aura, and we were invisible.

Although the trip took over twelve hours, it was pleasant enough. Our money and our passports ensured us a cordial welcome in Kolonia—a sleepy, tree-shaded settlement of six thousand. It's the main town of Pohnpei. We rented a tree-shaded home made of concrete and logs, with a corrugated tin roof, a long porch, and an open-sided pavilion for cooking and eating, cooled by the breeze from the sea.

Maya and Seela are opening a jewelry stand. Rafaelo and I are starting a dive business with the guy next door. And I'm doing some writing for the local paper. Our *woomo* Ned has taken up residence in a local reef, and we visit him from time to time. Rafaelo is making progress on his *Tierra Hueca* game. They don't have cows on Pohnpei—but I got us some chickens, and we're thinking about a pig.

Rudy mailed me his draft of *Return to the Hollow Earth*, and it reads as if I wrote it myself. I didn't find much of anything to change. Tekelili is amazing.

I used to dream of a literary career. But getting to know Eddie Poe took the bloom off that rose—as did Rudy's inability to sell our book to a commercial publisher who would actually pay us some money. He's printing the narrative himself, for what little that's worth. And he says nobody believes my story is true. To hell with them all.

We're starting to make friends in Pohnpei. Brumble has learned to lie on his stomach and lift his head. Maya calls it tummy time. Frida is almost talking. It's beautiful here—the flowers, the birds, the rain, the fruit, the fish, the waves, the faces. It's almost as good as the Hollow Earth.

And Ned is out there in the reef.

Editor's Note

In 1990, I edited Mason Reynolds's 1850 manuscript, *The Hollow Earth*, and I saw it into publication. *The Hollow Earth* ends with Mason and his wife Seela setting off for California aboard a clipper ship, the *Purple Whale*. Newspaper records of the time report that the *Purple Whale* sank off Cape Horn with no survivors.

For years I've wondered if Mason and Seela might somehow have made their way to California anyway—and whether they ever revisited the Hollow Earth.

In 2006, one of my woman readers emailed me that, while on a dive trip to Fiji, she'd spent a passionate night with a man named Alan Poague, who showed her an unfinished manuscript attributed to Mason Reynolds and entitled *Return to the Hollow Earth*.

By way of researching this, my wife and I took a cruise on a liveaboard dive boat in Fiji—great fun. In a village on one of the smaller islands, I met this Alan Poague, a Californian who'd gone native in the islands. A raffish and engaging man, he played a steel guitar in the lounge of an inn that catered to divers and surfers. I told him my story, and he readily showed me the manuscript pages that he'd shown the woman diver who'd emailed me.

Poague said he was familiar with my edition of *The Hollow Earth*, and that his manuscript was by Mason Reynolds as well. How so? Supposedly the words had come to Poague in a *kava* trance, that is, in a waking dream brought on by an intoxicating local plant. He'd typed the text without really having to think about it. He'd produced eleven pages this way, and then the flow had stopped, or he'd gotten distracted—and he'd moved onto other projects. He was now assembling a diving guidebook for the Great Astrolabe Reef. And he dreamed of writing a New Age work based on his notions of the thought-processes of the *woomo*. I made a copy of Poague's eleven pages and we returned home.

Ten years later, in April, 2017. I began having lucid dreams involving the Hollow Earth—in particular I was sensing the mind of the giant *woomo* whom Mason called Uxa. Uxa was extending her tendrils from the core, worming them through volcanic vents and ocean-floor holes. Upon reaching me, Uxa's fronds wrapped my body in a net of pale gold. Using this connection, the Great Old One was speaking to me—not in words nor in images, but via certain physical sensations. She was making my fingers twitch.

I had no writing project that April. Sitting at my computer keyboard one morning, I turned my thoughts to my dreams of Uxa. As I thought of her, my fingers began to move. Suddenly I realized that Uxa wanted me to type the second narrative of Mason Reynolds.

I knew this in the same non-verbal way that I might know the workings of a mathematical proof. Mason had written *Return to the Hollow Earth* in his head, Uxa had read his mind, and now she was using me to put Mason's words to paper. She'd tried earlier to use Alan Poague of Fiji for her scribe, but he hadn't had the patience. But now, with me already having edited *The Hollow Earth*, Uxa had found someone who would see the project through.

Smiling to myself, I unleashed my fingers and let the story flow. As my tekelili connection to Uxa sharpened, I began mentally hearing the words I wrote, and inwardly seeing the scenes I described.

The strange, intense transmission lasted several hours, and when I was done, I'd typed the first six pages of *Return to the Hollow Earth*. The next day I typed five more. I compared what I had to my copy of the Alan Poague manuscript. The two texts were word for word the same.

For a week nothing more came. I lost hope. Perhaps I'd unwittingly memorized Poague's manuscript and had merely retyped it. Perhaps there was no Uxa. Perhaps I was a doddering, self-deluded, borderline-senile old man. A writer at the end of his rope.

But then, *bam*, Uxa linked into me for three days in a row—and I was well into the second chapter. My joy mounted, and in the coming months my confidence steadily grow. I didn't like telling my wife or my friends exactly what I was up to. I just said I was working on a sequel to *The Hollow Earth*, and that I had no outline at all, and that I was depending entirely on the muse. My scribing continued, off and on, for nearly a year. Nobody paid me much mind. Writing is what I do.

On March 24, 2018, things got stranger. According to what I was transcribing in the pages of *Return to the Hollow Earth*, Mason had arrived that day in Big Sur! No longer was he a fictional or a historical figure. He was here and now, just down the coast from my Los Gatos home. A day later, I found myself typing that Mason and his family had moved in with four undocumented Latinos in the Beach Flats neighborhood of Santa Cruz. Should I go and meet him? I didn't quite dare.

How had Mason jumped so far forward in time? I had only to study the pages I'd written. Mason had spent over a hundred and sixty seven years stranded with the *woomo* Uxa in the slow time zone at the Hollow Earth's core. Evidently it was near the end of that stay when Uxa began using her tekelili to send out Mason's narrative for transcription. First she'd tried it with Alan Poague, and then she'd turned to me. And then Mason had escaped the slow time zone and he'd ridden to Big Sur in a live flying saucer made of two *veem*. And, now, even with Mason so far away from the Earth's core, Uxa was still picking up his mental narrative—and transmitting the updates to me.

On March 28, 2018, I found myself writing that Mason had sold an article to a Santa Cruz newspaper called *Good Times*, and that his article was appearing that day. I'd been leery of seeking him out, but this pushed me over the edge. I got in my car and drove to the *Good Times* editorial office in Santa Cruz, and asked where I could find Mason Reynolds. A young woman told me to check the crumbling old Evergreen Cemetery.

I hurried there—and I found Mason, along with his wife Seela, their baby Brumble, Mason's new friends Maya and Rafaelo, plus an inquisitive policeman, and none other than the recently resurrected Edgar Allan Poe, accompanied by his wife Ina. I felt like I was going crazy.

But yet, everything remained, in some ways, ordinary. Mason already knew that I'd edited and published his manuscript of the *Hollow Earth*, and he was interested in discussing this. He and his friends were on the point of being in trouble with the police, and I was able to talk our way past the problem.

And—Edgar Allan Poe? Was I really meeting Poe? It certainly seemed so, not that he was in good shape, having spent well over a century buried in a bronze casket, and then having immediately gotten drunk. But you know all this if you've read *Return to the Hollow Earth*. Mason describes these scenes better than I. He's a born writer, a natural.

Having grown used to the fluent, assured tone of Mason's two narratives, I was startled to see how young he was in person. Eighteen years old, or not quite that. He was dark-skinned from the *woomo* light, with the features of a slender, white, Southern boy, and with, of course, something of a Virginia accent. He was very articulate, and with a rich vocabulary. His speech had a leisurely pace that matched his origin in slower times. His eyes were quick, animated, and perhaps a bit haunted.

Seela was dark brown, with thin lips and a delicate nose, resembling the Melanesian women of Fiji. She was beautiful and lively, with a sharp tongue. Clearly she loved Mason and Brumble. The moment of her parting with them was very painful, and their reunion a joy.

Mason and Seela didn't like our present day world, and Mason himself was a bit let down that he hadn't traveled onward through that dubious tunnel in space with Eddie Poe. I was glad to give Mason and Seela some money—although he thinks it should have been more. I hope I did well in suggesting they move to Pohnpei. And I'm glad to have inherited their dog. Arf is good company, with deep wisdom in his eyes.

In my excitement, I didn't think to take any photos of Mason, nor of the epic scenes at Big Sur. But Arf is here in the flesh. As I like to tell people, "If you don't believe the Hollow Earth is real, come visit me and you can see the dog!"

As I write this, he's lying in a patch of sun, thumping his tail against the floor. Good dog. Arf is my proof that the Earth is hollow.

I'm no longer getting any tekelili updates from Uxa. Perhaps, from the *woomo* point of view, my mission is done— not that I'm certain what was the purpose of my mission. Perhaps Mason's two narratives are meant to prepare our society for an eventual merger with the civilizations of the Hollow Earth? The *woomo* take a long view.

I don't have any contact information for Mason, but I do have Rafaelo's email address. A couple of months ago I mailed a paper printout of my draft of *Return to the Hollow Earth* to Mason in care of General Delivery at Pohnpei. Rafaelo emailed me Mason's response, and this comprises the brief closing section of the book's final chapter. I've heard nothing more since then.

Judging from Mason's ending to the book, I think he's angry about his book being published with so little fanfare— and that he blames me. And never mind that I spent a year writing his book for him, and gave him ten thousand dollars! A slicker promoter might have found a way to package Mason's adventures into a best-seller. A wiser editor might not insist—in the face of universal derision—that Mason's two books are literally true.

The public is wary of nuts—and this category unfairly includes believers in the doctrine of the Hollow Earth. But Mason and I are right. As he puts it—*to hell with them all.* What matters is that we've managed to publish the truth, and nobody stopped us.

As a final point, note that definitive proofs of the Hollow Earth doctrine are in the offing. Eventually the passageways at the poles will reopen. As the Antarctic ice melts, the cap across the South Hole will crumble. And, as ice vanishes from the Arctic and the speed of the polar jet stream increases, the pre-1850 North Hole maelstrom will reemerge.

And then Mason Reynolds will be granted his just place in the Pantheon of great explorers!

By the way, in the 2021 editions of *The Hollow Earth* and *Return to the Hollow Earth*, I emended some disparaging racial epithets that were in *The Hollow Earth*.

 —Rudy Rucker, Los Gatos, California
 July 4, 2018 and May 29, 2021

Acknowledgements

Although it seemed obvious to me—and to those around me—that the public would welcome a new Hollow Earth novel, I could find no commercial publisher who agreed. So I turned once again to Kickstarter to crowd-source my funding, and it worked well. I raised enough money to make it feasible to publish *Return to the Hollow Earth*, along with a new edition of *The Hollow Earth*. Heartfelt thanks to my supporters!

Here's a list of their chosen names, alphabetized by their first letters.

@ofeenah, Adam Browne, Adrian Magni, AgentKaz, Al Billings, Alan Robson, Albert Henry Tyson, Alex McLaren, Alexander Pappajohn, Alexander the Drake, Allen Tollin, Allen Varney, Andrew Binder, Andrew Gordon White, Andrew Ward, Aris Alissandrakis, Arthur Murphy, Beat Suter, Benet Devereux, Benjamin H Henry, Bob Hearn, Bob Schoenholtz, Brian Anderson, Brian Dysart, Cameron Cooper, Carlos Pascual, Carrie G, Chad Bowden, Chris McLaren, Chuck Ivy, Chuck Shotton, Cliff Winnig, Collin Bennett, DaddyChurchill, Dan P, Daniel Rubin, Daniele A. Gewurz, Dave Bouvier, Dave Holets, David Chatterjee, David H. Adler, David Kirkpatrick, David Rains, David Schutt, Derek Bosch, Don and Harriet, Don Tardiff, Doug Bissell, Dwayne Plain, Eamon John Carrig, Ed Kirkland, Edward Marr, Eibo Thieme, Eli Tishberg, Elijah Wendell Cauley and Benjamin Harry Cauley, eorojas@gmail. com, Eric Wollesen, Erik Sowa, Fraser Lovatt, Gaia Maffini Mazzei, Gara Gaines, George Bendo & Hedvig Bartha, Grat Crabtree, Greg Deocampo, Gregory Scheckler, Hiroyuki OGINO, https://twitter.

com/cixelsyd, Ian Chung, Iggy Utah, Jayson Lorenzen, Jeffrey Ferrell, Jeremy W, Jerry Bonnell, Jim Anderson, Joe Sislow, Joel Ward, John, John C Monroe, John Kohler, John R Donald, John T. Baldwin, John Winkelman, Jon, Jon Cook, Jon Hamlow, Jon Kimmich, Jon Nebenfuhr, Josh Cooper, Julia Grillmayr, Karl W. Reinsch, Karl-Arthur Arlamovsky, kath odonnell, Kevin J. "Womzilla" Maroney, Kevin Wehner, Lee Fisher, Leland Poague, lord of anti-slack, Luke Gutzwiller, Mark Anderson, Mark Chatinsky, Mark L Cohen, Martin, Matthew Cox, Maxim Jakubowski, Mayer Brenner, Michael Becker, Michael W, Michail Sarigiannidis, Moshe Feder, None, Norbert Bruckner, Patrick Shettlesworth, Philip Rubin, Rafael Fajardo, Rafael Laguna de la Vera, Raja Thiagarajan, Ramon Cahenzli, Rebecca :), Richard J. Ohnemus, Richie O'Hara-Beamand, RJ Moore, rob alley, Robert Guffey, Rod Bartlett, Ronald Pottol, Ronan Waide, Ross Presser, Roy Berman, Sandor Silverman, Sandy McAuley, Scott and Annabelle Call, Scott G Lewis, Scott Lazerus, Seanstoppable, Stefan Schmiedl, Steve Hirst, The Hackers Conference, Theron Trowbridge, Thom Slattery, Thomas Gideon, Tim Conkling, Tim Gruchy, Timothy Lee Russell, Timothy M. Maroney, Todd Ellner, Todd Fincannon, Tom M, Tom Velebny, Walter F. Croft, William Sked, Yaro Godziumakha, and Yoshimichi Furusawa.

Thanks also to those backers who chose not to be listed here. And thanks to Michael Troutman and my wife Sylvia, who proofread my final manuscript. And thanks to John Douglas, who published the first edition of *The Hollow Earth*, and to Chris Roberson, who published the second.

In closing, I'll remind you of my website for the Hollow Earth novels of Mason Reynolds.

www.rudyrucker.com/thehollowearth

Yours in full *woomo* tekelili.

—Rudy Rucker, Los Gatos, California, July 4, 2018.